SEALED
with a Ring

MARY MARGRET DAUGHTRIDGE

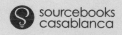
sourcebooks
casablanca

Published by Sourcebooks Casablanca, an imprint of Sourcebooks, Inc.
P.O. Box 4410, Naperville, Illinois 60567-4410
(630) 961-3900
FAX: (630) 961-2168
www.sourcebooks.com

Printed and bound in Canada
WC 10 9 8 7 6 5 4 3 2 1

"I consider myself blessed with the best things a man could ever hope for. I loved being a SEAL. If I died doing something for the Teams, then I died doing what made me happy. Very few people have the luxury of that."

—Neil Roberts, first SEAL to be killed in Afghanistan, in a letter to be opened in the event of his death.

Chapter 1

IT HAD BEEN A NICE WEDDING, IF YOU LIKED WEDDINGS. Davy didn't, much. It took too long to get to the good part. Davy set his almost full champagne glass on a table littered with other barely touched champagne glasses and dessert plates with half-eaten portions of wedding cake. They'd just spent a half hour on champagne and cake nobody wanted—proof of what he was saying.

SEALs didn't have a hell of a lot of free time. And he might have even less before long. The medical corpsman with a unit in Afghanistan had lost most of a leg in an IED ambush. Davy was tempted to volunteer to finish the corpsman's tour of duty. He was still weighing the pros and cons.

In the plus column, having been deployed there, Davy already knew the country, knew the language. He would be useful from the moment his plane touched down. The platoon wouldn't have to baby-sit him until he could fend for himself. In the minus column, he'd returned from deployment only a few months ago. He had used up almost none of his accumulated leave.

Back on the plus side, when he was operating, life was intense, flat out. All his skill, strength, and intelligence were employed to the max, with the added plus that his care made the difference in whether others returned alive.

He didn't know yet. But if he did go back to Afghanistan, he wouldn't want to think he'd wasted his time in America on drinks that weren't for the purpose of drinking and food that wasn't for the purpose of eating. He was ready to get down to business.

The upside of a wedding was the way it attracted girls all tricked out in pretty dresses and in the mood to hook up. Davy did love sex. Every time he looked in the mirror, he thanked the excellent genes that meant he'd never had to work very hard to get it. Nature had gifted him with black hair that, allowed to get the least bit long, had a tendency to curl around his ears, smooth olive skin, and large, wide-set brown eyes. His perfectly straight nose was neither too large nor too small, and his jaw was just wide enough to make his face strong and thoroughly masculine. Oh, and the coup de grâce, a dimple in his left cheek. SEAL training kept the body in perfect trim.

Life for Davy Graziano, usually called Doc by his buddies, was good.

He had his eye on a couple of pretty girls who had smiled a certain way when they found out he was a SEAL. Toasts out of the way, the bride and groom had started the dancing. Without being rude or making it too obvious that he hadn't come for the party, he could at last pick his partner for the night and get out of here.

Automatically, he checked the position of his SEAL teammates scattered throughout the well-dressed throng of guests. Until awareness was ingrained, SEAL instructors drilled the men in teamwork. Every exercise was a competition that could only be won by keeping up with every other man in the team. But in Davy's psyche, the habit was even more deeply embedded.

When someone called "Doc" or "Corpsman up!" he had the same combat duties as any other SEAL, and he also had to care for the wounded. To find them he had to scramble through disorienting smoke, confusion, din of gunfire, and exploding shells. Knowledge of where they were came through his muscles and bones and sometimes through the very pores of his skin. No way could he leave his buddies, even in a situation as tame as a wedding reception at a country club, until he knew everyone else was okay.

Most of the SEALs here were men he'd been deployed with in Afghanistan only a few months ago. The unit was scattered now, off to new assignments. The wedding of their commanding officer, Lt. Jax Graham, had offered a welcome chance for reunion. The groom, the best man, and Senior Chief Lon Swales were easy to spot in dress blues loaded with gold braid. Most of the others, like him, never wore a uniform if they could help it.

Jax was dancing with his bride, Pickett, holding her in one arm and the cute little boy, his son from his first marriage, in the other. The three of them twirled slowly, smiling into each other's eyes. It looked like Davy's CO was squared away and wouldn't be needing him.

Chief Petty Officer Caleb Dulaude—"Do-Lord" to his friends—was on the dance floor, too, with Emmie Caddington, Pickett's best friend. They were the best man and maid of honor. Emmie wasn't much to look at, but she didn't look quite so much like a dork tonight. Someone had done her makeup, and a strapless bronze-green bridesmaid dress hinted at world-class breasts (Davy considered himself a connoisseur). Like Do-Lord, she was really smart and courageous—but she wasn't date material. Do-Lord no doubt was dancing with her only because he thought good manners obliged him to, at least once.

Or maybe not. Davy rapidly revised his assessment when he saw Do-Lord's hand on the small of Emmie's back move in a slow circular caress. *Huh. Was Do-Lord really interested?* Davy just hoped Do-Lord understood that girl wasn't the fun-and-games type. A shy girl like that wouldn't know how *not* to take things seriously.

It was best, Davy had decided long ago, to let *women* do the picking up. If that limited his selection, hey, nobody scored every time. The important thing was, when women came on to him, he didn't have to worry. The women got what they wanted and knew what they were getting. When they were in charge of the signals, everyone came away happy.

Speaking of signals, *yo, mama*! The most beautiful woman he had ever seen—the most beautiful woman *most* men had ever seen—stood no more than twenty feet from him, looking straight at him. Strong, bold features, their incomparable proportions molded by a master, had been set in a classically oval face. She had large, intelligent green eyes, cheekbones as exquisite as they were uncompromising, and a sultry mouth, designed to make any man who saw it think x-rated thoughts. The whole was saved from too much perfection by an assertive little chin sporting just the hint of a cleft.

A gleaming waterfall of coffee-brown hair moved in a sinuous slide over the rosy apricot skin of her shoulders. Her dress, almost the same brown as her hair, traced every generous curve of a perfect hourglass figure. The slinky material ended just north of her knees, showing off long, strong dancer's legs, every curve shaped by muscle.

She was tall. In her heels, she'd probably be eye-to-eye with him. She sized him up with the confident self-possession of an older woman, though he guessed she was about his age. She looked like she'd had experience ordering men around. God, he hoped so. He liked a woman who could take over. When he turned the tables on her, it was so much more fun.

She was looking for someone. It might as well be him. He squared his shoulders, then sent her a devilish grin at the same time he preened and stroked an eyebrow.

Her large green eyes widened in surprise, her mouth dropped open, then she threw back her head and laughed as she caught the joke.

—✺—

Even though her cheeks got hot to be caught staring, JJ Caruthers laughed at his parody of his Greek-god looks. He was gorgeous, he knew it, and he was so confident that his worth did not lie in a pretty face, he could make jokes about it. She was surprised at his antics and even more surprised that she could laugh. Seconds before, she'd felt more utterly serious than she'd ever felt about anything in her life. She hadn't intentionally been staring at the young George Clooney look-alike, although the resemblance was amazing. Well, not at first anyway.

He was stare-worthy all right. Cheekbones to die for. Large, thickly lashed brown eyes. Black hair curling around his ears just begged to be twirled around a finger. Lips shaped into a sensual curve above a hard masculine chin and jaw. His olive complexion was so smooth, taut, and fine-grained it had a slight sheen, as if his flesh was covered with something finer than mortal skin. But it was the way the laughing look transformed him that made her feel as if the sun had come out in her heart.

A group of guests heading for the dance floor stepped between them.

Smile fading, she resumed her search for Alexander Garfield. She thought she'd seen her attorney's gray head and short, roundish body just behind the Greek god. She wouldn't have stayed at the wedding reception longer than required to congratulate the bride and groom, if she hadn't needed to talk to Garfield.

He was proving elusive.

Among the throng of mostly strangers, she was surprised to see one face she did know: Lauren Babcock. Lauren was fifty or so and still the most beautiful woman JJ knew, although the strapless gown she wore revealed painfully thin arms. Lauren stood alone, sipping a glass of champagne, an unfocused look in her eyes. Her grief surrounded her like a force field, separating her from the laughing, celebrating people all around. As always, Lauren's blond hair was skillfully highlighted and her makeup flawless, but the petal pink chiffon she wore, though exquisite, was a couple of years past the height of fashion, and more appropriate for spring than Thanksgiving. JJ's heart went out to her. Lauren defined the word *fashionista*. Nothing could have revealed more poignantly that Lauren had lost interest in life since the death of her daughter.

Watching the man who had once been married to her daughter start a new family—while her daughter lay dead and would never have a chance to find true and permanent love—had to be heart wrenching. JJ really should speak to her.

But JJ never had a chance. Just as Lauren walked, with less than her usual grace, over to a burly man with a kind, weathered face and an impressive amount of gold braid and shiny medals on his Navy uniform, JJ spotted the pink, balding head of her quarry.

At a table near Davy, the floor-length, green tablecloth lifted. A tot in one of those fluffy, little-girl dresses crawled from underneath. Davy grinned when she barreled past him as fast as her toddler legs would go. Obviously an escapee. He wasn't going to end her race, but he moved to where he could keep her in sight.

Her form was good; she had a winning attitude, which counts for a lot, but physics was against her. Her center of gravity was too high, necessitating a broad-based gait to maintain balance. Unfortunately she hadn't yet learned the importance of equipment. Tiny red shoes with a strap across the instep might be the envy of the nursery set, but they were too stiff and too slick soled for sprinting. She was going to come to grief, and in a second, the inevitable happened. She fell, splat, with enough force to make her little red heels fly up.

Before she had time to work up a good wail, he scooped her up.

He settled her on one arm so he could look into her face. Her chin puckered. Big blue eyes glared at him. "I wunnin'!"

"I saw that."

"Fall down!"

"Yes. I saw that, too."

"*Huht* Yay-ya."

Hurt, he could guess at, but he couldn't think of a body part that sounded like yay-ya. She wasn't acting like a kid who was injured.

"What did you hurt? Show me."

After a moment's cogitation, wispy brows drawn over her button nose, she presented him a tiny starfish hand, fingers outstretched.

Hiding a smile, he examined it. There *could* have been a red spot on the heel of the palm, but without a magnifying glass, he'd never know for sure. "I think it will be all right," he gravely reassured her. He tried to return the hand.

"No!" Her forehead crumpled. Her lower lip pulled down in a serious pout. "*Kiss* it!"

So, like a lot of patients, she thought the diagnosis was inadequate if she wasn't given some medicine. Applying the time-tested boo-boo remedy, he respectfully put his lips to the possibly imaginary red spot. To make her forget about it, he blew a raspberry into her palm.

He was rewarded with a chuckle, a surprisingly robust and knowing sound in one so young. He looked around for who she belonged to. Anyone running that hard usually had somebody chasing them.

The moppet put her head on his shoulder. She patted his cheek. Blue eyes peeped at him from under absurdly long, light-brown lashes. She smiled beguilingly. For good measure, she threw in a sigh, a head tilt, and a few lash flutters. "Kiss it? 'Gain, pease?"

Amazing how early they learned what it took to wrap a man's heart around their adorable fingers.

"Leila!" A young woman rushed up arms outstretched.

"Mommy!"

"Here's your speed demon," Davy passed his darling back where she belonged.

"Mommy! Me get kiss!"

"Purely medicinal, I promise. She fell down. She was more startled than hurt."

"Sweetie, I've warned you not to run like that."

Safe in her mother's arms, the miscreant nodded, the very picture of "sadder and wiser." "Huht Yay-ya."

"That's right. You'll hurt Leila."

By the time the toddler's mother had thanked him and borne Leila away, little starfish fingers squeezing a bye-bye "wave," the woman in the brown dress had been swallowed up by the crowd. Never mind. Her signals had been unmistakable. He'd find her again in a minute, or she'd find him.

Speaking of signals though, on the dance floor, even as Do-Lord smiled in response to something Emmie had said, he was hand-signaling to someone behind Emmie's back, asking if he wanted help.

Who did Do-Lord think needed help? Davy followed Do-Lord's line of sight. On the other side of the dance floor, Senior Chief Lon Swales had a slender woman in a pale pink gown draped all over him. For a second, Davy couldn't believe his eyes. Physical displays while in uniform were frowned upon—one reason Davy never wore a uniform socially if he could help it. But Lon? If Lon had a sex life, he kept it discreet to the point of invisibility.

The woman's head turned, and Davy caught sight of a classically perfect profile, marred by turned-down lips and a slack, unfocused look. Holy shit, the woman wrapped around Lon was Jax's ex-mother-in-law, Lauren Babcock, and she was drunk.

An uncoordinated fling of her thin arm almost overbalanced her. She was saved from falling only by Lon's arm around her. At first glance, her head on his shoulder might have looked intimate, but, in fact, she was close to passing out. It was only a little after eight. Too early to be that drunk. It looked like the scuttlebutt that Lauren had become an alcoholic since her daughter's death was true.

Lon's seemingly out-of-character behavior suddenly made sense. He was holding her up while he hustled her toward one set of the wide doors that stood open to the corridor.

That was the senior chief he admired. Making sure problems were taken care of before most people knew there was a problem. "I see what's happening. I'll assist," he signed to Lon.

Unhurried yet moving swiftly toward the corridor, Davy eased between laughing, chattering guests.

Waiting in the wide, cool hallway with its footstep-deadening turquoise carpet, Davy scanned the ballroom through the open doors for the hot babe in the brown dress. The crowd parted again in time for Davy to see her throw her arms around a balding, gray-haired man whose well-cut tuxedo only partly disguised his portliness.

Davy's diaphragm clenched in protest. The man was old enough to be her father—no competition at all—but still. Women didn't always go for looks in a man. A tux like that said money, and Davy would bet the woman's dress, for all its brevity, had cost as much as he made in a pay period.

She launched into a very serious-looking conversation, her shoulders square, feet in those fuck-me heels planted.

Davy relaxed.

For a SEAL, reading body language wasn't just a handy social shortcut to understanding; it was a survival skill. Every line in her killer bod said even if the man was old enough to be her father, she considered herself his equal; possibly his boss.

Whatever she was telling the man, being turned on was the farthest thing from her mind. And despite a dress that glimmered and slid sensuously with every movement, as if her nude body were clothed only in dark water, she clearly didn't plan to use seduction to get what she wanted.

Davy almost felt sorry for Gramps. No man—not even a guy that old—could think about anything but sex around her. Hours of sweaty sex, her hair drifting over him like cool, heavy silk, his hips caught in the clasp of those long, strong legs.

Lon had worked his way to the edge of the crowd. If the girl in the brown dress was gone by the time Davy got back, there would be others. But *damn*, Davy wished he'd had a chance to ask her to hang around until he returned.

His hospital corpsman identity took over as Lon steered his charge into the wide hall.

Davy was pretty sure Lauren was drunk, but other conditions could mimic alcohol intoxication—diabetic coma or stroke at the top of the list. Most he could rule out. Pulse and respiration were normal. He leaned forward to check her breath for the classic Juicy Fruit gum odor associated with diabetes but detected only the sour smell of wine.

Her eyes were open and she was still able to walk, but she was long past the point of being able to remember anything in the morning.

"We need to get her out of here. Look in her purse," Lon directed. "See if you can find out where she's staying."

Davy rifled the tiny silver bag. He withdrew a key card and held it up between two fingers. "She's at the Fairfield, same as us, but no room number. You'll have to ask at the desk."

"That'll call attention to her. The fewer people who know about this, the better."

"What do you care? She's trying to get Jax's kid. She doesn't deserve any TLC."

"I don't care about her. But I'm not going to let gossip about her ruin Pickett's wedding. I'll put her in my room, and I'll bunk in with you."

"Sorry. Other plans." Davy met the senior chief's eyes without a shred of guilt. It wasn't really a lie. Davy might not have anything lined up yet, but he didn't plan to sleep alone, and he sure didn't plan to sleep with Lon.

"Already?" Lon's bushy two-toned eyebrows drew together in disbelief. "We just finished dinner. You didn't have anything lined up fifteen minutes ago. How did you talk a girl into going back to the hotel with you that fast?"

A certain brown dress flickered in Davy's mind's eye. The grin he flashed was unrepentant. "Um, talking didn't have anything to do with it."

Lon grunted and shook his head, half-affectionate, half-disgusted. "Doc, you are pretty as a cupcake, but you are a *dog*." He shrugged. "Okay, there are two beds in my room. She can have one, and I'll take the other." He shifted the woman in his arms so he could fish his keys from his pocket. "Go get my car and bring it to the side entrance. You can drive it back here, if you want to, after you drop us off at the hotel."

Chapter 2

WHEN DAVY RETURNED TO THE COUNTRY CLUB, INSTEAD of parking out front, he drove Lon's car around to a service entrance. Lon had sworn him to secrecy; if no one saw Davy return, they'd likely never realize he'd been gone.

He pocketed Lon's keys, aware of a pleasant zing of anticipation and of an unusual urge to hurry. He wanted to find the tall woman in the brown dress before she found someone else. He hadn't been gone long—less than twenty minutes. Still, he quickened his pace until he was jogging toward the half-glassed service door.

Mostly he believed women were like buses. Miss one, and another would be along in a few minutes. *So what if she's gone? There'll be others.* Even so, this particular woman was one he was running to catch.

———

JJ's lawyer took a sip of champagne, a not-unsympathetic look in his shrewd eyes. "I'm sorry, JJ. Your grandfather is the sole owner of the business. He can sell it, and you can't stop him. He can do anything he wants with it."

JJ's heart battered her chest wall as if desperate to escape its cage of ribs. Her cheeks tingled as the blood drained from them, and her head swam. She had to get out of here before she fainted or screamed.

After her grandfather had slapped her with his ultimatum, she had had no desire to go to a wedding, but she had reasoned that catching her lawyer at the reception would be her best chance to talk to him before Monday. But consulting her lawyer at a country club crowded with well-dressed guests celebrating a wedding? *Bad* idea.

She had been clutching at straws, looking for reassurance, looking for any sliver of hope. She should have known he would only confirm her fear that everything she cared about really could be imperiled by the ego of one man.

"Th-thank you." JJ stifled a bubble of hysteria at the irony of thanking someone for news as bad as this. But the impeccable manners instilled by her grandmother demanded she maintain her poise, stay in control, and, even if her world was crumbling, think of others first. "Excuse me, please, I—um—uh—"

The noise from the orchestra and the babble of well-bred voices combined in a confusing roar that drowned out coherent speech. She backed away, knowing only that she had to get out.

The country club entrance was miles away, down a long hallway. She would never make it out that way before she broke down. JJ flung herself through a door marked *Staff Only.*

The narrow service corridor where she found herself was lit only by the red glow of the exit sign over the half-glass exterior door. Before her mind could even register that the dark shape silhouetted against the door was a man, she slammed into him, a small startled scream escaping her. Running into him was like hitting a concrete wall.

"Hey, slow down!" The man she'd crashed into laughed as he gently set her back on her feet. It didn't take a lot of brain power to guess he was one of the

SEALs—the ballroom was awash in them. The groom was a SEAL and apparently had invited his entire team to his wedding.

In her heels, she was almost the same height as him. JJ ducked her head to hide her face. "Sorry. I need to... um..." She tried to edge around him.

"Wait a minute." He snagged her arm and turned her so that he could see her face. "It's *you*. You're upset. Need me to take care of anybody for you?"

The cheerful bloodthirsty-ness of his offer almost failed to register, said as it was in a voice as smooth and dark as Dove chocolate. The incongruity surprised a laugh from her. Well... that, and the fact that he had no idea how much she'd like to take him up on it.

"No," she shook her head, cringing at how tear-clogged she sounded.

"Okay," he agreed easily. He stepped into her path before she could try to go around him again. "How about I take care of *you*? Want me to kiss it better?" he teased. Again there was the cheerfully competent, dimple-decorated smile—as if he never doubted he was just as good at kissing as he was at *taking care*.

JJ knew the correct answer: a cool *no thank you*.

She didn't kiss men she didn't know—not that she'd had a lot of offers—not from men her age, anyway. Men with the confidence to come on to the working head of one of the oldest and most successful car dealerships in the state were usually a lot older. They went for smoother, less direct moves—like sending her a drink.

Tears welled in her eyes again. Really, she had to get out of here before she made a spectacle of herself and bawled. "A kiss isn't going to make it better."

"Depends on where I kiss," his voice turned deeper, mellower, "don't you think?" Without appearing to move, he was suddenly nearer. She could feel his heat and smell the masculine musk of his body. It wrapped around her the same way the chocolate of his voice did.

"Like," he murmured, "suppose I kiss you here?" He brushed the backs of his fingers over her breast, unerringly grazing the nipple through the slinky silk jersey of her dress. Only the barest touch. She'd almost think it was accidental—except for the teasing glint of a smile as he gauged her reaction and waited to see if she would stop him.

Shocked, appalled, yet mesmerized by his audacity, she couldn't speak, couldn't move. Her face, then her whole chest, got hot, and her heart lurched into a slower, deeper rhythm.

He repeated the outrageous familiarity with the other breast. The dimple in his cheek deepened. He allowed his hand to slide down the front of her body, past her waist, across her belly, until it rested at the juncture of her thighs. "Sometimes a kiss here is the most effective cure of all. Would you like for me to kiss you here?"

Would she like it? JJ struggled to review her options in spite of the hot maelstrom of emotion that threatened to suck her under. JJ's other choice was to drive home to Wilmington where not even a dog waited to comfort her and keep her company.

At last, JJ found her voice. "Yes," she whispered. "Yes, I would."

Chapter 3

JJ SAT UP STEALTHILY, CAREFUL NOT TO SHAKE THE BED. When the man's even breathing told her he still slept, she eased her weight to her feet. She had no idea where her clothes were.

They hadn't drawn the hotel room's heavy drapes. Light from the hotel's parking lot sifted through the loose weave of the privacy curtains. She could make out dark shapes of chair and dresser.

The compressor on the room's HVAC rattled to life, making JJ jump. The man—Davy, she thought his friends had called him—sighed and turned on his side. She didn't know his last name. She hadn't told him *her* name at all.

He had pushed the sheet down around his hips. In the pinkish glow from the parking-lot lights, his skin gleamed faintly. The defined swells and dips of the muscles of his arms and chest looked carved. His features in profile on the pillow were so impossibly perfect she still found it hard to believe he was real.

She wished she believed none of it was real, but twinges and tiny aches and a deep, satisfied awareness of her body told her differently. Even now, although she knew she had to get away, if she thought about what they had done, deep shudders of pleasure ran through her.

In small, shuffling steps, tentatively feeling her way across the scratchy carpet with her toes, JJ crept around the dark room looking for her clothes. They had arrived in his hotel room in such a heated frenzy she didn't remember taking them off. She shuddered again in mingled pleasure and horror.

Her bare instep connected with one of her stiletto heels. A lightning bolt of pain unbalanced her. She staggered against the bed.

"What are you doing?"

She'd wakened him. *Damn*. She didn't want to deal with him. JJ blinked back anxious tears. Careful to keep her voice low, she picked up the shoe. "I need to be going."

"Why?" He yawned. "Sorry I went to sleep on you, but I'm good for a couple more times now." He extended a beautifully modeled arm. "Come here." The last was said with such sexy confidence her knees went weak and a throb began between her legs.

"No, I have to leave."

"It's oh-three-hundred. It's too late to go anywhere. You don't want to do it again? We don't have to. Come back to bed."

Without answering, JJ got down on her hands and knees at the foot of the bed. She swallowed her desperation to get out as she patted the carpet for her other shoe. She fought the memory of kneeling there between his legs, her arms balanced on the hot, living steel of his hair-roughened thighs, the musky male scent of him, the hunger to feel him with her tongue, the way he'd praised and encouraged her every move. "Oh, yeah, that's good… Right *there*… Do that again." Stroking her as she stroked him, holding her to him with his soft voice.

When she'd slammed into him in the service entrance, his voice was the first thing that had drawn her to him.

Oddly enough. You'd think it would be his amazing looks, but JJ had experience with people judging her by her beauty. While she could and did use people's assumptions to her advantage, she understood how much of herself she hid behind her looks. No, his extreme handsomeness did not account for her out-of-character behavior.

His voice wasn't soft as in *not loud*. It was soft as in *pillow-soft*. A voice to snuggle into and hug for comfort. A voice to ease weariness. A voice to convince anyone that voluptuous indulgence was safe. Desirable. When she knew better.

JJ rose, naked, holding a shoe in each hand. "I have to leave. Right now."

"Why? Is someone expecting you?" He pushed up on his elbows. "Hey, you're not married, are you?"

"No." The irony wrung a pained laugh that was close to a sob from her. Not being married was her problem, according to her grandfather. He was going to sell the business—the business she'd shaped her entire life to be owner and head of someday—if she didn't marry within a year. Her grandfather even had four prospective grooms all picked out for her. All were solvent, healthy scions of well-to-do families or professional men on their way up. All had stated their willingness to marry. She had only to choose which one.

"Then why won't you stay?" Davy crammed a pillow under his head and crossed his ankles, clearly settling in for a chat. "The sex was spectacular. We had this bed smokin'." Even in the shadowy room, his smile gleamed with such cheerfully practiced seduction it was impossible not to smile in return. In fact, he had a way of laughing at his whole I'm-a-god persona—as if he was perfectly willing to use his stunning good looks and yet refused to take them seriously—that added a devastating charm to his sexiness.

The charm dragged at JJ like undertow, pulling her toward the bed. It was why she had to leave—now.

She located her dress and bra on the floor near the room's door but gave up on finding her thong. She ducked toward the bathroom.

"Hey!" Too fast for her to see how he did it, he leaped from the bed and blocked her path to the bathroom. Naked, devoid of any veneer of civilization, he hulked before her. No drape of material softened the dangerous power and strength in every muscle of his body.

Now, too late, she realized how helpless she was. Every horror story she'd ever heard about what happens to girls who go off with men they don't know flashed through her mind.

She should have been terrified, but the combustible mix of anger at her grandfather, disgust at herself, and sexual thrall abruptly reignited. Suddenly her frustration had a target, and she was furious.

"Get the hell out of my way!" She took a better grip on the shoe in her right hand and raised it, stiletto heel pointed outward.

A trace of surprise crossed his too-handsome features, but then his dimple flashed as he looked her up and down. "Honey," he assured her, "you're a whole lot more dangerous wearing those shoes than brandishing them."

She raised the flimsy weapon higher. "I'm not joking. Don't make me regret sex with you more than I already do."

"Okay." Before her eyes, he did something with the broad set of his shoulders, and suddenly he looked just as strong but no longer threatening. Like she could put her head on his chest and his strength would shelter her. "Calm down," he urged. "I'm not going to stop you. I'm not going to hurt you. Just tell me why you're leaving."

God. She blinked away the hot pressure of tears she couldn't let fall. That was all she needed—for him to go all sweet and concerned. "Let me by." She squeezed past him into the bathroom and locked the door.

In the sudden brightness of the utilitarian, white-tiled room, she blinked and squinted, while with shaking fingers she fastened her bra and pulled the brown satin jersey over her head. Finally she steeled herself to face the mirror. Her cheeks were pink, and her green eyes seemed unnaturally bright. But her coffee-brown hair was a mess, and her lipstick was gone. Not wanting to go back where he was for her purse, she searched his shaving kit for a comb.

She found a short black one and dragged it through the tangles, relishing the painful tugs at her scalp. She felt raw, aghast, shattered. In the past several hours, she had allowed her emotional nature to rule her.

Angry, rebellious, and bitterly betrayed by her grandfather's willingness to destroy the foundation of her life, she had been a smoldering fire just waiting for the gasoline of a sexy and charming SEAL to explode into an excess of sensuality and chance-taking.

The scary thing was that it had worked. For a few hours, she had been transported out of herself. She had felt wild and free and magnificently alive. She hadn't thought once about the business or the seventy-five people who depended on her to keep it running smoothly and making a profit. She hadn't called to mind her relentless schedule or how fragile her grandfather had looked, his once broad shoulders rounded, his once iron-gray hair almost white.

She'd had a one-night stand with a man whose last name she didn't know and proved she was as capable of emotional extravagance as her parents. And that was the scariest thing of all.

Chapter 4

DAVY WOKE UP PISSED.

Royally pissed.

He'd lain awake until past four-thirty, cursing himself for an idiot.

Even when he finally fell asleep, he kept dreaming he was looking for her. They were in a bazaar in Afghanistan, and she had on one of those blue shuttlecock burqas—so called because the wearers looked like a giant blue badminton birdie had been tossed over their heads—obscuring not only her face but all hint of shape or individuality. All he wanted was to know her name, but without a name, he didn't have a chance of finding her among the other burqa-clad women.

He tossed back the covers. He was pissed at her for running off—as if what they'd had together wasn't spectacular—but he was more pissed at himself.

He'd had lots of time before he finally fell asleep to go over everything that had happened, to remember every word. It galled him that the situation had gotten so far out of control before he even realized something was wrong. His mother had warned him about treating girls as if they were interchangeable. He'd always protested that he didn't. Now he wasn't so sure. He'd been so eager he'd ignored everything else.

Too late, he saw all the signs of agitation he had ignored, the opportunities he'd let go by when he could have gathered intel about who she was, where she lived.

Girls didn't run away from him crying. They didn't threaten to beat him off with shoes.

Part of him knew it wasn't him. She had been upset when he ran into her at the service entrance to the country club. But the part of him that was a SEAL wouldn't let him evade responsibility. He had been so willing to assume she was too hot for him to want any preliminaries that he had ignored even the common decency of learning her name.

He shook his head, trying to dislodge the feelings of self-disgust. The gray light that seeped through the open weave of the curtain hinted at dawn. The red numbers on the bedside clock read six-thirteen. He had time for a run.

He pulled on shorts and a T-shirt and was tying his running shoes when he realized he had no idea where he'd put the key card after unlocking the room. The increasing daylight showed him a room that was a shambles. He righted a lamp that had been knocked over—but not broken, thank God—and pulled his tie from where it draped over the shade.

Images from the night before assaulted him. Underneath a tipped-over chair he found his dress shirt. Oh, yeah, the part about the chair had been *fine*. He'd still had on his shirt when she'd pushed him into the straight wooden chair and straddled him, her long legs reaching the floor easily. Already joined, lodged hot and tight within her, he had pulled the silky material of her dress over her head and unhooked her bra to reveal the perfect roundness of her breasts. The large, velvety brown areolas had been clearly visible even in the shadowy room. In his need to feel them against his mouth, he'd hampered her efforts to unbutton his shirt. They had laughed—*not* just him, dammit, they had both laughed— batting hands out of the way, moving together.

He felt the pockets of his slacks when he found them beside the bed. Nothing. His navy sport coat, unbelievably, was near the bathroom, and now he remembered standing on it when he'd blocked her way to the bathroom door.

And she'd defended herself with a shoe. And warned him not to make her regret it more than she already did. Only at that point had he realized how completely things had gone to shit.

The card wasn't in the sport coat either.

He hung up the coat. It was the only one he had and he didn't want a dry-cleaning bill. The key card wasn't on the dresser or the nightstand; it must have fallen on the floor. He gathered the bedspread from the carpet at the foot of the bed and shook it. The card fluttered to the floor. So did a scrap of brown lace.

Her panties. Thong, actually. He picked it up and spread it over his hand. The tiny flesh-colored triangle of transparent silk sported a running horse bordered by a rounded-off rectangle. Unless he missed his guess, that was a '64 Mustang logo embroidered smack-dab over the crucial spot.

Damn, he wished he'd seen that on her. He wished he'd insisted they turn on the lights and take their time. He wished she hadn't… He shook his head at the futility of the thought. He wished a lot of things. None of them made any difference.

He didn't want to keep the thong, but he didn't want the maids to find it when they came in to clean. If he didn't have any idea who the woman was, they couldn't, and yet he needed to protect her privacy. It was the least he could do.

He crammed the thong in his shorts pocket thinking he would toss it in a public trash can on his run. He wasn't one to collect souvenirs. Despite his Don Juan reputation, he wasn't motivated by the thrill of the chase. He really did just like sex.

Back in his room after his run, he showered and shaved and pulled on clean but worn jeans and a white T-shirt. After only a tiny hesitation, he retrieved the thong from the pocket of his discarded shorts.

He stuffed the silky trifle deep into a pocket of the navy blazer he'd worn the night before. After he'd passed the third trash can, he realized he wasn't going to toss the thong, and he didn't want to leave for the base until he found out the girl's name and at least tried to make sure she was all right.

Davy felt better now that he had a plan.

Davy's improved mood had gone sour again by the time he rendezvoused with Do-Lord in the hotel's coffee shop. Do-Lord was spiffy in new-looking jeans and an open-collared dress shirt topped by a sport coat.

Davy's plan to ask other wedding guests if they knew his mystery woman's identity had been a complete wash-out. He had even defied all common sense—an enlisted man didn't draw an officer's attention when it wasn't in his best interests to do so—and approached the bride and groom when he saw them loading their car.

"Sorry." Pickett shook her head when Davy's unknown was described to her. "My mother knows everybody in a radius of one hundred miles—"

"And is kin to half of them," Jax put in.

"No, if she were a cousin, I'd recognize her, I think. But Mother invited a lot of people she's met through business—people I don't know."

Jax made a restive movement. His tolerance for having his honeymoon interrupted wouldn't last much longer. He put a possessive arm around his bride's shoulder and rested his cheek on the top of her golden curls. Pickett returned the caress by rubbing the back of her head against his shoulder. The movement exposed her throat and a line of tiny pink bite-marks.

If he'd had any doubt (he hadn't), Davy now was sure Jax had had a good time last night—and with a woman who still wanted to be with him this morning.

Davy didn't need the "get lost" look Jax aimed at him over the top of Pickett's head. There was nothing to do but wish them both well.

Do-Lord, looking disgustingly cheerful, slid into the booth where Davy waited for him in the hotel coffee shop. "Before we head back to the base, listen. I just had a call from Pickett's sister. She says a whole tableful of wedding presents got left at the country club last night. She wanted to know if I would go get them and take them to Pickett's mother's house. You up for it?"

Forty-five minutes later, wedding presents retrieved and stowed under a tarp in the back of Do-Lord's big Ford Silverado, Davy and Do-Lord stood at the side door of a large brick colonial surrounded by a wide green lawn and sheltered by tall pines. The morning's earlier overcast had turned to a light drizzle that was bringing down pine needles in a steady brown rain.

A spray of needles landed on Davy's shoulder, pricking him through his T-shirt. "Are you sure anyone is here?" he asked when Do-Lord pressed the doorbell a second time.

"Even if everyone else has gone out, Emmie is staying here."

A note of eagerness in his voice made Davy glance at him sharply. Do-Lord usually met the world with laidback but distant good humor. "And you would know this, how?"

"I brought her home last night." There was undeniable satisfaction in the smile that lurked in the corners of his mouth.

Sheesh, Do-Lord and Emmie had gotten it on last night, too. It just kept getting better. Lon hadn't said anything about Lauren this morning when Davy had returned his car keys—but then, he wouldn't. Davy bet they had shared more than a room, too.

A particularly nasty blend of chagrin and guilt crawled around in his stomach. SEALs were intensely competitive. Jax, Do-Lord, and Lon had all gotten lucky, and *they* all knew where the lady in question was this morning.

He, on the other hand, had had the most awesome sex of his life with a woman whose name he had neglected to learn. He'd had the best one of all and let her get away. If the guys ever learned about it, they'd laugh themselves silly.

"Where the hell is she?" He stamped his feet impatiently. All he wanted was to get this over with. "Ring the bell again," he told Do-Lord.

"Give the girl a chance. Why are you so itchy?"

"I just want to get on the road, that's all."

"Got another hot date tonight?"

Davy imagined calling one of the girls who'd be glad to hear from him, but he knew a better way to blot out last night's fiasco. "Nah. I've got a rating coming up. I need to study."

Saying the words made Davy feel calmer. As soon as he was immersed again in his life as a SEAL, the river of time would flow over this incident and it would be as if it had never happened.

The sight of Emmie when she at last opened the door restored the rest of his good humor. Her face was puffy. Her not-quite-blond, not-quite-brown hair was stuck to her head on one side and standing up on the other. The shapeless terry bathrobe, a faded shade of blue, all but swallowed her, and it hung haphazardly because the collar had been pushed up by the cobalt blue sling that was back in evidence.

What a charity case! He rapidly revised the mental picture he had of her and Do-Lord. Come to think of it, he couldn't imagine Lon doing it with anyone as completely drunk as Lauren had been last night. Of the men he'd been comparing his performance to, that left only Jax.

Jax was the obvious winner in the satisfaction department, but hell, he'd had to get married to do it.

His inner equilibrium restored, Davy reverted to his hospital corpsman identity. Taking care of the wounded was what he did. "How's the shoulder this morning?" he asked Emmie.

"Better. You were right when you told me yesterday that taking my pain medicine on a schedule would help. I did sleep better. In fact, I slept so deeply I'm a little groggy this morning." She laughed sheepishly. "I could hear the doorbell ringing, but I couldn't figure out which door you were at."

"The dopey feeling is caused by the meds. Don't worry. It'll go away in a day or two." He pointed to where folds of the bathrobe were caught under the dark blue sling. With all that excess fabric and a shoulder that hurt with every movement, it was probably the best she could do. "That looks uncomfortable. Want me to help you adjust the sling?"

Emmie looked down at the faded robe as if surprised to learn she had it on. She blushed. "I need to get dressed for real."

Her cluelessness about how she looked had a certain dorky charm—but dorkiness wasn't on the list of what Davy looked for in a girl. He doubted if it made Do-Lord's list either.

"Be careful not to—"

"Put my hand behind my back, I know," Emmie finished.

Do-Lord clapped Davy on the shoulder—hard enough to make the gesture a friendly warning. He subtly interposed his body between Davy and Emmie. "Let the girl go, Doc. I know how much you like to take care of the wounded, but—enough!"

Davy simultaneously realized two things. One: Do-Lord, whom Davy had always found hard to read, was broadcasting, loud and clear, his interest in Emmie. Davy didn't get it, but there was no accounting for tastes.

And two: what was wrong, really wrong, with last night's debacle was that he had failed.

Despite his reputation, he didn't use women—at least not more than they used him. Because he did care what happened to them, he carefully stayed away from any girl who might mistake his intentions, and especially damsels in distress. They had a bad habit of thinking his willingness to try to help them fix their problems was the equivalent of an engagement ring. And when he had to let them down, he just felt like a jerk.

He had an alpha male's tendency to take charge and believe he was responsible in any situation. On top of this, he had more than his share of nurturance and protectiveness. It added up to more than a desire to help others. It was more like "white knight syndrome." He took plenty of teasing designed to remind him he couldn't fix every situation or help every person.

He had learned to temper his natural tendencies with a certain amount of ruthlessness, but at heart he believed, had to believe, he was one of the good guys. Last night he hadn't met even the minimum requirement. He hadn't returned the woman in as good condition as he found her. Whatever her problem was, he was sure he had made it worse.

His failure settled one question for him, though. God's gift to women he was not. If he could screw up an encounter with the most spectacular girl he'd ever met, fuck it. He was needed in Afghanistan.

Chapter 5

AT A LITTLE BEFORE SIX, IN THE UPSTAIRS BEDROOM WHERE she had slept since she was a child, JJ impatiently threw back the duvet. Lying in bed while going over what had happened last night would do no good. She shivered as the predawn chill coming in the open window washed over her naked skin.

JJ preferred to sleep in the nude. She was a restless sleeper. Anything she wore to bed seemed to get twisted around her during the night, winding tighter and tighter until a constricted, trussed-up, tied-down feeling woke her. In college she'd had four blessed years of freedom.

Sleeping in the buff had been out of the question, though, once she returned home. Her grandmother's, and later her grandfather's, illness meant she never knew when she would be needed and someone would come into her bedroom to waken her.

This was the first time she had slept naked since college. Technically, since she hadn't *slept*, she still hadn't done so—but that was going to change.

Chafing her arms, she scurried to the window, shut it, and closed the wide plantation blinds before switching on a bedside light.

———

With quick efficient movements, she made the cherry pencil-post bed and tidied the room. Near the head of the bed, her foot encountered Smiley's orthopedic dog bed. For a long moment, she studied it with a funny what's-wrong-with-this-picture feeling.

Then she remembered.

Yesterday had started with a call from her vet, with whom she had left her golden retriever of fourteen years, telling her Smiley had died. Smiley's death wasn't unexpected. She planned to ask the vet later that morning if it was time to put the dog to sleep. Still, her knees had gone rubbery, and the phone had become so slippery with sweat from her palms that she'd almost dropped it when she heard the news.

She had pulled herself together. With a few swift phone calls, she had postponed meetings with her sales manager and the president of the SPCA, moved a lunch meeting with the Azalea Festival Chair to breakfast, and shuffled everything in between. Not burying Smiley herself—whether her day was already packed or not— had never been a consideration.

After Ham, the Vietnam vet who did odd jobs for her grandfather, had dug the grave, she had laid Smiley to rest in his favorite cool, shady spot in the garden: at the foot of a fall-blooming, white *camellia sasanqua*. Burying him was wrenching, but oddly comforting, too. Smiley had been a good dog. He deserved to be laid to rest, not disposed of, like something used up.

While her grandfather, who had come outside in the unseasonably warm autumn sunshine to pay his respects, looked on, they had lined the grave with Smiley's Carolina blue UNC blanket and laid him in it. In old age, his silky coat had turned more blond than golden.

A light breeze ruffled the beautiful wavy fur, giving

the heart-clenching illusion that he had started breathing again. JJ knelt forward and rested her hand on his chest. Underneath the fur he was cold and the ribs were too stiff. She carefully pulled the edges of the blanket over him and smoothed it until he was hidden from her sight.

After that—after burying her dog—the thought of driving for an hour or so to another town to attend the wedding of a couple she hardly knew was almost unbearable.

Just this once, she would have disobeyed her grandmother's dictum that an invitation, once accepted, became an unbreakable obligation. But Mary Cole Sessoms, the mother of the bride, was a good friend and JJ's mentor.

She owed Mary Cole. Without Mary Cole to advise her, JJ thought she would have buckled under the load when she assumed leadership of Caruthers Automotive at the age of twenty-two. If the older woman wanted her at her daughter's wedding, then by God, JJ would be there. And, no matter how she felt, she would put a smile on her face and act delighted.

At last, she and Ham had redistributed the pine-straw mulch over the newly packed earth. She shook the dry, shoe-leather hand Ham offered in condolence. Her grandfather squeezed her shoulder in sympathy. Each in his own way loved her; she knew that. Their small gestures of comfort was as demonstrative as either of them got.

You'd think burying the only creature who had unfailingly rejoiced when he saw her—and had never been afraid to show it—was bad enough. But then her grandfather had said, "Jane Jessup, would you come into my office after you wash your hands?"

And her day got a great deal worse.

Chapter 6

JJ HAD TAKEN TIME NOT ONLY TO WASH HER HANDS BUT also to shower and change into the Donna Karan satin jersey dress she intended to wear to the wedding. JJ considered looking beautiful, fashionable, and perfectly turned out to be part of her job description. She'd been satisfied with her appearance until the three-way mirror revealed a panty line that marred the liquid fall of the material across her butt.

Aware she was keeping her grandfather waiting, she rifled hurriedly through the tiny drawer containing thongs. At the back of the drawer her fingers closed over a silken pouch, a gag gift from Bronwyn, her college roommate.

They had made bawdy jokes about thongs embroidered with a famous carmaker's logo in an eye-catching spot. Neither had guessed that in less than a year JJ would be the de facto head of the oldest car dealership in the state. That was almost six years ago. The frivolous little nothings had been crammed in the back of the lingerie drawer and forgotten.

The Ford Mustang one was an ecru color that would do. She stripped off the offending bikinis and pulled it on.

In twenty minutes, her strappy gladiator sandals with three-inch heels were carrying her down the curving staircase into the two-story entry with its Waterford chandelier and long, multipaned windows. The entry formed the center of the house. From there, she turned down the wide hall of her grandfather's wing.

Her grandfather spent most of his time these days in his "office," which still contained the massive walnut desk. Since little business was done there anymore, the office also now boasted recliners, a deep sofa, and a wide-screen TV. JJ thought it was really her grandfather's man-cave.

The walls were lined with photographs of Caruthers in all its incarnations. Over the mantel hung the framed artist's rendering of the modern white structure, built when JJ was seventeen. It lifted her spirits every time she saw it. She hadn't needed her grandfather to tell her it would all be hers someday. In letting her help design it, her grandfather had made it hers. It belonged to her and she to it.

Her grandfather's big, oxblood-leather desk chair was swiveled to face the long windows behind the desk. At her tap on the open door, he turned to face her. His still-shrewd green eyes peered over the tops of silver-framed reading glasses.

"You look nice," he said. He always acknowledged when he thought JJ had done well in any way, but he didn't heap praise. He made sure she understood that serious responsibility came with the wealth and privilege she enjoyed, remarking that he had indulged his son, JJ's father, too much.

"Thanks, Lucas." After college, when JJ had come into the business full time, it became obvious that the affectionate "Granddaddy" she had always called him made it difficult for others to understand the authority she had. However, the more formal "Grandfather" fell oddly on Southern ears.

Instead of taking a seat, she leaned one hip against the desk, hoping to make the point that although she had come at his request and was prepared to listen, she hadn't come to chat. "What's up?" She smiled a let's-move-this-along smile.

Lucas pushed back in his chair and allowed his elbows to rest on the wide chair arms. Despite his man-at-ease posture, JJ recognized an alpha male proclaiming his territory. A tiny tingle ran up her spine.

The tingle was her only warning that the foundation of her life was about to crumble.

Chapter 7

JJ STOOD IN HER BEDROOM AND CONSCIOUSLY LET GO OF yesterday's memories. Smiley would never sleep in his dog bed again. She would never see that SEAL again. She would never believe her grandfather was on her side again. All that had happened yesterday was over. The only thing she could do was move on. JJ breathed deeply to ease the tightness in her chest and picked up Smiley's bed.

Downstairs, she deposited the bed and four others she had gathered from around the house in the laundry room. Smiley, wherever he was, was out of pain now. She hoped someone was with him, someone to throw a ball so he could play his beloved fetch. She refused to dwell on how achingly silent the house was without him.

Beds large enough to accommodate a golden were not cheap. She would have Esperanza wash the covers tomorrow and donate the beds to a rescue organization for goldens in Smiley's name.

Yes. That would be the first item on the list. With that thought, JJ immediately felt better. In fact, she needed to make two lists, one for herself and one for Esperanza, the housekeeper who came in a couple of times a week. At the thought of two lists, JJ felt more firmly in control, more able to focus on the future rather than the past. Less cut in two by the hollow feeling in the pit of her stomach.

She loved lists. Her employees teased her, saying she had so many that she had to make lists of her lists to keep up with them. They weren't completely wrong.

She set two list pads on the table in the breakfast nook. She could have retrieved her PDA, but nothing was as satisfying as watching a pencil-and-paper list grow.

From a glass-front cabinet, JJ drew her favorite of her grandmother's hand-painted porcelain mugs: the one with a delicate spray of lily of the valley. JJ couldn't use one of the mugs without thinking of her. Her grandmother had been an ardent gardener and student of the art of flower arranging who had refused to drink from crockery, saying coffee only tasted right in porcelain. JJ had found the floral theme mugs, each one a work of art, in Belgium.

From the breakfast nook where she took her coffee, JJ could see the dark evergreen of the fall-blooming *camellia sasanqua* under which Smiley was buried.

Yesterday's warm, sunny weather was gone. Today, fat white blossoms brought down by the morning's heavy drizzle littered the pine needles and obscured the proof that the ground had been disturbed. Already the evidence of Smiley's life and death was vanishing.

JJ took a swallow of coffee and picked up her pencil.

When she had twenty-nine items on her list and eleven on Esperanza's, JJ put down her pencil and glanced at her watch. Seven-fifty. A little early to call anyone on Sunday morning, but Vanessa Clemmons was head of the real estate agency and understood that business came first.

"Good morning, JJ!" Vanessa seized the initiative before JJ could speak. Salesman to the bone, she sounded like nothing could have thrilled her more than to recognize JJ's caller ID. "How are you?"

"I'm fine, thank you. Hope you're well. How is Harold?" Harold was Vanessa's husband. Vanessa asked about JJ's grandfather and how business was at the "car place"—colloquial for car dealership. They agreed the long Indian summer Wilmington had enjoyed had come to an end and Christmas was right around the corner. They traded a few more of the social niceties without which business in the South could not be conducted before JJ said, "Vanessa, I apologize for calling you on a Sunday morning. I won't take but a minute. I'd like you to find me an apartment."

A pause. "For yourself?"

"For myself."

"Hmm." The line was silent while Vanessa absorbed that. "Well. Frankly, I think it's high time. Any requirements?"

"I'd like something immediately... and I'd like not to be the object of speculation. That's why I called *you*."

JJ had been the subject of gossip, most of it friendly, some of it not so much, all her life. People could hardly be blamed for finding everything a Caruthers or a Jessup did newsworthy. There were richer people in Wilmington and more distinguished families, but few were so visible to so many people as the owners of a hundred-year-old car dealership whose TV commercials ran every day.

Vanessa was right. JJ should have moved out years ago, right after college, but since she hadn't, suddenly getting a place of her own would attract a lot of attention.

The *real* story, that the future of Caruthers was threatened, was bad enough to make the banks that held their loans nervous. Automobile makers were going bankrupt, and dealerships were being forced out of business. The economy would eventually turn around, but it would take fancy footwork to keep Caruthers afloat until it did. But the real story would be nothing compared to the wild stories about a rift between her and Lucas that *could* circulate.

"When you say 'immediately…'" Vanessa probed delicately.

"I mean today wouldn't be too soon."

"Are you set on an apartment?" Vanessa inquired. "Let me tell you why I'm asking. Lauren Babcock—you know her, don't you? She wants me to list her beach cottage."

Lauren Babcock! JJ had seen her just last night, she remembered guiltily, and had been so wrapped up in her own problems that she hadn't crossed the room to speak to her—although she should have. Lauren had lost her grown daughter back in the summer. JJ had sent flowers and a handwritten condolence card. Still, she should have taken the opportunity last night to speak to Lauren and express her compassion personally.

There was always a huge outpouring of sympathy when a death occurred, but after the reality settled in, the bereaved were often treated as if their grief was an unmentionable disease, as contagious as it was embarrassing. JJ understood why. People never knew what to say and somehow seemed to feel avoidance was better than any possible verbal faux pas. They were wrong.

When her parents died, JJ had endured the other little girls staring at her with round, shocked eyes, pointing and whispering behind their hands. Clumps of little boys had scattered at her approach, taking to their heels as if fearful of getting caught. One little boy, who had once made excuses to sit by her, had turned and walked away when he saw her coming.

Only Bronwyn, her college roommate, had ever wanted to know how JJ felt to lose her parents at the age of nine.

Yes, JJ knew Lauren, and she didn't bother to think to herself, "Small world." The world of eastern North Carolina society *was* small. To her list JJ added: *30. Send "thinking of you" note to Lauren Babcock.*

"The thing is," Vanessa's voice continued, "this is a terrible time to list beach property. I hate to see it sit unsold or to sell for much less than it should. She doesn't need to liquidate. I think she's just reacting to the death of her daughter. Right this minute, the cottage has too many memories, but one day, those memories might be precious."

"The cottage is on Topsail Island, isn't it?" JJ liked the thought of helping Lauren out by saving her from a bad decision but Topsail was thirty miles north of Wilmington, and when traffic was heavy, the better part of an hour away. "I don't think I want to commute that far."

"Hear me out. The cottage comes completely furnished, turnkey ready. You won't even need to buy towels. It was redecorated a couple of years ago, so it's fresh and—you know Lauren—top of the line. I don't know any place else you'll find to rent furnished, and that's what you're used to."

"I don't think I'm ready to buy."

"That's good, because I don't think she's ready to sell—even if she says she is. I'll work a deal that leaves you free to move and her free to sell. Let me call her and tell her it's you. Oh, wait. I know how you love dogs. She's not going to allow pets."

"Smiley's gone."

"I'm sorry. You're not going to get another one?"

"It wouldn't be fair to the dog. I just don't have time for one."

"In that case, I think I can sell her that with you there, she really can safely put the cottage out of her mind—and I think that's what she really wants."

JJ couldn't help but smile to hear Vanessa's salesman wheels turning. "What are you going to sell me on?"

"Privacy," Vanessa answered without hesitation. "The cottages on either side are closed for the winter."

JJ and Vanessa discussed rents and a few safeguards before hanging up. Vanessa promised to call as soon as she had talked to Lauren.

The feeling of constriction in JJ's chest eased for the first time since her grandfather had called her into his office yesterday. Well, for the second time, if you counted the few hours she'd spent with the Navy SEAL, Davy No-last-name—but she wasn't going there.

"What time did you get in last night?" Lucas asked when he came into the kitchen a little after eight. He was dressed in the same slacks and gray and slate-blue, diamond-patterned golf sweater as yesterday.

Before she rose to pour him some coffee, JJ made a note on the separate list she was making for Esperanza to lay out fresh clothes for him.

Her grandfather was no male chauvinist. He believed women could do anything men could. He had never expressed the smallest doubt that JJ could inherit and command Caruthers. He would have rejected any notion that women existed to serve him. And yet, if he had thought about it, which he didn't, he would have believed he would be invading her territory had he poured his own coffee when she was there to do it.

The simple truth was some woman had always been there to put whatever he needed into his hand. His wife had bought his clothes and laid out what he was to wear every day, made his appointments, handed him his medicine and vitamins to take, bought the gifts he gave, and written his thank-you notes for the gifts he received.

When her grandmother had known she was dying, she had carefully instructed JJ on all she would need to do for Lucas. Lucas had become so lost, so befuddled, and then so sick that JJ had done it.

"Around four-thirty." She set the coffee—his mug was a blue delphinium—in front of him.

"What were you doing out so late? I don't like the idea of you being alone on the road at that hour. Anything could happen. You should have gotten a room."

"I had a lot to do this morning, but the drive home also gave me time to think about our discussion yesterday." Lucas looked at her expectantly, his green eyes sharp under his bushy white brows. "I'm not agreeing to your demands," she told him. "Howev—"

"Whether you agree or not," Lucas interrupted, "one year from today, if you're not married, I'll start selling off the business. If you are married and remain so for a year, I'll put the business in your name."

"*However*, I'm not opposed to marrying." *Although Lucas's timing couldn't be worse*. "I know you don't believe me. You think I don't act like a woman who wants a husband, but until the car business recovers more, I don't see how I can do more. If finding time for a boyfriend is this hard, imagine how hard finding time to keep a husband happy will be."

Lucas's bushy white brows lowered in a scowl. "You're giving your life to that business! Do you think the day will come when it will give you your life back?"

JJ let that go by. Lucas had raised her to think of Caruthers first, but now that she did it, he wanted more. JJ's fingernails cut into her palms as her hands unconsciously curled into fists. Her jaw clenched, and she fought to keep her voice level. "Anyway, looking at it objectively, I haven't been successful at finding a husband. I realized I shouldn't refuse, sight unseen, the men you picked out."

Lucas humphed, the grooves around his mouth going deeper. "Nothing like a wedding to make a woman think of marriage. Is that what changed your mind?"

JJ crossed her arms. "Hardly."

He gave her a sharp look. "Did something happen last night?"

Only wild, no-holds-barred sex with a stranger. Only the discovery that she was more dangerously like her parents than she had ever believed and that she must guard more scrupulously against emotion-based decisions if she hoped to live up to her responsibilities. JJ willed her expression not to change. "Like what?"

"I don't know. I didn't expect you to give in this easily."

JJ allowed herself a tight, cold smile. "Rest assured, Lucas, I haven't *given in*. However, if I'm going to begin dating seriously, I need a place of my own. I don't need a grandfather keeping track of what time I come in—or with whom." And the real reason: if she saw Lucas every day, her anger *would* boil over and she would do something rash.

"You're going to move out? But this is your home."

"Correction: it's your home. And, as you've forcibly reminded me, Caruthers is your business."

"Now wait a minute. You're taking this the wrong way."

"Did you think I would meekly continue to live here while you attempt to coerce me into living my life on your timetable?"

Lucas's intensified frown told her that was exactly what he had thought.

All his life, Lucas had issued orders and people had done as he said. Smart as he was about making money, careful as he was to treat his workers *his* idea of well, he had one weakness as a manager: he didn't anticipate how others would react emotionally. If he thought something was a good idea, he thought they should think it was equally good and be grateful.

JJ watched his face as he sought for some bargaining chips. There weren't any. JJ was of age, and she had her own money, the Jessup fortune, a legacy from her grandmother. She almost felt compassion for him as she saw how slowly he thought through his options and how poorly he hid the sadness in his eyes. Almost.

"I'm not going to back down," he said at last.

"I don't expect you to."

"Then why…?"

JJ shook her head. He didn't get it. Even when it was brought to his attention, he didn't understand that his actions had caused her to withdraw from him. If she tried to explain her feelings, he would only say she was wrong to feel that way.

For the first time, JJ felt a measure of compassion for her father. He had been forced to rebel to obtain any autonomy. One of his most important acts of rebellion had been marrying JJ's mother, a totally unsuitable woman.

On the drive home, through the darkest hours of the night, JJ had considered—and discarded—the same course. Her father had been heedless of the destruction left in his wake. JJ wasn't. Her mother had married her father for his money, as she freely admitted, and with no thought to the responsibilities she would acquire. Chaos had followed.

Hundreds of people, if you counted all JJ's employees and their families, depended on JJ to get this right. She had chosen, instead of mindless rebellion for which others would pay or committing acts that harmed no one but herself, to direct her anger toward its cause. Between yesterday and today, something had hardened within JJ.

There was no point in trying to explain why she was moving out. If she tried, they would only get into a shouting match.

JJ rose and carried her mug to the sink where she rinsed it and set it in the dishwasher. "You have my cell number. I'll write down the address and landline number. There are frozen dinners in the freezer if you don't want to go out to eat. Esperanza will be at church right now, but I'll call her later and arrange for her to start coming in every day." JJ smiled coolly as she replaced the sponge. "Is there anything else I can do for you before I leave?"

—⁓—

Lucas Caruthers looked at the set face of his grand-daughter. She had the sort of warm, apricot complexion that didn't pale easily. Except for her eyes, which she had gotten from him, she looked more like her mother, who had had a drop or two of Indian blood. He could see it in the strong curve of JJ's cheekbones and in moments like this when she could look so unmovable she appeared graven. He understood her, he thought, but he hadn't anticipated that she would move out as part of accepting his challenge.

JJ's problem was that there weren't a lot of men who were her match in drive, strength of character, and powerful will. Without some sort of come-ahead signal from her, most men weren't going to make a strong enough play to get themselves noticed. Lucas had hoped that if challenged, she would finally start looking at men as suitors. If she applied herself, he felt sure she would find someone worthy, someone to share her life with, someone to be there after he was gone.

He had thought long and hard before offering her the choice of finding a husband or losing Caruthers. He didn't believe in empty threats, didn't think he could have gotten by with one anyway. But he had tried every way he knew to make JJ see that she was letting Caruthers consume her.

He understood her drive—she got it from him—and, to an extent, he blamed himself. She was what he had trained her to be. But even when the tide of his young manhood had been in full competitive spate, he had had extracurricular activities. He'd loved taking the *Daddy Carbucks*, his twenty-six-foot Chris-Craft out to the Gulf Stream for some deep-sea fishing, and if he used the trips to do a little business, that was okay. He didn't invite anyone who didn't love the big sport fish as much as he did. There'd been other leisure activities that he wasn't so proud of, but the point was, he had them.

He'd also had Beth. In the early days of their marriage, he had thought she was his hood ornament. Too late, he realized she was his outrigger. Without her, he floundered.

He didn't want to take Caruthers away from JJ. He had given up the notion of leaving it to her father even before he died. When Lucas realized JJ liked it, even though she was just a little girl, he felt as if the meaning of life had been given back to him.

It would break his heart not to pass the business to another generation—she must see that—but he would.

If destroying Caruthers was the only way to free her from its thrall, then destroy it he would.

Chapter 8

Afghanistan

HE WAS GOING TO DIE TODAY.

Davy's eyes snapped open. In the east, a mountain crag that had no name was a dark smudge against a barely lighter sky as dawn came to the Afghanistan mountains. Around him, the other fifteen men of his SEAL platoon began to stir, grousing about the frigid morning. SEALs, both intrinsically and through training, had greater tolerance than most people for cold conditions, but that didn't mean they liked being chilled. Winter came early in the thin, dry air of the Hindu Kush, the westernmost finger of the Himalayas. Higher peaks were already capped with snow, even though it was only the second week in August.

Hearing his buddies complain assured Davy he was really awake *this* time.

He'd had one of those dreams in which you dream you wake up. In the dream, he'd been awakened by the sound of a woman crying. He'd gone looking for the source and found his mother, her plump shoulders rounded with grief, sobbing.

Davy rolled over in his sleeping bag to ease the crushing feeling in his chest. That was the part of the dream he hadn't liked. The rest of the dream, in which he saw a wooden coffin with row after row of golden

SEAL Tridents slapped against its gleaming walnut lid, had been okay. He had died doing what he loved, being who he had wanted to be. In the dream, he had not felt saddened to be dead weeks shy of his twenty-eighth birthday but incredibly fortunate to have had the life that fitted him perfectly.

Still, he didn't like for his mother to cry.

Raised with a matter-of-fact acceptance of ESP, Davy didn't question his dream's significance. Dreaming true ran in his Irish mother's side of the family, as did fore-knowledge of one's death. He'd rarely experienced a premonition himself.

On the other hand, he'd never died before, either. Davy chuckled, feeling for the sleeping bag's zipper. Maybe he'd never before needed a warning dream.

He sat up, still laughing, and rubbed his cheeks, finger-combing the glossy, black curls of his beard. With his black hair, large dark eyes, and olive skin, he blended into the local population, a fact he capitalized on by pulling a blue-checked shirt over his body armor. Close up, he wouldn't fool anyone, but from a distance, if his appearance made a shooter hesitate even for a sec-ond, it could save his life.

An hour later, Davy looked up from checking his medical supply kit in time to see McHale lead a kid in baggy, dusty black pants and a once-white shirt over to the platoon's lieutenant.

"Hey Doc." The platoon's lieutenant, Garth Vale, waved him over. "Lemme talk to you for a second." The lieutenant clapped Davy on the shoulder and drew him out of earshot. "The kid's name is Hamid. He says his sis-ter's in labor in the next village. Wants you to come."

"Shit." Davy stubbed at a pebble with the toe of his boot. He was often the platoon's goodwill ambassador—the first person villagers would open up to, the one whose help they would seek. He relished the role, even though what he could do for them was often a drop in the bucket compared to what they needed. But in a situation like this, he couldn't help anyone. He could lance an abscess, sew up a cut, or even set a bone in men and children, but he couldn't touch a woman.

The fundamentalist Muslim interpretation of modesty decreed that letting a woman die was preferable to allowing a man who wasn't a relative to see her body. "I can't do anything for her. They're not going to let me examine her. Her husband's not going to let another man look at his wife."

"The kid says he will. Says the husband sent him. But it's up to you. I'm taking the guys into a village south of there. We're going in like it's a 'search and apprehend.' Supposedly they're ready to talk about where some Taliban placements are. We'll make it look like we weren't invited—just in case the Taliban are watching."

Here in the mountains, villagers were often caught in a no-win situation between the Allied forces and the Taliban—since alliance with one invited attacks from the other. The media were quick to condemn any civilian deaths caused by the UN forces but slow to mention the unrelenting terrorism inflicted on their own people by the Taliban.

"I don't expect anything to come of it," the lieutenant added. "I can spare you."

Garth was leaving it up to him. This war would never be won without the aid of the Afghanis. Any amount of trust he won could make a difference. "If they've asked for help, I guess I ought to go. I probably can't do anything for the woman, but maybe some other villager needs me."

Seeing that Davy had made up his mind, the lieutenant clapped him on the shoulder. "All right. Do what you can. I've asked for extraction at fourteen-hundred. Stay in touch."

—⁓—

The woman died. There was nothing Davy could do. Nothing he *could* have done.

As his driver (the same twelve-year-old who had come for him) kept the rattletrap Toyota pickup hugging the mountain side of the dirt track, Davy fought the hot prickle at the back of his eyes. Woman hell, the *little girl*, barely fourteen, had bled to death. Her baby, still unborn, had died with her.

Since he rarely saw Afghani women except at a distance and swathed head to toe in their blue burqas, it was easy to forget that one cause of the country's dismal childbirth statistics lay in the practice of forced marriage. It wasn't uncommon for girls to be married before puberty—and not in name only. A girl of nine or ten could be married and her husband, a man three or four times her age, would insist on his rights.

Sure enough, when Davy got there, he'd found the husband, a forty-year-old man, arguing with the village headman, a man of sixty or so. If Davy's Dari, the local variant of Farsi, was up to the task of translation, the headman was the husband's father-in-law—the girl's father.

Finally the headman had given in, but only, Davy suspected, because he knew it was already too late. He could claim he had mercifully heard his son-in-law's pleas, and, at the same time, the smirch upon the family's honor, caused by letting a man other than a relative look upon her, wouldn't have to be expunged by killing her—if his daughter was already dead.

So Davy had entered the windowless room, the usual odors of spice and incense and unwashed bodies overwhelmed by primal birthing smells and the hot, sticky, metallic tang of blood thickening the air.

Even now, instead of the yellowish-tan monochrome of the landscape through which the Toyota traveled, he kept seeing her wide, emerald-green eyes set in black, curly lashes—all that was visible of her blue burqa-covered face.

She had opened those green eyes (all he knew of her), gazed at him with distant interest and, with a sigh, slowly closed them again as the last drops of life drained away.

He'd only seen eyes of that pure, intense green once in America. In Afghanistan, although the color was always startling, it wasn't rare. He'd encountered it over and over, and every time he did, he remembered the woman whose name he never knew.

The memory embarrassed him, but he couldn't seem to erase it. Fucking a woman whose name he couldn't remember afterward was one thing. He wasn't proud of it, but it happened. Carelessly not bothering to ask was inexcusable. He even dreamed occasionally that she was running away from him and he was running behind her, yelling, "What's your name?"

At the time, it hadn't seemed to matter.

At the time, all that had mattered was getting together with her as fast and in as many ways as possible. If he had thought about it at all, he'd probably assumed they'd talk the next morning—in between more languorous bouts of lovemaking. They'd certainly have exchanged names then. But her abrupt departure at oh-four-hundred had erased all assumptions about how they'd spend their next morning. Later, nobody seemed to know who the woman in the brown dress had been.

Careless. A mistake he could neither fix nor forget. But he'd made sure it would never happen again. These days he learned the names of women—all women—the instant he met them.

The road narrowed, and his kid driver edged the truck even closer to the mountain. It was a long way down on the other side. More important, staying in close also made them a little harder to target from above. They were so close to the top of the mountain now that there was little above them to worry about, but when they started their descent, it would be a different story. The back end of the Toyota fishtailed as nearly bald tires fought for purchase on the rough gravel track.

Davy absently thumbed the switch on the radio, not really surprised to hear nothing. He'd been trying to check in with the platoon since they started back, but the mountain was blocking reception. As soon as they rounded the next bend, they should be in line of sight with the village, and he'd get a signal again.

The tiny pickup shuddered. The boy had felt it, too, and braked before Davy could tell him to *tawaquf,* stop. With the whine of the motor silenced, both could hear thunder, sometimes seeming near, sometimes far, as the sound echoed back and forth between the mountains. The pickup shuddered again. Pebbles slithered down the sheer rock face.

Rocket-propelled grenades. This was very bad news because his platoon didn't carry any RPGs. The Russian-made weapons were cheap and easy to use, a favorite of the Taliban. Their presence indicated a planned, organized ambush, which was very bad news indeed.

Davy signaled the kid to stay where he was, and ran around the bend in the road. Below he could see the mud-walled village. On a saddleback ridge to the south, sun glinted on metal. He was above them, and they didn't know he was there. It was the first bit of luck.

He radioed headquarters and requested an air strike. He considered how to make maximum use of the small amount of tactical advantage he had. It wasn't in a SEAL's nature to sit back and wait while others did the heavy lifting. Every member of his platoon could be dead before help arrived. *Look after your buddies. They are your life insurance. A man alone in combat does not survive.* He was alone. He could still look after his buddies.

Everything about the Taliban force's placement spoke of a carefully planned trap. From his higher position, he could see the routes along which they intended to scatter before reinforcements arrived.

If he took the fight to the Taliban, he could distract them, keep them busy. He would also be inside the kill zone of the Apache helicopters. If the Taliban didn't kill him, friendly fire would. So be it.

He had surprise on his side. Violence of action was the SEAL credo. He would only get one chance to maximally confuse and disorganize their attack on the village.

He set his rifle on automatic and lobbed a grenade into their midst. Then before the first echoes of the explosion reached him, he charged down the hill.

Chapter 9

Charlottesville, VA

HIS MOTHER'S KITCHEN WAS THE MOST SILENT HE COULD ever remember. It was as if all the noise in the house had been sucked out by his mother's death.

Friends and neighbors had made pools of chatter as they cleaned the kitchen, stored the casseroles, and tidied the living room and dining room. After they departed into the September dusk, Davy and his brother and sister sat at the glass and wrought-iron kitchen table, idly turning cups of coffee on spongy plastic placemats shaped like sunflowers. They were trying to absorb the senior chief's verdict that there wasn't any money in their mother's estate.

Four days earlier, Davy had looked up from the Nintendo he was playing with in the hospital dayroom.

"Hey, guys. Garth. Lon," he amended, grateful their names had come to him in such a timely fashion. Davy's eyes went from one man to the other. Garth, injured in the same action as Davy, had graduated to a cane. Lon was his same burly, massively competent senior chief self. "This is bad news, isn't it?"

"Your sister has been trying to reach you," Garth began. "When she couldn't, she called me."

Garth faltered, and Lon, his eyes kind, took up the story. "Your mother passed away last night."

Davy's heart squeezed. "Last night? Was that yester-day?" Davy thought if he could get the time sequence right, he'd understand the rest of what Lon said.

"Yesterday, yes."

"That can't be right. I talked to her yesterday."

"It was last night. Late."

"How...?"

"She called your sister. Said she felt bad. Your sister called 911. By the time the paramedics got there, she was already gone."

Davy understood the words, and something more. He didn't remember being hit; he didn't remember what they said he'd done. The closest he could come to ac-knowledging it happened was recognizing that it was something he *would* have done—and been glad to.

What he did remember with perfect clarity was the dream he'd had that morning in Afghanistan and the certainty he'd felt that he was going to die. A thousand times, while he was recovering from surgeries to put the pieces of his face back together, he had pondered why he had dreamed of his mother and of dying when he hadn't died. Now he understood at a level far deeper than rational thought.

He had been right all along. He *was* supposed to die. His mother had known it. She had bargained with God or something—he was hazy on the details—and once she was sure he was safe and on the mend, she had taken his place.

———

Davy had asked Lon to stay behind after the other SEALs who had come to his mother's funeral had left.

Lon was the steadiest man he knew, and Lon had the experience to look at financial statements and sum up the situation.

Even with Lon's help, Davy had looked too long at papers, straining to read with eyes that weren't quite used to their new, slightly different positions. Davy ignored the hot ice-pick of pain that stabbed through the back of his left eye. The pain made the walls he'd always thought of as a cheerful yellow glare with nauseating intensity under the overhead fluorescents.

His pain would decrease as the swelling from his injuries abated. Being blown behind a rock by the rocket-propelled grenade had probably saved his life, but landing among rocks had smashed his cheekbone and fractured his eye socket.

Everyone said he was lucky. Lucky to be alive, lucky not to lose an eye, lucky the shard that had sliced open his cheek hadn't severed... that nerve. He knew the anatomical name—he was a hospital corpsman, for chrissake—but the word wouldn't come.

Yeah, he was lucky he wasn't killed or totally, permanently messed up, but he wasn't sure his family had been so fortunate.

Shit, if he'd been killed, at least his family would have had his life insurance.

"Is it true you might be up for the Medal of Honor?" Harris broke the silence, his steel-blue gaze both sharp and remote. He and his twin sister, Elle, short for Eleanor, had inherited their light brown hair and blue eyes from their father, Davy's stepfather, while Davy took his Italian looks from his own father. Harris's build was bonier than either his twin's or Davy's. He was an inch or so taller than Davy—or he would have been if not for an already noticeable scholar's slump.

"It's true." Lon affirmed from Davy's mother's home-office desk where he had sat while going over bank statements. "Unfortunately, there's no money in it, unless you write a best-selling book about it, the way Audie Murphy did."

"Who's Audie Murphy?" Harris asked.

"World War II hero," Lon told him. "Pretty as our Davy here. Went on to be a movie star."

Elle ignored the byplay. "Why didn't you tell us about the medal?" she demanded. "Didn't you know how proud we'd be?"

"I'd sort of forgotten about it. It isn't likely. They don't hand out many Medals of Honor."

"The men I overheard were talking about what you did. How you deliberately drew the Taliban fire until an air strike could arrive. Don't you think you deserve recognition?"

"I can't remember what I'm supposed to have done, but I know this much: I'm not a hero… The whole thing just embarrasses me."

Harris thought that over. "I guess that means 'no book.'"

"*Harris*!" Elle's round blue eyes widened in outrage. Unlike her twin, her gaze was rarely remote. "Even for you, that's insensitive. Don't you realize David is relating his feelings?"

"Oh. You mean because he said he was embarrassed? I'm sorry, David. But amnesia for the event is frequent in cases of traumatic brain injury," Harris informed them all, showing off his nascent medical knowledge. He and Elle were in their first year of medical school.

Davy didn't feel up to explaining that being called a hero was what embarrassed him, not the amnesia.

They all fell quiet again while Davy wondered how could he effortlessly use words like *nascent* and then blank on ordinary words that should have been easier to summon. It kept him constantly off balance, never knowing when he was going to hit a wall.

Elle began to cry again. She made no sound. She patiently wiped the tears from her round cheeks, as if dealing with a slow leak. Her round eyes puffy, she finally broke the silence.

"She told us everything was okay after Dad died."

Harris tossed aside the bank statement he'd been studying. "Did you know Riley's school was that expensive?"

"I feel so guilty," his older-by-fifteen-minutes twin said. "You and I should have gotten jobs when we graduated instead of going straight to med school. David's the only one who wasn't dependent on her."

That didn't let him off the hook. He was also the only one who had been an adult when Eleanor, Harris, and Riley's father had died. He'd accepted his mother's reassurances that his stepfather had left them well-provided for—it was what he wanted to hear.

He'd been totally engrossed by medical corpsman and SEAL training. When he'd made it home for Christmas or the occasional birthday, everything had seemed fine. Pretty much like always. He'd fixed a leaky faucet or cleaned the gutters and told himself what a good son he was.

Eleanor stiffened her shoulders. "Maybe if I get a job, Harris can stay in med school, and Riley can live with us."

It was typical that Eleanor had gone into problem-solving mode and was planning how to care for her twin. While unquestionably brilliant, Harris had always been willing to turn practicalities over to his more assertive sister.

Well, not on his watch was she going to sacrifice her dreams for Harris's. It was time for Davy to man up. He was the oldest, and he was already established. If they'd had his life insurance, there would have been enough money to get them past the shock, and to buy enough time to get their feet under them. Instead, he was alive. He'd just have to make sure the twins finished their education and Riley was taken care of.

"You're going to stay in medical school. Both of you."

"How?

"We'll sell the house. This semester is paid for. You might as well finish it. In the meantime, we'll find scholarships, loans, something."

"But what about Riley?"

"Lower your voice." Their fourteen-year-old brother, Riley, had bionic ears—when he chose to listen. He'd wandered off to the family room to play video games as soon as they got home from the funeral.

"But what *about* him? He doesn't adapt well to change. Our hours are crazy, but yours are crazier. I still think I should get a job. I can provide the stability he needs."

"Mom's will names me guardian," Davy reminded her, more sharply than he intended. The pain in his head was making him nauseated now. He needed to end this discussion.

"Sorry." Elle stiffened at his tone but didn't back down. "I didn't mean to step on your toes. But you haven't been around much. I don't think you know what you're letting yourself in for."

Davy lurched to his feet. The pain was affecting his balance. He had to get out of there before he threw up. "I'll figure something out."

―――∞―――

Davy woke up in his old room, now Elle's, with his sister standing over him holding a white Nike shoe box.

"Feeling better?" She sat down on the edge of the bed, shoe box in her lap.

He was. The headache had retreated.

"We've finished packing up personal items—things we need to remove if the house is to be unoccupied."

"Sorry I didn't help you."

"Lon kept us organized. You needed to rest. You're not recovered yet. Listen, I packed a box of the things Mother kept for you. I'm kind of embarrassed it's so small."

"I'm surprised there's anything. I didn't live here." For all practical purposes, he hadn't lived in this house since he left for military school when he was twelve. It had been ridiculous for his room to be unoccupied while the younger kids had to double up and ridiculous to hang on to mementoes that only cluttered up space needed by someone else.

Davy sat up. "Let's see what you've got."

"Here's the watch Daddy gave you for graduation. Some old coins. Dad's arrowheads. Ten or twelve. Not enough to be called a collection."

"His arrowheads? Why are they *mine*?"

"Mom put them away for you after he died. She said you loved them when you were a little boy." She turned over a photograph. "I found this in the bottom of her jewelry box. I thought you'd like to have it. That's Carl, isn't it?"

Carl was what the family had always called Davy's biological father. *Dad* was his stepfather. Frozen forever in time, Carl appeared younger than Davy was now. He was smiling just like—Davy glanced in the long dressing-table mirror—just like Davy used to. Before shrapnel had opened his cheek from the corner of his mouth almost to his ear.

Davy sifted among the items to uncover a tiny, square jeweler's box. He opened it. Against satin, yellowed and slightly grubby with age, nestled a woman's diamond ring, a solitaire set in platinum. He snapped it closed and offered it to Elle. "You should have this, shouldn't you?"

"I have the diamond Daddy gave her. This is the engagement ring from her first marriage. Mom said it should be yours." Elle's smile was a crumpled mix of sadness and affection. "To give to your bride—you know how sentimental she was."

"I know. But," he held it out again, "seriously, you take it."

"Seriously, no."

Davy tossed it back in the shoe box with the other forgotten pieces of his past.

Chapter 10

Wilmington, NC

JJ CARUTHERS' CELL PHONE CHIMED. CHECKING THE CALLER ID, she saw it was Blount Satterfield, her soon-to-be fiancé. She hand-motioned to her executive assistant, Katherine, that she needed to take the call. "Hello, Blount."

"Hey. I wanted to make sure we're on for tonight."

"Of course." JJ didn't understand why Blount so frequently had to call to find out if she was going to keep a date with him. She didn't say what she didn't mean, and when she made an agreement, she kept it.

"Well, you said you didn't like to go to weddings and I wasn't sure."

"Into every life, the occasional wedding must fall," JJ quipped. "Including mine. You took what I said about not liking them too seriously."

Attending weddings had never been a favorite part of her social duties, and, after last year's disaster, she liked them less. But since she had to attend one, there was no point in dwelling on the negative. She wished she'd never told Blount how she felt. She changed the subject. "Tell me again, whose wedding are we going to?"

"Emmie Caddington. A friend—well, more a former colleague. She was an instructor last year in the biology department. She's come back here to get married."

JJ wondered why Blount, a tenured professor at UNC-Wilmington, would want to attend the wedding of a lowly instructor—a lowly *former* instructor. "A good friend?"

"Just someone I used to know. But a lot of the faculty will be attending. Since I'm invited, and people like Senator Teague Calhoun will be there, it's an opportunity to network."

Having achieved the holy grail of tenure, Blount had ambitions on the administrative side of the university system. In these days of grant money drying up, an administrator with an inside track to the people who had money, or who could steer funds in a university's direction, was very valuable indeed.

JJ respected his ambition and his ability to stay focused on his goals. They had that in common. It would benefit them both to be seen in public together, while in private, their interests were separate enough to keep them out of each other's way.

He was fine with the prenup they had discussed. Married to her, he would be invited into a world of power and influence—something he valued more than money. She was ninety percent sure he would officially propose tonight, and she would officially say yes.

JJ checked the oversized stainless-steel clock on the wall of her office. "Listen, if I'm going to be ready for you to pick me up at the beach cottage by five-thirty, I'm going to have to leave soon, and I have a few more things to see to."

"I'll be so glad when you give up that place."

JJ was a little surprised by his vehemence. "I won't. I've loved living there. I didn't realize it bothered you."

"It's just that Topsail Island is so far from Wilmington. I have to factor in another thirty minutes."

"On a good day," JJ acknowledged. "But you know, I've almost enjoyed the commute. It gives me time to decompress a little. I don't take work home with me quite as much. You have a point though. It's a long way for you to go, only to turn around and go back to Wrightsville Beach. I can drive myself and meet you at the hotel, if you'd rather."

"No," Blount answered as she knew he would. "That's fine. I don't really mind picking you up."

Katherine stuck her head around the office door, waving the floor-plan inventory reconciliation report for her signature.

These days, the car business had more to do with massaging the numbers than with the glamour of cars, even the sexiest high-end foreign cars. Businesses selling high-ticket items like cars and boats survived on something called a floor plan.

A floor plan was a line of credit extended by a lender using the inventory as collateral. The lender kept a list of every car in the floor plan, and every month the car went unsold, interest had to be paid on that car. When a car was sold, the loan on it had to be paid in full immediately—not at the end of the month.

Every business that sold big-ticket items and depended on volume walked a tightrope between the amount of inventory they were required to carry and the interest they had to pay on that inventory. During economic downturns, businesses might be forced to carry more inventory than they could possibly sell. It took fancy footwork to maintain the cash flow and creative financing to stay in the black.

Sometime in the next week, the bank's floor-plan auditor would come around to check the vehicle identification number, or VIN, of every car on the lot against what was listed in the floor plan. Mistakes could be costly. If the auditor found cars unaccounted for and for which the bank hadn't been paid, the dealership was considered "out of trust." Being "out of trust" could spell doom. Car dealers everywhere had been forced out of business when they lost their line of credit.

JJ had invested in new software to keep more accurate, real-time data on exactly where Caruthers was with the floor plan. "Gotta go, Blount," JJ told him, already studying the numbers. "I'll see you later."

—∿∿—

Report signed and dispatched, JJ glanced at the wall clock again. She liked the clock for its polished face and cuneiform-like numerals. She especially liked the large distance that the sleek hands moved to measure the minutes. Unlike the relentlessly changing numbers on the digital clock on her desk, those on the wall clock gave time a sort of spaciousness. There was very little time left before her grandfather's deadline, but she had made it. By midnight, JJ would be engaged.

She had had a year in which to grow resigned to the inevitable.

A year in which to search for a legal way to stop her grandfather's machinations—and to learn there was none. The car business had been passed down in the family for three generations. Her great-great grandfather had insisted it not be divided among his heirs, and the tradition had continued. JJ's grandfather was the sole owner. He could do anything he wished with it, including dismantle it and sell the parts if she didn't get married.

A year to consult doctors about her grandfather's health—and learn that his heart condition might eventually kill him, but so slowly he could very well die of something else first. His mind was as sharp as ever and likely to remain so. Trying to wrest control of the business on the grounds of incompetence would be expensive and probably fail.

She'd learned a long time ago not to fight what couldn't be changed. Far better to adapt and make circumstances work for you.

By the time her parents' marriage had had its final eruption, she had already found more security than she'd ever had before in the dealership's active orderliness and purpose. She had somewhere to be other than on the battleground of her parents' marriage.

At the car place, there was always noise in the repair bays—whines of power screwdrivers and percussive bangs from compressed-air power wrenches tightening lug nuts—but never discord. People came and went (hired, fired, and retired) and car models changed with the years, but the purpose, the need, and the work of the business stayed exactly the same.

She couldn't remember the first time she'd come here. From her babyhood, the dealership had always been the background of her life. She starred in her first commercial at two. When she was thirteen, she had realized that Caruthers was hers—or would be one day. She had drawn the first unrestricted breath she'd known in years. And the business had moved into the foreground.

She'd had a year to get to know each of the four men her grandfather had selected.

The cardiac surgeon—that one had never gotten out of the parking lot. It was harder for him to find time to date than it was for her, and that was saying something.

She and the scion of the agribusiness family had become friends almost instantly and still were. But he had known exactly what he wanted in a wife—and it wasn't someone dedicated to a business of her own.

The lawyer was a decent man, one who shared her commitment to service in the community. But he was captivated by her beauty and looking for true love. He would have married her in a heartbeat, and she would have broken his heart in no time. Even with the future of Caruthers at stake, she couldn't use him without regard for his welfare.

That left Blount. She had always intended to marry some day. The last thing she needed was to get sentimental about marriage at this point. Blount would do very well. JJ scooped up a contract she wanted to study before Monday and tucked her purse under her arm. There was just time to check on the progress of the adoption fair. Several times a year, JJ invited animal rescue groups to use the parking lot to show off pets available for adoption and to raise money.

The phone clipped to the Italian leather belt of her black silk-crepe slacks sang "We Are the World" as she descended the white metal stairs from her office on the mezzanine to the polished black granite floor of the car showroom. A soaring, semicircular bank of windows filled the building with sunlight all day. She'd only been sixteen when the old headquarters was razed and the new building put in its place, but her grandfather had included her in every decision.

She loved the black, silver, and white color scheme; the clean serenity of the façade's classical proportions; and the efficiency and functionality of the back sections. It was she who had insisted on a spotless lounge for customers waiting for their cars to be serviced and a quiet room equipped with child-sized furniture and toys where tots could be entertained. Tires and motor oil, plastics and lubricants smelled like security to her.

She put the phone to her ear. She blessed the technology that had created cell phones. Their advent had eliminated the unending noise of a public address system that had to be audible over a fourteen-acre lot and kept her in touch no matter where she was—since she wasn't likely to be found in her office. And while her employees knew they could come to her at any time, she preferred for them not to have to. She preferred to be so visible and present in the workings of the business that she already knew of any problems before someone *had* to come to her.

While answering a salesman's question, JJ waved to Kelly at the concierge desk and held up her car keys to show she was leaving. From a rack near the door, she snagged stylish sunglasses, intertwined J's decorating the stems, and headed out to the sun-drenched lot.

The sunglasses were an innovation of JJ's that had evolved into a Caruthers tradition—a piece of its cachet.

Her eyes were sensitive to light. Without protection, she found spending time on the lot to be painful. In a seeming paradox, the problem was even worse in the fall and winter than in the summer. Even in winter, the sun was still plenty hot and bright, capable of burning. Being lower in the sky, the sun sent the millions of hot, sharp shards of reflection straight into the eyes.

Sunglasses were vital. And yet JJ couldn't seem to keep up with them. She replaced them so often that she finally resorted to buying them wholesale. They became a sort of personal trademark, and since whether she meant to or not, she left them wherever she went, she turned them into a calling card. Gold intertwined J's were added. All around Wilmington, people sported "Shades of JJ."

She didn't pass the glasses out wholesale. Customers had to ask for a pair, which meant salesmen had a chance to meet them even before they "looked." Customers were asked to return the glasses when they left the lot, giving salesmen another chance to establish a relationship when customers left. A lot of people didn't return the glasses, of course, but that was okay. Every time they looked at the glasses, they subconsciously remembered they had been given something and asked to return.

When a customer bought a car, a pair of the glasses in a special case was tucked into the glove compartment. The salesman would open the glove compartment and say, "Here is the manual, and here's your registration, and these are the sunglasses JJ wants you to have as a present and a thank you."

Other dealers had tried similar promotions, but none attained the cachet of Shades of JJ.

"Have my people looked after you?" JJ asked a few minutes later when she reached the rescue group's leader, a serious-looking young woman with short, straight hair, who was dressed in jeans and a plaid flannel shirt. Even though it was a beautiful fall day, JJ had resisted going to see the animals until now, knowing how hard it would be not to want one of the dogs.

"They've been wonderful, JJ. They always are. We really appreciate them setting up this tent."

JJ nodded with satisfaction at the temporary pens where a couple of older dogs snoozed at the back of the tent. "I thought the last time you came, it would be better if we could provide the dogs some shade. Today feels more like real summer than Indian summer. But it can get hot out here on the pavement, even on a cool day. Glad it's working. Is there anything else we can do for you?"

"We'll be packing up soon, but it's been a great day. I think we've found placements for three of the dogs. One family took a dog to the Land Rover they were looking at to see if he liked it."

"Did he?"

"They said he hopped right in and sat up like, 'Okay, I'm in. Where are we going?' I hope that was okay, to let a dog get in a car."

JJ dismissed her anxiety with a grin. "These days, if it will sell cars, I'll include a dog guaranteed to love rides in every deal."

"How about you? Isn't it time for a new dog for you?"

"Soon, maybe." Her golden retriever, Smiley, had been gone almost a year. But while JJ was ready for another dog, her soon-to-be-fiancé wasn't fond of animals. Since she agreed with the rescue organization's policy of only placing dogs in homes where they would live inside the house, she wasn't sure how she and Blount would work it out.

The cell phone at her waist vibrated. JJ smiled apologetically and mouthed, "See you soon," as she turned toward the corner of the lot where her sporty, red Lexus SC 430 was parked and brought the phone to her ear.

—◆◆◆—

JJ glanced at the man beside her in the late-afternoon sunlight and then back at the couple being married below on the beach. Only a handful of people had been escorted to the semicircle of plastic chairs set on the sand at the water's edge. The minister, JJ understood, was the missionary father of the bride. The only attendants, a matron of honor and a best man, didn't process. Instead, they walked shoulder to shoulder with their friends to where the minister stood.

The assemblage was simple and intimate, and despite the hotel's plummy reputation, oddly egalitarian. Beach walkers and their dogs stopped to watch. A pair of hotel maids in gray and maroon uniforms halted beside their laundry cart. All up the twenty-story face of the hotel, guests kibitzed from their balconies, peering down on the scene.

The crowd standing at the railing of the hotel's beach-side patio had gone silent, expectant, as if to catch the occasional syllable tossed up to them.

The bride looked as romantic and magical as a pre-Raphaelite painter's heroine in a simple white cotton dress ornamented only with delicate inserts of white lace in the bodice and down the long sleeves.

If the bride looked like a heroine from an ancient legend, the groom looked like the Viking hero who had claimed her, with his reddish hair and golden skin burnished by the setting sun and his Irish fisherman's sweater revealing the breadth of his shoulders and the depth of his chest. His strong-boned face bent tenderly to hers.

The ever-present wind off the ocean lifted the bride's white skirt from time to time and twined it round the groom's legs as if even the dress longed to press itself to him. The bride's full-length chiffon veil tried to do the same thing, until laughing, the groom captured it and, completely unself-consciously, draped its silken length across his broad shoulders like a stole. It was still attached to the bride's silvery-blond head, of course, so he drew her closer and tenderly adjusted it so that it was not so taut as to prevent her moving her head.

Exchanging rings was hardly necessary after that. Groom and bride had both made it clear how eagerly and completely they accepted the bonds of matrimony.

JJ tightened her jaw against tears caused, she reasoned, by the wind blowing in her eyes.

The groom slipped a ring onto the bride's finger, then bent to kiss her fingers in tender homage. A moment later when her turn came, the bride did the same. A collective sigh wafted among the watchers on the patio. Around JJ, several couples squeezed one another's hands.

JJ sneaked a glance at Blount's face to gauge his reaction to the moving scene. He wasn't watching it. He was looking over the crowd, probably making a mental list of who he needed to speak to.

Though they stood side by side, she and Blount weren't sharing this experience in any way. Before it could blossom and set fruit, JJ pinched off the sprout of disappointment. He was exactly what she needed him to be. JJ, with her championship of animals and children, had been accused of having a sentimental streak. If he had none at all, he could be a balance for her.

Blount caught her looking at him and smiled. Now he did cover her hand and squeeze it. He looked like he was anticipating sex tonight. So was she. It had been a long time for her—almost a year. Although she was trying to be rational about selecting a husband, something about knowing she was interviewing each of the four men her grandfather presented her with had prevented her from going to bed with any of them until she made her choice. It would have felt a little too much like she was trying them on for size. And really, she didn't want any part of her choice of husband to be based on sex.

Sexual compatibility was important, of course, but she saw no reason she wouldn't find it with Blount. His features were even and his light brown hair just long enough and raggedy enough to give him a *with it* look, while his charcoal sport coat, red tie, and white starched shirt would distinguish him from his students at the university. He was tall enough that she didn't have to worry about towering over him in three-inch heels.

He really was a very pleasant-looking man. She gave him a deliberately sultry look of promise and turned her attention back to the marriage ceremony.

The ceremony over, the groom helped an elderly lady to rise from a plastic chair while the best man did the same for a middle-aged woman. When the woman turned around, JJ, to her surprise, recognized Mary Cole Sessoms, her mentor. On the patio, someone cranked up the music.

"I'm ready for a drink," Blount announced. "Can I get you anything from the bar?"

"A gimlet, please."

Blount had no more than turned away when a man with silver-flecked hair slid an arm around her waist in a one-handed hug. "Hello, beautiful," He kissed her cheek lightly. "Don't marry that man," he whispered. "Marry me."

JJ returned the hug. "Henry. You are good for my ego."

"I could be good for more than that. I'm serious."

JJ looked into the eyes of the man who had been her friend the past five years. "You're not ready to give up your bachelor status." Divorced for years, Henry was known for the number of beautiful women he dated. She enjoyed Henry. He liked to shag. A laidback cousin of swing dance, the shag was the signature dance of several generations in the coastal Carolinas. He knew just how to flirt without ever getting heavy-handed, and he never pushed for sex although he'd made it clear he'd be ready anytime she was.

"I would for you."

"Oh, no. I value my own skin too much. At least twelve women would come gunning for me if I took you off the market." She patted his cheek. "Besides, I like you too much to marry you. I need you as a friend."

Though she had thousands of acquaintances, friendship was a rare commodity in JJ's life. Her position as the working head of a large, successful car dealership meant that men who were her natural equals—equally successful, equally depended upon by as many people—were twenty years older.

The same was true of women, except there were far fewer of them. Women hardly wanted to be compared with a woman just as smart and just as successful, but twenty years younger and possessed of the voluptuous body and sultry beauty of a young Ava Gardner.

Except for old movie buffs, most of the world had forgotten the fifties movie star, but not the folks of eastern North Carolina, who claimed her as one of their own.

Though nature had given JJ the emerald-green eyes and abundant black-coffee hair and the tiniest hint of a cleft in a very stubborn chin, the resemblance to the silver-screen siren wasn't totally accidental. JJ had recognized her beauty as a form of power and accentuated it, with the help of a hairdresser and judicious use of makeup. She'd have been well-known anyway. An almost iconic face meant she was recognized anywhere she went. This wedding, though she was acquainted with neither bride nor groom, was no exception.

JJ had just time to promise Henry a dance later before the head of the Wilmington choral society, one of the civic enhancements Caruthers supported, claimed her attention.

"Mary Cole!" JJ exclaimed an hour later, delighted to see the sixtyish insurance agent among the shifting groups of acquaintances. Despite their age difference, Mary Cole really was a friend. Living in different towns, they most often saw one another when business brought them together. Still, when her youngest daughter, Pickett, had married last year, Mary Cole had invited JJ to the wedding, and JJ had driven an hour and a half to attend. They air-kissed.

"You look beautiful." JJ pulled back to admire Mary Cole's full-length evening gown of silver silk that perfectly complemented her silver hair. "Didn't I see you down on the beach with the wedding party? How do you know the bride and groom?"

"You were at Pickett's wedding last year, right? Don't you remember?"

JJ nodded   a small social lie. In truth, JJ remembered almost nothing about that occasion except the talk with her lawyer that had confirmed her worst fears—and *that* she would never forget. She'd spent most of the last year trying to wiggle out of the marriage dictate before finally yielding to necessity.

The other part of the occasion that she hadn't been able to forget—although, God knows, she had tried—was wild, no-holds-barred sex with a stranger. A *stranger*. She had been beyond upset, but that was no excuse for abandoning all her self-control.

Mary Cole hardly waited for JJ's nod before she went on. "*Well*," she began portentously. "It's the most romantic story. The bride is Pickett's best friend, Emmie. She and Do-Lord met at Pickett's wedding. He was the best man, and she was Pickett's maid of honor. They hit it off, and the next thing you know, they were in love. Now they're married."

JJ went very still. "Do-Lord?" She'd heard the name before, and there was only one person she could have heard it from.

"He got the nickname in the Navy. His real name is Caleb. Emmie won't call him anything but that."

"I take it he's a SEAL, too?" JJ's stomach went cold and heavy—like she'd swallowed a whole slushy in one gulp. Although she had been horrified that she had had sex with a stranger, on the plus side, at least she been certain she'd never see him again. Fearing she was inquiring about her own doom, she asked, "Are a lot of his friends here?"

"Yes indeed, my dear!" Mary Cole winked conspiratorially. "Would you like to meet one or two? Pickett can take you around and introduce you. Pickett, come over here."

JJ wished she had kept her mouth shut. "That's not necessary."

"Pickett," Mary Cole said when the petite young woman JJ had seen on the beach joined them, "you remember my friend, JJ Caruthers, don't you? She was at your wedding."

No way did Pickett remember her. JJ had never actually spoken to the bride and groom.

"There were so many people there. I'm sure she doesn't." JJ forestalled the necessity for another social lie. She offered her hand. "It's nice to meet you now."

They shook hands while Mary Cole said, "Pickett, JJ wants to meet some of Jax's and Do-Lord's friends. Now, who do you think we should fix her up with?"

"Oh, no. Really!" JJ rushed in. "Please don't bother." The last thing she wanted was to meet her mystery SEAL with a bunch of people watching. Her greatest hope was that he had forgotten all about her.

Men talked. Having spent her whole life in a male-dominated industry she knew. If they had no personal experience of a woman's willingness, they speculated. If they did, they bragged.

Though sex without marriage might no longer soil a woman, the double standard was alive and well. Men respected women known to be selective in granting their favors, and that respect colored their every interaction.

If he wanted to brag, he wouldn't have to embellish. The absolute truth was as salacious as anyone could want. She had no desire to remind him.

The best thing would be to find Blount and get the two of them out of there. She wished she hadn't sent him to get her pashmina shawl from their hotel room a few minutes ago. Instead, she wished she'd used being a little chilly as a good reason to move their evening to the next phase.

"Don't look so worried," Pickett urged, chuckling. "Mother is a hopeless matchmaker. I'm not going to push guys at you. A SEAL wouldn't be to everyone's taste. Anyway, Mother, Jax is fixing to drag me out of here. I'm pregnant," she explained to JJ. "He thinks I get tired. To tell you the truth, I do."

"Does this mean you're going to listen to reason and not try to stay at the Snead's Ferry house while all the construction goes on this weekend?" her mother demanded.

"Yes, ma'am." Pickett turned to include JJ in the conversation. "Some of the men are going to help Jax finish a bathroom in the Snead's Ferry house this weekend. Then on Monday he'll take them diving on that shipwreck the last hurricane uncovered. Wisdom being the better part of valor, I'm going to stay here at the hotel."

"Alone?" Mary Cole fussed. "I thought you would spend the weekend with me."

"Being alone sounds wonderful. These days, anytime Jax is gone, Tyler's grandmother, Lauren, wants to come over to visit with Tyler."

"Is the tension between Jax and Lauren wearing you out?"

"No, ma'am, but this weekend Tyler is with his cousins, and Jax is *here*." A wicked light appeared in her deep aqua eyes. "And I," she tapped her chest, "intend to make the most of it."

A harsh-featured man with cold gray eyes stepped up beside Pickett. His eyes warmed when they rested on Pickett. He responded politely when Pickett introduced him as her husband, Jax, but it was clear he had eyes only for his tiny wife. "I warned you ten minutes ago it was time to get you off your feet, but did you listen? No. Now there are going to be consequences."

"Ooh! Consequences." Pickett fluttered her eyes. "I like the sound of that."

"Off your feet. Now." He swept her up into his arms.

Pickett reflexively put her arms around his neck. "Jax, for goodness sake! Put me down."

Jax ignored her and turned to his mother-in-law. In a long-suffering voice, he told her, "You have no idea what it takes to keep her in line."

Pickett gave him a narrow-eyed look. "Does this mean you intend ravishment?"

"Guaranteed."

Pickett swept a regal hand. "In that case, carry on!"

JJ followed Jax's progress as he threaded his way through the crowd, carrying his precious burden in strong, sure arms. Her heart pounded uncomfortably, and she had a strange lump in her throat.

Swamped by shame that she had dived into sex for a few hours of forgetfulness, JJ had pushed the details of the night with a man whose last name she didn't know from her mind. But if she were being honest, it hadn't been all hot monkey sex. For so many men (women, too, for all she knew), sex was hardly more momentous than a good sneeze. There was a certain satisfaction as a strong urge was relieved, but it wasn't anything worth stopping for. He, however, had been a man determined not merely to do it but to enjoy it. A man for whom sex was fun, and with a serious, focused playfulness, he had constantly engaged her, whispering sex words and naughty suggestions. At the memory, she smiled in spite of herself, feeling weak in the knees.

"Are you sure you don't want one of those?" Mary Cole inquired, not having missed how JJ's eyes followed the couple so obviously in love and secure in their love.

JJ shook her head. The *weak in the knees* part was what she needed to remember. "He looks hard to manage."

"You have no idea what a strategic thinker my daughter is. Unless I miss my guess, she set that whole thing up."

"Anyway, I'm here with someone else tonight. I ought to go find him."

"Did I see you with Blount Satterfield? Are you two getting serious?"

JJ read a look of disquiet in the other woman's eyes that made her answer less affirmatively than she might have. Mary Cole was one of the few people who knew of JJ's grandfather's ultimatum. "Possibly. Why?"

"Oh… nothing. He dated Emmie for awhile, that's all."

JJ nodded. "I gathered he and Emmie were colleagues."

"Is *that* what he told you?" Mary Cole made a sound that in anyone less ladylike would have been a snort. "It's true as far as it goes. But they also went together for long enough to make her think he was serious, and then he dumped her—went out with someone else very publicly, without so much as a by-your-leave."

From what JJ had seen of the barefoot bride and her far-from-traditional wedding, JJ doubted if Emmie and

Blount had ever suited one another. Breaking up was probably best for both of them. Still, he'd given the impression that he hardly knew Emmie.

"There are always two sides to any story," she told Mary Cole. "I'll bet he just wasn't really involved and assumed she wasn't either. I don't think he's the kind to have deep feelings for anyone."

Mary Cole's brows drew together. "Even you?"

"Even me. Frankly, I like that about him. I don't need to worry he'll feel jealous of my involvement with Caruthers."

"You mean you really *are* serious about him?"

"You sound upset. You're the one who told me maybe my grandfather was right. You said I *should* consider one of the men he had picked out."

"I meant I didn't think you had tried very hard on your own to find someone to marry. How could you expect to get to know a man if you saw him, at most, every two or three weeks? It's no surprise your relationships petered out before they ever got off the ground."

It was almost word for word what her grandfather had said. JJ tossed a long-fingered hand in a frustrated gesture. "Get real, Mary Cole. You know what it's like to be the female head of a large business. You have to do everything a man would do *and* everything his *wife* would do."

"Of course I do, but the insurance agency is not my whole existence. As long as I live, I'll regret that the needs of the business made me neglect Pickett."

JJ knew the story. "You did what you had to," she reassured Mary Cole, "to save the agency from bankruptcy after your husband died. A lot of people, not just Pickett, were depending on you."

"Maybe. But maybe I was also using work to bury my grief and my fury at him for dying suddenly and leaving us in that condition." She raised blue eyes heavenward. "An insurance agent who let his own insurance premiums lapse!"

"No matter how you felt, you didn't have a choice about what you had to do."

"There are always choices."

The older woman was sincere, JJ knew, but their situations weren't the same. "I thought you *agreed* with me that this was the best way."

Mary Cole sighed. "JJ, I'm not trying to argue with you. I'm on your side. I'll say this for your grandfather: he's not all that smart about women, but Lucas knows men. I thought he would select men who had the basic qualifications, and you would choose the one you had a real attraction to. I didn't mean you should marry someone who didn't love you!"

JJ's grandfather had taught her how to run a car business, but Mary Cole had taught her how to be a businesswoman. JJ admitted to a little hurt that her mentor didn't seem to be proud of her. It made her say, a little stiffly, "Since Blount and I are making a deal, I feel it's best not to let the decision be clouded by strong emotions. But I respect him. In time, I expect that will grow into real affection."

Blue eyes dark with distress, Mary Cole squeezed JJ's hand. "Oh, my darling JJ, what has *happened* to you?"

Chapter 11

ON THE OTHER SIDE OF THE HOTEL PATIO, DAVY HELD the cold beer bottle to the outer corner of his eyebrow where the red flashing pain had lodged. The doctors said his fractured eye socket was still healing and the pain would go away. He hadn't died in Afghanistan, but he wondered how long it would be before he felt alive again.

He hadn't been shipped home in a box. Instead it was his mother who had lain in a coffin only weeks after his first surgery, and Davy had become responsible for a much younger brother.

Now everybody wanted to know his plans, while he was trying to understand something he'd never looked into before. In the deepest part of himself, he had always known the present was all he had. Now it felt as if he was living someone else's future.

Lon, always looking after everybody, had talked him into coming to Do-Lord's wedding, saying it was better than brooding in his tiny three-room apartment while he had thirty days of convalescent leave. Davy wasn't so sure. These days following conversation, particularly in a group, took concentration. It was easier to let his mind drift away.

Garth Vale, a.k.a. Darth Vader, and who, like his namesake, was extremely fast and extremely dangerous, saw the action. "You got a hangover, already?"

"Hangover from the 'Stan. Headache. I still get them."

Garth nodded and hoisted his cane in salute. Being a SEAL was hard on a body. They all had paid with pain for their place among the world's finest warriors. Garth had been wounded in the same action Davy was and now had titanium where part of his thigh bone used to be. Hospitalized together, they'd gotten in the habit of hanging out. Garth was an officer and Davy enlisted, but that wasn't the same barrier among SEALs as in other services.

SEALs had a reputation for being clannish, for having their own hangouts, for not liking to mingle even with other Navy personnel. The reputation was deserved, but the charge of elitism and arrogance that often went with it wasn't. The simple truth was that life as a SEAL put them outside the mainstream. Even if they could talk about what they did, which they couldn't because everything they did was secret, most people couldn't understand it or even believe it. When they had time to relax, they relaxed with SEALs.

Gradually Davy and most of the other SEALs had gravitated to a corner table partly hidden by masonry pillars and sheltered from above by an overhanging balcony. It was no accident that the space had three exits and anyone approaching the table was clearly visible, while the table was in shadow. In some countries, eating out was the most dangerous thing SEALs did. In an unfamiliar place, they trusted only each other.

"Did you ever see that movie, *Wedding Crashers*?" Garth asked. "Do you think going to weddings is a good way to get laid?"

"What are you asking him for?" a SEAL whose name Davy couldn't call up snickered. It was embarrassing how often he couldn't recall people's names and was greeted by name by people he'd swear he'd never seen before. While in the hospital, it hadn't been a big problem—most people there had been strangers.

Since he was on convalescent leave, hanging out in Little Creek where more people knew him, it happened more frequently and was harder to cover up. He hoped the problem would go away on its own while he was on leave.

"All Doc's got to do to get laid," the SEAL continued, "is go anywhere girls are. Even getting hit by an RPG couldn't blow all the 'pretty' off that face the girls love so much." Davy wished he could think of the guy's name. It was *right there*.

"Hey, Doc, you think you've still got it—now that you got the scar and your cheekbone looks a little lumpy?"

The guys had always ribbed him about his looks. Intensely competitive men every one, at a glance they could estimate the height, weight, and fighting condition of every man they met—and what it would take to win against him. Unsurprisingly, their competitiveness included attracting females. It stood to reason his friends wouldn't ignore, or dismiss as unimportant, the change in his features.

Davy fingered the thin y-shaped scar that angled across his cheek from the corner of his mouth to his ear. The short leg of the y creased the cheek vertically. His cheek was as smooth as plastic surgery could make it, but there was no doubt that the perfect regularity of his features was gone for good.

"What do you look like when you smile?"

Davy obligingly spread his lips in a grimace. The other men watched his cheek crumple.

"Shit. You lost your killer dimple!"

"I've still got everything that matters," he parried, taking a confident swig of his beer.

What he didn't say was that ever since his injury, something felt… flat. Not The Admiral, thank God. But despite its reflexive interest in attractive women, getting it on with a girl lacked… He had actually ignored signals from a couple of nurses in the hospital—even once or twice pleaded a headache as an excuse. Him. A headache. It would be funny if it weren't pathetic.

Vic Littletree whistled under his breath. "Babe alert! Three o'clock."

Davy looked to his right and almost swallowed his tongue. "That's no babe," he corrected reverently. "That's a goddess."

The men were silent in appreciation of the vision the crowd on the patio had parted to reveal. Her back to them, she strolled not hurriedly, but purposefully, among the other guests. Her coffee-brown hair tumbled in loose, silky curls to her shoulder blades. Her short-sleeved dress, the dusty purple of ripe plums, was almost demure in its restraint.

She had no need to advertise her sexuality. It was there in the unconscious sway of her hips, the assertive set of her shoulders. Tall and statuesque, there was plenty of her, and every millimeter was in exactly the right place. A man would have no fear of crushing her or having a hard time finding her in bed.

He could imagine shaping the warm flesh of those hourglass curves with his hands—as if he already knew what she felt like. His whole body tightened. Weird—his imagination had never been that good before. He didn't take time to examine the feeling. It felt too damn good to feel a flood of genuine arousal for him to question where it came from.

He willed her to turn so he could see her left hand. Bare. Relief made him lightheaded. He didn't poach, not only because he thought there was plenty to go around and saw no need to covet what some other man had. He also believed marriage vows were sacred and hard enough to keep without interference from the outside. He sent thanks to whatever luck had kept her free. He might have howled if she had been taken.

He set his beer bottle on the plastic table. "Stand back, guys. This one's mine."

"We get to watch the operator operate!"

"We'll see how much the scar handicaps him."

"All right, I say we start a pool. How long is it going to take him? An hour?"

"Thirty minutes."

"Uh-oh. Subject is being approached from the right. Sorry, Doc. Looks like somebody's ahead of you."

Davy took his eyes from the woman long enough to watch as a man, with a shawl or something draped over his arm, approached her and handed it to her. What an idiot.

"No, she's not taken," Davy chortled. "See that? The schmuck blew it. He should have wrapped the shawl around her himself."

"Oh. Right! So he could put his arms around her."

"Are you going to go over there and muscle in?"

"Uncool. I don't want a pissing match with him; I want *her*. A fool like that will leave her alone again. When he does, I move in."

Across the patio, the woman turned. A face, so exquisite it was hard for him to breathe, turned toward him. She radiated feminine strength in the modeled cheekbones, high intelligent forehead, and very determined chin with the tiniest hint of cleft.

The sudden return of sexual interest was explained. What she had would bring a man back from the dead. And he knew her!

Every cell in his body recognized her. He'd heard people talk about seeing someone across the room and suddenly, indisputably, knowing they were the one. Elation and anticipation, far more complex than lust, expanded through his chest. And something that felt like relief heated his eyes with unshed tears. He had found her, the one for him.

"Darth, stay on her. No matter what, keep her in sight."

"What are you going to do?"

"Somebody here is bound to know her. I'm going to find out what her name is."

"Here's your shawl. What did you call it?"

"A pashmina." Smiling her thanks to Blount, JJ swirled the woven length of fine wool and silk around her shoulders. Woven in shades of lavender, blue, and earthy gold, it was gossamer light and amazingly warm. "Thanks for getting it from the room."

Now, without sounding too ditzy or like she didn't know her own mind, she had to convince him she was ready to go to the room. In a few minutes she would say the shawl wasn't warm enough and invite him to go with her.

"I hope this isn't a sign of things to come," he teased.

Had he read her mind? "What? Getting chilly?"

"You know, always expecting me to fetch and carry for you."

JJ took a sip of her drink. This wasn't the first time he'd acted a little put out, laughing but making the point that he thought he was indulging her excessively. She hadn't expected or wanted lover-like behavior, but was he already so sure of her that he thought he didn't need to court her at all? She wondered if Mary Cole was right about him.

"How does it feel," she studied his face as she asked, "to watch an old girlfriend get married?"

He didn't take his eyes from the crowd he was scanning. "What old girlfriend?"

"The bride, Emmie."

"Oh. We were never serious. Colleagues, that's all."

"There's gossip going around that you dumped her, callously."

Blount's snicker dismissed the rumor. "Who told you that? I didn't dump her. We saw each other a few times casually. Then she got mad because I went to a departmental dinner with someone else."

"Why didn't you go with her?"

"I told you… we weren't dating." Hearing the touch of asperity in his tone, he backtracked. "Just, you know, getting together sometimes. You don't know what she looked like in those days. I had to admire her scholarship—but, how can I say this? She wasn't the kind of girl you want to show off."

JJ understood the male psyche. She *was* the kind of girl men liked to show off. She used the fact to her advantage, but she had worked too damn hard to be who she was in her own right to want to be an ego prop for any man.

Blount gave a half-pained, half-philosophical laugh and continued. "I didn't find out until too late that she's extremely well-connected politically and the heir to a sizable estate."

He sounded rueful, like he'd messed up.

"You mean," she inquired in a carefully neutral voice, "if you'd known she was rich, you would have" —JJ made finger quotes—"dated her?"

Blount made a noncommittal sound and shrugged. "It wouldn't have worked out between us anyway." His tone said he was shutting the subject down.

One thing JJ's grandfather had taught her was that the true art of making a deal lay in understanding what people really want. The key was getting them to talk about themselves.

She leaned against the patio railing in a way that made maximum play of her breasts and legs. For good measure, she lazily stirred her gimlet and then lifted the swizzle stick to her lips to lick off a drop. "It wouldn't have worked out? Why not?"

"She has the money—though you would never have known it to look at her—and important friends, but she doesn't use them. To get ahead. Look at her. She's married a SEAL."

"What's wrong with that?"

"You don't think that's going to earn her any points in an academic setting, do you? Anyone who does what those guys do has got to be a little short on brains and way short on better choices."

"Actually, I've read there's a minimum requirement of some college, and that many have degrees, even advanced degrees. Other careers are open to them."

"Popular press," Blount dismissed. It was a trump card he often pulled when she questioned his facts. In fact her information did come from the popular press. The foiling of a pirate attack by SEALs had generated several newspaper and magazine articles that had caught her eye.

She adjusted the shawl to cover more of her arms, although her chill wasn't physical. She had accepted, even welcomed, Blount's essential self-interest since it made him simpler to deal with, and she had thought their differences would make boundaries and expectations easier to define.

In the last several minutes, though, she had seen that he didn't respect anyone. If there was one thing her grandmother's lessons on deportment had taught her, it was to take note of how people treated others. *Remember*, she had advised, *anytime they think they* can, *they will treat* you *the same way*.

The tiny flicker of hope that, in time, she might have something resembling a real marriage with Blount dimmed out. The challenge would be to live with him the year her grandfather stipulated.

It had only been a glimmer of hope. It was amazing that something so small could have held back the sick, black dread that rose up now to fill her chest.

"Blount, I need to visit the ladies' room, and I'm feeling a little chilled. I think I'll sit in the lobby for a few minutes."

"Why don't you go on up to the room? I want to talk to Senator Calhoun about a bill he's sponsoring—just show my interest, you know." He glanced around the wedding crowd, which was beginning to thin. "Actually, there are a couple more people I need to speak to, but I'll be up after a while."

"Up where? Oh. The room." For a moment she had forgotten they were sharing a room with the clear expectation that they would share more before the evening was out. She seemed to be looking at him from a great distance.

Insensitive as (she now realized) he was, he noticed something had happened. "I'll hurry," he reassured her with an intimate smile, patting a pocket. "There's something special I want to ask you."

He meant the proposal they both knew was coming. He must have the ring in his pocket.

The hard place inside her grew a little harder. *She didn't have to like him to marry him.* Still, she wasn't ready to be alone with him. Until she'd thought things through she didn't want to accept his ring and all that went with it. "I'll come back," she told him. "Or I'll wait for you in the lobby."

———

JJ Caruthers. JJ Caruthers. As Davy made his way through the thinning crowd back to Garth, he repeated the name. He liked it. Strong, up-front, challenging. It fit her.

Learning her name had been easy, which was good because, just as Davy had predicted, the idiot had already let go of her again. He was talking to an older man with thick silver hair. She was nowhere to be seen.

"She went toward the lobby," Garth reported. "Then she turned and went the other way. Look, there she is. Looks like she's going down to the beach." He slapped Davy on the back. "Go get her, tiger."

Chapter 12

AT THE FOOT OF THE CONCRETE STEPS LEADING DOWN to the beach, JJ balanced on one foot and then the other as she pulled off her high-heeled sandals. Sandals they might be, but she'd break her neck or at least an ankle if she tried to walk on the beach in them. She'd come down to the beach to be alone, to think. Disappointment made her eyes feel dry and tight, and made her cheeks stiff. JJ didn't want to talk to anyone, not until she had her game face back on.

It was darker near the ocean—or as dark as it ever got with Wilmington just over the bridge. The glow of a thousand streetlights and parking lots smudged the velvet blackness of the sky and faded the stars. She hadn't understood how much until over the last eleven months she had seen how different the night sky appeared on Topsail.

There were people who didn't know what stars looked like. She had tried talking to Blount one night about how in the modern world, a tiny handful of people could travel to the stars, but millions of people could no longer see them. The price of progress.

In the faint wash of light from the hotel patio, a colorless sand crab scuttled sideways in alarm.

JJ wished she could walk down the beach and just keep walking. But if she was capable of walking away from her responsibilities, she wouldn't have this problem.

She reached the firm, wet sand just beyond the tide line and turned right. Over and over, she had listed all the reasons to marry or not to marry Blount, and decided she should. No matter how disappointed she was now that she had seen his true colors, here was the bottom line: nothing had changed.

She'd always known they had an association of mutual benefit more than a grand love affair. What difference did it make now that she understood Blount was marrying her solely for her money? Her looks were a plus since he was proud to be seen with her, but money alone would do.

Despite the cold, slimy feeling of dread that made her pull the shawl tighter around her shoulders, she reminded herself that she had come to terms with harsh reality before. She would come to terms with this. She angled her wrist to see the face of her watch in the light that spilled from a nearby cottage. For those who wanted to dance and party, the reception would go on for a couple of hours, but the older guests were beginning to leave. She wanted to say good-bye to Mary Cole.

She turned back, angling across the soft sand on the shorter, more direct route to the hotel patio, although the walking was more difficult. Closer to the sea-oat-topped dunes, she heard the thin, high notes whistled by the wind blowing through the tall sea grass.

This sound always made JJ stop, take a deep breath of the salty air, and suddenly, consciously, appreciate where she was. The sound wasn't loud. Even a few feet away from the dunes, it was drowned out by the ever-present ocean roar. And it wasn't constant. The wind had to come from exactly the right direction to vibrate the blades of the five-foot stalks.

The experience of being on the beach could be simulated in pictures and recordings, even using canned scents. But none of those things could equal this reality. This was no dream, no memory, no ersatz association. There was a trueness to the beach, to the ocean, that brought her back to herself. Here she was able to think clearly.

The pieces came together, and her decision formed itself. She was going forward. She had no choice but to go forward, but she wasn't going to bed with Blount— not tonight.

Absorbed by the song of the dunes, she didn't notice the approach of the man until he was almost upon her.

"JJ."

He was a dark silhouette against the lights of the hotel patio. It didn't matter that she couldn't see his face. With knee-weakening certainty, she knew that voice, that smooth, smooth, Dove-bar-chocolate voice. He was here.

Thank God.

JJ fought her way clear of the crazy feeling of deliverance. What was the matter with her? If ever there was a man who was not the answer to a maiden's prayer, it was Mr. Davy Anonymous Sex. Mr. Opportunistic. Mr. I'm Too Sexy for My Shirt. She couldn't claim the moral high ground. He hadn't been by himself in that hotel room, but while it had been an aberration for her, she had no doubt it was business as usual for him.

She *wasn't* glad to see him. How could she have imagined even for an instant that she was? Still if she had to meet up with him, at least it was out here, privately.

She had kept an eye out for him ever since Mary Cole had said he might be among the SEALs at the wedding. When she hadn't seen him, she'd felt relieved, lucky. A greasy feeling of shame slid around in her stomach. She'd rather pretend she didn't recognize him, and that shamed her as much as acting so irresponsibly with him had. Had she now added hypocrisy to her other shortcomings?

"What are you doing here?" she demanded, heart pounding, heat flooding her face, sweat prickling in her hairline.

———— ·ᴗᴗ· ————

"JJ," Davy called to the woman standing so still near the dunes.

Her dress belled out like a dark sail. Her crossed arms held the shawl against her body. The long ends of the shawl rose up and flapped like the wings of a trapped creature fighting to get free. Her head was tilted as if she was listening to something.

She whirled at the sound of her name. "What are you doing here?"

"I know this is the oldest line in the world—" The irony killed him. The most beautiful girl he'd ever seen, and he was stuck with the lamest come-on ever. "But I swear it's the truth. I can't get past the feeling I know you from somewhere. Have we met?"

Chapter 13

SHE STILLED. THERE WAS A TINY PAUSE WHILE SHE batted down the fluttering end of her shawl. "You don't remember… meeting me?"

"No. But I'm not lying. I feel like I know you."

"I believe you." She laughed a little and shook her head. Then she smiled at him. *Kindly.* "Actually, people tell me that all the time. I do some of the commercials for Caruthers' Cars. That's probably why I seem familiar."

He tried to picture her against a background of cars. He couldn't. He hated the feelings of confusion, of not being able to call to mind things he should know. He felt like—like he was trying to play poker but cards were missing… like he *wasn't playing with a full deck. A few bricks shy of a load. Elevator doesn't go all the way to the top.* Shit. Those things said about people with impaired brain function—that was actually how he *felt.*

"JJ Caruthers, Caruthers Cars? You're the owner?"

"My grandfather owns it. I'm its… public face."

He heard the tiny pause. She'd meant to say one thing and changed it to something else. His gut told him she wasn't telling him the truth, not all of it anyway. But who cared? She was talking to him, and that's what he wanted. He ought to let the feeling of familiarity go, but he couldn't. "That might be it. But I don't think so. I'm not from around here. Are you saying you don't recognize me?"

She looked a little embarrassed. "I meet so many people." She spread her hands in a helpless gesture, and the ends of her shawl threatened to get away from her.

"Maybe you don't recognize me because of this." He angled his face so that the light spilling from the hotel patio fell on it and touched his cheek.

She recoiled. Took a step backward while her hand came up to stifle a gasp.

"Is it that bad?"

"No," she admitted slowly, "it's just... seeing you in the light, I realize now I do know you. You're Davy... Davy *Something*, aren't you?"

"You mean we really have met? Wow. That's a relief. You recognize me, too?"

"The scar doesn't change you that much. I was just startled to see you, that's all. I'm sorry it happened though. It must have... hurt."

He chuckled at the understatement. "You might say that."

"Apparently I just did." She rolled her eyes in embarrassment. "It was a stupid thing to say. Obviously, I have no idea how it felt. Okay, let's rewind. If you weren't sure you'd even met me, how did you know my name?"

"I asked around." He had hoped hearing her name would bring everything together. But it hadn't helped. Her name hadn't rung any bell at all. Every second he was around her, the sense of recognition grew and yet not one single fact or even a nebulous association came to mind. Weeks of frustrating encounters had taught him that the harder he tried, the less he would be able to recall.

"Look, I know it's unbelievable that I could have forgotten how I met a girl as beautiful as you... if I haven't completely screwed up, do you mind telling me where?"

—〰—

JJ hoped being recognized everywhere hadn't given her an inflated sense of her importance. She knew that night hadn't meant anything to him—hooking up with available women was something he did. JJ had been prepared to deal with their previous encounter, making it clear she wasn't offering anything like that again. What she hadn't considered was that she was so insignificant as to be completely forgettable.

Even as she dealt with the blow to her ego, she breathed a sigh of relief. This was better than the best she could have hoped for. If he didn't remember, she didn't need to persuade him not to talk. For a second, she considered lying, denying knowing him at all.

She might have, if he hadn't showed her the scar. If there hadn't been a touching vulnerability in the way he suggested it was why she didn't recognize him.

She understood that his vulnerability wasn't around loss of self-confidence or vanity. As scars went, it wasn't that disfiguring, something he probably knew, but it profoundly altered his identity.

Most people's identifying characteristics had to be built up like a mosaic. Age plus height plus weight plus hair color, eye color, tattoos, and identifying marks, all the way to "last seen wearing."

Not him. Likely all his life pointing him out in a crowd had been as simple as saying "the gorgeous one." For the rest of his life, he would be "the one with the scar."

JJ had heard people speak of having a soft spot in their hearts. When he had turned his ruined cheek to her, it literally felt as if a place in her chest underneath her breastbone went soft. She just couldn't let him think the scar made him unrecognizable.

"We met here in North Carolina," she answered. "I'm not surprised you don't remember. I'm sure you met a lot of people at that wedding, too." *And have probably done the same thing with too many other women too many times for one night to stand out,* she added silently.

"Whose wedding?" His brows drew together in lost-looking puzzlement.

"You were there as a friend of the groom, I guess." For a second, JJ drew a complete blank on the groom's name—even though she'd just met him. She was rattled by this encounter. Now that she knew she needn't fear he'd gossip, she only wanted to get away. She still had to deal with Blount. The name popped into her mind. "Jax... Jackson Graham."

Slowly his brow cleared. "Was that just a year ago? Seems longer." His gaze roamed over her in frank appreciation. "Hard to believe I could have forgotten you, though."

Davy hesitated, unsure what to say next. She wasn't giving him even a hint of a come-aboard signal.

She shrugged with a hint of self-deprecating humor. "What can I say?" She began to edge around him. "Well, nice running into you again."

"Stop," he caught her wrist. "*Wait.* How I screwed up and let you get away before, I don't know, but here we are. And now we get another chance. Do you know how rare those are? I want to get to know you. The guys in my unit call me Doc—sometimes Davy—but my full name is David Graziano. Is JJ what everyone calls you? What does it stand for?"

"Jane Jessup—and that's why I only answer to JJ. Nice to meet you. Now, I really need to—" She tugged on her wrist. "Let go," she ordered.

He should let her go. Any decent man would. But something like hot desperation flared in his chest. Most mistakes you only knew about after you made them, but somehow Davy knew that letting her go now would be the biggest mistake he'd ever made.

He couldn't summon the smooth moves, the ease-things-along, meaningless patter he'd used in the past to keep girls talking. He couldn't hold a girl against her will either. But if he couldn't think of how to talk, why not just do what he wanted to? It was audacious, but SEALs lived outside the box, and something about an audacious approach with this girl just felt right.

"Listen carefully." He made his voice slow, serious, and smooth. He wanted her to pay complete attention and understand he offered no threat. SEALs were drilled in split-second evaluation of the amount of resistance they were meeting and selection of the precise amount of force needed to overcome it. A confrontation could often be controlled simply by stating clearly what *would* happen, and what the other person needed to do to comply. "I'm going to drop your wrist. What you *need* to do, *JJ Caruthers*, is stand still while I kiss you."

He released her wrist, and she let her arm drop to her side. She didn't walk away. *Yes*. Time hung suspended while her eyes roamed his face, looked into his eyes, fixed on his mouth.

She blinked slowly and found his eyes again. "You can't kiss me."

He smiled at that. "Yes I can. There's a lot I can't do right now, but *that* I most certainly can."

"I mean, I can't kiss you. I came with someone else."

He stilled for half a blink, all urge to smile vanished. "Does he matter?"

"I'm going to marry him."

"You're engaged?" He brought her left hand up where he could see it. "No ring."

"It isn't official."

"Then you're not engaged. Not yet. And unless you tell me you don't want me to, I am going to kiss you."

Chapter 14

SHE WAS SUPPOSED TO TELL HIM SHE DIDN'T WANT HIM to kiss her.

She *intended* to.

She opened her mouth to do just that, in fact. But when he angled his head and, instead of going for her lips as any reasonable man would have, he settled his mouth against the crook of her neck, she was too surprised— and too flooded with knee-weakening hunger—to do anything but clutch at his shoulders just so she could stay upright.

The feel, the incredible, solid feel of him, the musky heat of his skin, the whispery, moist drift of lips and breath on her neck made her nipples tighten and her back arch.

She thought she had forgotten how *good* it was. God knows she had tried. She tightened her fingers into the crisp cotton of his shirt. Determined to hold on. Determined to push away.

"Take it easy." She felt rather than heard his chuckle. "I'm going to give you everything."

Oh, she remembered *that*, the easy, confident way he laughed. No sweat. Everything copacetic.

His arms came around her to hold, to cradle her to him, to nestle her against him, his strength so sure, so competent, so safe that she could let him take over. She dropped her head to his shoulder and inhaled the rich, warm, slightly musky, wholly masculine scent of him. Low in her body, hidden tissues recalled plea-sure and swelled and primed in anticipation. She could yield to the delicious sense of being unrestrained, yet secure—*no*!

What was the matter with her? She shoved uselessly at shoulders impossibly beyond her strength to move. He had to do no more than enfold her in his arms to make her feel safe—but it wasn't true. The morning-after always came. The scattered pieces always had to be picked up. She had been down this road before. She didn't know what he did to make her think forgetting her responsibilities was acceptable. She knew how fast everything came apart if one let down one's vigilance.

She wrenched her mouth away from his seeking lips. "No," she said.

He relaxed his hold but didn't release her. "How come? I was enjoying it—a lot."

"I can't. I can't kiss you and marry him."

"That's easy. Don't marry him."

The same no-sweat chuckle that had charmed her a minute ago made her furious now. "You don't know what you're talking about! There are obligations more important than an easy lay," JJ snapped and was in-stantly ashamed of herself. She had her faults, but she hoped self-righteousness wasn't one of them. She had only to look at his scars to know he understood both duty and sacrifice. "I'm sorry." She made herself meet his eyes. "I shouldn't have said that."

His hands had stayed at her waist, but now he slowly dropped them. The scarred side of his face was in deep shadow. But even on the perfect side, his face was harsh, his brows drawn down, the perfect bow of his lips compressed into a tight line.

"You shouldn't be out on the beach alone." His hard fingers closed around her upper arm, tight enough to show he meant business. "I'll walk you in."

The hair stood up on the back of her neck. Nobody told JJ Caruthers where she should and should not be. Apparently he intended to march her back to the hotel.

"I got my own self out here. I'll get my own self back."

"It isn't about you. Somebody needs to tell that friggin' fool you say you're *not* officially engaged to he needs to keep up with you better."

Chapter 15

"I DON'T UNDERSTAND WHY YOU DON'T WANT A CHURCH wedding." Blount slowed his Miata for the turn onto Military Cutoff, which would carry them to U.S. Highway 17. He shifted into second.

The Miata shuddered as Blount let out the clutch. As always, he gave it more gas a fraction too late. Some men shouldn't be allowed to buy a six-speed manual transmission.

JJ let her head fall back against the headrest and closed her eyes, trying to shut out both Blount's whiny tone and his driving. She made a mental note to insist upon driving her own car rather than riding with him from now on.

"I wouldn't want anything as hippie-ish as what we just went to," Blount continued when she refused to be drawn in, (or maybe he just wanted to complain and didn't notice she wasn't contributing). "But a marriage is an important event—not just to the couple, but to the entire community. You're always so aware of your civic responsibility—what's the matter with a church wedding all our friends can be invited to?"

Blount didn't understand that she simply didn't have the year of lead time it took to plan a large wedding. She hadn't told him about her grandfather's ultimatum and didn't intend to now.

"Blount, we've been over this before. We will have a large reception after we're married. We'll invite half of Wilmington, if you wish. But the sort of MGM extravaganza that is expected these days—even among people who aren't well-to-do—offends me. With the same money, they could put a kid through college, buy a house, fund an animal shelter, a women's shelter, a homeless shelter, an after-school program—something that would change people's lives.

"They could make a real difference, and instead they create a faux-Disneyland that will be gone in a day."

"Sometimes you talk like an old lady."

"I just don't like to spend money and, at the end of the day, have nothing to show for it."

"If you feel that way, I'm surprised you insisted on leaving the hotel even though we'd paid for the room," he needled her.

In point of fact, after finding a bellman and clearing the room of their things, JJ had put the room on her charge card. *He* hadn't paid a nickel, but she didn't correct him. Blount's disgruntlement with her unilateral decision to leave was the reason he was acting so pissy now.

Despite her irritation at his aggrieved tone, she allowed he had some right to be upset. She *had* given tacit, if not explicit, consent to spending the night with him. In simple fairness she had thought she should pay for the room. Dealing honestly and equitably meant a lot to JJ. Now, whether he knew it or not, he was doing her a favor. With every whiny word, any guilt she felt for backing out dissipated further.

In the last hour or so, she had realized she had a much larger problem than not wanting sex tonight.

Before tonight, she had convinced herself the very tame attraction she felt for Blount was what she wanted. Any time she'd found herself recalling the night of unleashed passion she'd shared with Davy, she intentionally made herself characterize it as tawdry and reinforced her sense of shock at herself, her shame. She repressed any memories of being in such perfect physical accord that her body sang.

Tonight he'd said his name was David, and she had to admit, with his scars and new air of gravity, a name like Davy no longer fit him. She had gotten rid of him in her mind, and yet tonight she hadn't been with him for five minutes before she craved his arms, his kisses. And arousal had begun melting her bones.

She hadn't felt the smallest fraction of that when Blount kissed her.

She had no choice but to marry Blount, but she was beginning to doubt if she would *ever* want sex with him. And if refusing to have sex once they were married wouldn't be backing out of an agreement, she didn't know what would.

"When we're married, will you insist on spending all our money on good works?" Blount broke in on her thoughts. Having failed to provoke her into an argument, he was trying a different tack.

JJ clamped down on the urge to snap, "*Our* money? I thought we had an understanding. My money will remain mine. Yours will be yours—to do with as you please."

"You mean the prenuptial agreement? Are you still set on that?"

"Correction. I'm not 'set' on it. I'm demanding it." He had agreed to it, although nothing was signed yet. JJ tried to soften her tone. "This discussion indicates we need to have money matters spelled out between us, don't you think?"

"Of course. All couples should discuss how they will handle money, but do we really need lawyers?"

"If we should talk about it, what's the objection to formalizing what we agree to? Unless you don't intend to keep your word." Even as she spoke, all the pieces that had been coming together tonight clicked into place, and JJ realized she was right. No matter what they agreed to, he would try to weasel, and no matter how much she gave him, he would always think he was owed more. The sick, black dread she'd steeled herself against earlier on the beach broke through again.

Not wanting to look at Blount, JJ focused on the nightscape out the passenger window.

It was late. The businesses along Military Cutoff were closed. Streetlamps glared on empty parking lots. The car's headlights bounced off wisps of fog whenever they crossed over one of the swampy creeks. For long stretches, fewer streetlights and the thick canopy of trees draped with Spanish moss made the thoroughfare darker. On the curb, a lone man, barely visible, walked hunched, as if he was carrying something heavy.

She craned forward to get a better look.

"JJ, you're misunderstanding what I'm trying to get at. A marriage cannot succeed in an atmosphere of distrust—"

"Blount," she interrupted him. "Was that man carrying a dog?"

"I didn't notice. As I was saying—"

"Stop. We have to go back."

"Are you crazy?"

"No, Blount, I'm not hallucinating. If it was a dog, it had to weigh sixty pounds. He wouldn't be carrying it unless it was sick or hurt. We have to see if we can help."

"I meant crazy to think I'm going to stop. In this neighborhood?"

"We don't have to get out of the car. We'll just find out what's going on and see if we can call someone for him."

"Call the police yourself. Let them take care of it." He gave the car more gas.

JJ turned as much as the seat belt would allow, trying to keep the man in sight. "For God's sake, Blount! The man's hands are *full*. He can't attack us. Are you afraid the dog's got a switchblade on him?" She glanced back at Blount and saw the set, disapproving line of his lips. Realization dawned.

"You don't intend to stop, do you? No matter what I say."

"No. It's good to be generous, but you can't go around impulsively—"

"Turn the car around, Blount, or I *will* call the police. I'll tell them I'm being kidnapped."

He gave her a furious look and, with jerky movements, slowed the car enough to make a U-turn in the almost deserted street.

Chapter 16

THE MAN, BAGGY JEANS DROOPING OVER RUN-DOWN cowboy boots, stopped walking when they pulled alongside him. Sure enough, in his arms he carried a reddish dog that looked like a chow-lab mix. The dog's big square head hung over the man's arm. From time to time, the animal stiffened as long shudders ran through him.

JJ lowered her window less than a hand's width. "What's the matter with your dog?"

"Don't know. Just found him like this. Some'un's been poisoning dogs in my neighborhood." The man had the deep-grooved, hollow cheeks of someone who had spent too much time in the sun, smoked too many cigarettes, and drunk too much whiskey. Thinning graying hair was pulled back in a ponytail. His faded denim jacket and jeans hung on his slight frame. He shifted the dog higher up his chest.

"Where are you going with him?"

"Car won't start. I'm hoping my buddy lives over on Ewell will give me 'n' Snake a ride to the vet'narin."

Snake? JJ repressed a shudder at the macho moniker. No dog in the world had ever looked less like his name. But that was none of her business. She didn't have to name him; she just needed to help him. "Is your buddy expecting you? Couldn't you call him?"

"No'm. I ain't been working regular for some time. Phone's been shut off."

"Ewell is a good ways from here."

The man shrugged as much as a man with a sixty-pound dog in his arms could. "It's near 'bout as far to the pay phone as to my buddy's house. Figured I was just as well to pick up Snake here and start walking his direction," he added with philosophical acceptance of a life that had never been easy.

"What's your friend's number? I'll call him."

She put the cell phone on speaker and dialed. In a few minutes she heard, "Yo! I'm not here. You know what to do," followed by the beep of voice mail.

"Don't even think about it!" Blount shook her arm less than gently. "We're *not* going to take him to the vet." He shot a suspicious glance at the man and lowered his voice to a hiss. "I draw the line at letting a man that dirty—much less a dog that's sick and likely to throw up—into the car."

"Got it covered," she agreed, already dialing. "I'm calling Ham, my grandfather's handyman."

"Ham," she said as soon as he answered. "I need you to bring your pickup. I've got a man with a sick dog that we need to transport to the emergency vet. Throw some old towels or a blanket in the back."

She gave Ham the location and hung up. "He'll be here in a few minutes," she told the man. "Why don't you put the dog down and rest your arms."

At her suggestion, the man carefully laid the dog in the grass. Squatting beside the animal, he kept one thick-fingered hand on him, while with the other hand he pulled on the bill of his stained Evinrude cap. "Name's Grady, ma'am, and you, you're one of God's own angels."

Blount spoke through gritted teeth. "You have the situation all taken care of. Now can we get out of here?"

"We're going to wait for Ham."

"Come on, JJ! Enough is enough."

"When Ham gets here," she told him. "Not before."

———⁂———

In less than ten minutes, the headlights of Ham's big,
red Chevrolet truck penetrated the frozen atmosphere
within the Miata. JJ had her seat belt unhooked and
was out the door before Blount could say anything—
fortunately for him.

Ham climbed down from the cab. "Blankets ain't
clean," he said going around to the back of the truck
and opening the tailgate. "Had to take 'em off my bed.
Reckon a dog won't mind."

"Off your bed? I told you to bring old ones." JJ took
the wool blanket he handed her and folded it down to
pallet size for a dog.

Ham grunted. "Don't got nothing *but* old ones."

Together, Ham and Grady shifted Snake onto the
blanket. Taking the four corners like a stretcher, they
lifted him to the truck's bed. Grady climbed on beside
him. The dog's shudders were coming at longer intervals. JJ didn't know if that was a good thing.

"Here's something to cover him with." Ham passed
him a knitted, cotton summer blanket. Clearly, Ham had
stripped his entire bed for a dog.

JJ went back to the Miata, where a stiff-faced Blount
stared straight ahead. Rigid with disapproval, he hung
onto the steering wheel as if the car wanted to run away
and he was holding it back by main force. Wonderful.

He hadn't gotten his way so now he was sulking. What an ass. She retrieved her purse and quilted, Waverly tote from behind the seat.

"What are you doing?" Blount yelped, breaking his stony silence. "Get back in the car!"

JJ, respecter of good machinery, if not of its owner, closed the car gently. "Earlier, you asked if I was crazy. Apparently I was—I thought I could marry you. Fortunately," she gave him her sunniest smile, "in the last several minutes, I seem to have had a miraculous recovery."

"Come on, JJ. Don't do this. This is another example of your impulsive sentimentality. You're going to regret this."

"Not as much as I would regret being married to you."

"What about your grandfather?"

JJ went cold. "What about him?"

"He thinks you're going to marry me. What are you going to tell him?"

"I'll tell him I realized I could have you or a dog. I chose the dog."

Chapter 17

BY THE TIME HAM AND JJ TRANSPORTED GRADY AND Snake to the vet, waited while the dog was stabilized, took Grady home, and then drove to JJ's cottage on Topsail Island, she was too tired to do anything but strip and fall in bed.

In spite of her late night, JJ woke when the red rays of morning sun rising over the ocean filled her bedroom. She loved having her first sight in the morning be the ocean. She always opened the curtains before she went to sleep—even when, as now, she knew the sun would wake her before she'd slept long enough.

JJ slipped into the thigh-length silk gown she kept always close at hand—because really, you never knew—and padded into the cottage's kitchen.

By today's standards, when newer cottages were the size of mini-hotels, this one was small, only three bedrooms, but as promised, it was elegantly decorated in shades of periwinkle, sand, and pale coral. The kitchen area of the great room boasted every gourmet chef's dream appliance. Floor-to-ceiling windows took up the entire front wall, making the house seem continuous with the beach and flooding the interior with light even on the grayest days.

Outside the window, the rising sun tinted the light fog, present most autumn mornings, a pearly pink. As the sun climbed higher, the fog would draw back until it was a solid-looking cloud out over the ocean. For now, it drew the horizon closer and forced the watcher to notice only what was close at hand. Only the sea oats atop the dunes next to the deck were clearly visible. They stood motionless.

JJ watched day come while she waited for the coffee to drip.

She often had a fancy that the alternating land and ocean breezes were caused by the land breathing. In the daytime, air rushed into the land; at night, it rushed out. Moments of utter stillness like this were the relaxed pause before the invigoration of the next in-breath.

This morning, she felt as if she, too, hung between the night and the day, between one breath and the next. She kept waiting for the gasp when the terrible reality of what she had done would burst upon her.

Idly, JJ pictured herself as a cartoon character with a huge wave rising up behind her, cresting, beginning to curl over her. Only, in the cartoon, the hapless character was always blissfully oblivious to the wave. That was the joke.

She, on the other hand, was completely conscious of the onrushing tsunami. She knew it was there and knew it would sweep away and destroy everything when it crashed down.

For a long time, like a cartoon figure, she had managed to run ahead of it, but in one moment of impatience and intolerance, she had stumbled, and now it was gaining. Not only was it coming closer, but it also seemed now the disastrous wave was pulling her toward it.

The coffeemaker hissed and sputtered, signaling the end of the drip cycle. She left the window to pour herself a cup and then returned to look out again, holding the cup against her heart while the coffee warmed the slick china of the mug from within.

In a few minutes, the quiver of one tall sea-grass stalk and the swaying of another told her the great cycle of inspiration had started again.

For a year, she had tried so hard to shape a future that compromised between her grandfather's demands and Caruthers' needs. She'd been so sure only Caruthers mattered. And yet, in one lightning flash of passion, she had dumped the well-being of Caruthers in an argument about a scruffy mongrel and his equally scruffy owner.

JJ drew a deep breath. Her mind could not encompass the enormity of the tidal wave of change about to crash down on her head, but she accepted that it was going to. Still, for the first time in a long time, the sense of being slowly and relentlessly strangled had eased.

After watching the fog dissipate for a few more minutes, JJ poured herself more coffee and perched on a stool at the counter. Habitually, she reached for a list pad, but the feeling of unreality persisted. For once, she had difficulty thinking of anything that really needed doing. She filled the first four lines with doodles.

Finally she wrote, "Call vet, check on Snake," which led to thoughts of Ham's generosity—or unworldiness, she wasn't sure which. He had assured her he'd be warm enough last night, and fortunately the mild Indian summer weather had held. Winter was coming though.

She wrote, "Blankets for Ham," then checked her watch. If she called right now, she could probably catch Esperanza before she left for mass.

"Esperanza," JJ asked, when she heard the house-keeper's Mexican-flavored English, "do you remember when you complained that Lucas wouldn't let you replace the blankets on his bed?"

"Yes, Miss JJ. They're so faded. But he don't let me, still."

"Can you go to that bed specialty store at the mall this afternoon and get some new ones? Get sheets, too. Use the household charge—I'll authorize it. And I'll pay you for your time."

"Oh, Miss JJ. You don't got to pay me. I *love* that store. But, you don't want to pick them out?"

"No. I don't live there anymore."

"Miss JJ." Esperanza's sigh came over the line. "When you coming back? He don't let me do nothing except clean and cook him breakfast. He say leave his dinner in the refrigerator—he'll heat it up. But he don't. He don't eat half of it."

Esperanza had been with them since before her grandmother died. When JJ had moved out, she'd increased Esperanza's hours from a couple of days a week to full time. She couldn't stand the thought of her grandfather alone in the big house.

He'd never done for himself while her grandmother was alive, and now, no matter how willing, he wouldn't know how to. A thousand details would slip away because he wouldn't know to attend to them before they became problems. And like a lot of old people, he constantly suffered sticker shock, and not just on big-ticket items. He got upset over the cost of what JJ considered trifles and refused to buy ordinary things needed to keep the house in good order.

Lucas wasn't an easy man to live with. He'd always been autocratic and demanding, and he'd seen himself as entitled to the final say about everything. But he'd also always been willing to listen to advice. Only JJ and Esperanza saw how irrational and intransigent he had become in the last couple of years.

"I know what he's like, Esperanza. Just do the best you can."

Esperanza hesitated. Then, practical woman that she was, moved on. "Well, I think he needs blankets and a down comforter, too, and if *I'm* going to pick out the sheets, I'm going to buy the Egyptian cotton, 800 thread-count kind that cost four hundred dollars!"

"You are one dangerous woman," JJ chuckled at Esperanza's idea of rebellion. "Go for it! While you're at it, get him some new towels, too. Box up the old stuff, and I'll be by to pick it up in the morning."

"I knew it! What are you up to?"

"Ham needs new linens, but if I buy him *new,* new ones—even from Target, he'll say they're too nice to use. He'll probably sell them to some flea-market dealer."

Esperanza tsked. "That's the truth. Mr. Lucas, he looks after Ham, but he don't think about things like sheets. You, you look after Mr. Lucas. You look after the car place. You look after all the peoples there. Who's looking after you?"

Chapter 18

"SO. YOU'VE KICKED ANOTHER ONE TO THE CURB." HER grandfather barked from behind his desk. "Well, I'm done helping you."

Courtesy demanded she stop to speak to her grandfather when she picked up the linens for Ham, so here she stood in the doorway of his home office. The shield she had put up to guard her feelings held, mostly. After all, she knew where Lucas got his information. "Esperanza told me Blount was here yesterday," she affirmed. "What do you mean, 'helping me'?"

"He came by here a month or so ago. Showed me the prenuptial agreement you wanted him to sign. Pretty upset."

"He didn't think I'd marry him without a prenup, did he?"

"The man's a big fish in a little pond there at the university. He's got the book learning, but he's a little naïve. I was surprised you chose him over some of the others."

"You mean: of the four grooms you picked out for me? Do you think the others would have been happy with the prenup?"

"I think Halston Ferguson," he named the agribusinessman, "would have understood business is business."

That was true. "So what do you mean you're done with helping me?"

"He was the one you wanted. I thought I'd sweeten the deal a little."

Heat flooded her body. "You *paid* him?"

"Said I would as soon as the ring was on your finger."

"How much? No, don't answer that. I don't want to know." The amount wasn't important. What mattered was that she had been trying to accede to her grandfather's wishes, to figure out a way to make some kind of marriage work and, at the same time, keep everything else going, while her grandfather had understood Blount's real motivation for over a month. Hadn't warned her. She never would have imagined that he had so little regard for her.

"Okay, I have to ask this: Why? Why on earth did you imagine paying him to marry me was *helping* me?"

"I gave you a year to find a husband. Time is running out. I don't *want* to sell the business—that's been in the family for five generations—out from under you. I was afraid if this one didn't stick... and I had to follow through..." Lucas's eyes fell. "Well, I was afraid I would lose you."

He didn't want to *lose* her? He should have thought of that before. Her grandfather's intransigence stole her breath. She had hoped, had tried to believe he didn't really anticipate what would happen if he destroyed the business. She wouldn't be able to find pieces of *their* relationship large enough to pick up. She would never forgive him.

"If you don't want to, then don't!"

"No, I've made my decision. You've found a reason to turn down all the men I found for you. You're on your own. But the deadline, November 27, stays the same."

JJ hadn't believed her grandfather would relent—she knew him too well—and yet, the hope had always been there. Her mind worked frantically to find a solution while the strange, cold numbness she had lived with for the last year solidified.

She had been trying to hold everything together and, in spite of the distance that had grown between her and Lucas, to salvage what she could of their relationship. Blount had seemed to be the best compromise between bowing to her grandfather's will and keeping Caruthers firmly anchored.

She had been mistaken in Blount, but her grandfather had known for a month what the man really wanted. He hadn't warned her when, maybe, there would still have been time to change course. Only one conclusion was possible. Lucas didn't care what kind of man she married as long as he got his way. Whether she saved Caruthers or not, there wasn't anything *to* salvage between her and Lucas. There was only one good thing about it. She didn't have to worry any more about what he thought about anything.

Freedom, as the old Kris Kristofferson song said, was *just another word for nothing left to lose*.

Chapter 19

TO CALL THE PLACE HAM LIVED A CABIN WOULD BE TO flatter it past recognition. It was a shack. To reach it, JJ turned off the highway onto a blacktop that wound its way through pine and holly thickets. She continued onto another, narrower blacktop where small unprepossessing fishing cottages could be seen through the thick, leaning trunks of yaupon.

Ham's packed sand-and-oyster-shell driveway could be hard to spot. JJ slowed, keeping an eye out for his truck, to make sure she didn't pass it.

Having been built with no thought to aesthetics, weathered until it was the same gray as the leaning yaupon under which it crouched, and half-hidden by veils of Spanish moss, Ham's house was almost invisible. Even when found, it gave the impression of something that grew there, rather than a human habitation.

JJ had taken her grandfather to task once when she was sixteen or so for "allowing" Ham to live as he did.

"This is the best Ham can do," Lucas had explained. "He stripped off civilization to survive in Vietnam. He was never able to put it back on again. He's fine as long as someone manages the interface with society for him. At least he's not homeless. And he hasn't committed suicide."

Ham put it more simply. "I got what I want, JJ. Any more'n what you want is a burden."

He rarely went on binges anymore—in the last several years, not at all—but the arrangements he and her grandfather had made many years ago continued. Her grandfather cashed Ham's disability check and gave him only the amount that would get him through a week. JJ wasn't sure if Ham understood that her grandfather paid the taxes on his property and had the utility companies notify him whenever Ham's accounts went past due.

Ham appeared beside the car as soon as the crunch of the wheels on the drive stopped. He had a way of doing that, as if he materialized.

"Esperanza was throwing out some sheets and things, Ham, so I thought I'd see if you could use them."

Ham dipped his head in acknowledgment. "All right."

That was Ham. He wasn't ungrateful, she knew. It was just that he had come to a profound acceptance that in life, things come and things go.

"Well, I'll get back to town then."

"You come out here just to give 'em to me? I'll be at the house day after tomorrow."

"You gave a dog the blankets off your bed—because of me. It didn't seem right for you to do without. Nights are getting chilly now."

"JJ, you done the right thing. Gettin' rid of that parasite."

"Parasite?"

"A man like that will eat you from the inside. I told Lucas to leave it alone."

"You knew Lucas offered him money to marry me?"

"Know about the whole thing. Lucas don't like to drive at night anymore. He calls me to come get him, take him around. Never thought I'd be sixty-five and be the young one." The fan of lines around his eyes deepened. "Never thought I'd live to see sixty-five at all."

"You know he's going to sell Caruthers if I don't get married?"

"Yep. Stupid-ass thing to do. Told him so. Told him it was time to let you grow up. Let you go your own way. Stop trying to mold you." He looked her up and down, a frank masculine twinkle in his eyes. "You look molded to me."

"I hate him."

"Yep. Told him that, too."

"What am I going to do?"

"Figure out what matters. You made a start with dog-man. People are like cups. Some are sixteen-ounce super-Slushee size. Some are little ketchup cups at Hardee's. Don't matter. Brimmin' over is brimmin' over. Get it?"

JJ didn't. "Are you saying I'm trying to take on more than my capacity?"

"I'm saying you've had your eye on one thing all your life—that's Caruthers. You've been and done whatever your grandparents said you had to do to fit yourself to it. I'm saying you ain't never measured *your* capacity."

Chapter 20

"JJ," KELLY AT THE CONCIERGE DESK SAID, "MRS. BABCOCK is here and would like to see you."

JJ tore her eyes from the computer-screen display of the last quarter's sales, which were finally showing some turnaround. For three months last winter, she'd taken out loans to meet payroll, and there had been more months when the cash flow was so tight she hadn't paid herself. They'd held it together though. She hadn't laid off anyone. Now they were so close, *so close*, to being solidly in the black again. It made the thought of Caruthers being scuttled and sold for scrap doubly poignant.

She had returned to Caruthers after leaving Ham because, really, what else was there to do? Until it wasn't hers anymore, she had the responsibility to stay at the helm. Tomorrow, she'd try to cobble together a plan that would take care of her people. She knew what a lame duck felt like.

"*Lauren* Babcock?" she asked.

"That's right," Kelly confirmed. "She wants you to show her some cars."

Lauren was her landlord, the owner of the Topsail Beach cottage, and also a longtime and loyal Caruthers customer. JJ always felt a little hot lick of satisfaction that Lauren, who could have bought cars anywhere, preferred to deal with them. If she wanted the VIP treatment, she would get it.

JJ wouldn't have said they were friends, but she liked Lauren, even though they rarely saw one another. When Lauren's daughter died unexpectedly, JJ had sent flowers and a handwritten condolence note. She'd seen Lauren at Mary Cole's daughter's wedding but had neglected to speak to her and so had written again. Come to think of it, that wedding was the last time she'd seen Lauren. But she'd heard her name mentioned just this last weekend, and now here she was. JJ searched for the word for that kind of meaningful coincidence. *Synchronicity.*

"Lauren!" JJ held out her hands to the woman standing in the square of yellow sunlight the two-story windows threw across the black polished granite of the showroom floor. Lauren had been a fashion model as a young woman and still knew how to find the best light and arrange her limbs so that even standing still, she looked dramatic and dynamic.

"Lauren, I hardly know what to say!" How *did* one say, *You look better than I've seen you look in a couple of years* without sounding grudging or offering, at best, a back-handed compliment. The gray look of dissipation was gone, as was the hard, glossy shell she'd worn before Danielle's death. "You look so… beautiful," she finished lamely.

"Better than the last time you saw me?" Lauren met the issue head-on with a wry smile.

"Yes." There was no point in denying that grief and drinking had taken their toll on Lauren's looks when last JJ saw her. "You've always been beautiful, and now you look healthy, too. I'm glad."

"Stopping drinking will do that. I've been sober for eleven months now."

"Good for you." JJ quickly did the math. Eleven months ago was significant for her, too. It was when her grandfather had struck her—she'd never be able to think of it in any other way—with his ultimatum. "So, you stopped right around last Thanksgiving? Did seeing Jax remarry the Saturday after Thanksgiving have something to do with quitting?"

For the first time, Lauren seemed embarrassed. Her lovely hazel eyes clouded. Still, after a brief internal struggle, she answered. "Only indirectly. I was drunk that night. One of the wedding guests, a SEAL who didn't even know me, told me how disgusting I was."

"*Ouch.*"

"Yes. He was completely heartless. He said I was a lousy grandmother."

"That's not true!" JJ rushed to her defense. "You've always adored Tyler. You would do anything for him."

"Thanks. But when I finally took a look at myself, I agreed with him. No matter how much I drank, it wasn't going to make the pain of losing Danielle go away. I wasn't thinking about how much Tyler needed me, only how much I needed him. I let him down. I'm not going to do that again, though. And I'm not going to let Jax Graham keep me away from my grandson." Lauren visibly shook off the darkness of the past.

"But I didn't come here to tell you my story. I've rented an apartment in Virginia Beach to be near Tyler. However, he's outgrown the car seat I had for him. I need a new car seat for Tyler, and I thought I'd get a new car to go with it."

"Only you." JJ laughed and shook her head. "Wait.

Are you saying you came all the way from Virginia Beach to buy a car from Caruthers?"

"Of course."

"Oh, Lauren, I'm touched. And honored. When dealerships are going under right and left, it means a lot that you would go out of your way to deal with us."

"Not so far. Tyler's out of town anyway so I couldn't see him, even if I stayed in Virginia Beach. Since I had business in North Carolina, I decided to combine it with a trip here." Lauren dropped her social smile. "I, um, I kind of needed to see a friendly face. The note you sent… It arrived after I went into rehab, and they held all our mail, so I didn't see it until after Christmas. I have so many amends to make to so many people—I can't tell you how much it meant to know I wasn't forever beyond the pale to at least one person."

JJ squeezed Lauren's fingers. "Well, I'm still honored by your loyalty. Okay, what kind of car are you looking for? You're going to get the very best deal and the best service Caruthers can offer."

———※———

They stopped at the concierge desk to get sunglasses. "Kelly, I'll be out on the lot with Mrs. Babcock. I'm going to forward my calls to you," JJ said punching numbers into her cell. "Hold everything for me, will you?"

"Uhh…" Kelly looked uncomfortable.

"What is it?"

"You have a call holding right now. It's Dr. Satterfield. I told him you were with a customer, but he demands I interrupt you."

JJ had expected Blount to call sooner or later. Little as

she wanted to talk to him, she guessed she owed him a "closure talk," but trust him to go through the switchboard so there would be no chance of keeping things private.

"Tell him you've talked to me. Tell him I'm aware of his call and will call him back as soon as I can." JJ smiled with more confidence than she felt. "He understands that at Caruthers, customers come first."

―――∞―――

"So how are *you*?" Lauren asked as they walked between the rows of gleaming automobiles. "I heard you're engaged."

"Not exactly. I thought I was ready to say yes, but he turned out to be a man I couldn't marry."

Lauren pulled dramatic black-framed reading glasses from her Prada handbag. She carefully adjusted the sunglasses over them and leaned forward to study the sticker on a car window. "Why not?"

"He was marrying me for my money."

"The louse," Lauren murmured without heat. She moved to the next car. "I'll say one thing for my ex-son-in-law. He didn't marry Danielle for her money. And believe it or not" —she trailed a finger down the accessories list— "I didn't marry Daniel Babcock for his money. Everyone thought I was a trophy wife, but I honestly thought I loved him. Still, once the romance wore off, I'll admit I stayed because of Danielle—and the money." Lauren's light hazel eyes swept JJ up and down in a measuring glance. "You don't look brokenhearted."

"I'm not. It doesn't excuse Blount, but I was being a hypocrite, too. I led him to believe I wanted a real marriage, but really, of the men I knew, he seemed the most likely to go his way and let me go mine." JJ sucked in a big breath and let it out. "It feels good to tell the unvarnished truth."

To JJ's surprise, Lauren chortled. "Oh, my darling, if what you *want* is a husband you won't have to see much of, what you *need* is a SEAL!"

"A Navy SEAL?"

"Trust me on this." Lauren's voice shook with amusement. "Danielle always said, 'Being married to Jax was almost the same as being divorced from him.'"

In the end, they didn't find a model with all the features Lauren was looking for. Once Lauren had selected the correct-sized child seat for Tyler, JJ turned Lauren over to a salesman who would receive the commission to help her write up a factory order.

With Lauren's laughingly tossed-off words seemingly stuck on an endless tape loop in her head, JJ went up to her office where, for once, she closed the door. She turned off her phone. She sat at her desk and held herself just as still as she could.

If what you want is a husband you won't see much of, what you need is a SEAL.

The daring, the sheer recklessness of the idea Lauren had put in her head, made sweat prickle in her hairline and left handprints on the desk blotter. Her heart pounded. Her entire body shook with each thud. She wanted to laugh. She wanted to yell.

She recognized her impulse to throw caution and good sense to the winds as hysteria-driven. Everything she knew about him told her less likely husband material there never was, but really, she wasn't wife material either. The very first time she had needed to compromise with Blount, to find common ground and work together, she had blown it.

If what you want is a husband you won't see much of, what you need is a SEAL.

As it happened, she knew a SEAL. Having talked with her friend Mary Cole this morning, she even knew where he was. *Knowing where a SEAL was*, she gathered from Lauren, was an accomplishment in itself.

So she might be inviting disaster. So? The tsunami was going to tear loose the moorings of everything she cared about anyway.

Why not?

Why the hell not?

Chapter 21

IT WAS HER! SITTING ON THE BIG, RED FLOWERED SOFA that occupied the center of Pickett's living room. It was… dammit, her name had taken unauthorized leave again. He'd been able to remember it an hour ago, and now it was gone again. And he was so gobsmacked to think that by some magical somehow she had appeared that he couldn't think of anything to say. Not *Hello Beautiful*, not *How are you*, not even *What the hell is going on*?

Then, cooler than cool, perfect features composed, magnificent rack framed by a contour-hugging red leather jacket, she raised emerald-green eyes and said, "I would like to marry you."

Davy threw back his head and laughed. His scar, still new enough to be red, ached when the muscles in his cheek flexed. He didn't let the pain hold him back; he laughed anyway. "This cannot be happening! Okay, where'd the guys hide the cameras?"

They had ragged on him all yesterday as they installed sinks, sanded drywall, and set cabinets and countertops in the bathroom Jax and Pickett were adding to Pickett's Snead's Ferry house. They thought it was a hoot that he had gone chasing after her and had come back empty handed. This practical joke was SEAL humor at its most inventive. They must have planned the whole thing for when he'd be alone in the house with Lon while everyone else went off to dive.

He should have been suspicious when Lon had come into the bathroom where he was finishing painting and said, "There's a woman who says she knows you. In the living room. I suggest you talk to her."

Now here he stood in grubby shorts and even grubbier running shoes, shirtless because it was stuffy in the windowless bathroom, spattered with blue-green droplets of something called *Spruce Mist*, and his hair matted and gray with sanding dust.

Her air of self-possession didn't alter. She smiled politely. "I don't know what you're talking about. What cameras?"

She was a cool one. He raised his hands in mock surrender. "You got me, okay? I didn't see it coming, and you can tell the guys they gave me the best laugh I've had in weeks. This is one hell of a practical joke. How'd they get the senior chief and you to go along with it?"

"I'm not joking."

Either she was one hell of an actress or she was serious. Or nuts. Regardless, it was time to call this to a halt. He crossed his arms over his chest knowing it made him look intimidating. The scar on his cheek added to the effect. One thing about his little gift from the Taliban, he didn't have to work to look tough anymore.

"You want to marry me?" He loaded his tone with sarcasm. "The other night you said you were engaged. Close to it anyway. Now you want me? What the hell are you up to?"

A shadow flickered in the intense green depths of her eyes, but they didn't waver. "Let me make myself clearer. I am in *need* of a husband, whether I *want* one or not. I'm prepared to offer you a lot of money."

Whoever had come up with this little gag had gone too far. His worry about how he was going to scrape up the money for his little brother's tuition wasn't funny. Nor was the implication that someone had been talking about him. He made his voice hard. "What makes you think I need money?"

With one graceful hand, she batted the question away. "Most people want more than they have." Not taking her eyes off his, she said, "Would you sit down, please? Glowering at me really won't help."

Davy had started to settle into the green leather easy chair near the fireplace before he caught himself. Shit. He was too dirty to sit on the upholstery. He'd almost sat down just because she told him to. This lady had thrown him more completely than anything—even his mother's unexpected death. He straightened slowly. "You're not joking."

Her full lips tightened. "I said I wasn't."

The lady wasn't used to having her word doubted. He smiled—yeah, he liked knowing he'd discomposed her a little. If she could do it to him, he could do it to her. He didn't like the feeling that he had been set up, or that this woman, Lon, and God knew who else—*everyone* but him—knew what was going down.

Still he didn't need to be so heavy-handed. He knew his way around women, and when it came to the fair sex, he'd much rather make love than war. "Pardon me while I put on a shirt, and then let's go out on the porch," he suggested, "where I can sit without ruining anything." And where, just in case this was a joke, hopefully there were no cameras.

On the porch, he indicated one of the rockers pulled up near the railing for her. Instead of taking the chair beside it, he settled a hip on the rail in front of her.

To make the point that he wasn't going to be messed with, he was deliberately crowding her space, intimidating her, but he didn't want to scare her to death, so he folded his hands loosely on his thighs. People relaxed better when they could see his hands had been taken out of play.

He weighted a smile with carefully calibrated sexiness. "Okay, you've gone to the trouble to find me here. Maybe you'd better begin at the beginning. But first," he added a charmingly diffident chuckle, "I'm sorry, but... you mind telling me your name again?"

Twice. He'd come on to her *twice*, and he still didn't know her name. It wasn't flattering, but it *was* reassuring in a way. For her, their first meeting had been an aberration, and if she gave him the benefit of the doubt, maybe hooking up without so much as a preliminary drink was unusual for him, too.

Now all doubt was eliminated. She could dismiss the last of her reservations about the wisdom of her proposal. When it came to women, it was obviously out of sight, out of mind for him. She didn't need to fear she would be raising false hopes or keeping him from finding the right woman—her reasons for eliminating Henry and the lawyer as candidates.

Obviously, he was one of those men for whom the woman in front of him was the right one. And she left no more lasting impression than a plane does on a radar screen once it moves out of range.

The way he perched on the rail, lazily swinging one leg, the long muscles of his thigh knotting and smoothing out under their covering of black hair, said he intended to dominate and trusted his charm was sufficient to let him get by with it.

This wasn't going at all the way she had imagined it in her head. She'd planned a rational discussion in which she would explain what she needed and what she was offering. The nice man who had answered the door had been perfectly polite, but by the way he had smiled at her so kindly, she'd known he thought she was one in a long line of girls who ran after Davy. She doubted if his scars had changed a thing. Her pride had gotten up.

And then David had come in, and oh, my God—she'd seen him in full daylight. He may have been Davy when she knew him before, but he was David now.

His bare shoulders and chest were speckled with blue-green paint. His khaki shorts rode low on his hips, as if he'd lost weight.

His face was thinner, too. Before, the flair of his jaw had given his face weight and kept the perfection of his features from being pretty. Now, honed by God knew what sufferings seen, suffering endured, it had rock-like strength. Then he had recognized her, and joy had blazed across his face. In a face tanned by foreign suns, his teeth had flashed white, and his brown eyes, which should have seemed dark, were full of light.

Desperate to get things back on a track she understood, she'd said the first thing that came into her mind. And he'd laughed. Long. Uproariously.

Now he'd managed to arrange how they sat so she felt trapped. She *hated* to feel trapped. She hated to feel like her back was to the wall.

She stiffened her shoulders. Her back *was* to the wall or she wouldn't be here, but she was tired of letting others make the moves while she adapted. If she was going to do this, she was going to do it *her* way.

"My name is JJ Caruthers." She scooted her chair back and stood so forcefully the rocker threatened to tip. "Stop trying to tie me up with sexy charm. It won't work any better than the tough-guy act you tried a minute ago. I've come here to make you a deal."

He stood when she did. Now they were hardly a hand's width apart. He smelled, not unpleasantly, of paint and drywall dust and working man. JJ's stomach did a backflip. She knew his smell, and every cell in her body responded to the memory. She searched his face for the man she'd known before. The man she had thought she would be dealing with.

Before, with perfectly proportioned features and skin so smooth and fine-grained it had a light sheen, he'd looked plastic. Now, damaged, in that totally unfair advantage men had over women, he was actually better looking. The scar matured him. It revealed him as the kind of man who would walk into the kind of danger that left scars like that.

He fingered the red line, and she knew she'd looked at it too long. She felt herself coloring. "I'm sorry. I didn't mean to stare, but it does change you. *Now*, I do have a proposal for you, and I think it would be worth your while to listen. So can we both sit down" —she eyed the rockers significantly—"and get to business?"

⁓

Davy could not believe what he was hearing. "Are you telling me your grandfather is making you get married—and you're letting him get away with it? This is twenty-first-century America, woman! Forced marriage isn't legal. Fight him."

"Fight him!" JJ slapped her forehead. "What's the matter with me? Why didn't *I* think of that?" JJ rolled her eyes and huffed a pained-sounding chuckle. "Do you think I haven't spent the last year looking for a way out? There isn't one."

"Okay, okay. You did think of fighting him. But he's got to be crazy."

"His lawyer solemnly swears that if I challenge Lucas's competence, he'll call the whole town to testify that Lucas is as wily as ever. I won't win, but a trial will provide grist for Wilmington's gossip mill for a couple of years. I'll destroy my reputation, his reputation, and the family business's reputation. I can't win, but I can lose everything."

So this was all about holding onto an easy life and not airing dirty laundry. "Lose everything, huh? What's he going to do? Cut you out of his will? What's the matter, little rich girl? Would you have to go to work?"

JJ gave him a reproving look. "I'll overlook your nasty tone. I didn't explain myself very well. The car business has been hit hard the last year or two. When carmakers fail, there's a ripple effect throughout the whole economy. Dealerships go belly-up, too." Her words were mild, but her eyes blazed with green fires.

"I've kept Caruthers strong, and because of the business, one hundred families have paid their mortgages. *They still have homes.* They've gotten the medical care they needed when they needed it, because *they still have insurance.* They're not afraid of the future. *They still have pensions. Their kids are still in college.* Christmas is good at their houses.

"And that's just the start of the prosperity and peace of mind Caruthers generates. It doesn't include the Little League teams, the United Way campaigns, the civic improvement projects it spearheads."

"But still, you'd get married? To save a business?"

"Throughout the ages, women have married for reasons that have more to do with protecting property and providing for those who depend on them than with love. For me, this business and the people who are part of it are inseparable from my family. It is the soil my roots are set down deep into. Yes. I will do what it takes."

Her green eyes lit with passion; her voice throbbed with fervor. That cool exterior hid passionate depths. He could see her like a latter-day Joan of Arc, mounted on a black horse, dressed in chain mail, fearlessly moving into holy battle.

"One more question. You're a beautiful woman. Are all the men in Wilmington blind or something? With your looks and money, I bet men would line up around the block if you put the word out."

"It's possible," she acknowledged.

"Then, why me?"

"I've already tried putting the word out—as much as I'm willing to. Strange as it might seem," she quirked an ironic eyebrow, "I don't really want to be wooed for either my looks or my money. I'm not an ornament for a man's ego, and I don't want someone kissing up to me so he can move up a few price points on the loafers he buys. I prefer a straightforward business arrangement. What you see on the table is all there is. No hidden agendas, no hidden expectations. As for why you—you're a SEAL."

"A lot of women who are marriage-minded think that's a problem."

Her full lips moved in the first genuinely pleased smile he'd seen. She leaned forward eagerly. "No, it's perfect! I don't know why I didn't think of this solution a year ago."

"Then clue me in, how 'bout it, because I don't see the connection."

"It's obvious the business won't allow me to live anywhere but Wilmington. I understand you're out of the country most of the time, but even when you're here, there are no SEAL bases in North Carolina. We won't have to live together except in the most nominal sense. I can be married to you and not need to see you more than a couple of times a year."

That killed any hope that she was harboring a secret yearning for him. "Damn. That's cold."

She looked down and blushed—which was interesting. "I didn't mean to sound indifferent to your welfare. Let me put it this way. You would also be free to live as you please. Get married one day, return to your old life the next. I don't expect you to be faithful—although I would appreciate discretion."

"What's the catch?"

"You'll have to sign a prenuptial agreement. Whatever payment we agree on, that's it. I don't intend to support you the rest of your life." She pulled a paper from her briefcase. "I have it here if you'd like to read it."

He waved it aside. He could read it, sure, but he'd have to go over it several times to comprehend it. Better to do that when he was alone.

She knew when to be silent; he'd give her that. In fact, he'd bet she was a hell of a businesswoman. She waited for his decision, her perfect features composed, a tiny smile at the corners of her mouth. Her green gaze was steady but just a touch weary, he thought.

The strange, nagging feeling that had rolled around the edge of his consciousness like a basketball circling and circling the rim finally dropped in. Her eyes were the same color as the little girl's in Afghanistan! It hadn't made sense that he would feel so moved by a woman he had barely met—a woman obviously able to look after herself. But if she reminded him of the child, that explained it. The death of a patient had rarely left him feeling so helpless or inadequate, or made him wish more wholeheartedly that he could have done more. It felt unbelievably good to have solved at least one mystery in a brain that half the time seemed to belong to someone else.

"You know, your eyes are the same color green as a little girl's in Afghanistan." He touched his cheek. "I don't remember getting this. Seeing her is the last thing I remember before coming to in a hospital in Germany."

"You don't look like that's a happy memory."

"She died. In childbirth. Fourteen years old. Forced into marriage with a man in his forties. So many things could have saved her. If she hadn't been forced into marriage. If her husband had at least waited to get her pregnant. If someone had recognized that a pregnancy in a girl that young is high-risk. If a competent midwife had been available. If it hadn't been forbidden to let a man, not her husband, look at her—even to save her life."

"You," she whispered, looking at him with unflinching kindness. "You were the 'man.'"

He nodded and swallowed, unable to speak.

She averted her eyes, a courtesy he appreciated. Since his injury, emotions sometimes caught him unaware, spilling over before he knew they were so close to the surface.

Even when he had control again, she continued to look into the distance.

She chewed her lip, scraping at it slowly and thoughtfully with her upper teeth. It didn't look like a nervous habit—more something she did when she was thinking deeply. Mostly she seemed to have the strength, poise, and power of an older woman. It turned him on, big time. This gesture though, this made her look young, earnest, and vulnerable. It went straight to his softest soft spot.

After a while she said, "I understand. My marriage problems must seem picayune compared to that. I'm not a victim of oppression. Legally, I can't be forced. Because I didn't like the choices I saw, I refused to acknowledge that I was making a choice. But I am. The one that seems to be in the best interests of the most people."

There was a quiet dignity about the way she spoke, neither arguing nor pleading her case. He liked it. In fact, he liked her. He liked the passion with which she embraced responsibility for those in her care. He liked her ability to stay focused on her goals even when he goaded her. He liked that she didn't candy-coat. He was aware of her allure, but she didn't use it to get her way. They were from different worlds, and yet it was surprising how well he understood what mattered to her.

No, she wasn't being forced. And when all was said and done, she wasn't proposing marriage. She was making a deal. It was time to get down to terms.

"How much money are we talking about?"

Chapter 22

"HOW MUCH DO YOU THINK A KITCHEN RENOVATION LIKE this costs?"

Lon ran a practiced eye over the room, figuring costs on the glowing, hand-rubbed cherry cabinets, the state-of-the-art appliances, the green granite countertops. As a sideline, Lon flipped houses. In the booming housing market in San Diego, he'd made some serious money. "Sixty, seventy thou."

Davy whistled silently.

"It's a good investment. In this location, they'll get back every penny."

"I thought Pickett's mother gave them the renovation as an enticement to keep the house, not sell it."

Lon's smile held a touch of cynicism. "She said it was a wedding present, but, yeah, that probably was her real agenda. She wants to give them a reason to always come back here, no matter where Jax is stationed. I've gathered Mama Sessoms likes to hold on to her kids."

Davy wondered if his mother had wanted to hold on to her kids—not him—his half-brothers and sister. Somehow he always thought of *them* as her children. She would have moved heaven and earth to get anything they needed—he knew that. Which circled his thoughts back to how he was going to provide for them. "Is it going to take a kitchen re-do to get my mother's house to sell?"

"Kitchens and baths sell houses, no doubt about that, but even if it does sell, you won't realize the kind of money you need." Lon had helped him with settling his mother's estate. He knew how things had been left. "Want something to drink?" Lon asked, going to the refrigerator.

"I need to finish painting the bathroom."

"Done."

"You finished it?"

"Finished, brushes washed, everything."

"Thanks, bro."

Lon grabbed two cans of Pepsi from the refrigerator and set one in front of Davy. He pulled a stool opposite Davy and perched on it, gingerly pulling his pants leg away from the groin. After a day doing the same work Davy had, Lon's cargo shorts were pristine. Davy didn't know how he did it.

"How's the leg?" An injury at the top of the thigh, requiring stitches, was the reason Lon was here, not diving with the rest of the guys.

"Still a little sore."

"Are you really going to baby-sit Jax's mother-in-law while you're on limited duty?" Davy asked, aware he was stalling. "That woman is a drunk."

"*Ex*-mother-in-law," Lon corrected. He wasn't going to discuss the arrangement he'd made with Jax to supervise Lauren's visits with her grandson. "Lauren's trying to turn her life around. That's not easy. I guess you're thinking about when we hustled her, drunk, out of the wedding reception when Jax and Pickett got married?"

"Umm-mmm." Davy's murmur might have been an affirmative, might have been an invitation to Lon to keep talking. It was a sound he'd gotten good at in the last

several months. If he could keep people talking, sometimes he could figure out what they were talking about
without revealing that he had lost track of the conversation. The silence between them lengthened. Davy rolled
the cold red, white, and blue can between his hands. Lon
was waiting for him to start.

———

"So what are you going to do?" Lon asked after he'd
heard the whole story.

"I don't know. A chance to earn the money I need by
getting married—it still feels like a practical joke—one
that God is playing on me."

"Listen, losing your mom so soon after nearly dying
yourself is bound to make you examine your life. But
you need to chill. You're taking on too much. Eleanor
and Harris are adults—help them if you can, but let them
figure out how to stay in school."

"That's not the way Mom would see it. Anyway,
Riley's just fourteen. My mom's will names me guardian. You know what that school is costing."

"You can get help. The Navy has a lot of support for
sailors with special-needs kids."

"It's still better for him if he stays in his school. Riley
doesn't handle change well."

"So what *do* you want?" Lon asked after a while.

"I just want my life back. I feel like the person I'd
been all my life died in Afghanistan, and now I'm walking around as someone I don't recognize. I want out of
this limbo I've floated in ever since I was shipped back.
I want to operate again. When I'm a SEAL, I know who
I am. I know where I belong. Even the bad days are

good. Now, I wake up every day hoping today's the day I'm finally going to feel like myself again."

He couldn't explain what he had to do. He didn't try. His mind squirrel-caged as he tried to find his way through all the variables. It settled on the one moment of—he sought a word for that incandescent, miraculous peace he'd felt when he'd walked into the living room and there she sat.

Joy.

And then she had said, "I want to marry you." It had felt like a joke, but now he thought it was a sign.

Whenever he had thought about getting married, it had seemed like a vague possibility in some unimaginable future. He wasn't against it; he just hadn't been able to see it. He'd always put off the thought for when he'd had enough of operating. Until then, being faithful through the inevitable separations would be too much of a hardship. Operate single, and have all the sex he wanted, or operate married, knowing he got none until he got home. It was a no-brainer.

Marriage was a sacrament. He'd feel dirty turning it into a commodity. But a marriage on paper only? Maybe it was the answer to what had looked like a hopeless problem. He had told himself it was time to man up. To take care of his family—if he made sure no money came to him—he could go through with it.

"I don't want to do it on her terms," he told Lon. "Will you help me come up with a counteroffer?"

Chapter 23

"THANKS FOR THE RIDE," DAVID CALLED TO LON. HE waited until Lon drove off to knock on the paneled redwood door of JJ's beach cottage. Lon hadn't been crazy about what David was proposing to do. David didn't like it either, but it solved his problems. With a clear conscience, knowing his brothers and sister were taken care of, as soon as he was healed up, he could have his life back.

The door opened. A wet tendril of dark hair hung over the one green eye he could see peeking through at him. Through the crack of the door, he could smell her, warm and moist from her bath. Girly soap and shampoo and clean woman essence—it went to his head and weakened him with longing. "Aren't you ready?"

"It's only four-thirty. I wasn't expecting you until five-thirty. I was in the shower."

Shit. Had he gotten the time mixed up again? His problem wasn't forgetting. He remembered, but when he got to appointments, he was wrong. He should have written it down—not that even that always helped, because sometimes he wrote it down wrong. Didn't matter. With Lon gone, he couldn't offer to go away and come back. A little surprise might be to his advantage. He pushed against the door. "That's okay. I'll wait."

She let go of the door in favor of clutching together the lapels of the white terry robe she wore. Which was a damn shame. The glimpse of leg he'd gotten was fine.

He watched the action with a knowing and very appreciative smile.

She fell back a couple of steps, but she didn't let him fluster her. "Come in," she invited, ignoring the fact that he was already in. "Why don't you have a seat while I put on some clothes?" She waved him toward a grouping of sofas and chairs near the huge windows that looked out on the ocean and took up one wall.

Trained in situation awareness, he took in the layout of the room, the position of every door and window, every structure that could conceivably hide a shooter. Moisture escaping from the bathroom intensified odors. The room was full of her personal smell. Through the open door to her bedroom, he could see the red leather jacket and green wool slacks she had been wearing earlier, now draped across the foot of the bed, the yellow heels on the floor beneath them.

Reconstructing the scene, he could imagine her stepping out of the heels, undressing, walking naked to the bathroom. Just for a second, he could see how her round, high breasts tipped with large, velvety-brown areolas swung as she bent over. He inhaled reflexively as his whole body tightened. Damn. There went that feeling that he *knew* her again. His imagination had never been that good before. The head doctors talked about a lowering of inhibition thresholds as a result of traumatic brain injury, or TBI, but he'd thought they meant acting more emotional.

Focus. This was no time to start thinking with his dick. People who paid you thought they owned you. He had to make sure JJ knew she wasn't going to get a lapdog. To cover his reaction, he gave her a deliberately suggestive chuckle. "Don't get dressed on my account."

Her green eyes narrowed, and the corners of her lips tightened. "Trust me, I'm not."

—∿∿—

JJ toddled toward her bedroom with as much barefoot dignity as she could achieve while holding fistfuls of terry robe together at the waist and top of her thighs. She hadn't been able to find the sash. Comfortable naked, she'd rarely used the robe since she'd moved to the cottage. Drat the man for destroying her carefully orchestrated scenario.

She'd had a dress all picked out. One that said she was fully aware of her power and able to be in charge. She had intended to take him to one of the gourmet restaurants on the sound side of the island for a nice dinner over which they could come to terms.

Now she had to regroup. She took a deep breath and focused on what she wanted, not what wasn't working. She had achieved part of her goal. He was here. He hadn't said no.

As if delighted with the change in plan, she put a smile in her voice and called over her shoulder as she gained the dressing alcove, "I put some soft drinks in the refrigerator, or you can pour yourself something at the bar. I'll be out in a minute."

In the bathroom, she abandoned her plan to blow-dry her hair straight and then iron it into silky smoothness. Her thick hair would take too long to dry completely. Instead, she dried the ends enough to prevent them from clinging wet and cold to the back of her neck and shoulders, then combed her hair back and clipped it at the nape.

She did take the time to slick on some lip gloss and a little mascara. In the vanity mirror, she checked the black wide-leg jeans and baby-doll top she'd grabbed on the way into the bathroom. It wasn't what she had intended to wear for this meeting, but he didn't need to know that. The jeans showed off her most excellent butt, one payoff of her ballroom-dancing hobby.

When she came out of the bathroom, she grabbed the initiative. "Can I take your early arrival to mean you're eager to accept my offer?" she asked over her shoulder as she slipped on lollipop-red Manolos.

"Not exactly."

JJ whirled at the sound of his voice right behind her.

He leaned against the opening of the dressing alcove, a can of Coke in one hand. He gave her a slow, frankly approving appraisal.

He was trying to rattle her to gain an advantage. She told her heart to slow down and her body to ignore his proximity. As if she'd expected him to turn down her first offer, she gave him a knowing smile. "And yet, you are here," she told him. "Sounds like we need to talk. I think I'll have some wine."

She led the way into the great room. A glass of white wine already stood on the placemat at one end of the dining table. Piled with papers, the other end of the table had slowly turned into JJ's home office.

He grinned. "I already poured your wine."

"How did you know I'd want it?"

"Open bottle in the fridge. Wine glasses in the dishwasher. You told me you had bought soft drinks, which made me think you didn't always keep them on hand."

"Oh. Thanks. Can I get you something else?"

He lifted the Coke can. "This is fine." He pulled the prenuptial agreement from a back pocket and tossed it on the table before seating himself. "You can tear this up. I'm not signing it."

The trick to staying in control of a negotiation was to remain flexible. JJ ignored the icy weight in her stomach and smiled ruefully. "Too bad. Out of curiosity—how large would the offer need to be to be attractive?"

He laced his fingers around the Coke can as if he needed to anchor them. "Here's the deal. I don't want your money, and I don't need it," he stated in a flat, throaty growl. "I won't take a cent from you. Not now, not ever. No perks, no expensive presents."

He was turning her down. The tsunami loomed closer. JJ fought dry-mouthed panic to say smoothly, "But you want something or you wouldn't be here."

Her phone, where she had left it on the granite countertop, made a loud buzzing noise. She had set her phone to vibrate since she didn't want any distractions. It was probably Blount again. She swallowed her frustration.

"You want to get that?"

"Let me see what it is, then I'll turn it off."

But the text message read GF 911.

She had bought Ham a cell and taught him to text, but he had neither the patience nor the comfort with technology to learn anything fancy. They had settled on a few simple codes. GF 911 meant an emergency concerning her grandfather.

"I'm sorry. I have to take this," she told Davy as she punched in Ham's number. "What is it?" she asked when he answered on the first ring.

"Lucas and me, we're at the hospital. He had some shortness of breath."

"Is he okay?"

"I think he is. The doctor's in with him now."

Davy was listening to her half of the conversation with frank interest. If only she could have finished negotiations with him before this call. If they broke off now, the deal was going to go cold. But neither her grandfather nor Ham dealt well with modern medicine. Ham shut down and became robotic. Lucas combated helplessness by giving orders. "Is Esperanza with you?" she asked Ham.

"She's got the flu. Lucas sent her home."

"So he was home alone and called you? He should have called 911. No, forget I said that. At least he had the sense to call you. He didn't attempt to drive himself." She would deal with the guilt that he hadn't called *her*, later.

She came to what had always been a foregone conclusion. "I'll be there as soon as I can, but I'm on Topsail. It will be thirty minutes—at the very least."

"Trouble?" Davy asked when she ended the call.

"My grandfather. He's in the ER with shortness of breath. I guess you and I will to have to talk later. Maybe I can—"

"How 'bout if I ride with you? Thirty minutes, you said. That should be plenty of time."

"You know what emergency rooms are like. I have no idea how long I will be."

"No problem."

"But what if you miss your ride? Don't you have to be back at the base by a certain time? I guess Ham could drive you back here, or I could ask—"

"Don't worry about it. It's not a problem. I can get myself where I need to be."

Fear for her grandfather, relief that this window of opportunity with David wasn't lost, hope that her life could get back on track again produced a roller coaster of emotions. "Okay. *Okay*! If worse comes to worst, there's always a plane. I'll call my assistant and have her check flights to—Norfolk? Is that the best airport?"

He closed his fingers over hers and gently forced her to close her phone. "I said I'll take care of it. I can look after myself. Do you always make yourself responsible for everyone?"

The warmth of his fingers spread up her arms. The man exuded reassurance. "I guess I do." She thought about it a second and chuckled tiredly. "Actually, most of the time, I *am* responsible."

"No. It's my duty to get myself back to base. Mine alone. Now, do you have a raincoat or something? There's weather coming in."

—∞—

The cloud ceiling had lowered, and an early dusk turned the pines beside the road black. At Hampstead, where 210 left U.S.17, the stoplights bounced and swayed in the gusts. The closer they got to Wilmington, the heavier the five o'clock traffic became.

Even though the cockpit of JJ's red Lexus was roomier than many sports cars, with David in the passenger seat, it suddenly felt small. He wasn't taller than average, but somehow there seemed to be an awful lot of him. Even separated by the gearshift, their shoulders almost touched. She was aware of his masculine scent and the warmth his body heat added to the small confines.

She hadn't brought up the subject of marriage again. She usually faced things head on. She was the kind of person who liked to hear the bad news first. Though it might be cowardly, if there wasn't a chance they could come to terms, she didn't want to know—not right now.

Instead, David had asked her questions about her grandfather's heart condition, and she'd wound up telling him her grandfather's entire medical history. He was a good listener. JJ tapped the breaks when an SUV pulled out in front of them. The speed limit through here was 45, but she wasn't doing even that. A fine mist covered the windshield. She switched on the wipers and headlights. She sighed.

"Are you okay?" he asked in his dark, smooth, comforting voice. He sounded like he really cared.

"To tell you the truth, I don't know what I am. For the past year, I've lived with my eyes on the future and one goal: find a man I could marry so I could save Caruthers. I didn't hope... I didn't despair... I didn't anything. I just kept moving. In the last forty-eight hours, it's all falling apart, and I can't seem to put it together again. I can't even find all the pieces."

JJ waited for David to say something. The car filled with the hiss of tires on wet pavement. The swish-slap of the wipers.

"*I'm so angry at him.*" There. She'd finally said it.

"Your grandfather?"

"I don't want to care that Lucas is sick, but I do. We had an argument earlier today. I'm afraid it caused a heart attack or something, and now he's in the hospital and it's my fault. And here I am, rushing to the hospital—rushing as much as I can in five o'clock traffic—which I wouldn't be in, not like this, if I hadn't moved to the beach to get away from him."

"Why did you dump the idiot?"

"The idi—? Oh, Blount." She sniggered. "Lost my mind?"

"Seriously. Why?"

Why. JJ had asked herself that over and over. David's "why" wasn't an accusation the way hers had been. It was a simple request for information. She searched for how to explain it. "Watching Emmie and What's-his-name get married—"

"Do-Lord."

"Anyone could see how in love they are, how right for each other. I've never been in love like that—have you?"

"Like that? No. Not yet."

"And Jax and Pickett. The air between them sizzles."

"So, you were envious of them."

"Maybe. Partly. I could have dealt with that. But then I almost kissed you. And I thought, 'Where did my integrity go?'"

"Huh."

JJ wouldn't have thought one grunt could contain that much satisfaction. She stole a sideways glance. She'd already noted that the scarred side of his face was less moveable, but even so, she could see the way he held back a smile.

JJ laughed against her will. "Oh, wipe that smirk off your face!"

"One almost-kiss, and you ditch him? Come on, girl, a kiss that powerful is smirk-worthy."

"It's not, and that's not the way it was." She smacked him on the arm with the back of her hand. "It's just that when I couldn't make myself spend the night with him because I felt so guilty, *he* got pissy and acted like a jackass.

"I had to threaten to call 911 and say I was being kidnapped before he would stop the car to help a dog. A *dog*." Her ire rose again at the memory of Blount's cowardice. "Nobody was asking him to run into a burning building. A phone call was all it took. And I lost my temper."

"I'll bet that doesn't happen much. How did it feel?"

"Better than most sex I ever had."

"Huh."

"Are you smirking again?" she asked dangerously.

"No, ma'am! Not me!"

"You are. I can *feel* you over there, laughing."

"No, I'm not. Sex that bad is serious!"

"I didn't say I had bad sex."

"You didn't have to."

"Be that as it may, good or bad, the high afterwards was just as short-lived. I had blown my future and the future of everything I cared about. I walked around in a daze for about twenty-four hours. Then I had the idea of asking you to marry me. I had hope again."

"Tell me again, why me?"

"Because you're the only SEAL I know."

"Oh, right. And SEALs are never around. You wouldn't have to face me at breakfast."

"I didn't mean it that way. I meant your time is already occupied. It's also that you don't care anything about me. I didn't have to worry about hurting your feelings every time I put Caruthers first. Not even to save Caruthers am I willing to break someone's heart or ruin their life. But you're not in love with me, and I'm not in love with you. Best of all, SEALs have a ninety-five percent divorce rate. It would come as no surprise to anyone when we split up."

JJ put on her signal to make the turn onto the U.S. 17 Bypass. They would make better time now. "It doesn't matter now. You're not interested in what I have to offer. So you ask me if I'm okay. Well, I'm worried and guilty and angry and sad and hopeless. And I'm off to the bedside of a man I'm not ever going to forgive—" Her stomach shook with pained laughter at what a mess she was. "But I'll probably be at his bedside the next time he needs me, even so."

Chapter 24

HER PAINED LITTLE LAUGH WAS FULL OF AFFECTIONATE irony. Like the precordial thump—a blow to the sternum administered before initiating the chest compression part of CPR—it surprised his heart into a different rhythm. She was a woman of deep feelings who didn't give in to them—not when they conflicted with her principles. She would never abandon those for whom she was responsible. She wouldn't cut and run when the going got tough.

Morally, he was turned off by her cold-blooded offer. Marriage was only a means to an end with her, but even if he'd never thought it was in his future, it meant something to him. At the same time, she had qualities he admired in a man but that he'd never sought in a woman. Her fundamental kindness, her strength, her unflinching shouldering of responsibility, and her willingness to do what had to be done were qualities he respected and were a surprising turn-on. He had come to her beach house prepared to make her an equally cold-blooded counteroffer, but now he knew there was no way. This wasn't a woman he could marry and walk away from.

She reached for his hand. "Even though you're turning me down, I appreciate your coming with me. I'm glad I'm not making this drive alone."

Her fingers were chilly, revealing the stress she didn't allow to show on her face. She withdrew them quicker than he wanted her to.

"I didn't say I'm not interested in marrying you," he told her.

She flicked her eyes from the rain-washed street to give him a disbelieving look. "Sounded like it to me. You don't want money or presents or I forget what else. You have your own money—I remember that part. You don't have to try to soften the blow. It's fine."

"I'm not softening anything. I've got another deal I want to talk to you about."

"Fine." She flicked on the turn signal and moved into a right turn lane. "You want to make me a deal. Talk fast. We're only a couple of blocks from New Hanover County Hospital."

"I'm serious."

"Okay. But pardon me if I don't get my hopes up again." Her phone rang and she brought it to her ear. "Hey, Ham, I'm almost there… Yes, I know Lucas *made* you call me… It's okay. I'm turning into the parking lot now… Okay." She closed the phone with a sigh and a bewildered shake of her head. "I guess you heard. I don't know what Lucas thought Ham could do to make me go any faster!" He could see her mentally shifting gears as she spied a parking place and expertly whipped the Lexus into it. She switched off the ignition. "Now, you were saying something?"

"This isn't the right time." She wasn't listening. Not really. Her mind was already on what she would find when she saw her grandfather. She was always two or three steps into the future.

"Maybe this will grab your attention." He slid his hand under her hair. He grasped her nape firmly enough to immobilize her head and captured her mouth with his. He suspected she opened her mouth more in surprise than anything else, but he was too much a SEAL to let an opportunity like that pass. He ran his tongue over the silky inner face of her lips before sealing his mouth to hers.

He had intended to make it quick. As soon as he felt her tongue move in response, he decided to go for *thorough*. She tasted incredible. Her breathing quickened. He damned the console that separated them. He wanted to feel her breasts flatten against his chest. He angled his head for a deeper taste. He wanted to taste her everywhere.

When he slowly let her go, there was something thoroughly satisfying about the startled look in her green eyes and her soft, slightly parted lips. "Just don't go offering your hand in marriage to the first doctor or orderly or hospital security guard you see. Keep in mind that we are still in negotiation. You're not free to make any other deals until you've heard me out."

She blinked the startled look from her eyes. "Ooo-kaay."

He reached for the door handle. "We'll talk about it later. Let's go see how your grandfather is."

The tired-looking doctor, short and dumpy in her white lab coat, was with Lucas when they arrived at the ER. She told JJ they had run an EKG and drawn blood to check for cardiac enzymes but had found nothing alarming.

"Can you tell me what medications he's on?"

JJ produced a card from her wallet. "Here's the list with dosages and schedules. On the other side are contacts for his family doctors and his cardiologist."

The doctor's eyes lit with respect. "This is great. I wish everyone came in with something like this."

"Lucas has a card just like it in his wallet."

"He was a little disoriented when he came in. He probably didn't remember it." She glanced at the chart again. "We'll run some more blood work," she added, "but I really think his symptoms were caused by dehydration."

"Dehydration?"

"It's one of the commonest reasons for admission of elderly patients. Sometimes there's an underlying problem, but sometimes it's just that they don't drink enough water. Older people don't always feel thirst the way younger people do."

JJ wondered if Lucas had faked his symptoms to get her to come to him, but she abandoned that theory when she saw how pale his papery cheeks were. The thin hospital gown revealed only jutting bones and deep hollows where his strong shoulders used to be.

Anger and betrayal, pity for the loss of his power, fear that she would have to face life without him someday, relief that he wasn't going to die today, and love—spine-softening love—all clashed together under her breastbone. She had the disorienting sensation that the floor beneath her feet was sinking.

"Sit down, JJ." Davy's strong arm supported her back.

JJ stiffened her back. "I'm fine."

"Gotta hang tough, huh?" His clear brown eyes twinkled. "Okay. Sit down *please*—as a favor to me."

He was maneuvering and manipulating her, charmingly. He had her number, no doubt about it, and it felt so comforting to be understood that she couldn't object. She allowed him to push her gently onto a rolling stool. He stood beside her, one hand resting on her shoulder, while he questioned the doctor about Lucas's condition.

"If there's someone who can stay with him, he'll be better off at home," the doctor finished. "Then you could take him to his regular doctor in the morning for follow-up."

If there was one thing in the world JJ didn't want to do, it was take Lucas home and care for him. The anger burning in her chest made her long to fling Lucas's words back at him and tell him he was on his own. She calculated how many hours she would have to stay before the home nursing agency they had used for her grandmother would be able to send someone.

"No problem," she heard Davy say, as if from a long distance. "We've got it covered."

Chapter 25

DAVY KNEW JJ WAS RICH. HE HADN'T GIVEN A LOT OF thought to her lifestyle, though, until they had followed the Lexus 460L carrying Mr. Caruthers and Ham to a floodlit house built of yellowish stone. Through a silvery curtain of rain, he had the impression of soaring two-story columns at least six feet in diameter across the front of a central section, flanked on either side by single-story wings. The place was a frigging mansion.

They had gone in through a rear entrance, with JJ leading the way and turning on lights, as he and Ham had helped Mr. Caruthers to the master suite, which contained, beyond the predictable bedroom and bath, an office and a short hallway that led to an indoor pool. In a bathroom larger than his mother's dining room and tiled in travertine marble, he had helped Mr. Caruthers brush his teeth and use the toilet.

The old man's urine was clear and pale yellow, a good sign that he was no longer dehydrated. After David saw that the old man was managing fairly well on his own, with no signs of dizziness or disorientation, he moved to the doorway—close enough to be at hand if he was needed but far enough away so that Mr. Caruthers wouldn't feel hovered over.

When David was growing up, his stepfather, a CPA, had provided a comfortable living. His mother, a nurse practitioner, had worked mainly because she wanted to. As David had told Lon, he had never thought much about money. What he had wanted was to test himself outside the safe boundaries of middle-class normality. And that seemed to have nothing to do with a world in which you got good grades so you could get into a good college which would allow you to get a good job that would provide enough money to send your kids to a good school so they could get good jobs—and so on to infinity.

For the first time, he was looking at the difference between a three-hundred-thousand-dollar house—the absolute most he could hope to sell his mother's house for—and one that would never change hands for less than a couple of million. And that was just the house. He didn't know what you called the simple yet sumptuous style of the king-size four-poster bed and dressers. The greens, yellows, and blues in the rug and upholstery fabrics on the small grouping of sofa and chairs around a marble fireplace gave the room the feel of a magically secluded springtime garden. Even by his inexperienced calculations, it was obvious you couldn't furnish a room like this for double what he made in a year.

When she had said that she didn't want to be married for her money, he'd had no clue how much money was in the equation. He had been salving his conscience with the thought that since he was taking nothing for himself, he was clean.

SEALs were sometimes accused of not respecting authority, and in a way, it was true. SEALs were a meritocracy. Officer or enlisted, nothing—not money, not background, not skin color, not even size (there were SEALs who were 5'2" and SEALs who were 6'7") would make a man a SEAL except his intelligence, ability, and indefatigable spirit. SEALs respected character and competence.

Right now, recovering from traumatic brain injury, his competence might be in doubt, but he still had his character. He had never done anything only to make money. It didn't set well with him that the first time he did, he was starting with marriage.

It was ironic. He couldn't have taken on a wife at this point in his life—not with Riley, Harris, and Eleanor to take care of until they were independent. Marriage would be out of the question for him if his bride didn't have money.

He was more determined than ever not to accept any money for himself.

For himself, he wanted only her. And want her, he did. That much had become clear to him as they drove to the hospital.

He wasn't going sign a few papers, call himself married, and walk away.

Back in the bedroom, David poured Caruthers a glass of water and handed it to him. "Have you been having trouble with peeing too frequently? Is that why you haven't been drinking enough? So you wouldn't have to get up so often at night?"

The old man ignored the question. "Where'd my granddaughter find a male nurse this time of night?" he demanded as he dried his hands on a monogrammed, sea-foam green towel.

"I'm not a nurse. I'm a hospital corpsman."

"Navy medic?"

"Yes, sir."

"My brother was in the Army. He joined because he had flunked out of college, and it was that or be drafted, but I think he took a notion he wanted to be a Green Beret, and that's why he flunked out. Our daddy would have had a fit if he'd known that's what Clive was up to."

As soon as he told older people he was in the Navy, they had to tell him about some family member who had served. Like he had to know they, too, had stood up for their country. It was good the old man wanted to chat. David had some things he wanted to bring up himself. To keep Mr. Caruthers talking while he looked for an opening, David asked, "Did he make it—become a Green Beret?"

"Oh, yeah. He got to go to Vietnam, just like he wanted to. Three tours. They took him to Japan when he was wounded the last time. Couldn't save him. Where did they take you—when you got that?" He waved toward David's face.

"Germany."

"We got on a plane, my brother's fiancée and I. We were there when he died. Did any of your family come to Germany?"

"My mother. Where do you keep your pajamas? I'll get them for you."

"Can't stand the damn things, but since JJ is in the house and will probably come in here to check on me, I reckon I better put on something. Get me a T-shirt from that top dresser drawer. I'll keep on my shorts."

David extracted a shirt from the drawer while Mr. Caruthers sat down to untie his shoes. "While you have your shirt off, I need to listen to your chest. JJ said you have a stethoscope and blood-pressure cuff here."

"I don't know where the damn things are. You'll have to ask JJ. What did you say your name was?"

"David Graziano." He glanced around the room for a likely storage place for medical equipment. "She said they were in here. Mind if I look?" He opened another dresser drawer.

"Graziano. That's Italian. Are you Catholic?"

Nothing but clothes in the dresser. He moved to the armoire. "My father was," he answered Mr. Caruthers.

"He's dead?"

"He died when I was three. My stepfather was Congregational or something. We didn't go much." David shut the doors of the armoire. Nothing there.

"Look in the credenza."

"What's that?" These people didn't just have fancy furniture. They had fancy-*named* furniture.

"That cabinet over against the wall."

David went to the piece of furniture he pointed out—a long, tallish thing with doors, made of swirly-grained wood.

The pressure cuff and stethoscope were behind the first door he opened. *That did it*.

He extracted them and turned to face his patient. "You manipulative old coot. You knew where these were all the time, didn't you? You were looking for an excuse to call JJ in here."

The old man shot him a wily look and snorted. David figured that was a yes. Mr. Caruthers' green eyes, the color of JJ's, were shrewd as he continued questioning David. "The Episcopal church recognizes Catholic baptism. Would you be willing to have your kids raised Episcopal?"

"I never thought about it." David suddenly understood where the idle-seeming inquisition was headed. He leaned against the credenza and folded his arms across his chest. "Why do you ask?"

Chapter 26

"YOU MARRIED?"

"Not yet. Hope to be soon."

"That's too bad. I hoped to fix you up with my granddaughter."

"She told me about your husband list. Your granddaughter is who I hope to marry."

The wily look in Lucas's eyes was supplanted by surprise. "You want to marry my granddaughter?" David could see the wheels turning in the old man's head. "Don't you be put off by that prenup she'll insist on. Tell you what, I'll give you a hundred thousand now, a hundred thousand after the birth of my first great-grandbaby."

Now he understood where JJ got some of her cold-blooded ideas about marriage. "As a matter of curiosity, is two hundred grand all you think it will take to buy me or all you think she's worth?"

"What?"

"What the hell is the matter with you?" David let his voice go dangerous and low. "Offering a bribe to a man you don't know, like JJ is some kind of excess baggage you need to unload."

"No! That's not it."

"It's not? Then how about treating her with some respect."

"Respect? What are you talking about? I love JJ!"

"Then why aren't you willing to let her live life her own way? Why did you threaten to sell Caruthers if she didn't get married?"

A stubborn look dug the wrinkles around Lucas's mouth deeper. "Had to."

"Come on. If I'm going to talk her into marrying me on my terms, I need more to work with than that."

"Year by year, I was watching her disappear into the business—like she was slowly being eaten by it. It wasn't what I wanted for her."

"You never intended her to inherit the business?"

"What the hell is the matter with everybody I try to explain this to? You've got it all wrong. I raised her to know it would come to her—wanted it to stay in the family. But if I'd known what was going to happen, I would have sold it ten years ago. You know what they say about twenty-twenty hindsight? I thought I had years before she would have to take it over. She'd be settled by then, maybe have a nice husband who could help her with it. I never meant for her to have to manage everything before she was out of her twenties. Not what I meant."

The old man suddenly looked frail. The sparse hair on his chest gleamed silver in the lamplight. The skin on his arms, mottled with large brown sunspots, hung in crepey swags. He had the height and bone structure to weigh a good thirty pounds more than he did.

"She's had too much responsibility," Lucas went on. "First her grandmother had cancer. We kept her at home—it's what she wanted. JJ would say, 'Granddaddy, I know you want to stay home with Grammy today. Why don't you?' So I did."

He raised his eyes—the same shade of green as JJ's—as if he was imploring David's understanding. "Every hour with her was precious. I was a fool. I didn't understand what she meant to me until it was almost too late."

His eyes took on a thousand-yard stare—a look David had seen many times on the faces of men who had been through a trial that had forever changed them and could never be put into words. Then Lucas visibly returned to the present. He straightened his shoulders.

"After my wife died, I went to pieces—I admit it. Then I had my heart attack. By the time I recovered and got my head back on straight enough to see that JJ didn't have a life, the economy tanked and the car business took a direct hit. She was working harder than ever and too caught up in keeping Caruthers going to hear me when I told her she needed more out of life, deserved more."

He aimlessly picked up his water glass and moved it to a different spot on the nightstand. "You want to know the worst part? It's my fault. *I'm* the one who taught her that Caruthers was the be-all, end-all of existence—who told her anything that didn't affect the Caruthers bottom line wasn't important. I thought it was great that she wanted to spend all her time there, even when she was a teenager. Beth, her grandmother, tried to tell me I was wrong."

David didn't want to, but he felt a little sympathy for the old man. Even when they know they're wrong, people always have a reason that convinces them that *in this case* what they're doing is the right thing.

He picked up the cuff and stethoscope from where he'd laid them on top of the credenza. "Let's go ahead and check your vitals now."

Chapter 27

"You haven't eaten much. Can I get you something else?"

David surveyed JJ's plate. "You haven't eaten much either. Are you too tired to eat?"

For a moment her gaze was blank, her eyes dull, as if she didn't know what he was talking about. David recognized the exhaustion of unremitting stress, but she didn't admit it. She pushed away from the table. "I'm not as hungry as I thought I was." She picked up a plate of half-eaten lasagna. "I guess I need to put this food away."

Outside, the wind tossed fistfuls of rain against the windows that half encircled the table in what JJ called the breakfast nook. On the table were the remains of the lasagna, salad, and breadsticks she had ordered delivered after she ordered the hospital equipment from the rental agency.

David had wondered how she was going to procure the equipment after closing hours. Simple. She had called the owner at home, told him who she was, told him what was needed, and said, "Pay your driver as much overtime as it takes, and don't worry about whether insurance will cover it."

In fact, the owner himself was driving the delivery truck that pulled into the drive minutes after they arrived.

To the restaurant she had said, "I understand it's outside your delivery radius. There will be a very nice tip for the driver, and if you'd like to add a tip for yourself, that will be fine."

Money was her weapon, her power, and her insulation. Anything she asked for, she got, speedily. The hospital staff had offered coffee, water, a private room in which to wait. They had assured her they were doing everything for her grandfather. But at least ten people—nurses, orderlies, techs, security—people who should have been doing their jobs—had stopped her to ask if she was JJ Caruthers and to tell her how they watched her commercials. Others had grown silent when she approached. Watched her.

She was unfailingly courteous, smiling, and warm as she responded to their intrusion.

Only one person, a brown-skinned woman in peach scrubs, David couldn't make out what her badge said, had squeezed JJ's fingers, offering comfort.

After observing her in the hospital, he could almost see why she preferred to buy a husband so she wouldn't have to care, wouldn't have to wonder what he really wanted.

David gathered the utensils and their glasses and followed her to the sink.

"Thanks," she told him. "I'll take it from here."

He ignored her. While she rinsed the dishes and put them in the dishwasher, he retrieved the aluminum containers the food had come in and covered them with foil. He located the foil and tucked the pans in the refrigerator as if he had worked in this kitchen a hundred times before.

He found a sponge and leaned over her shoulder to wet it under the stream of water from the faucet. His chest grazed her back; his arm brushed hers. His forearm was brown, sprinkled with black springy hair and corded with muscle. The wrist was easily twice as thick as hers. A prominent vein looped over it. She wanted to touch it.

His long, powerful fingers with strong oval nails squeezed the sponge.

He drew back and began wiping the counter, as if nothing had happened except the casual intimacy of two people sharing the sink—something that happened every day. But something had happened. In her life, that sort of casual intimacy *didn't* happen every day.

She shut off the water. "I haven't thanked you," she said.

He paused in his wiping to smile inquiringly at her. The smile was a little crooked, his upper lip pulled unevenly. "For what?"

"Going with me to the hospital. Helping me bring Granddaddy home. I'm glad you were there. I know it's best for him, but I don't think I would have done it. I'm still angry, but I'm grateful that you are so gentle with him. I was falling apart a little."

He rinsed the sponge and set it on the sink rim. He dried his fingers on a dish towel and rested one hand on JJ's shoulder. "JJ, you're allowed to be upset."

"No, I'm not."

"You are. By me." He ran his hand under her hair, gently stroking and massaging the tight muscles in her neck.

"Don't do that if you don't want me to start bawling."

He pulled her into his arms. "I don't want you to cry, but I do want to make it better for you. Something about you makes me want to make it all better." The gentle circles he was rubbing on her back stopped. "Do you ever get déjà vu?"

"Why? Did you just have one?"

"Yeah. It felt like we'd been here before and I'd said that to you."

Want me to kiss it better? That's what he had said. He'd probably used the line too frequently to remember *who* and *when*. "Memory is a funny thing." JJ wiggled out of his arms. She had been *this* close to letting go.

The more she was around him today, the less she saw of that live-for-the-moment, devil-may-care, all-fun-and-games man she'd first met. She had seen at the time how easy it was for him to hook up with a woman he didn't know, and she'd been willing to bet he was probably a good SEAL.

In his own way, he was gentle and considerate. He might be careless but never cruel. She didn't doubt that, without a qualm, he'd tell any lie he needed to, but where he gave his loyalty, he would be dependable no matter what the cost. Those were the qualities she needed. A man like that would be able to see the advantages of the deal she had to offer.

This David seemed so different that it was easy to convince herself he was somebody else. When the time came, it wouldn't be so easy for her to let him go. And she was not immune to either David physically. She had needed the reminder that when it came to women, it was still easy come, easy go for him.

She changed the subject. "Do you think Lucas is all right? Did I do the right thing, bringing him home?"

"I'll check him in a few minutes, but on the whole I think he's better off. His temp has come down and his pulse is more regular. His pulse ox is 98."

"But he was so exhausted by the trip home."

"He was exhausted anyway. In the hospital, he was fighting sleep. He'll rest here." David reached across the table to squeeze her arm. "Stop worrying, JJ."

"Did you mean what you said in the car," JJ asked, "about marriage still being negotiable?" She felt oddly shy. Proposing a straight business deal to a man she hardly knew was one thing. Talking about marriage while they cleaned up a kitchen together was something else. The very homeliness encased them in a kind of intimacy.

"There are things you need to know about me."

"Like what?" JJ closed the dishwasher and turned around to find David wiping the table with a damp sponge. The table had been cleared and the food put away with such quiet efficiency that she'd hardly noticed what he was doing. At the Topsail beach house, his calm assumption that he could go through her kitchen without permission had seemed invasive. Now she saw he was just one of those competent people—the kind who intuitively knew where things were and who saw what needed to be done and did it.

David realized JJ was ready to listen now. He explained to her about his mother's death and about his determination that his siblings finish their schooling, in spite of the financial condition in which the family had been left.

"Stop. Are you saying that on top of being badly injured, your mother just died? Oh, I'm so sorry. You must feel like something or someone is out to get you."

He hadn't expected such instant comprehension from her. He waved her sympathy away. He couldn't let her throw him off track. Whether or not it was rational, whenever he tried to sort out the pieces of his life, he could never shake the feeling that some terrible mix-up had substituted his mother's life for his. He'd seen in JJ's proposal a way to discharge the duty he had to his mother. If he could do that, he would finally, maybe, feel free to feel *alive* again.

"Anyway, I have to ask myself what happens to him if something happens to me?"

"Go on."

"Riley has Asperger's syndrome."

"I know about Asperger's. I'm on the advisory board of an autism group. People with Asperger's have normal intelligence, don't they, but they have some autistic characteristics like trouble relating to people. Is that what he's like?"

"He takes things literally, and he doesn't pick up on social cues. He seriously lacks street smarts. My mother got him into a special school and pretty much drained the estate to keep him there."

"So you want money for his tuition? I don't get it. Why didn't you take my first offer?"

"I told you. I don't want to touch your money. I want you to set up a trust for him—enough to care for him and keep him in school through college."

"That would be a condition?" She thought about it a minute. "All right. I can do that."

"So that there won't be any reason for jealousy, you will also arrange scholarships for Eleanor and Harris. I want to know that, no matter what happens to me, they'll have what they need to get through med school." He paused to give JJ some time to think it over. She nodded slowly. "That's not all. I want you to be Riley's guardian if I'm killed or incapacitated."

"But why? Surely your other brother and sister—"

"Harris will get caught up in some fascinating research and forget Riley exists. Any time Riley hits a rough spot, Eleanor will let her studies slide while she looks after him. One of the reasons I have to provide for Riley is because if I don't, Eleanor will drop out of med school and do it herself."

"But isn't there another member of the family who would be a better choice?"

"I've seen what you are. You're willing to marry a man you don't know in order to take care of your employees. Riley isn't easy to warm up to. But even though you felt angry and betrayed by your grandfather, when he needed you, you were there. You'll do what you have to, and if you give your word, you'll keep it. I trust you."

Of all the outcomes JJ had anticipated when she decided to propose to David, the one she'd never thought of was that she would have to take responsibility for three more people. A lot of the work could be turned over to lawyers. They would figure out how to set up the trust and the scholarships, but she understood that David wanted her personal oversight. He wanted her involved. Another duty. Another strain on a load that was already close to unbearable. This was not the simple contract she'd been aiming for.

"This is getting complicated," she told him. "Let me get my laptop so we can make some notes about what we are agreeing to."

"Okay," David agreed. "And there's one more thing."

JJ paused in the act of opening a shiny, apple-red laptop. "One more thing?"

God, she was beautiful. A tendril of dark hair had escaped its clasp. It framed the perfect curve of her cheek. The dark wings of her brows were lifted in inquiry.

That feeling slammed him in the chest again, stealing his breath and making him feel weightless at the same time. Brilliantly overflowing peace. *Joy*. Spreading over the always-present arousal that throbbed through him, its power certain and available, even when it idled.

She had given him everything he'd come hoping to achieve. He'd known, regardless of how he felt, he was not going to allow this opportunity to create security for his brothers and sister escape him—not when all she wanted was his name on a marriage certificate. He ought to leave well enough alone.

He was sweating, his heart pounding. Everything in him said if the kids were taken care of, that was enough. He didn't want to blow what he'd already secured.

He shouldered past the guilt that told him to shut up. Because it *wasn't* enough.

"One more thing. I want you."

The bottom dropped out of her stomach. "Me? What do you mean?"

"None of this half-married, 'married in name only' bull. For as long as we're married, we're married."

She couldn't think of what to say. Images filled her mind. The sight of his strong, tanned fingers on her breast. His laughter. The casual strength he picked her up with. The feel of his hips clasped in her legs.

"Is it this?" He fingered the scar.

"What?" She jerked her mind back. "No. If you want to know the truth, it makes you more attractive."

"The hell you say. I don't remember some things, but I remember how I looked before. This isn't better."

He met the issue head on, without flinching. He even met it with bravado, but she had already seen his vulnerability around it. His question wasn't about vanity. He had never drawn his self-worth from his beauty. But in a burst of insight, she understood he had used it as a shield, as armor for his heart.

Men's hearts were more delicate than women's, and she suspected his heart was softer than most. While he had his unmarred beauty, he had never had to expose his heart and thus become vulnerable.

Merry. It wasn't a word people used much anymore. Because he'd had so much less to lose than most people, it's what he had been. Merry. Coming at life, coming at her with such gaiety, such promise of fun—did he but know it, it had been the greatest part of his attraction.

In time, he'd probably grow some calluses over his heart. People did. But he didn't have them now. Though she would have run from him, would have put any barrier between herself and the danger of what he was suggesting, she could not use the scar.

"I didn't say 'more handsome.' Before you looked… I don't know… too perfect or something. Like you inhabited a different plane of existence. Now you look… real."

Before, she'd only had to recall her responsibilities to walk away from the devastatingly handsome and charming man he had been. She wouldn't be able to walk away from this man who would marry her if she would look after his little brother.

There must be something else he wanted. Something that would allow them to come to an agreement. She stalled for time.

"Let's talk about it in the morning, shall we?" She turned toward the back stairs. "Let's go upstairs and pick you out a bedroom."

―――

"Pick out a bedroom?" he laughed as they moved up the stairs side by side. "How many are there?"

"Not counting mine, three. One on this side of the staircase, two on the other."

He pointed to the room straight ahead, door open. "What is that room?"

"Mine—it *was* mine."

"Can I see it?" He was already in the doorway.

"Sure, go on in."

"It's huge. It's bigger than my apartment." He had wanted to see this room because he was looking for some trace of her in this house she had lived in over half her life.

This room was so serious. No hint of the little girl or the teenager she had been lingered here. No trace of exuberant enthusiasm, no dreams, no leftover teenaged angst.

He contrasted it with his sister Elle's room where beloved dolls and stuffed toys were still given space on a shelf, the walls rocked with bold energy of posters, and child-sized skis and poles leaned in a corner.

―――

JJ's heart thumped and skipped to see him in her old bedroom. He touched the bedspread and moved a curtain to peer out the dark window.

JJ had accepted Smiley's absence from the rest of the house, but she never entered this room without expecting to see him get up from the floor to greet her. Something must have showed in her face.

"What is it?"

"My dog. He died the day before I moved to the beach house. I always miss him most in this room."

"Did he sleep with you?"

She smiled a touch guiltily. "Most nights. My grand-mother wanted him to sleep in the garage, but I had nightmares without him. Anyway, he slept with me until his arthritis got too bad and he couldn't jump up anymore. Then his bed was right here."

"By yourself in this big, lonely room? It would give any kid nightmares."

"You think this room is lonely?"

A quick flick of his eyes dismissed the room. "I think you're lonely."

"I don't have time to be lonely."

He might have lived at a distance from his own, but he knew what a family was. No family lived in this house. The only emotional security, the only warmth, the only unconditional love JJ had known in this house, had come from a dog. And yet she showed no signs of being emotionally stunted. She wasn't greedy, miserly, or self-absorbed. She was amazing.

He traced the smooth curve of her cheek with one finger. "Time has nothing to do with it."

After a long moment in which he thought about kissing her and decided not to—if he started he wasn't going to stop—he turned to leave. "I'll see you in the morning."

She came out of her daze. "Wait. We didn't pick you out a room."

"Find me a pillow and blanket. I can nap on the sofa in your grandfather's room."

"Oh, yes, of course." She went to a linen closet and came back with the requested items. "I'm not thinking very clearly. I also forgot to discuss how much I'm paying you for staying with him."

Just when he thought they were reaching some kind of understanding, there she went with the money again. "Five hundred thousand," he snapped.

"But that's—"

"The amount you were going to pay me to marry you. I've already told you," he spoke through gritted teeth. "I don't want your money."

JJ blinked. "I was *going* to say, 'That's outrageous.' But I see now I offended you by offering to pay you. That was clumsy of me. Forgive me."

There was just the right amount of contrition in her voice, just the right amount of winsomeness in her smile. She was all contained again. Shit. He wished he hadn't popped off at her. He respected the hell out of her ability to control her emotions, but he didn't want her to suppress her reactions around him. He admired the strength, the self-control, the willingness to shoulder responsibilities far beyond her years. Still, she might as well learn that maintaining a cool, restrained exterior would not keep him at a distance.

Her arms were full of blanket and pillow. Perfect. He leaned forward and found her lips with his. After a shocked moment, hers softened and parted just enough to give him a hint of her taste. He wanted more, much more, but, for now, he had made his point. He forced himself to pull back. "Forget it. No harm done. Get some sleep."

Chapter 28

UNABLE TO SLEEP, UNABLE TO LIE STILL ANY LONGER, JJ threw back the sheet. The rain had ended. Cold patches of moonlight draped her legs. JJ loved the feeling of moonlight on her bare skin. She'd read an article once about the pagan religion Wicca. Most of the beliefs were foreign to her way of thinking, but at some primal level she understood the Wiccan custom of dancing naked at the full of the moon.

It was too cold to go outside, but when they remodeled the house, JJ's grandparents had added an indoor pool with tall Palladian windows down one wall and skylights. The pool area would glow with moonlight, and nothing relaxed her as swimming did.

She swung out of bed and went to the built-in drawers of her closet for a swimsuit. All her tank suits were at the beach house, and she discarded the bikinis she found as too uncomfortable to swim in. She was ready to reject a moonlight swim as unfeasible when it occurred to her to wonder why she needed a suit at all. She put on an old, wine-red hoodie beach cover-up and headed for the stairs.

The pool had been added at the same time as her grandparents' downstairs master suite. It was accessed through a short tiled hallway in their wing. JJ listened carefully as she passed her grandfather's door. There were no signs that anyone was awake.

The latch on the door to the pool area made a heavy clicking sound when she turned the knob. To silence it she quickly depressed it with her finger as she edged around the door. On the other side, she very slowly released the knob. There was still a small click, but she doubted it was enough to wake anyone.

As she had thought, silvery sheets of moonlight made the area more than light enough to see. She unzipped her jersey cover-up and tossed it over a deck chair before slipping into the water.

David woke to sharp, shooting pain on the left side of his face. He fought the upwelling of despair. Two weeks had passed since his latest surgery. He had been free of pain all day and had allowed hope that the pain was finally going away to steal in. He was already on the thin edge of remaining a SEAL, since the repetitive jarring of spine and skull when he ran made the pain worse. If the pain didn't get better, the next thing the docs would want to try would be anticonvulsants. That would finish him.

The pain wasn't bad yet. Dwelling on the grim possibility that he'd be forced to leave the Teams wouldn't help.

JJ wanted him because he was a SEAL. He hadn't told her that was by no means a sure thing. Anyway, if she wanted a husband who stayed gone, he could arrange that. The important thing was that his brothers and sister would be taken care of. In the bathroom, he helped himself to two aspirin and checked his patient. Lucas was sleeping so deeply he didn't rouse as David gently felt for his pulse. It was strong and steady.

A metallic click, like from a door latch, came from the hall. He looked out in time to see a shadowy figure on the other side of the translucent glass door that opened to the indoor pool. No lights came on. JJ or a housebreaker? He needed to make sure. He hastily pulled on jeans and, shirtless and barefoot, let himself into the hall.

Someone was in the pool. As soon as he opened the pool door, he could hear faint splashing sounds.

Moonlight streaming in the tall Palladian windows on the south wall rendered the scene in silver and black.

"Don't turn the lights on." JJ's voice, pitched to bounce as little as possible, came from a patch of shadow.

"Why not?" Realization dawned. "Oh." A grin spread over his face. This was better than he had any right to hope for. Water and darkness were a SEAL's friend, but it was almost too good if she was already naked. "Good idea. I think I'll join you." His hands went to the zipper of the jeans.

"If you'll give me a minute, I'll get out. You can have the pool to yourself."

"Pool's big enough for both of us." He shucked jeans and briefs together.

"Don't dive!" Seeing that her protests didn't stop him, she warned him hastily. "It's too shallow."

He hadn't been going to, but he appreciated the warning. He let himself over the side without making a ripple. He had achieved the first part of his aim. He was in the water before she could organize her resistance. Now he needed to lull her. "How deep is the deep end?"

"Seven feet."

She was in the pool's back corner in a patch of shadow. Lucky for him, he had better night vision than most. The light-colored and hard surfaces all around reflected light almost as well as sound. The dark shape of her head, the glisten of her eyes, was perfectly visible. Keeping close to the wall, he glided slowly toward the deep end.

"No. Stay there. Don't come closer."

"Don't you know you shouldn't be swimming without a…" he let the taunt trail away.

"A what?"

"A… buddy," he supplied, full of innocence. "I'll just be your buddy, here to save you if you get into trouble. Don't worry. I'll stay on this side. You stay over there." What a liar he was. *Oh, he was bad,* he thought without a trace of remorse.

"I think you *are* the trouble."

"Nah. We'll swim laps. Plenty of room for two swimmers side by side." He put a hint of challenge in his voice. "I'll race you."

"We have to be quiet," she objected. "The crawl will make too much noise."

"All right. You choose. Breaststroke or underwater?"

Her head disappeared. His cheek pulled as he allowed himself a smile. She had taken the bait without ever seeing the hook. He took a deep breath and went under himself. Underwater she was visible.

She was halfway down the pool, not desperate for air yet. The water at eighty-two degrees was a silky caress over her breasts, her belly, her buttocks. Especially her buttocks. Eddies titillated her most sensitive tissues. Suddenly she knew *he* was doing it. She couldn't imagine how, but he *was*. If she hesitated and she was wrong, she was going to lose the race to the shallow end—she had no chance without a head start. She felt the lightest, but unmistakable, brush of fingers. Reflexively, she drew her legs up and twisted in the water to find his grinning face no more than a hand's width away.

The concentration it took to suppress the urge to breathe was broken. She gasped water. Her trachea burned. She squeezed her throat against the urge to cough. She had only an instant to surface before the need to cough would overwhelm her conscious control. Almost before she could take in her danger, strong hands grasped her rib cage and shot her to the surface.

While she coughed and sputtered, her eyes streaming, he kept one strong, warm arm around her and guided her to the side.

"Relax." He took her hand and placed it on the rough, dry, unpainted, cement coping. There was a sensitivity to the action, a deep understanding of what would reassure her body, that in that moment changed something. He might try her patience a thousand ways, disturb her, and shake her up, but he knew what it took to make her safe.

"You're okay." The arm around her wasn't needed now, but he kept it there anyway, and she was glad. His skin was warmer than the water. "Relax. Just let yourself breathe." He lifted a hank of hair away from her face, and then another one, until he could look into her eyes. "Okay now?"

He had taken them to a patch of moonlight. His irises were colorlessly dark but even clearer than usual—eyes one could literally look into. His clumped, spiky, absurdly long and thick lashes radiated like a dark sunburst.

There was concern in his eyes and also the avid glint of hunting instinct.

She wiped water out of her eyes. "You *made* me do that!"

His grin was unrepentant, in fact, satisfied. "Not the breathing water part. You did that on your own. See there. I told you, you needed a swim buddy."

~~~

Breasts floated, and wasn't that one of the best ideas God ever had? He wanted to feel them mold against his chest, but it was too soon. Anyway, from this distance he could see them while keeping his eyes on her face.

The conical mounds gleamed white, chased with silver where water streamed across them. He loved breasts, the soft firm feel of them, the way they were cool on their tops and warm underneath. The texture change between skin and areola.

Her areolas were dark—just like he knew they would be. They played dark peekaboo as bright water first lapped over them, then receded with every breath. Breasts clothed in dark water. The déjà vu feeling nudged at the base of his skull again. He didn't have a poetic bone in his body, but he knew he'd had that thought before. Chasing it, he let his eyes drop.

She gave a gasp of disgust and slapped one arm across her chest. Fortunately, it didn't do much good.

"You jerk!"

"You're the one swimming naked."

"Alone!"

"You stayed."

"I could hardly get out."

"Yes, you could. You're not embarrassed to be naked."

"How do you know that?" The challenge surprised him with its sharpness.

He gave her a knowing grin. "Don't deny it." Truth was, he didn't know how he knew, but he did.

"Just because I enjoy swimming naked doesn't mean I'm immodest."

"Hell, no. It means you enjoy your body. You like moving and letting air or water touch every inch of it." She was listening now, eyes wide. He wasn't sure what he had said that had gotten her attention, but he decided to go with it. "It feels good," he put the full import of what he meant by *good* in his voice, "doesn't it? It can feel even better."

Above the quiet lapping of water, he heard her breath hitch. She was responding to his arousal—he knew it better than he knew the feel of his own heartbeat. *Now* was the moment to kiss her. This moment wasn't about dominance or bending her to his will. Now he could invite her to love play.

He cupped her shoulder, relishing the vital, pulsing-with-feminine-power feel of her. He skimmed his hand over her shoulder and up her neck. "I love how good your body feels," he murmured, "and I love knowing it feels just as good to you."

He drew her to him, letting them both savor the extra sensual dimension the water added. The suddenness of added heat, skin clinging to skin. How good it felt to know he wasn't taking or demanding. He was giving his desire to her. When their lips met, it was to further mingle their delight with twining tongues and toying nips.

Her long, strong fingers restlessly kneaded muscles on his back and then dug into his shoulders so that she could take advantage of the buoyancy of the water to stroke herself against him side to side, up and down, and in sinuous belly-dancer moves. With exquisite control, she made sure his erection received full attention. He caught the two globes of her buttocks in his hands, insinuating his fingers between the silken folds, letting her move but staying with her so that a teasing touch from him was added to her every movement.

She made a sound, a tiny gurgle of delight. He wasn't sure she knew she did it, but it filled up his chest and made him feel like the king of everything.

He hadn't come this far to fail to render this goddess her full homage. He wanted to see her, to fill his hands with the bounty of her breasts, to draw the nipples deep into his mouth. Still, he'd rather not drown himself while he did it. He clamped his hands on either side of her rib cage and lifted her out of the water. "Extend your arms along the gutter," he commanded.

"Why? What are you going to do?"

"You know what I'm going to do."

As if her hands had a will of their own, she felt for the slick, curved tiles of the overflow channel with one hand and then the other. Warm water lapped over her arms and made soft slurping, sloshing sounds. The position arched her back and lifted her breasts above the surface. With her body no longer vertical in the water, her legs wanted to float.

Before she could think of what to do with them, he calmly stepped between her legs and pulled them around his waist. She could feel the thickness of his arousal, its heat, against her buttocks. With his thumbs, he opened her so that the swollen center of her excitement was in

full contact with him. Something about the sheer competence of the move penetrated the hypnotic sensual haze
that his voice had sent her into.

"You've done it in a pool before." She pulled her legs
away and stood. If the water didn't cover her, so what?
Once again, she had been *this close* to giving in, just
going with the flow, letting the tide take her—just like
before. What this man could do to her should be illegal.

He didn't deny it. He also didn't move away. "You're
a passionate woman. We would be good together.
What's the objection?"

"The truth?"

"That would be best, yes."

"I know what you're like. You see a pretty girl, decide
you're going to have her, you do, and then you see the
next pretty girl and it's the same moves; rinse, repeat.
A week or so later, you don't remember her any better
than you remember what you had for lunch that day. I
can deal with that—in fact, I prefer it—but not if I'm the
one you can't remember."

She turned her back to him to hoist herself from the
pool—the coping was too high for her to manage the
more graceful lift—even though her position would
give him an eyeful. At this point she didn't care what
he saw.

Out of the water, sticking to the earth as land creatures do, she felt heavy. Her feet made wet slaps on the
concrete. She crossed to the chair where she had draped
the towel brought from her bathroom. She wrapped it
around herself, tucking it securely under one arm.

He lifted himself to the coping as she had but far
more easily. If there was one thing her ballroom-dancing

hobby had taught her, it was that grace was a combination of strength and of always knowing where all parts of your body were. The sight of his shoulders and sculpted back rising from the water, silver water sheeting from him, the shape of his buttocks, the perfect timing as he caught the coping with his foot—his consummate coordination, caught her breath.

His feet on the concrete made almost no sound. Disregarding his nudity and his still more than half-aroused state, he came to stand in front of her. "You think I'm pretty much a lightweight, don't you?"

"Not in every way. I can see you're devoted to your family. I don't think you got to be a SEAL without an unusual degree of dedication and determination, plus willingness to make sacrifices." She tilted her head, testing the fairness of her assessment. "I'm not even sure it's your fault, but women drop into your hands like ripe plums. And you don't turn them down."

"You seem very sure of that."

"Oh, I am."

"Did you know someone like me—like you think I am?"

JJ chuckled cynically. "You could say that."

"What does that mean?"

"Nothing. The experience taught me not to do something I was going to regret. I had the same problems in the morning, but, in addition, I had to recover my self-respect."

David couldn't believe what he was hearing. "So, you're willing to marry me, but you're not willing to have sex with me?" Oh man, did they need to talk. "I'm not going without sex."

"I've already told you I don't expect you to. I'd just rather you didn't do it in Wilmington. But I have no control over that."

"I meant sex with you."

"Think again, stud. Anyone you want, but not me."

"You."

"Why?"

"I don't screw around."

"I find that hard to believe. Are you saying you've ever been faithful in the past?"

He'd usually—once he was out of his teens—limited himself to one girl at a time, but he admitted it never lasted long, and he stuck to his rule largely because it made one less thing to keep up with. Best not to go there. If he could have what he knew *she* had to give, he'd have no need to look elsewhere.

"You don't think much of me, do you?" he countered.

"I told you I admire your dedication. Frankly I'm awed by the sacrifices you have made."

"Dipoma—diplomatic answer. I mean what you think of *me*. The man, not the SEAL."

"I think you're intelligent and you can be trusted to do your duty—to put duty first. I believe those qualities would allow us to be on the same page."

"Well, let me tell you something else about me. As long as I'm married, I intend to be as married as I know how to be. I don't do anything halfway. I will give you the best I have. But I won't do it, I can't even think about doing it, if there's no way you'll give yourself to me."

His sincerity rang through every note in his dark, smooth voice, was written on every line of his stance, could be read in the vulnerable look in his eyes. She might doubt his ability to live up to his words, but he believed what he was saying. That kind of genuineness could create the mother of all con jobs. "Don't tell me you're in love with me!"

To her surprise the uncompromising lines of his face shifted. He looked a little sheepish, adorably boyish. He didn't let his eyes waver, though she thought they looked a little pained. "Well, maybe. Some."

She laughed in disbelief. *"Some?"*

In his life he had never heard one syllable packed with such incredulity and indignation. "How the hell do I know?" He lifted a frustrated hand, reaching for what he didn't know, and let it fall to his side. "All right, that sounded lame, but what do you expect me to say? I'm attracted to you."

The pain, which had been just inside the threshold of awareness, suddenly twanged hotter, harder, longer. Sometimes it escalated; sometimes it didn't. He needed to finish this up and get out of here.

"I don't know about love. I get wanting sex, you know? But sex with someone else isn't going to satisfy. I want you. I know that much. Girl, you say yes, and I'll do you in every one of the eighty-six *Kama Sutra* positions. Twice. But now... I can wait. I'm not going to force you. I'm just telling you where it's going to end up. Take it or leave it."

"You want me?"

"You are the stubbornest woman in the world. What part of *want* don't you get?"

"And you'd be willing to turn down everything else I have to offer, if you don't have that, too?"

"Is *that* what I said?" The words he meant were not always the words that came out. He mentally replayed his words. The pain in his skull flared with acetylene torch intensity with every heartbeat. He couldn't believe he'd found a way to take care of everyone, to be free to return to the Teams as soon as he was better, and he was getting ready to throw it all away. Had he lost his mind as well as scrambled his brain?

And yet whether he had thought it through beforehand or not, he *had* said what he meant. He and Riley might wind up living on his disability and eating a lot of beans, but so be it.

Pain lashed at him. Nausea. He couldn't think. Couldn't explain or argue any longer. He spotted his jeans, a dark heap against the lighter concrete. He scooped them up. "Look, JJ, we've talked enough. Go to bed. Think it over."

Lucas rarely slept long or deeply anymore. He heard the distinctive click of the door to the pool. In a few minutes, he opened his eyes long enough to see the young man, Dave, slip from the room.

Didn't take an Einstein to figure out where he was going.

While Dave had made himself a bed with sheets and blankets on the sofa, Lucas had probed but learned nothing of how the courtship, if that's what you could call it, was progressing.

Lucas had been clumsy with the young man earlier. It was never good to look too eager. He could blame it on the fact that he had been rattled, badly.

In the ER, he'd faced the truth that so far his strategy, every part of it, had backfired, and he really might not live to see this thing all the way though. But when JJ showed up with Dave, Lucas recognized the kind of luck a man doesn't get but two or three times in his life.

He didn't see how his granddaughter could be indifferent to this young Adonis—no, not an Adonis. Adonis made him think of empty perfection.

Lucas wasn't a sensitive man. He'd never understood why people would want to look at art. Sure, he could appreciate beauty or great design, but that wasn't what art aficionados (what kind of a word was that—aficionado?) were talking about. He'd had the liberal education of his day, which damn well wasn't an education in how to be a liberal. He'd only gotten art once when Beth had hauled him through Florence, through hoards of tourists, to view Michelangelo's David.

He looked at it and felt like he had been opened just as easily as you sink a knife into the heart of a ripe watermelon. The humanity-saturated air of the place had hit his soul. Now, the state of his soul he considered to be the Lord's business, and, since there was no need for him to worry over it, he'd just as soon not have to feel it.

This Dave looked like the man Michelangelo's David might have been when he was fully grown—deep chested, shoulders padded thick with muscle, and arms

those of a man, the marks of experience as well as character on his face. Still, you never knew.

He'd almost dozed off again when something made
him open his eyes and he saw Dave walking toward his
bathroom. He turned on the light, and, in the second before the door closed, Lucas saw quite clearly that Dave
was wet, naked, and carrying his jeans.

So. His granddaughter and this young man.

So. The two had been skinny-dipping.

Skinny-dipping was good.

Chapter 29

THE NEXT MORNING, JJ SURVEYED HERSELF IN THE THREE-way dressing-room mirror.

From the cocoa-colored sweater, which had seemed stylish when she bought it but had proved to be a mistake, to black patent sling-back pumps that snagged at the hem of her trousers with every step, she was wearing clothes she didn't like.

Not really intended as a year-round residence, the cottage didn't have a lot of closet space. JJ stored there only those items she needed for each season. The closet in this house had become a repository of clothes she didn't wear. On her list of Sunday chores had to go weeding it out.

She'd had to make do with the lipstick and mascara in her purse. She'd dealt with her hair by twisting it up and securing the twist with a faux tortoise-shell pin-through clasp.

Fortunately, her office at Caruthers had a small bathroom completely stocked with makeup, hair dryers, and curling irons for times when a complete change was required and her schedule too crowded to run to Topsail. As she had so many times before, JJ comforted herself that she would be all right once she got to Caruthers.

She wasn't all right now though. She glanced at the clock and wondered if David would be up yet. Wondered if it would be cowardly to sneak out without talking to him. After a nearly sleepless night, she still didn't know what she was going to say to his counteroffer.

On impulse, she pulled her cell from her purse and dialed Bronwyn.

———

"JJ." Uh-oh. Only Bronwyn was allowed to shorten JJ's name to Jay. When she didn't, it was a bad sign. "Did you, *seriously*, wake up a woman who has *just come off a thirty-six-hour shift* to ask me *that*?" Bronwyn's disgruntled tone was scratchy with sleep.

"Bronwyn, you've got to talk to me. I've already apologized for waking you. You're the only one who knows the entire story."

"I thought you told Mary Cole."

"About Lucas yes, but I can't tell her what happened at *her daughter's* wedding. If it had been someone else's daughter maybe—no. Not even then."

Bronwyn yawned. "I guess I see your point—although technically, the hot sex didn't occur *at* the wedding."

"Close enough. Anyway, you're the only one I can talk to about it. I've gone around and around so many times, I'm dizzy. It feels like the world is turning backwards."

Bronwyn huffed. "You already know what I think you should do: tell your grandfather to take Caruthers and shove it! I know, I *know*," Bronwyn raced on. Her tone dripped long-suffering. "It's just for a year, and you have all those people who trust you, and, at the end of the year, you will have everything you want finally and forever."

"That's right. And now I've found the perfect man to have a non-marriage with, except he insists on sex."

"Let's recap. You were willing to go to bed with Blount the Bland but not the man you know for sure can make you see stars when you come."

"I never said 'see stars.'"

"Don't quibble. You called me; I didn't call you. Bland Blount or Super-SEAL? Which one would it be a hardship to have sex with? Let me see."

"You don't understand. He's unpredictable. He takes over. He does what he pleases without a by-your-leave."

"Aha. The light dawns! He stands up to you, does he? Not impressed by your money or job title. Gets in your face a little?"

"Bronwyn, that's an unfair picture of me. You know I don't walk over people."

"I know you don't *like* to walk over people. There's a difference."

"You make me sound like a terrible person."

"Jay, hon." Bronwyn's voice softened. "Listen to me. Some people are too intimidated to speak up to you. You know it, and you bend over backwards to be considerate. Wouldn't it be nice once in a while not to *have to*—with someone besides me? Like, a man your own age?"

Her and Bronwyn's friendship had endured the years since college because they didn't need kid gloves. Each paid the other the respect of believing her friend could take care of herself.

"Here's the way I see it," Bronwyn went on. "You're hesitating to marry him because he insists upon his conjugal rights. And your problem with *conjugation* is that you know you would enjoy same. So guaranteed enjoyment of sanctioned sex is why you don't want to marry him. We in the medical field have a word for that. Nuts!"

JJ rubbed her forehead. "Somehow it made more sense in the wee hours of the morning," she acknowledged wryly. "I guess all he's really doing with his demand is forcing me to get honest. Agreement or not, he's right. Sooner or later, it would happen, and it would just as likely be me who started it as him."

"Let me go on record as saying I do not think you should let yourself be coerced into a marriage at all, but if you believe you must, then you owe it to yourself to enjoy it."

Chapter 30

SHE COULD HAVE ACCEPTED HIS PROPOSAL (IF YOU COULD call it that) a little more gracefully, JJ admitted to herself as she guided the Lexus into the Caruthers lot.

She had found David in the kitchen cooking breakfast for Lucas. She called him into the dim family room where the blinds hadn't yet been opened, and said, "Take it or leave it? You win. I'll take it."

He had cupped her shoulders with his strong, warm hands and gazed into her face a long time, an odd look of pain tightening the corners of his eyes. "For real?"

She was ashamed of herself. Grudging acceptance was no acceptance at all. Around a strange lump in her throat, she whispered, "For real."

He *had* smiled then—a sort of covered smile that was really more teasing light in his eyes than movement of his face. "A marriage deal should be *sealed*," the corner of his eyebrow twitched, proving the pun was intentional, "with a kiss."

He had taken her mouth with gentle ruthlessness, courting, seducing, tempting, each stroke of his tongue both threat of possession and promise of fulfillment.

Her breath hitched even at the memory.

The man took pride in his work—she'd grant him that.

The phone chat with Bronwyn had convinced her to accede to his demands. They weren't unreasonable, and she didn't find him repulsive. Her pride would take a beating if her heart got involved before he moved on, but that was no reason to jeopardize the well-being of those who depended on her.

Still, she hadn't expected to feel something close to lighthearted once the die was cast. Her body hummed, and she felt hope. Maybe the irrational feeling she always had around him, that everything was going to be all right, had finally melted away all her natural leeriness.

Regardless, going into Caruthers after being thoroughly kissed made for a novel experience.

The false summer that had made time feel suspended in the past few weeks had been washed away by the previous night's rain. The sky this morning was deep robin's egg blue, and the air was impossibly clear. All across the lot, glass and chrome and multiple colors of metal sparkled as if the whole place smiled. Overhead the blue triangle flags snapped with jaunty energy.

The salesman of the month's parking place at the door was empty, which surprised her a little. "Red" Attenborough won the coveted space two months out of three, and he didn't do it by waiting for sales to come to him. To cover the busiest times as well as give them some days off, the salesmen worked a complex rotation. Maybe she misremembered who was supposed to be in early today.

Employees and a few customers called out greetings. She answered with a wave. She stopped at the concierge desk. "Where's Red this morning?"

"He traded with Robert. Robert's son has a soccer game this afternoon."

JJ nodded, her mind already on the next thing. "All right. Get out the sunglasses, Kelly. We're going to need them today."

━━ᨆ━━

That night, back in his tiny garage apartment in Virginia Beach, David methodically filled a suitcase. He'd returned only to replenish his wardrobe. He'd be back in North Carolina in the morning. He was getting married

You said take it or leave it. You win. I'll take it. That's what JJ had said when she came downstairs the morning after the scene in the pool.

He ought to feel more triumphant than he did. *It pays to be a winner.* Wasn't that what instructors yelled at trainee SEALs over and over?

David added more T-shirts to the clothes he was packing. He'd need enough for the ten days until his medical leave ran out and he'd have to return to base. A ten-day marriage. He counted on his fingers, glad no one was there to see him resort to that. Not ten, five. They wouldn't be married until Saturday.

He and JJ had presented their plan to marry to Lucas. To JJ's surprise, but not to his, Lucas had been delighted but had nixed their idea of a quick trip to a justice of the peace.

"Weddings are about bringing together a man and woman to make a new family," Lucas had said. "Dave, don't you want your brothers and sister to be with you? They'll have time off from their schools over Thanksgiving, won't they? Plenty of room. You should invite them here."

So what had been a thirty-minute deal they could have taken care of that very day, since North Carolina had no waiting period, was now going to take three days by the time they had Thanksgiving dinner, an engagement party Friday night, and the wedding on Saturday. David doubted if there was a chance in hell he'd get near JJ in all that time.

David went to his closet. He would need his sport coat. He only had one, an all-purpose navy that hadn't been worn in a year or more. Thinking it ought to go to the cleaners, he quickly checked the pockets. And pulled out a woman's thong.

With a car logo in the crucial spot. *Whoa*. Talk about hot.

The name of the car tickled at the back of his mind, but he couldn't retrieve it.

How the heck had that gotten in his pocket? It must represent a good time, and yet something about it made him uncomfortable. He tossed it on the bed and returned to his packing.

He stopped counting out sock pairs when he uncovered the shoe box he'd shoved into the drawer after he'd gotten back from his mother's funeral. It contained personal items removed from his mother's house since it was going to be sold.

Not much in it, nothing he needed, so he'd forgotten it. Now he opened it. There was the watch his stepfather had given him, some old coins, some of his stepfather's arrowhead collection. And in a tiny, square, velvet-covered box, a ring.

He took out the ring, replaced the lid of the shoe box, and returned it to his sock drawer. His gaze fell on the thong. Who knew where it had come from? He reopened the box and tossed it in.

"Pass the ketchup," Lucas told Ham. They were eating French fries at Hardee's. Hardee's had a twofer coupon for seniors.

Ham shoved the little cup closer to Lucas's hand. "You're making a mistake." Ham gave Lucas a squinty-eyed look.

"The French fries need ketchup."

"That's not what the hell I'm talking about. You're ridin' high 'cause you think you're winning. You let JJ go through with this, you're gonna lose. Big time."

"I'm not doing it to win."

"Why then?"

"JJ has got to change while she still can. Young people think old people resist change because they're set in their ways. Fossils frozen in rocks who can't see that the world has moved on. That's not it."

"Then what is it?"

"Energy. Change requires energy. The time comes when it takes more energy than you can muster. Young people? Young people don't even know that they have energy. They think that's just the way it is. I look at JJ. Her train is ready to leave the station, and she's not on it. I gotta do this."

"Hey, JJ, how was lunch?" Kelly called from the concierge desk.

JJ pulled down her sunglasses to give Kelly a dry look. "The Rotary Club sends their regards."

"Did you manage to leave behind any sunglasses?"

"In the ladies' room."

Kelly reached under the counter. "I have two things for you. First..." She passed JJ a sheaf of papers.

"They finally located the model Mrs. Babcock was looking for. And second…" She handed over a paperback book with a magnificent masculine torso on the cover. "The girls in accounting finished *Star-Spangled Heart*. Do you want to read it next, or should I send it to the detail shop?"

JJ sighed. She allowed herself a moment of longing. Reading romances was something she shared with most of her female employees, though there was rarely time anymore. "Is it good?"

"Not as good as *Twilight's Last Gleaming*. But still good."

JJ passed the colorfully jacketed book back. "Better send it to them. I don't know when I'll get a chance to read it."

In her office, JJ stowed her purse in a desk drawer, checked her makeup in the bathroom, and phoned Lauren Babcock.

"Good news, Lauren. We've located the make and model you're looking for, and it's actually at a dealership in Virginia Beach. You can pick it up tomorrow."

They chatted for a minute about logistics before JJ said, "There's another reason I called. I'm getting married the Saturday after Thanksgiving."

Lauren was satisfyingly intrigued. "You are? Who? How? Did you get back together with what's his name?"

"Not him." JJ was enjoying drawing the moment out. She'd had to listen to people's surprise over and over as she made her bombshell announcement. It was fun to be telling someone who would see the wacky humor of the situation.

"Well then, who?"

"To a SEAL, actually. We're having a very small home wedding—family and a few friends. I know it's short notice, but I'd like for you to come."

The long, stunned pause on the other end was everything she wished for. The laughter, when it came, was even more. "You're getting married. To a SEAL. When I told you you needed to marry a SEAL... shoot! I thought my advice was like the old country granny's recipe for rabbit stew. 'Well,' said the granny, 'first, you catch a rabbit.'

"I should have known if I told you to get a SEAL, you'd... just... do it! I can see you walking into some commander's office and saying, 'I'd like to choose a SEAL. Send me in a selection please.'"

When Lauren had sobered, JJ asked her, "So will you come for Thanksgiving?"

"I appreciate your wanting me. As it happens, I'm spending Thanksgiving with my grandson. I've been invited to join Jax and Pickett and Tyler for Thanksgiving."

"Does this mean Jax has forgiven you?"

"That would be too much to hope for. It will be a long time before I earn his trust." Lauren sighed philosophically. "God hasn't given me any of those things I wailed and stamped my feet and demanded He give me after Danielle died, but the more I practice my serenity, the more I see He has given me much better."

There was a long pause. JJ was getting ready to wind up the call when, in an oddly shy and serious tone, Lauren went on. "JJ, you haven't told me why you're bent on avoiding a fairy-tale marriage—and I'm not asking. One of our AA slogans is 'Mind your own business.'

"Goodness knows, I'm the last person in this world to pass out relationship advice, but listen. Don't go by my experience or Danielle's. There is such a thing as love that survives marriage. Some marriages are easy; some are hard. Marriages to SEALs can be very hard. But you can't judge them by that. The issue is not how hard they are, but whether they are worth it. Don't turn down love."

Chapter 31

"HARRIS AND I WANT TO TALK TO YOU." DAVID'S SISTER, Eleanor, spoke from the doorway of the bedroom David had been assigned in Lucas's house. Her round blue eyes were grim, the soft line of her lips spoiled by tight grooves at the corners.

Behind her stood her twin, Harris. Both were already dressed for the wedding. Elle's simple blue dress brought out her blue eyes and fair skin. Everything about Elle was round. Round face, round cheeks, and a pleasing roundness to her figure. David saw a resemblance to their mother he'd never noticed before.

Harris wore a brown tweed sport coat, a little baggy at the elbows. Being fraternal, the twins looked no more alike than any brother and sister. Neither looked at all like dark-haired, olive-skinned David, a circumstance that had made people ask more than once if one of them was adopted.

David stopped tying his own tie to wave them in.

"We don't believe you're in love," Elle stated flatly once they were inside. "We think you're only doing this for us."

David caught Harris's eye. "You've seen JJ," he grinned man to man. "Does it look like I'm sacrificing myself?"

"Deal with *me*," Elle snapped. "Stop making jokes and skipping away. I don't understand what's going on here."

"What's to understand? Men and women get married all the time."

"Yeah, well *you* don't. You've never acted serious about anybody. Mom was afraid you would never settle down. She thought it was her fault."

"Her fault? No. It was because I was too much like my da—" David caught himself before the wrong word slipped out. "My father, Carl," he amended. David was the child of his mother's first marriage. Try as he would, he'd never been able to be like the gentle, thoughtful man who was David's stepfather and the only "dad" he'd ever known.

Elle gave him one of those *I am female, and so I understand things forever beyond your ken* looks. "She thought it was because she sent you to military school," she explained, carefully spacing her words. "She was afraid you felt squeezed out of the family when Riley came along, and so you turned your back on us. And that's why you never brought any girls home for us to meet. You showed no signs of wanting a family of your own."

Squeezed out was exactly how he had felt, but you'd think enough years had passed for his eyes not to get hot and wet when that time was mentioned. He'd been a wild kid, skipping school, into mischief, with too few outlets for his energy. When Riley with his special needs was born, his mother had been overwhelmed by a baby who screamed if you put him down, screamed if you picked him up, screamed if you changed his diapers or dressed him, and often screamed for no reason at all.

The strain on the family had to be relieved somewhere. The twins, Eleanor and Harris, were too young to leave home. They still needed their mother. David was a problem, and so he had to go. He, at least, was old enough to take care of himself. He'd long since accepted responsibility for being sent away.

"Nah. Mom and Dad did the right thing. Who knows what kind of a juvenile delinquent I would have turned into?" He pressed the bridge of his nose.

"Headache?"

"Trigeminal neuralgia. Maybe. It's atypical."

"Bad?"

"It's okay. It makes my eyes water."

"Can I get you anything for the pain?" Elle asked.

"I took some aspirin."

"Then can we please get back to the subject? You're marrying her for her money, and there's only one reason you would do that. We can't let you—" Elle stabbed her chest with a forefinger. "*I* won't let you—sacrifice yourself for us."

The backs of his eyes burned again. When had she turned from a little girl into a lovely woman capable of fiercely protecting her own? David suspected Harris would be happy not to look too closely at whatever fate was keeping him in med school.

David and JJ had a story prepared about meeting a year ago, falling in love but not being ready to commit— not until his brush with death had shown them both his mortality. They'd been given a second chance and this time were determined to take it.

He didn't want to lie to Elle—she deserved better than that.

"Mom was wrong to think I turned my back on family life. I was just…" he struggled for a word that would encompass what it meant to be a SEAL—the joyful absorption that dimmed everything else in comparison. He couldn't think of one. He shrugged. "Just... busy, you know? Even though I haven't been around much, I care about you guys. I'll never be half the man Dad was, but I did learn one important thing from him. A man looks after his family."

Elle's eyes narrowed. "I was right. You *are* marrying a woman for her money—for us."

"For me. I'm already sleeping better. No matter what happens to me, Riley is secure. He will be cared for the rest of his life, and you and Harris will finish your educations."

"But you don't love her!"

"She's beautiful, smart, and kind—better than I deserve. I'm happy with my choice."

"Then what's the matter with her that she's got to buy herself a husband?" Harris asked.

"Nothing." He gave Harris a warning look. "And you'd better not ever imply anything is."

"I'm not. I'm just saying... why aren't guys throwing themselves at her feet?"

"Because I'm damn lucky, that's why."

"Hmm." Elle tilted her head. "You *want* to marry her."

"I told you I did."

Elle nodded slowly, a little smile playing around her mouth. "So you did." She hugged him and patted his cheek.

The gesture made something go all mushy all around his heart. Starting when she was a baby, Elle had always liked to pat cheeks, and she'd never outgrown it. All of a sudden he remembered how he'd sprawl on the sofa watching TV. Elle would be playing on the floor with

Harris and, for no reason David could see, would leave
Harris and scramble onto the sofa beside him, crawl into
his lap, and pat his face. When she had his attention,
she'd say, "Lub you, Dabid." She wouldn't leave him
alone until he said "lub you" back.

He tightened his arms and kissed the top of her head.
"Lub you, Elle."

She smiled a little mistily. "Lub Harris, too?"

He grabbed Harris's shoulder and shook it affection-
ately. Unlike Elle, Harris had never seemed to like hugs.
"Love Harris, too. Now you two get out of here and let
me finish dressing."

"I wouldn't worry. The maid of honor still isn't here."

David smothered his impatience. He was ready to
have the ceremony done with, but every time he turned
around, this wedding business got more complicated.
Lucas had been right about one thing though. He'd insisted on waiting until the Thanksgiving break so that
David's brothers and sister could come. And David was
glad. "Okay, tell everyone I'll be down in a minute."

Great-aunt Althea snagged JJ's hand and peered up at her
through dirty bifocals. Althea was Lucas's sister, older
by almost ten years. In her cracked, old-lady voice she
snorted, "You aren't acting much like a bride, Jane Jessup.
Aren't you afraid of bad luck if the groom sees your dress
before the ceremony? Or has he already seen too much of
you, making your wedding night an anticlimax?"

Aunt Althea cackled at her poor-taste pun. She was
just trying to stir something up. It was what she did.
Anytime she thought things were getting a little dull,

she'd see if she couldn't make someone uncomfortable enough to start a scene. And God knows, this wedding was dull.

Trying to look on the bright side, JJ had hoped the delay while they waited for the maid of honor to arrive would give the sprinkling of guests assembled in the formal living room of her grandfather's house a chance to mingle and grow more comfortable with each other. It hadn't worked that way. They stood around in tight little knots, even though she had broken with tradition and come downstairs in her borrowed wedding dress to play the role of hostess.

As JJ sank down on the brocade sofa beside the old lady, she wracked her brain for a topic that would keep her entertained. She didn't want to talk about herself. That was the crux of the problem.

JJ didn't like to lie. Even in sticky situations, rather than manipulating, she preferred to tell the truth and live with the consequences. She had found being absolutely up front about her reasons and requirements to be a more efficient way of having events turn out the way she wanted.

She been forced over and over to lie as people inevitably asked when she and David had met, why they were marrying so suddenly, why not a large wedding. But until she had her hands firmly on the business, until she was the legal head, not just the de facto one, no one could know.

If the banks lost confidence in Caruthers' leadership, the effects would be disastrous in today's economy. If they thought Caruthers might close its doors and sell out, they would start calling in loans, which could precipitate a chain of events that would make it a sort of self-fulfilling prophecy.

She just wanted the wedding over with, which was the reason for a gathering limited to family and closest friends.

"Oh, stop being rude just to get a rise out of me, you old bat. That's none of your business."

Aunt Althea laughed gustily. Far from being offended when someone called her on her outrageousness, she appeared to enjoy it.

"These days, pregnancy doesn't seem to make young people hurry up a marriage," she allowed. Unfortunately, since she spoke at the top of her lungs, everyone had heard her. There was a moment of silence while everyone assembled pointedly didn't look at her.

The last time JJ had seen David, he had been on the other side of the room talking to his friend and fellow SEAL, Garth, and yet he seemed to appear at JJ's side. He perched on the arm of the sofa. With casual possessiveness, he dropped a kiss on the top of her head. "Are you giving my bride a hard time?" he challenged the old lady in his warm, soothing voice.

"I'm just saying—getting married in such an all-fired hurry—willing to show herself in her wedding dress before the wedding, she doesn't care very much how the marriage turns out."

"Dress?" He looked confused. "What's wrong with it?"

He looked so adorably, helplessly masculine, JJ couldn't help smiling up at him and patting him on the thigh. "She means letting you see the dress is supposed to be bad luck."

He gave her an intimate smile and trapped her hand. "What kind of bad luck?"

"It might jinx the marriage."

"Gotta see it sooner or later. Hard to see how it makes much difference when." He lifted her hand to his lips. "Fate brought us together. One dress won't take us apart."

JJ heard her best friend, Bronwyn, at the front door and hurriedly excused herself from Aunt Althea. The scalloped-lace, trailing skirt of the late-sixties wedding gown belled behind JJ on the oriental carpet of the broad entry.

"Oh, Bronwyn, you're here!" she exclaimed folding her friend, damp trench coat and all, in her arms.

"Am I in time? The plane was late taking off in Baltimore, and Ham here kept having to detour around flooded streets."

JJ extended her hand to Ham, who was standing in the doorway behind Bronwyn. "Thank you for going to the airport to pick her up. I knew if anyone could get her here," she told the ex-Marine, "it would be you. I wish you would change your mind and stay for the wedding."

Ham looked down. "I cain't do that. Ain't dressed. Wouldn't be right." He slapped his grimy ball cap against his legs. "Well, you have your maid of honor now, so I guess you're ready to get married. I'll shove off." His gray eyes, set in a permanent fisherman's squint, softened. "You look beautiful, JJ. You be happy now."

A gust of damp air blew in the door as he let himself out.

Bronwyn stared at the closing door in consternation. "Are you sure this isn't a hurricane?"

"It's just a tropical depression, and, really, there's not much wind. Was the turbulence bad?" Bronwyn, for all her cool-headedness under stress in the ER, was a white-knuckle flyer. "I'm sorry you had to fly in this weather."

"Don't be silly. I would have come no matter what." Her chestnut brown eyes misted as she looked at her friend. "Oh, Jay, you do look beautiful. This dress is exquisite. Where did it come from? I thought you were going to wear a suit."

"My friend, Mary Cole Sessoms, convinced me I couldn't let the wedding look like I was ashamed. This is the wedding dress she wore in 1967."

"I'm glad." Bronwyn touched white lace set into the dress's sheer georgette sleeve with reverent fingers. "But this pantsuit," she indicated her gray slacks and jacket, the pants darker from the knees down where her raincoat's protection from the downpour had ended, "is the fanciest thing I own."

Mary Cole, elegant in a street-length dress in one of the silvery fabrics she wore so well, came up in time to hear Bronwyn's protest. "You must be Bronwyn. Don't worry about a thing. My daughters raided their closets and sent dresses they thought would work, but really now that I see your dark red hair, I think the emerald-green silk will be perfect. Come upstairs with me now, and we'll get you changed. Give us twenty minutes," she told JJ over her shoulder.

JJ watched as her friend was borne away up the curving staircase garlanded with white satin ribbon and caught up at intervals with nosegays of burgundy and tealight roses and white baby's breath—the work of an army of florists who had arrived at 6 a.m. A jeweler had arrived last night with a selection of rings. It was amazing what a few phone calls and enough money could accomplish.

Her eye was caught by an unaccustomed sparkle on her finger. David had surprised her last night with his mother's diamond ring—a gesture more sensitive and sentimental than she would have thought him likely to make.

"I don't know if you'd like to wear this. It was my mother's engagement ring from her first marriage—to my father. She said the stone is small but good quality."

"Oh…!" She'd done her best to hang on to the notion that the marriage was a contract. She'd congratulated herself that she'd found a man who, if he was marrying her for her money, at least wasn't doing so out of greed and who expected no more from the marriage than she did. JJ fought her thudding heart and thickening throat. "Uh—no—I—you shouldn't—I can't take this."

He turned her hand palm up and placed the shabby but obviously treasured little box in it. "She always said it was for my bride. You're my bride."

JJ detected a flicker of pain in the clear depths of his eyes. "Please don't get the wrong idea. I didn't mean to reject the ring. It's only that, well, don't you want to wait?"

"For what?"

"Wait until it's real. What if you find the perfect woman? Someone you want to be with forever. You don't want to give her a ring that's used."

"What if this is as real as it gets?" he countered. "What if you're the only wife I'll ever have? I have knocked on the doors of heaven. They are closer than anyone thinks. When my number's up, I have to know

I did all I could. That I gave everything I had. I have a ring. For my bride."

"I feel like I'm stealing something—something precious. I ought to call this off now. If I had any other option, I would."

"If you don't want it, you don't have to wear it. It doesn't look like much compared to rings you have."

"It isn't that. But shouldn't it go to your sister or your brothers?"

"This is mine. It's the ring my father gave to my mother. When Mom remarried, she put it away for me. It's just about the only thing I have to give you."

"It's beautiful. I'll treasure it. And if you ever want it back—"

His face went grim. "Don't say it."

"All right, but…" JJ made a mental note to call her lawyer Monday and have him add a codicil to her will, leaving the ring to David's sister in the event of JJ's death.

"Don't say 'but' either. If you don't count Mrs. Gutierrez, my kindergarten teacher; my aunt Katherine; and Serena Brancuzzi in the fourth grade, I've never proposed before."

"You asked that many before you were—what, nine?"

"I didn't exactly understand that you're supposed to ask—at least not my kindergarten teacher and Aunt Katherine."

"How about Serena?"

"Her, I asked."

She was being charmed and maneuvered. It was impossible not to know it but equally impossible not to smile. "What happened?"

"She slugged me. I took that as a 'no.'"

"Oh, I don't know about that. It might have meant she really liked you."

"Doesn't matter. She taught me not to go for girls who could hit harder than I could. It was about then that I began to see that girls had more going for them than a solid right hook. But I learned not to take a girl by surprise with a thing like marriage. Would you mind if I propose now?"

"Propose? Marriage?"

"It sort of goes with the ring—if you know what I mean." He carefully extracted the ring, a diamond solitaire in a simple Tiffany setting, and holding it out, went down on one knee. "I've always wanted to do this. I'm not going to miss my chance. Will you marry me?"

"Yes, I will."

If she'd had a choice, JJ didn't believe she would have said no.

"Someone put flowers on the stairs," David's brother Riley jerked JJ from her reverie of rings and SEALs and the first real marriage proposal she'd ever received.

"Were you speaking to me?" she asked the teen. It wasn't always easy to tell since Riley rarely made eye contact.

"Yes, I was," speaking in his oddly precise way, Riley answered. "No one can hear me when I do not speak aloud."

Though there was a shapeliness about his stripling build that spoke of working out, his clothes seemed to fit him oddly. His gray slacks sat too high at his waist. His white dress shirt, buttoned at wrist and throat, was too large in the neck. His military-short hair was the same light brown as the twins'. She had been standing in the middle of the entry, lost in thought. She had neither seen nor heard him come into the soaring two-story space.

"Okay. What about the flowers?"

"Flowers do not go on balustrades. They were not there yesterday," he added as if that clinched his argument.

JJ *had* been staring into space, in the direction of the broad, curving flight of steps. Maybe he had interpreted her bemusement as disapproval. People with Asperger's had difficulty reading body language and often mistook others' intentions. "They're meant to be pretty," she corrected gently. "The florist came this morning and put them there."

"Why?"

"They're decorations for the wedding."

He looked up and down at her dress as if he'd just taken in its significance. "Are you the bride?"

"Didn't anyone tell you your brother and I are getting married this afternoon?"

"Yes." Riley shambled away in his uncoordinated gait.

JJ shook her head at the strangeness of the encounter. His brothers and sister said Riley had a genius IQ, but he seemed to her to lack even common sense, as well as being what most people would take as rude. As the baby, according to them, he'd been spoiled by their mother and allowed to get his way with tantrums. Recognizing he did better in a more structured environment and thinking he needed a man's discipline, his mother had enrolled him in Dempsey Hall, a quasi-military school in North Carolina's Piedmont Region. The twins would return him there in the morning on their way back to Charlottesville, Virginia.

This was the teenager she'd agreed to be the guardian of if anything happened to David. Well, thank God there was a school that seemed to know what to do with him. She was fairly sure she didn't.

—◆◆◆—

"David, take Jane Jessup's right hand and repeat after me, 'I, David Christopher, take you Jane Jessup…'"

David's warm, hard fingers closed around her icy ones and tugged JJ back to reality. Her heart skipped a beat as she realized she had no idea where they were in the service. Was it time for her to say something?

"I, David Christopher, take you, Jane Jessup, to be my lawful wedded wife…" she heard David say. She was okay then. In her moment of inattention she hadn't flubbed anything. She forced herself to focus and found herself wondering how the shade of brown of his eyes would be described. Liquid chocolate, maybe. The trouble was that no color described how warm and sparkly they were. Was there such a thing as a merry shade of brown?

His eyes had drawn her from the beginning. In a face so perfect it almost looked artificial, his eyes had laughed at the huge joke of it all and sparkled in carefree anticipation of the next adventure.

"To have and to hold from this day forward…"

"For richer or for poorer…"

"To love and to cherish…"

The joking twinkle disappeared. My God, he looked serious. Why hadn't she remembered she would have to promise to love and cherish him?

JJ made as many empty promises and told as many social lies as the next person, but her word meant something to her. She had always been proud that her customers knew her personal integrity stood behind Caruthers, and her dedication to the stewardship of family business had always been the central pillar of her integrity. To save the business, to marry David, she had to say words she didn't mean. The monstrous wrongness filled her throat.

Until this moment, Caruthers had never required more than she was willing to give. She should have found another way to save the dealership. She should stop this farce right now. She was no child to cross her fingers behind her back.

She had been so focused on what the business would gain that she had given no thought to what she would lose. The pounding of her heart shook her entire body. For the first time in her life, JJ thought she might collapse.

"This is my solemn vow," David finished. His left hand came up to cover her hand where he held it, as if he sought to warm her icy fingers before he let them go.

"Jane Jessup, take David's right hand and repeat after me…"

The fingers with which she took David's hand were shaking so badly, she closed her left hand over their joined hands lest she drop them. Through lips that felt frozen she spoke her vows.

Chapter 32

DAVID LET HIMSELF INTO JJ'S BEDROOM AND INHALED the subtly flowery, spicy smell he associated with her. He'd like to take the time to go through her things, but she probably wouldn't appreciate it. He went quickly to her huge walk-in closet, where clothes hung organized by season and category. She would need a coat. As predicted, the storm which had kept the coastal city a muggy sixty degrees was being chased by a cold front. He selected a ruby red, down-filled parka as the most likely to be comfortable and warm.

What else would she need? Most of the clothes she wore frequently were already at the house on Topsail. Her purse! Never separate a woman from her purse. He went to the bank of built-in drawers surrounding the three-way mirror. Aware of an illicit thrill, he opened one that was too shallow to hold purses. Oh man! Thongs. He wished he had time to look at them one by one. In the back of the drawer, a silken pouch, embroidered with "It's all about the ride," teased him to open the snap and explore its contents. Aware time was slipping away, reluctantly he replaced the pouch exactly as he had found it.

He opened a deep drawer near the bottom as more likely to contain what he was looking for and was rewarded with more sizes, shapes, and colors of handbags than he had ever known existed. How was he to know which one she would need? He didn't. He'd seen her wallet and keys on a dresser in her bedroom. He'd just tuck them into the deep pockets of the parka. He was at the closet door when, on impulse, he turned back and went to the little drawer. It glided open as slickly and silently as before. He palmed the little silken pouch.

Back in the living room, David watched his bride circulate among the wedding guests. His bride. God, she was beautiful.

A flare of elemental possessiveness heated his chest. In all the strange, out-of-sync confusion of the past months since his injury, this one thing he knew he'd done right. Peace, he'd always thought, was a lack of anything happening—something that had never seemed worth seeking. But he thought this feeling of rightness, this lack of shadow, might be a kind of peace.

He wasn't there yet though. Ceremony notwithstanding, he wasn't sure she understood that she was his wife. She hadn't given herself to him, not *herself*. He knew he would never be satisfied and completely at peace until she did.

He'd made a start last night by giving her a ring. He thought he'd gotten to her with that. He'd seen how she lifted her hand from time to time and the soft expression of bemusement that came into her eyes as she looked at it. It was time for the next step.

———

"What do you mean we're leaving?" JJ protested when he'd lured her away from the crowd in the living room. Behind them, two of the caterer's staff worked quietly. "We can't leave."

He grinned. She said it the way you explain which way the earth turns, like it was an irrefutable fact. He admired her strength, her competence, her ability to take charge. He did. But he had areas of competence of his own, and she was about to meet up with them.

He slid an arm around her waist and moved her toward the door to the garage. "I'm kidnapping you."

She stopped to search his face. "You're kidding."

He tilted his head. "You want me to get out the duct tape?"

"But I need to change out of this wedding dress. It's not mine."

He put her in motion again. "Change when we get to the cottage."

"It's not right to just go off and leave Lucas with all of those people to entertain—three of whom are your siblings, and we're just abandoning them!"

"He needs a challenge." In fact, when David had told him what he was going to do, Lucas had all but rubbed his hands in glee and offered him the keys to the Rover.

"And there's the clean-up."

David grinned inwardly. She was reaching if she pulled out that one. He gave her a warning look. "I have two words for you. Duct. Tape. Here's your coat."

"My purse."

"Wallet and keys are in the left pocket. Anything else?"

"I, at least, need to take leave of my guests."

He hoped she didn't think that prim tone would put him in his place. "You just got married, JJ. They will guess where you're off to." She was skittish, not used to going with the flow. Once they had made love, she'd be all right. It was just a matter of getting over the first hill. After that, they would have all the momentum they needed. "Now, do I have to carry you, or are you going to come quietly?"

Chapter 33

ON THE COTTAGE STAIRS, THE WIND WHIPPED HER SKIRTS, tangling them in her legs. More fearful that she would step on the precious dress and tear it than that she would stumble, JJ gathered the material over one arm, exposing her legs to the sharp wind.

"Brrr. It's cold!" She glanced up. "But my goodness, look at the stars! The sky is so clear. A clear atmosphere is the best thing about winter. I love to look at them."

"Yeah, it's a good thing about being a SEAL. We operate—do what we do—undercover at night. Except in the jungle, where the tree canopy is so dense there's no sky at all, the stars are always there. Aboard ship in the middle of the ocean, they're really good."

JJ shivered. "Too bad we can't stay out here to look at them."

David dropped his duffle bag and unlocked the cottage's beautiful, paneled redwood door. When JJ would have gone ahead of him, he stopped her. "Wait. There's one more tradition. I have to carry you over the threshold."

He reached inside to turn on a wall switch and scooped her in his arms.

A couple of times during the day, she had doubted if she knew what she was getting into with David. Blount at least had been predictable. He would never, never have carried her over the threshold. The sheer romance of the gesture caught her unawares and scrambled her breathing circuits. As a result, she was a little shy, a little breathless when he put her down.

With her still in his arms, he closed the door by backing up against it until the latch clicked. "Welcome home, Mrs. Graziano," he said in his creamy chocolate voice. He set her on her feet but kept his hands at her waist.

She couldn't meet his eye. She was unsettled. Off balance. Fragile. Tenuous-feeling.

Funny she should feel so shy when she already knew this man's body. But that one night had been all heat and madness and impulse—a delirium. She could claim afterwards she didn't intend it. This... *this* was real.

He tilted her face up. She steeled herself not to give in too much to his kiss.

David felt her resistance. The darling. He understood her well enough by now to know she wasn't unwilling; she was unsure. He liked her a little off balance. It was only fair. He felt a little off balance himself. He had remembered the bit about the threshold in the nick of time. His heart was pounding, and it wasn't from carrying her. He hadn't expected the lump in his throat when he called her Mrs. Graziano. She was his. His wife.

He wanted her. Hot and urgent. Mingled together until they were one flesh. Not yet though. Under his hands, he felt the tiniest tremor. He brushed his lips across hers. Once. Twice. He released her.

"Why don't you change out of that wedding dress? Put on something warmer." She looked a little hesitant. "Go."

While she was in the bedroom, he had time to reconnoiter. He opened the sliders to the deck. Was he living right or what? The wind tonight was out of the northwest. As he had guessed, the south-facing deck was protected. Although it was chilly, probably around fifty degrees, wrapped up, they would be okay.

The next problem was some place to lie down. The deck's planking was thoroughly wet from the storm, as was the redwood lounge chair. Damp, he and JJ would lose body heat quickly, and *losing* heat was not part of his plan.

Loungers like that didn't come cheap, and he'd bet they didn't come without cushions. Which would have been stored for the winter. A smile spread across his face. Wherever it was, the cushion was nice and dry.

He lowered the back of the chair from its upright position. Shortly he had everything ready.

"What were you doing out on the deck?" JJ asked when he opened the sliders after arranging everything. She had changed into loose, stretchy pants in a deep-teal velour with a matching long-sleeved, zippered top. She was barefoot. Perfect. She probably had chosen it believing it wasn't sexy. Little did she know there was nothing she could put on that would keep him from thinking about sex around her.

He wasn't going to be able to see her tonight, which was a damn shame, but tonight wasn't for him. "Stay right there," he said. "Don't move." He went to her bedroom and pulled the king-size comforter from the bed. He returned to the living room and bundled it around her.

"I'm not cold. What are you doing?"

"Keep it around you." He opened the slider, then picked her up.

"The deck? What's going on?"

"I'm giving you the stars."

———

"Warm enough?"

"Toasty." The lounger was a tight fit for two abreast. He had turned out all the house lights before kicking off his shoes, lifting an edge of the comforter, and crawling in beside her. His body heat quickly erased the chill. They were lying pressed so close together she could feel the vibration in his chest when he spoke.

In an oddly innocent gesture, he had entwined his fingers with hers and lifted both their hands and carried them to his thigh. She wiggled a little to allow more of her arm to rest on him.

Little pats of wind occasionally tumbled past the shelter of the house, but only enough to make them conscious of the snugness of their haven. Up and down the beach, a mile in each direction, the houses were dark, closed for the winter. Starshine was their only companion. On the beach, long, slow breakers crashed and made the funny hissing noise as the spume of their crests was blown backwards.

She had lived at the cottage for a year and had never once thought to lie on the deck at night to watch the sky. But really she could hardly remember the last time she let herself stop and do anything for the simple pleasure of doing it.

"I haven't looked at the stars like this since I was a little kid."

"Didn't you ever camp out?"

"In a tent."

"Not the same. You ought to see the stars in Afghanistan. In the mountains, the air is so dry and clear. They don't twinkle. Even the faintest constellations jump out at you." He turned his head on the pillow they shared. His breath was warm on the side of her face. "Which is your favorite constellation?"

"I don't know them, except for the Big Dipper. The Little Dipper. That's all. I never studied the stars. I just like to look at them."

"The Big Dipper and Little Dipper are both in the north, behind the house. I'm afraid we can't see them."

JJ chuckled. "*That's* why I'm never able to find them when I'm out here on the deck."

"But we do have a perfect view of the Milky Way." It sounded like he was attempting to console her with an exchange.

Some hitherto unexperienced combination of wonder and affection bloomed in her chest. In spite of his masterful, take-charge—not to say occasionally overbearing—behavior, he wanted her approval of his "gift" of stars. Feeling oddly tender and protective, JJ squeezed the hard warm fingers entwined with hers.

"What, exactly, *is* the Milky Way?" she asked, wanting to extend the moment. "I've heard about it all my life, but I don't even know what I should look for."

"See that long smear of light directly overhead? Looks like a thin high cloud? That's it. As for what it is—it's actually one of the spiral arms of our own galaxy. And there's Cassiopeia."

"Where?"

He slid his arm under her neck to bring his face next to hers, then pointed to the sky. "Put your hand on top of mine. Follow your finger. See the five stars on the Milky Way that look like a W?"

"Yes."

"That's Cassiopeia." He moved his arm. "And there's Andromeda. And Pisces." He moved his arm further to the left. "And there's Aquarius."

"Where's Orion? I've heard of it."

"It's visible in winter. We ought to be able to see it. Look there. Over the ocean. See the three bright stars? They form Orion's belt."

"That's what people always say. But I don't see a belt. And I certainly don't see a man."

"I admit the Greeks had a lot of imagination."

"Well, do you see a man?"

"No, not really. Orion is just coming over the horizon. We're not able to see all of it."

"Maybe you should show me something easier to see. Where's the North Star? Everybody always says you can navigate by it, but I don't know how. I've never known how to find it."

"Polaris? We can't see it." He brought their hands down. He placed a kiss in her palm before he tucked her arm back under the comforter. When he had re-tucked the comforter under her chin, leaving no gaps to leak cold air, he rested his arm over hers at her waist. With his thumb, he idly stroked a slow pattern on the underside of her breast. "We'd have to face north to see Polaris," he told her, a touch apologetically. "It's in the Little Dipper."

She turned her face to his. So close her nose brushed his cheek. His hand left her waist and moved higher. He gathered the fullness of her breast, which had slipped to the side, and cupped it, testing its weight. "Oh." She tried very hard not to think about what he was doing. "You mean if you face north, you see the North Star?

And if the North Star is directly ahead of you, you're facing north."

"Uh, yeah." She saw the corner of his mouth curve upward. "You didn't know that?"

"Oh, go ahead and laugh at me. Not that I think understanding the connection will help. I don't have any sense of direction at all. None. GPS is the greatest thing ever invented."

He rolled his head toward her. She could see the glisten of his eyes, his teeth. She wondered if she imagined the tenderness of his smile.

"I'm not laughing." His fingers kneaded the softness they had found. Every now and then grazing to the nipple, never quite landing exactly where she wanted them.

Warm puffs of air, smelling attractively of him, batted her face, as if he'd found a way to caress her with every syllable. She was a little breathless when she asked, "Did you learn the constellations so you would know how to navigate?"

"SEALs learn several methods of navigation, but, to tell you the truth, I'd rather depend on GPS, too."

She wiggled, trying to bring her breast into the contact she desired. "Never have to ask for directions again, huh?"

"I need to ask for directions right now." He hesitated. "I need to know if you've looked at the stars enough."

His hand on her breast stilled. She wanted more of his touch. But she hated to let go of this moment, this sense of communion. "If I say no?"

"Then we'll look at them longer. As long as you want to."

"Will you keep doing that?"

He gently squeezed her breast. "This? As long as you like."

She wondered if he meant it, if he would let her have what she wanted, or if he was setting her up. Sometimes he was so sweet; sometimes he was aggressive. She had a hard time knowing which to expect.

"Don't be on your guard around me, JJ," he whispered. "You want me to play with your breasts while you look at the stars? I could play with your breasts for hours." He found the zipper tab and opened her top. He pushed aside the material and covered her flesh with his warm, hard hand. His strong fingers began again their slow kneading. With the new intensity, skin to skin, excitement twisted through her deep inside, then in a ripple that took her whole body.

"Trust me to have your back. This is about pleasure. You're a passionate woman who likes to look at the stars for the sheer pleasure of doing so. I want you free to let yourself go."

Her mind slipped back to that night, exactly a year ago. They had already made love once. Had been lying in each other's arms like they were now. She had turned her head, burrowing against him.

She opened her mouth over his shoulder, enticed by the thought of tasting him, feeling his skin with her tongue.

"A biter, are you?"

She pulled back. "I don't know. I just wanted to put my mouth on you." The interpretation he would put on her words didn't occur to her until she saw the hope that widened his eyes. "I can't. I'm sorry."

"Hey, it's okay. I don't want you to do anything you don't want to."

"I—" she finished with a helpless shrug. She *did* want her mouth on him—exactly *there*. She wanted to taste him and feel him against her lips. "It isn't that I don't want to. I truly mean I *can't*." The couple of times she'd tried had been embarrassing and a complete turn-off for herself and her partner.

"Don't worry about it. It's okay."

"But can I touch it? Just touch it? With my mouth?"

"Exactly as much as you want to."

She leaned over with one arm across him to brace herself.

"Wait," he said. "Let's sit you where your neck and throat can stay as relaxed as possible. Kneel on the floor. I'll come to you."

"You won't push my head down, will you?"

"You'll be in complete control. All the time."

He hadn't known who she was or what she was. She had been a temporary woman whom he would forget. He'd been audacious, pushing the limits over and over—and in that way he certainly hadn't changed—and yet he'd somehow made a safe space to let herself go.

She believed him. He wanted her to be free. Free to look at stars. Free to trust her sensual side. "Can we stay out here?"

He raised up on his elbow. "Tell you what. You look at the stars. I'm going to do a little undercover work."

He ducked down and pulled the comforter over his head. He continued his lazy stroking of her breasts, one and then the other.

She felt his lips, the faint scraping of his chin. For long moments he licked at their hardened peaks, tantalizing the very tip. When at last he took it into his mouth, she groaned.

He lifted his head. "Good, huh?"

A waft of chilled air hit the wet skin. Her nipple contracted with a tight ache she felt in her bones. She gasped.

The heat of his mouth when it closed over her again took her breath away. He suckled. Hard.

Every muscle in her body tightened. Her back arched off the lounger.

"Very good, huh?" she heard him murmur. Felt his breath against her skin. Could have sworn she felt him smile.

He gave the other breast the same merciless loving attention until she was panting steamy puffs into the cold night air. And writhing. And making hungry little sounds that surprised her.

She pushed down their covering. "Getting hot."

She urged him up until their mouths met. She ran her fingers under the soft cotton of his T-shirt, seeking the warm, solid feel of him. The long muscles of his back. The deep groove of his spine.

It wasn't quite enough. She snagged fistfuls of his shirt and dragged upwards, but she succeeded only in tangling her hands.

She grunted in frustration. "Off!"

He chuckled at her imperious tone. He withdrew his lips long enough to whip the shirt over his head one-handed.

He came back down, and it was exactly what she wanted. Exactly the muted drag of hot skin on her skin, his vital heat, the knowledge of bone and sinew and coiled strength feeding some hunger that existed deep in the deepest part of her soul.

She pushed at his chest, intent on rolling him over so she could gain control of the kiss.

He went, and caught himself just in time to keep from tumbling off the narrow lounger.

"Wrestling isn't on the list of approved uses for this lounger, I'm afraid. Let's do it this way." He lifted her up out of the way while sliding under her. "How's this?"

They fitted exactly. She centered the notch of her thighs over the hard bulge of his erection. Bracing her hands on his shoulders, she dragged her breasts through his sprinkling of chest hair, relishing the light rasp against their sensitive tips. When she lowered herself, he obligingly opened his mouth for her exploration.

Long, leisurely mating of mouths, lips lingering, tongues tangling. Sighs sifting breaths between the drawn-out hiss of breakers.

———

"My turn." He rolled them onto their sides, again in a casual display of strength lifting them both so that they lay in the center of the lounger. He had the most remarkable awareness of where his body was, and more amazingly, where her body was. Fleetingly, she wondered what it would be like to dance with him but instantly forgot it as his hand insinuated itself under the elastic waist of her pants, stroking her belly and then lower.

Stopped. Tentatively cruised lower.

On a whim she couldn't explain, JJ had left work early on Tuesday to get a Brazilian wax. She wasn't used to the strange feel of it herself. His one questing finger traced the seam of the outer lips.

They said when all the pubic hair was removed, the area became even more sensitive. They were right. She shuddered violently.

"Jesus, Mary, and Joseph."

Chapter 34

"JESUS, MARY, AND JOSEPH." AND HE MEANT THAT WITH full reverence. Again, he drifted his fingers over the petal-smooth feminine essence he had found. He had seen her in the shadowy swimming pool and remembered seeing the dark strip at the juncture of her thighs, as if an extra portion of night covered her secrets. "What... when?"

"Tuesday."

"Are you going to get upset if I ask you why?"

"An impulse. I just wanted something to make me different."

He knew about women wanting to change their appearance to give themselves confidence, especially when they felt a little low or unattractive. That wasn't what he heard in her voice though. "Different, how?"

She pulled away. Not on the outside—on the outside, they touched everywhere—still, he felt her shrink inside herself. "Does it bother you?" she asked. "It will grow back."

The last thing he wanted to do was make her self-conscious. He brushed his lips across her velvety cheeks, kissed the tip of her nose. "Surprised, that's all." His diaphragm shook in a silent, self-amused chuckle. "I thought I knew what you looked like." His fingers found the moisture at her heated center and spread it over the silken inner folds. "I was planning this for later, but you know what this means I'm going to have to do, don't you?"

Know what he had to do? "Uh-uh."

He pulled the comforter up to her chin. "Stay right there." He rolled off the lounger, catching himself on his hands.

In seconds she felt him untuck her feet. "Scoot down." He placed his hands on her hips to guide her. "Perfect."

"Lift up." Grasping the elastic, he eased the stretchy pants over her hips and down her legs.

"You'll get cold."

His smile was a glisten of eyes and teeth as he peered over her raised knees. "Trust me. I won't."

He gently pushed her knees apart. The comforter became an obscuring tent, one he disappeared into.

Unseen hands of a magic, invisible lover drifted over her calves, traced delicate patterns on her inner thighs, trailed unreal, dreamlike strokes across the epicenter of her desire.

Above her, the heavens sparkled with cold glory.

And then his mouth was there with hot, insistent pressure, tracing every hill and valley, seeking the pathway of every nerve. Scalding, soothing, stirring currents of pleasure that surged and sank in waves as timeless and inevitable as the sea.

Time stopped. Forget her clock with the spacious minutes she loved. She had found the unmarked time that lay between those minutes. She was oddly disembodied. No, that wasn't the right word. *Dis-worlded*, if there was such a thing. Drifting in unfathomable mystery, she had no point of familiarity to cling to. She was utterly lost. She felt found.

He entered her with a finger. Withdrew. Two fingers. She heard a sound like deep pleasure.

The ocean shushed and crashed. Slow rising tide of sensation, slow layer upon layer, held in thrall by hot, silken swirl, and then her climax was upon her, lifting her, crashing through her with shudders and shocks. One wave subsided only to build into the crest of another.

He stayed with her until he had drawn the last quiver, the last of the tiny internal shocks.

She opened her eyes and saw stars.

―∾∾―

She opened her arms to him when he slipped back under the comforter.

He was hard enough to drive nails. The thought of losing himself in her tight heat was a red throb, but *she opened her arms to him*. He had never before thought of the meaning of welcome with open arms. It humbled him and enriched him at the same time. Much as he wanted her roused and ready, he couldn't take her from the satisfaction of her afterglow.

He drew her softness close. As close as she drew him. She nestled her head into the crook of his neck, languorously drawing her fingernails back and forth across his chest. After a while, he realized the scraping across his nipples wasn't accidental.

She rose over him and added kisses. The skin of his cheeks was cool, a shivery contrast to the humid warmth under the comforter. With her lips, she dabbed dots of heat over his face, which changed to dots of cool as soon as she moved on and the moisture of her breath evaporated. She kissed his eyes, his nose, his forehead and moved on to the other cheek.

He waited to see if she would avoid the scar. He would be all right if she did; he honestly didn't know which he preferred. She answered the unasked question by moving her lips across it and then tracing it lightly with her tongue. The sudden warming was like she had touched it with a branding iron. Branched lightning of pain seared through his skull.

Against his will, he stiffened. His gasp was only partially stifled. He sat up, fighting nausea.

"What's the matter?" She sat up beside him and reached out. "What happened?" Lest she touch his face, he batted her hand away. She dropped it. "What's going on?"

Slowly the pain receded, leaving a cold, hollow tracing behind. The sensation wasn't pain, but in its own way, it was almost as unpleasant. "It's all right."

"It isn't. You're not. It happened when I touched the scar. I'm so sorry, but you should have told me."

"Not your fault. I didn't think. Cold, heat, shaving, sometimes nothing at all sets it off."

She thought about the delicious contrast between his chilled skin and his hot-feeling mouth. She had been kissing his cheek, wanting in her heart to kiss it better.

"Can't the doctors do anything?"

"The doctors hoped this last surgery would fix it—the scar had healed crooked. They hoped that a nerve had become entrapped and, by doing a scar revision, they could free it."

"I take it that's not working."

"It's still healing. There might be inflammation that needs to subside. It's going to get better."

He said that, but his eyes were dark, wounded-looking.

"We shouldn't be out here. Crammed in here, I could accidentally touch it at any time."

"I'm telling you, JJ… it's all right."

She pushed the comforter aside and stood. The deck boards were cold, wet, and gritty beneath her bare feet. Her pants were too clammy to put back on. Even the comforter was already heavy from the ever-present moisture in the ocean air. She had seen masterfulness and strategy when he had bundled her up and swept her off her feet. Now she saw detailed attention to her comfort and prioritizing her desires over everything. She gathered up the comforter. "Save your breath. I'm taking us in."

———

"Okay." He opened the slider for her. "We go in on one condition."

"What's that?"

"We keep the lights on."

He had a thousand fantasies, and the last hour had just added a thousand more. The most recent ones required light.

She lifted the bundle in her arms. "I need to put these things in the dryer."

His impulse was to take them from her and throw them on the floor. Slow, he reminded himself. She resisted being overwhelmed. He started toward the kitchen area.

A light came on automatically when the door to the closet where the washer and dryer were stacked was opened. JJ quickly grabbed a towel and wrapped it around her sarong style.

As she bundled the comforter and her clothes into the dryer, he leaned against the wall, enjoying the sight of her, anticipating all he wanted to do. It reminded of something he needed to ask. "Are you protected?"

"Against what?"

"I mean, are you on the pill?"

"Yes, but…"

"I know. There's still the issue of disease. Trust me, in the last few months, every inch of my body has had the once-over. I don't have anything. And there hasn't been anyone in… I don't know… anyway, not since Afghanistan."

"But would you remember?" Her disbelief was obvious.

"Yes!"

JJ crossed her arms under her breasts. "Remember every one, do you?"

"For God's sake. I'm not lying. I'm not that shallow, either. I may have forgotten a couple of girls' names over the years, but I remember being with them. In fact the day I got this, the little girl I told you about with eyes like yours? She reminded me of—" There was that feeling again. That certainty that he knew something—if he could just put the pieces together.

"What?"

Of you. No, that was backwards. JJ made him think of the little girl, not the other way around. But the little girl had reminded him of someone, he thought. Someone he associated with a feeling of loss… regret… failure. "The worst mistake I ever made—"

"Which was?"

He didn't know. He could remember being in a hotel… with Do-Lord… but where? There had been so damn many hotels in so many countries. Suddenly he could see Jax and Pickett in front of a hotel, loading a car with baggage. When would he have seen that? Their wedding? JJ said the wedding was where they met, but, as usual, the images felt jumbled, out of order.

They resisted all his efforts to sort them. He was probably making something out of nothing. The truth was, he constantly had feelings of déjà vu around JJ, as if something about her reminded him of someone, as if his unconscious were tapping him on the shoulder. But he couldn't ask her if there had been more to their meeting than she had told him. It would prove everything she thought about him.

"The time you failed to use protection?" JJ prompted, smiling with false helpfulness.

"No, it was—" He stopped himself. He read the disbelief in JJ's eyes. There was no way to defend himself against her suspicion. If there was one thing that wasn't smart, it was talking about old girlfriends. "Never mind. Forget it. I'm happy to use protection. I always have been. It's easier to get in the mood when you're not worried about some pathogen hitching a ride."

Chapter 35

JJ ROLLED OVER AND SQUINTED AT THE RED NUMBERS ON the digital clock. She was by nature an early riser, but this morning she could have happily stayed in bed another couple of hours.

Throughout the night, David had been endlessly inventive, playful, and tender by turns. Unhampered by any touch of fastidiousness, he had an earthy enjoyment of everything about her body and his.

Her problem this morning wasn't that she didn't wish to stay with him. It was that she wanted to stay too much. Resolutely, she pushed back the covers and sat up. It was a good thing she planned to go to work today. She needed to be reminded of what was important. Of what her life was really supposed to be about.

"Where do you think you're going?"

A hard hand closed over her upper arm. With breathtaking efficiency, she was tugged backwards, and in a second he had her draped on top of him.

He smiled sleepily. Through the sheet, she could feel his morning erection.

His hands closed over her naked buttocks and kneaded.

She moaned.

"Sore?"

"Mmm."

"Muscles or other?"

"Muscles *and* other."

"Wuss." But the rhythm of his hands changed to long, slow pressure that moved deep into the over-taxed muscles of her thighs and hips.

"Lie back down on your stomach. I could do this better if you lie on your front and let me work on you properly."

JJ stifled a moan when his talented fingers found a particularly tender place. "I can't. I have to get ready for work."

"Work?"

"It's what I do, remember?"

"But..."

"I mean it." She squirmed away from his too-skillful hands. "Let me up."

"But you just got married. They can't be expecting you to come in today."

"Would the Navy think you automatically got time off, just because you got married?"

"No. But I don't own the Navy. Caruthers is yours. You make the rules."

"I don't own it yet. Not for a year. And the fact that I make the rules means I have to be there when I am supposed to be."

"Are you afraid something will happen to it if you're not there?"

No, I'm afraid of what will happen to me.

JJ knew the exact day she had become aware that having a future and Caruthers were the same—and if she wanted to have one, she had to cling to the other. It was the day the *Daddy Carbucks* had been found adrift, her parents missing. Before then, what would happen to her tomorrow or the next day or next week had been some- thing her parents, in their own haphazard way, were in charge of. That day, she had realized that she had to look to the future for herself.

Even had her parents not died suddenly, mysteriously, she would still have eventually come to the same conclusion. They had not been good parents.

Around David, it was much too easy to go with her feelings and to forget that Caruthers was her safe haven, her sure anchor. She had drifted last night in the timeless time—and there was no future in it. Literally.

"Shit. You're not planning on any honeymoon."

"Well, no, it's not like we need to— what do they call it?—bond. You'll be gone at the end of the week. And I'll still have a business to run."

He swung out of bed. "Whatever you're thinking, you're wrong."

"You don't have to get up."

He gave a glimpse of world-class glutes on the way out the door. "I'll shower in the other bathroom."

David wandered the car lot looking at Jags, BMWs, Lexuses—lots of Lexuses—and waving salesmen away. He hadn't imagined Caruthers was this big. The glass-and-chrome showroom with its two-story front of curved glass was sophisticated, functional, classical, and modern all at once. It looked like JJ. Pride in her almost edged out the irritation that had made him decide to come see Caruthers himself, since she hadn't offered to show it to him.

This was her, the center point of her life, and it apparently had never occurred to her that he would be interested, want to see it, want to meet the people who worked for her.

He had had thirty-seven hours of her. That was not enough. He had to leave early Friday morning to make the appointment with his surgeon. That gave him four days and... he gave up trying to count how many hours.

Among the glittering, late-model, high-end foreign cars ranked row on row under the flapping blue triangular flags, the ancient Chevy pickup couldn't have looked more out of place. It was faded to an unlikely shade of pink and dabbed in so many places with gray primer that it looked piebald. No one could mistake its driver for a customer, but heedless of "No Parking" signs, he had stopped directly in front of the door.

The pickup's driver—white male, fifty, medium height and build, one-forty, gray hair in ponytail—exited the truck and walked around to the passenger door.

He bent over, and when he rose, he had a large yellow dog in his arms. He carefully set the dog down on the pavement where it swayed on wobbly legs. Black sutures bristled along the dog's spine where a wide swath of fur had been shaved.

A salesman, his name badge flashing in the sun, came running up. "You can't park here," he told the dog's owner. "And dogs can't come on the lot without a leash."

The dog took a painful step and then another, almost losing his balance.

"I brung 'im to JJ," the man explained. "This here's where she works, ain't it? Snake can stand, but he cain't walk more'n a few steps yet."

David surged forward, his hand out. "Maybe I can help. I'm JJ's husband." David saw the salesman's eyes go wide. "You brought this dog for JJ, you say?"

"His name's Snake. I want JJ to have him."

"Well, I'm sure she'll be honored. Let's take him to her. He looks like we'd better get him inside before he falls down."

"Might have to carry 'im."

"No problem." David offered Snake his hand to smell, then squatted beside him. "Hey, old Snake. Looks like you've had some surgery. Will you let me pick you up?"

Snake offered no objection. When David carefully lifted the dog, one arm under his chest, one arm supporting his rump, the listless animal grunted softly. The line of sutures looked clean, but he was clearly in a lot of pain.

"What's the matter with him?"

"Had to have an operation for things, kinda like deep dimples, on his spine—I forget what the vet called it—that got infected. Made 'im real sick. Vet said if he didn't take 'em out, they'd just keep on getting infected."

"Fistulas?"

"No. I don't think that was the word. Said dogs with Rhodesian ridgeback blood get them. I always thought Snake was more Lab, myself."

A young woman rushed over as soon as they were through the door.

"You can't bring… that in here."

Arms full of dog, David smiled at her. "Where's JJ?"

"She's in a sales meeting."

"I hate to disturb her, but as you can see, Snake here isn't in any condition to wait."

"Who *are* you?"

"JJ's husband." Oh, yeah. Every time he said it, it sounded better. "Which way to the meeting?"

"Um, I'll call her."

Somebody apparently beat her to it. A door opened, and JJ emerged from a room where a group sat around a large table.

"David? Grady? Is that Snake? What is going on?"

―――∞―――

"What am I thinking?" JJ grabbed her head. "Turn the car around. We can't take a dog to the cottage."

"No?"

Exactly how she had come to have a dog, JJ didn't know, except that she had taken events as they came—and here she was. The dog-rescue organization's leader had almost tripped on her tongue trying to apologize for not taking a dog at the request of one of their largest supporters.

"The thing is," she'd told JJ over the phone, "I'm over capacity now. One of our people is out of town on a family emergency. Everyone is having to carry her load in addition to their own."

And so now a new dog bed, bowls, lead and collar, dry and canned dog food were all piled in the backseat. In her purse were the pain meds David had demanded from the vet, as well as an in-depth explanation of Snake's condition. She had everything she needed for a dog except a place for him to live.

"My rental agreement with Lauren specifies no pets."

"Does she ever have to know?"

"I'll know. She only rented me the cottage because she knows me. I can't betray her trust. Okay. Let me call her."

After a few rings, the voice mail picked up. "Lauren, I was wondering if you would be willing to change our rental agreement," JJ told the recorder, "to allow me to have a dog. I'll be happy to pay you a deposit against damages. Or if you'd rather, I'll just agree right now to replace all the carpet when I leave, whether it's damaged or not." She added a callback number and hung up. "Well, that's the best I can do."

David took his eyes from the road to shoot her a speculative glance. "How much do you estimate carpet would run?"

"It's not a big place. Based on what I spent on carpet for Granddaddy's suite, it probably wouldn't be more than ten thousand dollars."

"Not more than ten thousand." David's tone was colorless.

"What? You think that's too little? Too much?"

He just shook his head, a disbelieving twist to his lips. After a pause, he went back to the subject. "How about your grandfather's house? If your grandfather doesn't want Snake inside the house, we can keep him out in the garage. It's heated."

JJ rolled her eyes. She had already seen her grandfather more in the last couple of weeks than in the year before. She had hoped she wouldn't need to be around him for another year. She didn't trust him and the last thing she wanted was to be beholden to him. But she called him. When her grandfather answered, she explained the problem.

She didn't even finish before he interrupted. "Y'all can look after him here. No problem. This big old house has plenty of room for a dog. Come on. I'll tell Esperanza to make up your bed and put fresh towels out."

JJ thanked her grandfather and pressed the end button. "'Step into my parlor,' said the spider to the fly.

He's been trying to lure me back for a year. He practically chortled with glee." She turned to glare at the dog, who was stretched on his side in the cargo area. "See what you just made me do, you Snake you? What kind of a name is Snake, anyway?" she grumbled.

Hearing his name, Snake opened his yellow-brown eyes. He flicked one ear forward. He rolled his eyes a little anxiously from JJ to David as if to say, *I didn't mean to do it*.

"So we're going to your grandfather's house?"

"Looks like it." Before she could tell him to, David unerringly made a right on College Boulevard.

"How did you know which way to turn? Have you driven to Lucas's house from this direction?"

He gave her his innocent look. "It's all a matter of knowing where the North Star is."

They were almost to Lucas's house when JJ thought of something that had been bothering her. "Why were you at Caruthers today?"

"I wanted to see you."

"To see me—about what?"

"I just wanted to see you and to see where you worked."

"Why?"

"What kind of question is that? Because I wanted to."

"So why did you come in with Grady and Snake?"

"You hadn't invited me to come by. I couldn't go barging in and say, 'Here I am,' and expect you to drop everything, could I?" He gave her a look of wide-eyed innocence. "*That* would be rude!"

"Do you ever play fair?"

"I play to win. If I'd strolled in and said, 'I've come to take you to lunch,' you would have said you were in a meeting or something. The same kind of reason you gave when you disappeared out the cottage door this morning."

"So you grabbed the dog out of his hands and marched in. You took shameless advantage of that situation, didn't you?"

"I figured as long as I kept hold of the dog, you would have to deal with me. You couldn't be 'too busy.'"

David put down food and water next to where Snake lay on his new dog bed in a corner of Lucas's kitchen. Snake turned his nose toward the food, and, with a sigh, turned it away. He was in too much pain to eat. David knew how that felt. "Where did you put the morphine for this poor animal whose name isn't Snake?" he asked JJ.

"In the refrigerator. On the door, second shelf down. I put the syringes in there, too. They're in a plastic bag in the crisper drawer."

Between the mustard and the steak sauce, David located the square-shouldered, brown glass container of morphine mixed in a flavored liquid. They'd had to go to a special compounding pharmacy to get it.

David carefully read the directions on the morphine bottle. *Give 1.0 ml by mouth every two to four hours as needed for pain.* Numbers slid around on him. Did it say point one milliliter or one milliliter? He looked at the little lines on the syringe. Cc's were the same as milliliters, right? Shouldn't that be cm? He knew this! Why wouldn't it come to him?

There was no rush. He took a deep breath and centered himself. All he had to do was think it though. A milliliter was one thousandth of a liter, and that would be point zero, zero, zero, zero one, so that would—No, it would be point zero, zero, zero one, which would mean he should fill the syringe to the first long line.

Frustration tightened his shoulders. He knew this! He rubbed his neck and widened his eyes to push back tears. He couldn't chance making a mistake. If he didn't give enough, the dog would be in pain—pain he couldn't tell anyone about. If he gave too much, he could kill the poor bastard.

He hated to feel stupid. *And* to see the looks of incomprehension on people's faces turn to irritation or pity or cunning when they realized he didn't know something a competent person should know. But he couldn't risk this creature's life to save his feelings, and JJ would have to find out sooner or later that she had married a man who might not be a SEAL much longer.

"JJ," he called, "do you know the metric system?"

"Sure." She paused in unloading the Chinese takeout they'd stopped to pick up on the way. It appeared he'd married a woman who didn't cook.

"Then I need you to come here and fill this syringe."

"What's the matter?" JJ crossed the kitchen to Snake's bed and knelt beside him.

"It's numbers. I can read them, but if I need to transfer them from one application to another, I get confused. I make mistakes."

Reflexively, JJ took the morphine bottle, but didn't look at it. "Wait a minute. That doesn't make sense.

How could you be a hospital corpsman if you can't read directions and then measure medication?"

He couldn't. That was the fear that hung over him all the time.

She sat back on her heels, comprehension darkening her green eyes. "You have a head injury. Of course you do—I mean I knew you had injuries to your head—"

"Brain injury."

"But you don't seem like other brain-injured people I've known."

He couldn't talk about it. Not with his inability to help even a dog right in front of him. "Measure the dog's morphine."

JJ read the bottle, then looked at the syringe. "Well, I see part of the problem. The directions say ml, but the syringe says cc."

She retrieved her phone from her purse. "Bronwyn, quick medical question. I've got to give medication to a dog... Yes, Snake... No, we haven't renamed him yet... Is a cc the same thing as an ml? Okay, I have this syringe that measures three cc's. Which line do I fill it to, to arrive at one ml? The first long line. Got it. Thanks."

She lifted the syringe and pointed. "We fill it to this line."

———

Lucas speared a kung pao shrimp. They were eating at the kitchen table, open Chinese food containers in front of them. Serving a meal this way didn't look right to Lucas, but it was the way JJ had fixed it.

The atmosphere was strained. Young people didn't need an old man horning in on their fun. Lucas was having supper with the kids, and then he intended to make it clear that he had television to watch and did not wish to be disturbed. To make conversation, Lucas asked David, "How long is your leave?"

"I have to go back Friday."

"That soon? I guess you'll be coming home weekends."

"David and I have discussed it," JJ answered for him. "As much as he travels, he won't want to came here for hardly more than twenty-four hours—if you subtract travel time. He's keeping his apartment in Virginia Beach, and he'll stay there until he has real leave."

Lucas frowned. "How often will that be?"

David forked up a green pepper. "Hard to say."

Lucas studied the tight, closed expression on JJ's face. The truth dawned. The boy wasn't going to come home but once in every blue moon. She'd known it all the time. Marrying someone who wouldn't be part of her life was deliberate.

"Will you be going to Virginia Beach to be with him, JJ?" he asked, just to make certain.

"I'm sure I will. Occasionally. But you know how often I have obligations on the weekends."

Damn, he should have known she had something up her sleeve. The story about meeting last year, meeting again and deciding he was someone she wanted to marry... Lucas should have known it was too easy and too convenient. He'd swallowed the tale because he had believed Dave really wanted JJ. Shoot, Dave had lit into him—like *he* was the bad guy—for offering to sweeten the deal. Lucas had admired him for championing JJ. He thought he'd gotten lucky. Lucas swallowed the bitter taste of disappointment. He'd only heard what he wanted to hear.

She had figured out the way around him. JJ had figured out a way to be married and not change her life a single bit.

—∕∕∕—

"If I'm going to keep him, we've got to give him another name," JJ told David as they unloaded the dishwasher. Lucas had excused himself and gone to his office—to watch TV, he said. The dog did look better. About thirty minutes after receiving the morphine, he had gotten very slowly to his feet and gone to his food bowl. Now he lay awake but relaxed, his eyes following them. "I just cannot have a dog named 'Snake.'"

David took a stainless-steel fork and dried it. "Where do these go?"

"Drawer to the right of the dishwasher."

He opened the drawer and slid the fork in. "What's the matter with 'Snake'?"

JJ studied the dog, who lay on his side. Sometimes he looked more yellowish, sometimes more reddish. "I'm thinking... Dagmar."

"You cannot name him Dagmar."

"Why not?"

"It's a girl's name, that's why. It will make him neurotic. All the other dogs will laugh at him. He'll get into fights all the time. He'll probably grow up to be a psychopath."

"Well, what did you have in mind? Butch?"

"Not some girl's name."

"Vidalia."

"Chip."

"Telluride."

"Duke."

"Dakota."

David paused. She almost had him with that one. "Chuck," he countered.

"Beaufort."

"Buick."

"Impala."

"Pinto."

"Beowulf."

"Chase."

"Chase? Do you really want to give him a name like a hero in a romance novel would have?"

"Really?" he gave her a sexy smile. "They don't have names like David?"

"No. It has to be really testosterone heavy—with lots of hard consonants. Like the names you keep wanting to give this poor dog whose sex life is over."

David slowly dried a spoon. "Then I guess you won't like Snatch, either."

On the floor, the dog flicked his dark amber eyes from one to the other, as if he were suddenly interested.

"See," David latched onto the dog's apparent response. "He likes it. It will help him maintain his self-image now that he's you-know."

"Snatch?" JJ asked the dog. "Is that what you want your name to be?"

His long, tapered tail thumped the floor.

"Well, at least it isn't dangerous sounding, like Killer."

———

JJ entered her grandfather's kitchen the next morning more than a trifle out of sorts. Once again, she was dressed in clothes she didn't like. It was a good thing she'd been too busy with all the wedding preparation to clear out the closet here, or she'd have nothing at all.

Once again, she promised herself she'd be all right as soon as she got to Caruthers. Although thinking of how yesterday had turned out—with a dog to care for, a husband who apparently needed to be entertained, and winding up back in her old bedroom—she wasn't sure she had problems Caruthers could fix.

Therefore, it didn't do her heart nearly as much good as it should have when she entered the kitchen to see her grandfather perched on one of the barstools at the counter, looking absolutely chipper.

David was manning the stove, very competently scrambling eggs in one skillet and turning home fries in another, while bacon hissed and popped in the microwave. Without missing a beat, he listened with apparent enjoyment to the tale about a marlin-fishing tournament Lucas was regaling him with. The tournament must have happened before she was born. She couldn't remember Lucas ever going marlin fishing.

David chuckled in all the right places, maintaining an easy camaraderie and stirring the eggs gently over a low flame—which JJ knew was the correct way but never had the patience for.

"You want to know why JJ and I didn't get together before?" David was saying. "She thought I couldn't be faithful."

"Can you?"

"Yes, sir."

"All right then."

That, apparently, in male-speak, was all there was to say about that.

David carefully lifted the potatoes with the spatula to check the underside for browning. "What happened to JJ's parents?"

"They went out on the *Daddy Carbucks*, my cabin cruiser." Lucas was silent a long time. "They didn't come back, and we couldn't raise them on the radio. The Coast Guard found my boat the next day, adrift, but no sign of either of them. A shrimp boat found my son's body. A while later, my daughter-in-law's washed up north of here."

"What happened?"

"Nobody knows why they took the boat out. They were in the midst of an ugly divorce, big custody fight. All we know for sure is that they both drowned. She had a skull fracture, but they said it didn't cause her death. Maybe he hit her. Maybe she went over the side and then hit her head and he went in after her—but the boat started to drift away from them. He couldn't get back to it, not while trying to swim with her."

Lucas took a contemplative sip of his coffee. "Or maybe it was a murder-suicide—we'll never know. Coroner ruled accidental death for both. They both had a lot of alcohol in their systems."

"How old was JJ?"

"Nine."

"She told me she had nightmares."

"That's right."

"About her parents?"

"That's what Beth, JJ's grandmother, thought. JJ couldn't tell us. She was better after Ham got her the dog."

JJ listened to the bare-bones account of her parents' death. She'd heard it many times before. Unfortunately, there weren't many additional facts to flesh the story out with. There was only the nightmare image of her parents in the water, caught in destructive currents of their own willfulness, drifting further and further from the boat.

Since she was nine, she had lived with and, with everything in her power, warded off the nightmarish mystery of her parents' disappearance. They had left eternally unanswered questions: Why had they gone out on the *Daddy Carbucks* that day? Why had they left the boat? Why hadn't they loved her enough? Understanding even the facts, much less the reasons behind them, would forever elude her.

Anyone could see that was the crux of her need for permanence and, above all, for never emotionally depending on people who could *for no reason* do something stupid—maybe.

Of course, she recognized that the events that day had merely been the culmination of hundreds of abandonments. Even before her parents died, she had decided she was safer and better off with Caruthers.

Chapter 36

"GOOD MORNING, GENTLEMEN," JJ SAID.

"Here you are!" David smiled like his welcome was a gift he'd made just for her. A few days ago she would have discounted his smile completely. Today? More like fifty percent. She was beginning to believe his assertion that he wanted her for herself.

"I was getting ready to call you," Lucas said. "I told Dave if we waited for you to cook, we'd get mighty hungry."

JJ forced the corners of her mouth to move at the joke gone stale long ago. Nobody expected men to be born with a skillet in their hands, and she doubted if Lucas had ever fixed anything more complicated than microwave popcorn.

"No time for breakfast." Her mind was already on how she would juggle her schedule today. The bank's loan manager wanted yet another meeting, and Lucas had to see his cardiologist. "I'm glad I caught both of you together. I hate to dump dog care on Esperanza, but I don't see any other way." she informed them. "I don't think he'll be a lot of trouble. If he gets worse, she can call Ham—"

"Don't go bothering Ham or Esperanza," her grandfather interrupted.

JJ's short fuse ignited. "Granddaddy, you know you cannot get him into a car by yourself!"

"Young lady, I reckon I can figure out how—" Lucas snapped back. Abruptly, he switched tracks and whipped out a salesman's smile. "But I knew you were going to say that, and I don't want you to worry. Dave and I have got it covered."

"Covered, how?"

"Now, now, we have it all worked out. He's going to hang around here, and maybe we'll ride around awhile. Esperanza can call us if she needs us. I thought I'd show him the marina, and then while we're out, we'll go to Topsail and pick up some clean clothes for him."

"If you don't mind letting me have a key to the cottage," David inserted. "Tell me what you need, and I'll bring clothes for you too."

"We'll take the Rover—it's four-wheel drive—that way we can ride down to the inlet, if we want to," Lucas expanded his plans. "Wish we still had the Jeep. We'll stop and get some barbeque sandwiches."

JJ didn't know when she'd seen her grandfather so enthused. Too bad he'd chosen today of all days to want to do something besides sit in his office. "I hate to rain on your parade, but Lucas, what are you thinking? You have a doctor's appointment today."

Behind Lucas's back, David shook his head in warning. With hand gestures so clear it was like hearing every word, he signaled, "Leave him to me. I'll take care of everything." He added a mischievous grin and a thumbs-up.

Aloud he said, "Since we just simplified your day, you've got time to eat."

JJ goggled at him, unable to articulate her feelings. She had spent a restless night that these two men, both singly and combined, had been the cause of. She'd lain awake mulling over the fact that she now had not one, but two men who would disrupt her life at will. And now *they* were male bonding, planning joyrides, and getting ready to eat perfectly scrambled eggs.

She didn't know how the hell she had failed to foresee this. Not the part about the scrambled eggs, but that these two would like each other.

In each, a charm that drew both men and women overlaid a ruthless will. Unfettered by society's restrictions, they adhered to principles they had hammered out for themselves—which made them very reliable friends and very dangerous enemies. Even the age gap and their widely divergent lifestyles worked against her, since their differences buffered their tendency to compete with each other for dominance. They would still both try to dominate her.

She knew how much these men *took*. She didn't know how much thinner she could spread herself. Neither was the kind of man who could be controlled, but singly she could have managed them. Allied, she didn't have a chance. She watched every bit of leverage she had had circle the drain.

"The eggs are almost ready to take up," David said, taking her silence for consent to join them for breakfast—which it probably was. "Have we got plates?"

"Ready," said Lucas. "I got out the breakfast china," he told JJ with pride. "Your grandmother isn't here, but it's what she'd say to do. Do you know which napkins go with it?"

Breakfast china? Lucas had never set a table in his life, that she knew of, and suddenly he wanted the "breakfast" china and coordinating cloth napkins. The plates he'd gotten out were part of a very old set. She

had no idea what made them, in Lucas' mind, breakfast china.

"Which ones, JJ?"

"Which plates are you using? The blue willow? This
close to Thanksgiving, grandmother always liked to use
the pumpkin napkins."

"Pumpkin."

"The orange-y brown ones."

He extracted three and piled the rest—the entire contents of the drawer they usually resided in—on the end
of the counter. She wondered fleetingly if he'd realized
for himself the damask ones were inappropriate, or if he
hadn't found them.

"And in the fall, she liked to use the oak leaf placemats," she told him.

"Placemats."

"Dining room sideboard, second drawer down."

JJ braced herself for her grandfather's impatient,
"Well, get them," or for him to say the everyday ones
were fine. Instead, with more jauntiness than she'd seen
in a while, he made his way to the dining room.

"Don't forget the *breakfast* forks," David called out.
He threw her a conspiratorial grin while keeping his
voice smooth and innocent. There was a drawer full of
stainless-steel flatware right at David's hip, as he very
well knew, having dried the flatware and put it away last
night. Clearly amused by Lucas's need to set an elabo-
rate table David was adding elaborations of his own.

Again she was struck by how his brown eyes always
seemed so clear and full of light.

Lucas laid down the placemats and returned to the
sideboard where he opened the silverware drawer. In it,

twenty-two dividers organized the accumulated silver of several generations of Caruthers and Jessups. Though if he were seated at a table, he would have unerringly picked up the right fork, no matter how complex the place setting, he stared into the drawer overwhelmed by choice. "JJ?"

He was so out of his element and yet so touchingly eager to get it right that JJ took pity on him. "I'll get them," she told him.

As far as she knew, while there were luncheon forks and dinner forks, there was no such thing as a breakfast fork. She selected medium-sized forks with more slender tines than salad forks, but shorter and lighter than dinner forks. No reason they couldn't be "breakfast" forks—if she said they were.

On impulse, she rejected the Chantilly (official pattern of Air Force One—Grandmother had loved knowing that!) as too classical in mood. Instead, since this breakfast seemed to be in the spirit of her grandmother, she put back the ones she'd chosen and found the Audubon pattern by Tiffany.

It was a set her grandmother had bought for herself. The restrained bird and leaf design evoked, as nothing else could, her love of nature, art, and elegance. JJ gathered knives and spoons as well.

JJ had never seen Lucas in quite this mood. He seemed to feel some extraordinary hospitality was called for, and there was something touching about his fumbling efforts. He knew what a well-laid table should look like, but he had no idea how to assemble one. Since she knew he wouldn't think of them, she asked him, "Would you like for me to bring the coffee cups that go with the 'breakfast' china?"

When she returned with them to the kitchen, her grandfather took a fork and hefted it. "*These* are the breakfast forks? Huh." He shook his head. "She saw them some place on our honeymoon. Loved them on sight. I should have bought them for her then, but I told her we had no need to be spending money that way. Her mother and mine had housefuls of silver that would come to us, and God knows how much more we'd gotten for wedding presents."

"Did you refuse because you didn't have the money?" David asked, spooning eggs onto the plates.

"Well, our parents didn't support us. We only had what I made working at the car place. But the car business was incredible in the sixties and seventies. Into the eighties. Making money hand over fist."

"Besides that," JJ reminded him, "Grandmother was the only heir to the Jessup half of the Caruthers and Jessup partnership. You and your father saved a bundle by creating a marriage merger rather than having to buy her father out when he wanted to retire."

Nobody ever said her grandparent's marriage had been dynastically motivated. Still it had guaranteed Lucas's father would leave his share of the business to him rather than his brothers—and everybody in Wilmington knew it.

"We've been through several name changes," she explained to David, "but the business was actually started in 1907 by my something-great-grandfather George Jessup."

"It was George Jessup and Sons," Lucas added, "until the thirties when my father bought in and the name changed to Caruthers and Jessup."

"So your grandmother was a Jessup, and that's why you're named Jane Jessup?" David asked when they were all seated, plates piled with fluffy golden eggs, crisp bacon, hash browns, and muffins David had found in the fridge and reheated in the oven. He had been listening and drawing conclusions.

JJ nodded. "And now the business is Caruthers. I once suggested it should be changed to Caruthers and Caruthers." That was back when she had considered herself an owner, rather than an employee. "But since then I've changed *my* name. It looks like a Caruthers and Caruthers will never happen."

JJ didn't like the tinge of bitterness that crept into her voice. She went back to the original subject. "I never knew Grandmother asked you for the silver."

Her grandfather's gaze roamed over a past only he could see and then returned to her. "I don't know that she did ask, directly. I knew she wanted it. She didn't say anything else, and I forgot all about it." He turned to Dave. "Listen to me." He lifted a spoon and pointed it at the younger man. "If you want to be a happy man, make agreeing with your wife your first priority. Women never forget." The corners of his mouth turned down. "She never used these after she got them."

JJ stared at him in surprise. "Yes, she did."

Granddaddy's hooded green eyes lit with a heated mixture of doubt and hope. "When?"

JJ thought back. "Let me see, she always used the Audubon when her garden club met here, even if it was just a committee meeting and she only served coffee."

"No!" He huffed a couple of times. "Did she really? Every time Mary Ann McCready came here?"

"I guess." Mrs. McCready had been ten or fifteen years younger than her grandmother, an acknowledged beauty in her youth. They hadn't been friends as far as JJ knew. "I mean, I don't think Mrs. McCready visited except with the garden club."

Granddaddy's huffing turned to outright chuckles and then to guffaws. He slapped the table hard enough to make the coffee cups rattle and a knife jump from the edge of a plate. "Audubon silver for the garden club!"

The corners of David's mouth lifted. He jerked his head toward Lucas, both black eyebrows lifted in inquiry over twinkling eyes. JJ could only shrug. "Don't ask me."

Sitting there at the round breakfast table set with the good silver, blue willow china, and pumpkin napkins, bright sun making hot puddles of light on the polished floor, JJ had one of those wake-up moments when an angel taps your shoulder and says "Pay attention. Don't see what you *think* you see. See what's really there."

Across from her, in a white dress shirt open at the neck, sat her grandfather, laughing at a joke only he understood. On his right, David picked up a fork and turned it over in his strong, brown fingers, his brown eyes alight with humor and curiosity.

It had not occurred to her that everything could be different if she had someone to share Lucas with. Someone whose mind wasn't already shaped by the same stories told again and again—one hundred years of Caruthers history absorbed with his breakfast cereal. Someone not the least bit intimidated. Someone who found the whole scene amusing.

David being there changed her. If Lucas was behaving uncharacteristically, so was she. If she had been alone with Lucas, she would have been sharp or impatient. Most likely, she would have told him wanting to set the table was ridiculous—assuming she had stayed long enough to see him set it. When was the last time her mind had been open enough to be curious? To not automatically react to what was going on, but instead to wonder what was going on?

Chapter 37

EYES STILL BRIMMING WITH LAUGHTER, LUCAS LOOKED from one young face to the other. God, it was good to spend time with young people. Last night he'd made a point to stay out of their way. As much as possible he'd wanted them to feel like they had the house to themselves.

This morning he had come into the kitchen to find David and the dog already there, and it was the most natural thing in the world to start talking. And now, to have JJ sitting at his table, sharing Caruthers's history with someone to whom it was a new story—he felt like they were a family in a way he hadn't in far too long— maybe since they'd lost Beth.

The idea for breakfast had come to him this morning when he'd been thinking about what Beth would have told him he had been doing wrong. Which would be pretty much everything. If he could lure JJ to sit down and eat with him, he decided, then he would see that the meal was done right—the way Beth would have approved.

It was working. David was smitten. Every time he looked at JJ, his gaze was hot and hungry and tender. Lucas might have doubts about what had brought them together, but he had none that David wanted his granddaughter—and would be good for her. JJ had that *look everywhere but at him* look girls get when they feel the same way but haven't made up their minds to capitulate. Yet.

Yes, JJ was acting girlish. His heart squeezed to see her young and tender and vulnerable. He had discouraged her from acting this way when she was younger, but he now admitted it was because he couldn't stand the pain of watching her get hurt.

Beth had accused him more than once of stealing JJ's girlhood. When she should have been hanging out with the other kids, talking for hours on the phone and giggling about boys, she had been at the car place. It was true, he hadn't *made* her spend time there, but when she was there, he could feel proud of her—she had been an unusually responsible kid—and guide her and see her safe. He didn't have to live with fear she was doing the wild, uncontrolled things teenagers are famous for.

He had loved her, but it had been a selfish, controlling love. It took losing Beth for him to finally see how constricted JJ's life was. Not a fit life for a young woman. He'd tried to tell her to date, to have fun, experiment some, fall in love, but all she'd heard was more of him trying to control her.

His threat was finally having the effect he had intended. Whether she meant to or not, JJ was reaching beyond her tightly organized world. He wasn't going to make the mistake of telling her she ought to try make this marriage a real one though. He would have to study on ways to foster a courtship without appearing to.

"You're wondering what's so funny," he told the two puzzled young people. "Well, I might as well tell you. God knows, I'm not the hero of this story, but everyone else with the right to tell it is dead."

"When I was young, I did my best to follow in my father's footsteps. A lot of years went by before I realized he was a strong man, and by the time he died, he was a rich man, but he wasn't a good husband—and I wasn't one either."

David was watching JJ, not Lucas, as the old man began his story. JJ was looking down, drawing the tines of her fork through her eggs.

Lucas quirked an inquiring white eyebrow. "Surprised, JJ?"

JJ looked up, her green gaze cool. "Surprised to hear you admit it."

Well, wasn't that interesting? JJ apparently believed her grandfather had been a bad husband.

"Officially the Caruthers were farmers," Lucas returned to his tale, addressing David. "Truth was, my granddaddy ran moonshine, and my daddy, too. Moonshine's where our money came from."

Moonshine. David hadn't expected to learn his mansion-dwelling bride was the recipient of a fortune made illegally. He didn't look down on it. Hell, his great-grandfather had been a rumrunner. He'd used his fishing boat to bring in bootleg. When Prohibition ended, he'd gone back to fishing.

"Moonshine's the reason my daddy had money when old John Jessup ran into trouble during the Depression. He gave old John the money to keep the doors open in return for a partnership. But my daddy kept right on being a tobacco farmer and a moonshiner, and let the Jessups run the business. That was a couple of years before I was born."

JJ presumably knew all this. David wondered when Lucas would get to the point.

"I set my sights. My brothers could have the land, and Daddy was going to leave *me* the car business. I started there when I was just fourteen. Worked summers while I was in college. I'm making too long a tale of this."

He waved the past away with a gnarled hand. After a pause to gather his thoughts, he aimed a shrewd look at David. "You know what the Bible says a man does when he finds a pearl beyond price?" Lucas asked David.

"He goes out and sells all that he has to acquire it."

"I wish I could exculpate myself and tell you I didn't know what a pearl beyond price my Beth was. I knew. She was lovely, refined, a real lady."

He stroked a table knife between thumb and forefinger. "I didn't sell all I had. No, sir. Not me. I was a hotshot. Gonna modernize Caruthers, take it straight to the top. High, wide, and handsome, as we used to say—that was me. Business was my god, and I served it. The Caruthers weren't respectable. The Jessups were. The exact right wife was necessary to my vision of what I was. My ego was big enough to think I'd earned her.

"The other women—they meant no more than a good cigar, a moment of pleasure, a little recreation. I worked damn hard. I had earned a little play."

Lucas's sort of reasoning wasn't uncommon among SEALs, many of whom felt their life when they were operating had nothing to do with their marriage, but David hoped Lucas didn't think that explanation would excuse him in JJ's eyes. In fact, the self-centeredness of it probably confirmed the worst of what she thought of her grandfather. *And explains her extremely low expectations of me.*

David checked JJ's reaction to Lucas's bald admissions. JJ was again looking down, hiding her expression.

Lucas put down the knife he'd been toying with. "Everybody knew what Caruthers men were like. Hell, I had three half-brothers and two half-sisters, all by different women. My daddy sent every one of them to college. One's a state supreme court judge now."

JJ's eyes got wide. "I have a half-great uncle on the supreme court? I didn't know that!"

Lucas grinned, obviously pleased he had managed to surprise her. "It's not a secret, but the connection was never flaunted." Almost immediately he looked contrite. "I should have told you. I should have known Beth wouldn't—not that I blame her. It wasn't her duty to make sure you understood your Caruthers kin. It was mine. I should have taken you to meet them. The judge was the one who convinced Daddy it was time to stop moonshine. But that's a story for another day.

"Anyway, there were women, but I knew what was due my wife, and it was that she should never cross paths with them. Beth was my wife, and the women were nothing, nothing to me! Until Mary Ann McCready."

"Wasn't she married to Ben McCready? The lawyer," JJ asked. Lucas should have stuck to talk of moonshine and bastard kin. JJ's polite mask had returned.

"That's right. They moved here from Wendell, and he set up a practice. She was one good-looking woman. Red hair. A figure that would stop traffic, and she was looking to trade up.

"I didn't see her coming. She had me so wrapped up—it's the only time I ever considered leaving Beth. Wasn't long before Mary Ann was zipping around town in a brand new Corvette and suggesting if she had a country-club membership it would be easier for the two of us to meet. Then she got greedy. She called Beth."

JJ gasped softly, making it clear where all her sympathy lay. "Was Grandmother crushed?"

Lucas took a sip of coffee, enjoying spinning out the story. "Beth didn't even break stride," he assured them with smiling pride. "She told me she had learned to live without me, but I had married her to get Caruthers, and, if I wanted to keep it, I could stay married to her. She told me she had made the life she wanted—without me—and she didn't care to change it. She told me to tell Mary Ann it was over. She would take care of the rest."

He shook his head, laughing. "Now, you got to get the whole picture: she did this with a smile on her face, in the middle of the celebration gala for the symphony, which she had worked for ten years to bring into being. All the time we're talking, people are coming up to congratulate her, and tell me what a fine woman she is, and I'm having to say, 'Yes, I know,' and how proud I am. Over and over, I have to tell the mayor and couple of judges and state senators that I know what a lucky man I am to have Beth Caruthers for a wife. Even Teague Calhoun was there. He was running for his first Senate seat.

"Beth knew me. Yes, she did. I told her I'd get rid of Mary Ann. 'Don't humiliate her,' Beth told me. 'Someone has said to keep your friends close and your enemies closer. I say, it is better to destroy your enemies by making them need you. Mary Ann is ambitious and energetic. With some guidance, she could do well for herself and her husband.'"

Lucas turned to JJ. "Do you remember how Beth used to tap her lips, and then s-m-i-i-l-e, JJ? Well, she tapped her lips and said, 'I believe I will invite her to join the garden club. She'll make the contacts there that will boost her husband's career.'"

Lucas paused, like the good raconteur he was, to let the significance sink in with his listeners. "And then, like she was changing the subject, she said, 'Oh, and by the way. You'll be getting a bill for that silver pattern I've been wanting. I'm afraid it costs more than a new car. I ought to get something from this deal.'"

"Oh my goodness, that's diabolical!" JJ laughed. "She had the whole thing planned. She probably started strategizing the minute she heard Mrs. McCready was flashing a new car she couldn't afford."

"See why I laughed when you said she used the silver for the garden club? I always wondered how she made Mary Ann pay."

"How about you?" David asked him. "How did she make you pay? I don't think being out of pocket for some silver meant anything to you."

"You're right about that. But trust me, she got me, too. I don't know who she told, but next morning all over town, people were saying, 'Did you hear? Beth found out about Mary Ann, and Lucas had to buy her a whole set of silver from Tiffany's to calm her down.' And then the punch line: 'It cost a lot more than a car!'"

He laughed again. "I'm telling you, for years, every couple of months, some good ole boy 'ould slap me on the back and say: 'How's the car bid'nis Lucas? Had to invest in silver lately to keep it going?' That was my Beth. You didn't mess with her."

"Then what happened?" JJ asked.

"Beth lived up to her word. She never bad-mouthed Mary Ann. She whispered into the right ears, and Mary Ann and her husband got the invitations they needed. Over the years, they prospered. Beth was a lady to her fingertips. She had class. But JJ, you tell me, every time Mary Ann came to this house, Beth served her with the silver. Now *that* was diabolical!"

"Were you faithful to her after that?" David asked.

Lucas sighed. "I wasn't that smart. The emptier serving the god of success became, the harder I tried. I'll tell you one thing, though. From then on, I respected her. If she said she wanted something—anything—she got it."

"Did she ever ask you to be faithful?" JJ wanted to know.

"No. She had too much pride." His lips pressed together. His green eyes grew round and sad. "But she thought I was still tomcatting long after I'd realized she was worth everything."

"I never heard that story," JJ said, a bemused look on her face.

"It was before you were born. Still, I'm surprised no one ever told you. The whole town knew it." Lucas looked down a minute. "I should have told you. I should have made sure you understood I regretted not valuing your grandmother as she deserved."

—⁂—

JJ lifted a set of keys from the rack where all the household keys hung. "I don't feel right about this. Lucas shouldn't have asked you to spend your leave looking after him."

Yesterday, she had looked a little tired. Today, signs of strain around her emerald eyes and plump, shapely lips were even more evident. He wanted to kiss them away. He wanted to fold her against his chest and tell her to sleep while he kept watch.

Having listened to Lucas's story, and having done a good bit of reading between the lines based on what else he'd seen in this house, David understood JJ much better.

Beth, JJ's grandmother, should have used her rolling pin on Lucas instead of buying herself expensive presents. It was a different time back then, but she was obviously able and intelligent. She could have gotten along without him. Instead she'd made a god out of hanging onto her position and her status. Breakfast china, breakfast forks, breakfast napkins—an infinite replication of utensils all for the same purpose.

As for Lucas, he admitted he hadn't been a good husband. David thought he probably hadn't been a great father or grandfather either.

JJ hadn't heard this particular story, but it was obvious she knew her grandfather's reputation. No wonder JJ didn't trust him to be faithful. No wonder, having watched her grandmother's style of coping, she had tried to design a shell of a marriage rather than expect someone to want her. That was the essential point of the story. It was clear Lucas had been proud of Beth's means of revenge and willing to assign her the victory in that skirmish. But when it came to his tomcatting, as he called it, while he hadn't gone over the boundaries again, he hadn't changed.

The point of Lucas's story was that he had missed the point of life. He had thrown away all the blessings life had given him and kept the box they came in.

David had been close to doing the same thing. He'd seen how much alike he and Lucas were. Before Afghanistan, David had thought he was hot shit. He'd thought he deserved for girls to throw themselves at him. He'd compared himself favorably to leaders like Lon and Jax, geniuses like Do-Lord, and had had the gall to compare their girls to his and think he got all the best. He'd been a good SEAL, but he hadn't been much of a man at all.

He had woken up one morning knowing that, except for being a SEAL, he didn't have much to offer anyone. He had gone to Afghanistan where being a good SEAL gave his life all the meaning it needed and was a goal he could reach.

Lucas and he had some of the same character traits. Lucky for him, his dad *had* been a good man and a good husband. David knew what a good husband looked like.

He wouldn't be JJ's husband for long, but as long as he was, he would give her all he had to give. He would start with sharing some of her load.

He stroked one finger down her cheek. "Give in gracefully, JJ."

She straightened her shoulders and nodded. "I'll figure out something so tomorrow—"

She had already jumped to how to handle tomorrow. Did she ever live in the present? "JJ, how 'bout we take this one day at a time. Snatch would probably be all right, but you'll feel better if he's not alone today. I won't let Lucas overdo, but I can let him show me around. I think he's enjoyed having someone new to tell his stories to."

"But I'm sure you have things you'd rather do."

"I'd rather be operating." Too late he realized how that sounded, but there was no way to backtrack. "I can hang around here as good as I can Virginia Beach."

He stroked her cheek. "What will you do today since I've got Lucas and the dog handled?"

"I'll go to my ballroom dance lesson at five o'clock. I had thought I would have to be here to relieve whoever was with Snatch."

"Ballroom dance?"

"My indulgence. I justify it by saying it's great exercise."

"Why do you have to justify it?"

"It doesn't have much to do with the car business. I throw away a lot of money on it with nothing to show for it. The exercise is just a side benefit." She ducked her head, as if she was embarrassed. "I only do it because I like it. Lucas doesn't know. Don't tell him, okay?"

Just for a second, she looked adorably young, anxious, yet thrilled by her daring. There was no trace of the cool, strategizing businesswoman, the harried executive. The emerald of her eyes lit with deep-green fire. The protectiveness he always seemed to feel around her (even though she had no use for it) turned into something warmer, softer, more encompassing. He smiled into the heart of that green fire.

"What are you thinking?" she asked.

"That I'd like to kiss you."

She scraped her full lower lip with her shapely white teeth. Thinking. The lip was plumper, redder, shining with moisture. "Maybe you should."

Was she flirting? "*Maybe?*"

She swept her lashes down, then up. "We won't know for sure unless you try."

She was flirting all right. Tilting her head at the same time, she set her jaw at a challenging angle. He wanted to crow in triumph. He *got* flirting.

With one finger, he traced the neckline of her sweater. He made his voice deeper. Smoother. "So. You're proposing an experiment?"

"Right." She did the lash-sweep thing again. Tiny mysterious smile. "For science."

He closed the space between them. Their shoes met. "Then you know it will take more than one trial to be sure of the results?"

Her breath hitched. Delicate nostrils flared. But she didn't fall back, body language for "I'm not ready," or move sideways, body language for "I want more play before we go to the next level." Her eyes went to his lips. "I guess."

He drew her toward him slowly, smiling into her eyes, forcing her just a little off balance, and, *yes*, her arms went to his shoulders. Oh yeah, he liked her off balance, and this time it felt good, purely good. Her lips opened. He was about to die from the sleek, soft female feel of her. Even touching her back turned him on. And her scent. He could get drunk on it. He had her, and by God, she had him. Some demon made him want to tease her just a little bit more. He let her feel his arousal. "In fact, we may need a series of trials before we have anything statistically significant."

She dug her fingers into his shoulder impatiently. "Don't you think we should get started then?"

"Oh, well." He drew her closer. Her breasts flattened against his chest. With his lips hovering just an inch above hers, he whispered, "A SEAL will do anything for science."

———

"What did you finally name the dog?" Bronwyn's voice coming from the cell phone asked. She had caught JJ on her way to her dance lesson.

"Snatch."

"*Snatch*? No! Tell me you didn't."

JJ signaled a left turn and moved into the center lane. "What's the matter with Snatch?"

"I know you hang around socially with people twice your age, but do you live in a glass bubble? Do you never get around anyone who talks trash?"

The stoplight changed from amber to red just as JJ reached the intersection. "Trash? Like slang? Uh-oh. I'm getting a bad feeling. What does it mean?"

"A portion of the female anatomy. Female genitalia. The mons. The vulva."

"*Really?*" JJ gasped. "No. Employees use euphemisms, but no one would ever use crude slang around me, unless I used it first. And I wouldn't."

Bronwyn, the ER doctor, had no such hesitation. "*Cunt, pussy.* Actually some authorities believe *pussy* originated as a slang form of the Greek word *pudendum*, which was a Victorian euphemism." Sometimes Bronwyn liked to show off her brains.

"*Pudendum*? That sounds worse than snatch."

"Maybe it is. Translated literally, snatch just means, well, snatch. *Pudendum* means shame."

"*Eeww*. And yet it was considered a *nice* word?"

"Well, I'm telling you, snatch isn't. In slang, *snatch* is on a par with *cunt*."

The light finally changed to a green arrow. "That

man! If you could have *seen* the offhand way he said, 'Then I suppose you wouldn't like Snatch.' Just wait. I'm going to get him. I'm going to get him good."

"What are you going to do?"

"I don't know yet."

Chapter 38

JJ WHIPPED THE LEXUS INTO THE PARKING LOT OF THE dance studio, dodged two new potholes, and pulled into a parking space at two past five. She grabbed a tote containing a cobalt-blue practice skirt, a cotton-and-Lycra T-shirt, and her dancing shoes; shoved her purse under the seat; and jumped from the car, already racing for the wide concrete steps.

Penned in between two strip malls, defrocked of crosses and stained glass, the brick building still was identifiable as a former church by its high roof and the spacing of the tall windows. Once inside the glass doors, JJ turned toward what, formerly, would have been the sanctuary. It was one big open space now. Red slants of westering sun made long, glowing streaks on gleaming, *real* hardwood floors. In the back, an overhanging balcony kept part of the floor shadowy even when all the lights were on.

Salsa music thumped from gigantic speakers. Somehow it didn't clash with the room's aura of spacious peace. Though its purpose was a very different sort of communion, the room still felt like sanctuary.

"JJ, you are *here*!" Illarion, her Russian-born dance instructor rushed toward her, arms outstretched, and wrapped her in a sandalwood-scented hug. The room whirled as she was picked up and twirled, so strong and sure and fast that her legs were lifted by centrifugal force. "Oh, I am so *happy* you are here!" Without the smallest bobble, he set her back on her feet.

JJ laughed. Illarion's over-the-top ardor was impossible to take seriously. His joy was part of his professional persona.

A canny capitalist, he never forgot he was in the business of giving people a pleasant hour of recreation. Yet, in its own way, his pleasure was also sincere—and another reason he was a sought-out dance instructor. He always made her feel desired and desirable, as if every moment in her company was a special treat, and yet he never stepped over the line that would have made her wonder what he was buttering her up for.

"How are you?" he asked now, his bright, intense blue eyes looking deeply into hers with real pleasure—and no small amount of shrewd assessment. He never failed to notice if she changed her hair, lost a pound, or wore a different scent. "Are you well? What is different? You look…?"

Illarion could read bodies the way other people read the newspaper. JJ wondered if he could see the emotional whirl one Navy SEAL had thrown her into. Illarion dismissed his question with a flick of his narrow fingers. "We dance. When we will dance, day is happy, yes?"

"I'm sorry I'm late. Two minutes," JJ promised, re-shouldering her tote and dashing toward the ladies' room. "Two minutes, and I'll be ready."

A few minutes later, Illarion stopped their waltz to grasp the back of her skull and chin. The first time she'd tried the waltz, she'd been shocked by how different it was from what romance writers described. With gentle, masterful pressure, he corrected the position of her head.

He made her elongate her neck and lift her chin and turn more so that her chin was almost over her left shoulder.

Any kind of eye contact was impossible, and her partner's right hand, far from being at her waist, rested precisely one inch below her left shoulder blade. Her left hand wasn't on his shoulder. The palm lay on his right bicep, the forefinger extended across the deltoid. They were "locked in an embrace," only compared to *not touching* at all. How anyone would think to hold an intense conversation under these conditions, JJ couldn't imagine.

Nevertheless, the writers weren't wrong about the nature of the dance. Romance infused the gliding steps. When in tune with a partner, one floated as if in love and walking on air. Union through perfectly timed cooperation in every movement, plus the woman's total dependence on her partner's guidance (the dance *never* moved her in the direction she was looking), elicited almost mystical exhilaration.

If she could see Illarion's face, she would find pride of possession and restrained tenderness in his blue eyes. Illarion was very good at what he did. JJ was philosophical. The waltz gave a lovely facsimile of romance.

Illarion led JJ into a variation of the grapevine step before he remembered she hadn't been taught it yet. Not to his surprise, she followed without hesitation.

"JJ, you are so *good*!" She stiffened slightly. He quickly swung them into a promenade, a turn, and then a deep dip that had her laughing. He had to be careful to temper the praise he gave her. Too much, and she thought he was—what did they say?—slick.

In fact, he didn't praise as much as she deserved. She didn't know what a rewarding student she was. She swore she hadn't danced before, wasn't an athlete. Even so, she responded instantly and accurately to every instruction; she knew where her body was.

"Doesn't everyone?" was all she had said when he remarked on it. Furthermore, she forgot nothing between lessons, something else he'd learned not to praise since she only gave him a puzzled look. As her strength and stamina increased, he had pushed her faster and faster. She was already several levels beyond what most of his students achieved.

She never protested when he stopped her to correct her technique. Instead, she gravely thanked him. If she wasn't satisfied with her execution of a step, she demanded repetitions.

Above all, she had the passion, the soul of a dancer. Oh, if he could have taught her when she was younger! Before muscles had tightened and ligaments shortened.

While he had worked with JJ, the studio tempo had picked up. Instructors of evening lessons drifted in, greeted clients. A man Illarion hadn't seen before entered.

People did just wander in off the street, but this one, despite his friendly smile and cloak of casual curiosity, hadn't.

He had a face like a wounded angel, and the dark-green polo shirt revealed arms and shoulders to make a sculptor weep. His roving eyes fixed on JJ. He was hunting for her.

The man, whoever he was, wanted JJ for himself. Illarion felt a little zing of heightened alertness, an atavistic response to challenge, which he was too naturally competitive to ignore.

"JJ, no arms." He removed his hands from her. JJ obediently dropped her arms and closed the distance between them. From chest to knees, they pressed together, offset so that his thigh rubbed hers with each step. JJ was past needing the rapport-building exercise designed to force a pair to sense the other's body. Illarion intended it for her watcher's benefit.

Illarion began a simple box pattern, keeping JJ's back to the man.

He had the satisfaction of seeing the angel's ruined face tighten.

Men were such primitive creatures. Illarion should know; he was one. A romantic atmosphere was his stock in trade—ballroom dance made the promise of passion into an art form. Beneath the polished veneer, in seething messiness lay the real drama of desire and capitulation. He accepted his nature with a Russian's earthiness and a dancer's celebration of the body. This hard-faced man wanted JJ and, just possibly, was worthy of her. Illarion also had a Russian's love of intrigue and a dancer's love of drama. The wounded angel was on Illarion's ground now. The rules of engagement were Illarion's rules. This man it would be fun and very fulfilling to test.

———◊———

"David!" JJ saw him standing near the front desk and deserted Illarion to rush over to him. "Lucas? Is he…?"

"Lucas is fine." David's brown eyes heated with appreciation as they traveled over her form-fitting dance clothes. "Tonight," he grinned, "for those in the know,

is barbeque chicken night at the VFW. Before 5:30, seniors eat for half-price. Hard as it was to turn down, I
wanted to see you dance. Ham picked him up."

"You didn't tell Lucas I take dance lessons, did you?"

"No, but I think Ham knows." He looked behind her.
"This is where you come?"

Illarion had been standing behind her. He thrust out
his hand, lips spread in an enthusiastic smile. "Welcome.
You are friend of JJ? You hear about us through her?"

David's smile was all geniality and gave nothing
away. "Will you mind if I watch you?"

"JJ does not mind audience," Illarion answered for
her. "She likes. Soon she is ready to compete. A little
experience, she takes first place."

Ballroom dance was now an Olympic-recognized
sport, and competitions were a huge moneymaker for
studios like Illarion's. JJ enjoyed competition. Measuring
herself against other dancers tempted her. Although
money wasn't a problem, JJ had so far resisted Illarion's
encouragements. As it was, she stole time for lessons.
How she would carve out more, she didn't know.

Expecting polite interest in her hobby, she was surprised to see David's brown eyes warm with approval
and something that looked like pride. "First place, huh?
She has winning instincts, all right."

"You dance?" Illarion asked.

"Not much. Not ballroom."

"Oksanna!" Illarion called over one of the female
teachers. "Have you time to give introductory lesson?
First three lessons are free," he told David, not giving him
a chance to refuse. "Is good to watch beautiful woman
dance. Anyone can do. Is better to dance with her."

Despite self-confident smiles reeking of geniality, the exchange between Illarion and David was bursting with subtext. No one could have missed the gauntlet thrown down by Illarion, or that it was picked up by David's, "Lead on, Oksanna."

———

JJ was sorry the next dance Illarion led her into was the rumba. Despite proficiency in the steps, despite following every instruction, JJ always felt she wasn't doing it well. Illarion was asking for something more.

She intuited what the more was. Unlike the playfully flirty cha-cha or the intense, sharp battle of the sexes of the tango, the rumba was explicitly sexy, frank seduction—a celebration of attraction and desire. She wasn't holding back. She just couldn't make herself one with the movements.

Illarion was as patient, as encouraging, as pleased with any effort as always. He led her to the mirrored wall to demonstrate how to extend her arm with her fingers spread wide. Again.

Behind her in the mirror on the other side of the room, Oksanna had David rumba-ing in the face-to-face closed position—already. Nobody taught JJ that in her first lesson! Unbelievably, even as JJ watched, Oksanna showed him the open position and the same arm extension Illarion wanted her to perfect.

"Energy!" Illarion demanded.

Attempting to emulate him, JJ made her fingers tenser. Stiffer. Behind her, David and Oksanna had returned to closed position. His hips swiveled smoothly. His footwork was accurate.

Illarion followed her gaze. Nodded. To JJ, he said, "*Energy*!"

The energy he was looking for—suddenly, she knew how to access it. JJ allowed a hot surge of hunger for David to fill her. She invited it. She chose it. She let herself consciously, deliberately experience her woman's capacity for desire. Every muscle clenched. At the moment the sensual charge peaked, she flung out her hand. The energy shot out her fingertips.

"Yes, JJ! That! That is rumba!"

━━

"Will you give me some more dance lessons?" David asked as he unlocked the door into the house and disarmed the security system. After leaving the dance studio, they had stopped at JJ's favorite Thai restaurant for dinner.

"Illarion was right to only let us partner each other about two minutes. I'm not ready to teach. It's that sense of direction thing, I think. I can do *my* steps, but when I try to reverse them to show a partner, I get all confused. But you were amazing. You were doing moves I didn't learn in a month."

In the kitchen, the misnamed mongrel rose from his hunter-green dog bed. He still moved gingerly, but his amber eyes were bright, his velvety ears at a jaunty, alert angle. It was amazing what twenty-four hours of being out of pain had done for him.

David gently pulled the dog's ears and then went to the sink to refill his water bowl. He looked at JJ over his shoulder and returned to the subject of dancing. "A SEAL is expected to pay attention. Something as simple as where to put his feet, he should do after being shown once. It might take repetitions to become skillful, but when he's told by an instructor, 'Do this, this way,' that's what he does—or gets his ass chewed."

"Once?"

David set the water bowl down. "As our instructors are fond of saying, 'There are no second-place wins in a gunfight.'"

JJ's heartbeat stumbled at the laconic understatement with which he spoke of his deadly work. He told funny stories, and he chatted easily on almost any subject, but he rarely alluded to the purpose of what he did. It was written on his face that he went into harm's way, but to her the scar had become just part of how he looked. No more significant than hair color. It was easy to forget what it meant.

He cocked his head at her silence. "What?"

"Why did you come to the dance studio?"

"I wanted to see you. I wanted to know you. What time is it?" He changed the subject abruptly.

JJ glanced at her watch. "Seven-twenty."

"I need to take Snatch outside." He gave her the totally bland, completely straight-faced look she had come to profoundly mistrust. It was exactly how he looked when he had suggested Snatch as a dog's name. He reached for the simple loop leash they were using until the dog could wear a collar.

He disarmed the security system and opened the patio door. Then he said, "Did I mention that Ham has promised to keep your grandfather busy until nine-thirty?"

A man could accomplish a lot in an hour and... David slammed into one of the concrete barriers in his mind.

He shouldn't have to think about how many minutes lay between seven-twenty-five and nine-thirty. He should know, and the crazy thing was he *did* know, but he reached for it… and whammo! Concrete wall.

He clinched his teeth, fighting the mind-bending, skull-tightening, stomach-knotting frustration. The biggest single difference between those who made it as SEALs and those who didn't was that SEALs didn't quit. Confronted with a challenge, they had an almost overwhelming drive to keep trying, to push harder. But trying would only push the goal further away.

Let it go. With a conscious act of will, he wrested his attention back to his task. There was *enough* time. That was all that mattered.

He tugged Snatch's leash. Snatch obligingly stopped sniffing the tires of the Land Rover and followed him to the Lexus he'd parked minutes before. David retrieved JJ's dancing tote from the trunk.

He had followed her to the dance studio tonight because he wanted to get to know her. Dancing was the only thing she had ever mentioned that seemed to be about her. Something she did for herself, because she was herself, not the head of Caruthers, not the charity or civic leader. Just herself.

Back in the kitchen, Snatch went to his bowl and lapped a bit, then collapsed with a deep, grateful sounding sigh onto his bed. He'd been much more willing to go outside tonight, but movement was still painful for the guy.

To make sure it wasn't time for more pain meds, David slipped the medication schedule he'd made from his pocket, although JJ had written out a schedule and taped it on the inside of a cabinet door. Numbers could be slippery. On the schedule he'd made, drawn clock faces showed each dose. Needing pictures embarrassed him. It looked kindergarten-ish. Looked… hell, it was. He unfolded it and compared his drawing to the kitchen wall clock—which had flowers instead of numbers anyway. A corner of his mouth quirked in philosophical humor. At least in this place, pictures made as much sense as numbers.

He listened for JJ, not that he expected to hear her if she was upstairs. This house made silence into an art form. Even the refrigerator motor kept its workings to itself. Some intuition sent him into the dark family room.

She perched on the arm of a sofa, head tilted as if she was listening to something.

JJ, sitting still, doing nothing. Something he'd never seen before. He paused on the threshold. "Am I interrupting anything?"

JJ leaned over to switch on a lamp. She was smiling. He'd seen her smile before, but not like this. JJ kept her beautiful features composed most of the time, giving away little of what she thought or felt. Now her whole face was softened. In the lamplight, her green eyes twinkled, and her disbelieving smile held affection. She quirked an eyebrow. "Since when do you mind interrupting me?"

He shrugged. "Bothering you when you're rushing around, already ten minutes into the future—that's one thing. Breaking in when you've found something important enough to bring you to a full stop—that's something else." He sat on the couch and hauled her down beside him.

She swiveled her hips so that she landed perfectly in his lap. God, he loved the way she could take care of herself. Around her, he could get physical with a spontaneity that had rarely been possible since he couldn't take a chance on hurting a woman. He couldn't wait to see what else was possible. "So, what made you hit the pause button?"

"You wanted to watch me dance—that's what you said."

"Watching you do almost anything would be worthwhile. Watching you dance? It was beautiful. Anyone would want to."

"Do you think Lucas would?"

"You think he wouldn't? Is that why you don't want him to know?"

"I've been thinking he would say it was a waste of time. One time I asked my grandmother for ballet lessons. She said okay. The next morning at breakfast, she mentioned to Lucas she was looking around for a ballet teacher. He said, 'All right, Beth. You know how to raise a girl. Me, I'd rather see her spend her time learning something that'll make a difference.' So I told her I'd changed my mind, I didn't want to. But he didn't say I couldn't take lessons. He just wasn't interested. Now I wonder how many opportunities I've missed because of what I thought he wanted."

David struggled to see the connection. He understood enough about women to know that they weren't talking about nothing when their logical leaps baffled him. He went back to the part he understood. She liked that he wanted to watch her dance. And he had known watching her dance would be a way to get to know her.

"JJ. Tell me about dancing."

"When I'm dancing, I think of nothing. I'm dancing, and that's all I'm doing."

"Is it like focus?"

"Like on a video game? No."

"Like intense concentration?"

"No, it's like the *opposite* of concentration. But it isn't spaciness. That implies an out-of-it, out-of-touch condition. I would have to say space-fullness. I am there, and what I'm doing is dancing. If this is how athletes feel about their sport, then I understand how they can dedicate their lives to it."

Again, though he might not have understood all she meant by her words, he understood the arms spread wide to encompass and embrace the totality of all-that-there-is.

People thought SEALs were adrenaline junkies in constant need for excitement. To an extent that was true. But there was something else. Something harder to talk about because there weren't any words and the experience was rare. SEALs practiced various movement sequences until anywhere, under any conditions, their bodies would respond flawlessly. At the same time, they practiced what JJ had called space-fullness—it was as good a word as any. Every iota of their being was in whatever space they were in.

He looked into her face. "Dance with me. Do it. Put your dancing clothes back on."

"My clothes are out in the car."

"I brought them in."

"You planned this?"

"I plan for what I want."

He understood what he had to give her. Freedom. Freedom of her body.

In her bedroom, JJ trailed her fingers over the dress's glistening white satin jersey.

As well as being too short, the skirt had an off-center sarong drape that allowed way too much thigh. The halter top plunged way too deep between her breasts in the front and exposed all of her back to a couple of inches below her waist. Only ingenious internal construction and the miracle of Lycra would keep the top on.

The dress might have done for Hollywood, but it was too extreme in every way for Wilmington society. It was a dancing dress. Expressly designed to display a female body. When she bought it, she had doubted she'd ever wear it, but she'd had to have it.

She finished buckling the collection of straps that made dancing in five-inch heels possible and quickly checked herself in the mirror. Oh yeah. The dress looked like it would go gliding off at any moment. And since there wasn't a man in the world who didn't think makeup on a woman was sexy, whether he approved of makeup or not, she had added lots of dramatic eyeliner and smoky shadow and Carmen red lipstick.

Downstairs, David quickly confirmed for himself that the front entry had the most clear floor space. He ruthlessly rolled up the undoubtedly irreplaceable oriental rug and dragged it into the hall of Lucas's wing. The wide polished boards gleamed bare and ready.

He had just finished when he heard soft footfalls on the stairs. His heartbeat faltered. Then it chugged into a deeper, stronger rhythm while he took in long, long legs, and bare shoulders and arms. The white dress displayed the rosy apricot swells of her breasts in mouthwatering lusciousness. It flowed over them to the deep curve of her waist. It swirled around her hips as if it were made of white water and depended on magic to keep it on, which of course riveted him on the possibility that at any moment it would let go.

She'd made her eyes look huge and mysterious, her mouth—oh well, her lips were x-rated.

He had once said she was a goddess. Now she came down the stairs without hurry, a woman fully aware of her feminine power and ready to wield it.

His.

Lest the harsh, atavistic, triumphant, totally retro thought show on his face, he inclined his head in grave obeisance. He lifted his hand to her. "Would you like to dance?"

She moved down another step and bestowed her hand in his. "I would," she answered, gracious acceptance curving those hot, hot lips.

"There's the question of music." He handed her the remote to the 800-channel satellite system. "I thought you would know which channels have the best dance music."

"Actually, I don't." She clicked through the menu. "I've never done this before." She paused to smile warmly into his eyes. "Okay, here's Latin. Do you want to rumba?"

"Sorta got to. It's all I know."

He raised his left palm. There was the tiniest tremor, the slightest coolness in her fingertips as she fitted her palm to his. The trust and faith she was showing humbled him.

He stepped into the music.

Chapter 39

JJ WAS DETERMINED TO LET HIM LEAD, NO MATTER what. IN those two minutes Illarion had allowed them to dance together, David had shown amazing proficiency, but he was, after all, a beginner. Even a dancing genius could learn only so many steps in a half hour. Still, the heart of ballroom was not fancy footwork. It was synergy of partnership.

For the first half of the song, he kept to a simple box step. He adjusted the size of his step to hers. His timing was flawless. With the simplicity of the steps, JJ relaxed into a deeper, smoother swivel of her hips. Felt him feel it happen.

So smoothly she hardly knew he had done it, he led her into an underarm turn. She rewarded him with a flirtatious glance over her shoulder.

The underarm turn in the rumba is slow, taken through four steps to return to the partner. He took his time to play his eyes over her, letting his gaze linger on her breasts and hips in frank, masculine greed.

She returned the look with a knowing smile and one eyebrow lifted in challenge.

After that, who knew if they danced steps ever seen before on a ballroom floor? With his lead so sure, so indisputable, so perfectly timed, her response was instinctual.

―~~~―

They danced.

Quick-quick-slow.

The music throbbed in leisurely undulations.

Quick-quick-slow.

Golden droplets of light sprinkled by the chandelier trickled over the rosy apricot of her cheeks. He took his hand from beneath her shoulder blade and stroked down her arm to signal open position so that he could better view the light slipping across the swells of her breasts. The skin between them gleamed from the heat of lazily relentless *quick-quick-slow.*

"Oksanna told me this step says I am dancing with the most beautiful woman in the room. I am showing her off to make all the men envy me."

Quick-quick-slow.

JJ peeped from the corner of her eyes. "I am the only woman in the room."

Quick-quick-slow.

"You are the most beautiful woman in this room or in any room in the world. And you— "

Quick-quick-slow.

"Are the only woman—"

Quick-quick-slow.

"In the world."

Quick-quick-slow.

"When I think the other men have admired her enough," he gave the authoritative snap that would cause her to pivot on the ball of her foot. He loved doing that. "I bring her back."

Her eyes were dark with desire. He drew her closer. With every sway of their torsos, her breasts brushed his chest. His erection brushed her mound. His lips found hers. Took.

After a good bit of reconnaissance, he had spotted the tiny hooks that restrained the halter top of her dress. Never letting the rhythm falter, never yielding his claim to her mouth, he brought his hands to her nape and released them.

Their steps faltered as they sought to get closer. He relished the fluid feel of her breasts against his chest. He filled his hands with her buttocks pressing her closer. She twined one leg around his.

"I want skin." Her hands tugged at his polo shirt.

What the lady wanted, the lady got. He pulled it over his head and sent it flying. It landed on the newel post, not that he knew it at the time.

"Hang on." He grasped her waist and lifted. She instantly clasped her legs around his middle. With them in better line with his mouth, he nuzzled her breasts.

"Oh yes!" She arched her back to give him better access.

She clung to his neck with one hand while, with the other, she offered her breast like luscious fruit. Her core was hot against his abdomen. He suckled hard. Her passion ratcheted up another notch. With each climb, her torso undulated, her legs tightened. The heels of her shoes dug into his buttocks.

Knowing each exact moment her arousal surged filled him with a heady rush of power, as arousing as anything he'd ever experienced. His forearms supporting her thighs, he dug his fingers into her hot, wet center. A silky barrier blocked his way. He ruthlessly found the seam and ripped it.

He pushed one finger, two, into her tight, wet heat. He experimented until he found the rhythm she was looking for.

She could come like this. She would.

———

JJ had, once before in her life, yielded to desire; this time she exulted in wild, unfettered freedom. She felt him tear through the sewn-in panty of the dress, and then his hand was there. *There*. With the same perfectly timed rhythm as his ministrations at her breasts.

His hard arms secure under her thighs, her hair brushing her bare back, the chandelier with its hundred glittering prisms above her, sinuous, seductive music—this moment filled her entire world. She heard herself crying "Good, good," in laughing sobs.

He urged her to climb to the peak with triumphant resolution. And then she shattered. She clung to his shoulders, pulling his wild, hot, male scent deep into her lungs as wave after wave gripped then released her.

He gently set her on her feet, continuing to support most of her weight. While she rested her head on his shoulder, he murmured praise and printed kisses on her throat.

As her breathing evened out, his kisses became more insistent, as did the fierce urgency with which he kneaded her back and molded her closer to him. He claimed her mouth in hot, hard demand, gripped the back of her head to keep her exactly where he wanted her and, with his other hand, pushed her against his arousal.

Not to her surprise, the searing throb at her core was already back. In fact, it had never faded. It had simply found a plateau and rested there. She insinuated a hand between his ridged belly and slacks, seeking him. She caught his gaze, letting him read her intention that she *would* have him.

He opened his slacks for her explorations, toeing off his loafers.

She hooked one leg around his to bring him to her. She had never pushed the bottom half of her dress the rest of the way off, but after what he'd done to it, it offered no impediment. The fine tremor in the leg bearing her weight increased, but she denied it. He gently pushed the leg she'd wrapped around him back down. "No, I want—"

"I know what you want. Your legs are too tired."

She would have protested except it was the truth. "What then? The floor's too hard. And cold. The stairs are worse."

"Now I get what *I* want." He stepped out of his slacks.

He looked a little scary all of a sudden. All powerful muscle and hard intent. Not bad scary. More big male animal scary. Make that big, male, *aroused* animal scary.

Reflexively, JJ backed away, half-laughing, half-nervous. "Um, let's talk this over."

"No talking." He came after her, stalking her step for step. As if it were a new dance. Rumba music still played, but their moves had the edgy tension of a tango.

She backed into the umbrella stand, which didn't contain umbrellas but a collection of walking canes acquired over the generations. JJ grabbed for it, but it went over. Wooden canes spilled everywhere, their clatter loud.

"See what you did," he chided, nimbly stepping over the small obstacles.

JJ backed around a corner and, not looking where she was going, caught her heel in the rolled-up rug. One hand flew out and knocked a painting askew.

Going down, she grabbed for anything and found his hands already on her waist, already setting her on her feet.

"Failure to watch your six," he tsked. "You are not practicing proper safety awareness," he told her sternly. "There will be penalties." Not giving her time to think, he scooped her into his arms. He headed down the hall toward Lucas's suite.

He turned into the much narrower hall where the door to the pool was. One of JJ's feet, still shod in her dancing heels, collided with a wall sconce. Its bulb went out, plunging them into shadows.

"All right." He put her on her feet. "Better take it single file from here. But first, now that it has served its purpose, we need to get you out of this." He pushed the bottom half of her dress off her hips. "Will you wear it for me again sometime?"

He stripped her efficiently. JJ couldn't get a reading on his half-joking, wholly intense mien, the feral light in his eyes, the low, growly, uninflected voice. She could feel her eyes get wider. Her heart kept skipping little beats. Her breath exploded in sharp pants.

He paused, one hand firmly gripping her upper arm, one hand on the doorknob. "Do exactly as I say, and nobody gets hurt."

He sounded so serious. Her heart stumbled, badly, before it found its beat again. "Come off it. Nobody's going to get hurt."

His implacable, graven look said more clearly than any words that she was in his power, they both knew it, and whether anyone got hurt was totally up to him. "Will you do as I say?"

Then she saw—even in the shadowy hall with only a vague luminance coming through the glass pool door— the glint of teasing deadpan humor. He was playing. And making it just real enough to be thoroughly thrilling. Something like a warm spring from deep within the earth bubbled to the surface, moistening and heating all the cold dry places in her soul.

As clearly as if he'd spoken aloud, she heard, "Trust me." It really was that simple. She could do what he said, and nobody would get hurt.

Trusting was a huge leap for her. It wasn't about admitting him access to her body. This was about stepping away from the control she sought to maintain over her world, the boundaries she stayed in charge of so that she always knew where they were. This was about learning to swim with the chaos of life instead of erecting barriers against it. This was about letting go of the anchors, moving away from all that tied her in one place.

This was about not managing life but participating in it.

She raised her hand, schoolgirl polite. "May I ask a question?"

"What is it?" He growled. He opened the door. One hand on the small of her back urged her into the thick, humid atmosphere of the pool.

She tossed him a smile over her shoulder. "If you're going to throw me in the pool, do you mind if I take off my shoes first?"

—◆◆◆—

"I like the shoes." God, he did. He flipped on the underwater lights. The shimmering light licked over every perfect, soft curve of breasts and hips and graceful line of long, long leg. Whatever you called the peachy color of the shoes, it almost perfectly matched her skin tone, making her look even more naked than if her feet were bare. "The shoes come off when I take them off."

His groin hardened even more. His heart thudded. Reluctantly he admitted he was never going to last through the love play he had planned. Meticulous planning and attention to detail were the keys to success. He had stored a selection of floats as well as silicone gel that maximized sensual water play. But they would have to wait for another time.

She was enjoying their little game of domination. A SEAL stayed flexible and took advantage of opportunities.

The thing was, he wasn't playing now. It no longer mattered how many other women there were in the world. He finally had her complete attention, and he wanted her. He wanted to master her. He wanted to take her into the fire and let it consume them both.

"Do you understand that I have you in my power?"

"Yes."

"And that I can do anything I want to with you?"

"Yes."

"Are you going to stop with the smart mouth?"

"No."

"So you're going to need a demonstration of just what I can do to you?"

"Probably." She let a dark tress fall over one eye. "I am bad, and I am thoroughly out of control."

"Are you saying I might need to restrain you?"

"You might."

"I'd better search you first. Up against the wall."

"Aren't you supposed to say, 'On the ground! Get on the ground!'"

"The wall."

She sauntered to one of the tiled walls, hips moving in slow undulation. He had to fight not to laugh aloud at the amount of sexy insolence she managed to put into it.

"Spread 'em." She moved her feet apart. He looked her up and down. "Even though nothing is concealed, I'd better pat you down."

"I'll need both hands free so I'll restrain you this way." He leaned against her letting her feel his weight. He traced her outline, in light lingering caress not neglecting any part.

"Now we do the cavity checks." He knelt in front of her.

"That's not how you do it."

He gripped her hips. "Who's had more experience here?"

"You."

"Then trust me when I say this is the only way to be thorough."

When her legs trembled, he inquired in his smooth voice, "Are you ready to cooperate now?"

He swept her up in his arms and carried her to a padded vinyl-covered bench. "What can I do to you?"

"Anything you want to."

"That's right." He positioned her so that her buttocks were at the end. He lifted one of her feet and then the other to his shoulders. "Now, I'm going to make you scream."

Much later, they lay in JJ's bed, spooned together, one of David's beautiful, strong arms a comforting weight across her midsection—the way sleeping together had already begun to feel natural.

JJ waited until she felt his arm grow heavier as David gave in to complete relaxation. "I've been thinking," she announced. "Snatch isn't quite the right name. He needs something a little more dignified."

The arm tensed. "Dignified."

"Snatch doesn't give him enough to live up to, if you know what I mean."

"Did you have another name in mind?"

"What do you think of Pudendum? It means…"

"I know what it means."

JJ flipped herself over. She twisted her fingers in the hair of his chest. "Shame! And you're the one who should be ashamed."

"Oh, I am."

She gave a good yank. "You're not."

"Okay. I'm not."

The man was laughing. Not out loud maybe, but she could tell.

She flipped over on her back. "Bronwyn told me it's a bad word, really dirty. As bad as cu—I can't make myself say it."

He rose on one elbow to look into her face. "I look at you, and I can't think any of those words that refer to that part of you are dirty or ugly."

That was so *sweet*. She couldn't give in yet. She crossed her arms over her chest. Added a pout. "You're trying to butter me up."

"How am I doing?"

"Terrible. You're supposed to be contrite. You should have seen some of the looks I got today."

"Tell me who they were. I'll beat 'em up."

"You can't. I told people I chose it because it was macho-sounding!... Oh, my God! Macho-sounding." She giggled. "I name the dog—you know—and think it's macho!" She laughed harder. "No wonder they were *looking* at me." Every time she thought of their faces, she went off into more gales of laughter. She began to roll around on the bed. "Macho!"

David grabbed her and began to roll with her, both of them shouting with laughter. After a while they weren't laughing.

———————

Spooned together again, JJ placed one of David's arms across her midsection. Comfortable now, JJ yawned and said, "His name is Brinkley."

"*Brinkley*?"

"Do. Not. Argue. I'm going to sleep now."

David squeezed her lightly. "Good night, Jane."

"Good night, David."

———————

David dreamed.

It was the prettiest meadow he'd seen in Afghanistan. A fresh breeze rippled lush grass into satiny-looking waves. Overhead, the sky was so blue his heart lifted in joy just to look at it. Perfect, cottony clouds sailed and trailed shadows from one side of the meadow to the other and across the encircling mountains.

It was the perfect place for horses, and sure enough there were two—a black one and a brown one, their coats gleaming in the sunlight, drinking from the shallow stream that gurgled through the grass.

"I need to get back." Garth stood and dusted off his camo. The desert gray and tan looked out of place in this verdant spot. "You coming?"

David leaned back against the grassy knoll that fit his shoulders and supported his head as if designed for him. "I don't think so. This spot is perfect. The sun is warm the air is cool... I smell flowers and pine trees. Pine trees! Can you believe it? This place looks more like a high meadow in the Rockies than Afghanistan."

"You can't stay here."

David laughed at the absurdity of that. "Why not? I like it here. I like it better than Afghanistan."

"You just can't."

Somewhere in the distance a bird called. "I don't have the energy to move right now, but when I do, I'm going to ride the horses."

"Doc. Davy. Listen, you've got to come back. They think you're dead."

"I am."

"No, you're not!"

"If I don't have a problem with it, Lieutenant, I don't see why you do."

"Get up. That's an order."

"Go to hell, Lieutenant." David smiled to show he meant no offense. *Go to hell*. It seemed like a really funny thing for somebody who was dead to say.

"They're searching for you right now, Doc. I don't know how long I can keep them searching. We're losing light."

"Tell them to go on without me."

"You know I can't do that. SEALs never abandon a fallen comrade. And nobody saw where you went after you flushed the bad guys from their position. Nobody saw you hit," Darth insisted. "You might be alive."

"I told you I'm not."

"How can you be so sure?"

"I never wanted anything but to be a SEAL. Never. I got to be a SEAL, and I got to be there for my buddies. I couldn't have gotten any luckier than that. I fulfilled my destiny."

"So you're letting yourself die."

"I think it was the Plan." Cool, sparkling joy welled up in him again. "You know, what I was born to do."

"Bullshit! There is no destiny except the destiny we make by making choices."

"Fine. I chose to die. I knew I wouldn't survive as soon as I took the first shot. You know how the instructors always used to say 'A man alone in battle will not survive.'"

"Isn't there anything you want to live for?"

"To be a SEAL."

"Then isn't there anything you regret?"

"Yeah. When I was a teenager, I gave my mom a hard time. I was so wild she had to send me to military school. I wish now I'd helped her instead. And I could be a prize jackass. I wish I could apologize."

"Isn't there anyone you hate to leave?"

"No one who needs me."

"How about a girl?"

"There was someone… but I totally screwed that up. Talk about a *dead* end. I didn't even get her name." All that seemed to have happened too long time ago to be worth worrying about now. "I'm real tired. I think I'll take a nap now."

"Okay, I'll carry you."

David looked at the blood that soaked Garth's camo pants from his hip to his knee. Funny that he hadn't noticed it before. "You've lost a lot of blood."

"I'm losing more while I'm standing here talking to you."

David fought his lethargy. Garth needed him. "Where are you hit?"

"Hip, top of the thigh, something."

"How's the pain? Need something for the pain?" David felt for his field pack.

"It was bad at first," he heard Garth say while he searched frantically for his pack. "I don't feel it much now."

"Where the hell is my field pack?"

"I'm not leaving you. You wouldn't be alone if I hadn't sent you on that pointless errand of mercy."

"He's got a pulse," Davy heard someone say. "Tell the lieutenant we've found him."

Chapter 40

JJ SWAM UP THROUGH THE DARK WATERS OF PROFOUND sleep. She put layers of consciousness on, one at a time. She was in her bed. She was in her grandfather's house. The warm presence, the exquisite balance of male to her femaleness that she had grown used to sleeping beside in only five nights was gone.

She could hear David murmuring somewhere. She pushed herself up and finally found him in the shadowy room on his haunches beside Brinkley.

"Is Brinkley all right?"

"Yes."

"What's the matter?"

"Nothing."

"Then come back to bed. It's the middle of the night."

After a long moment, he rose in one of those lithe movements full of strength and control so characteristic of him.

When he lifted the covers and got in beside her, she snuggled against him. As he always did, he folded her against him.

She gave in to the luxury of pressing her nose against his skin to inhale the wonderful masculine scent of him. "What woke you?"

He stroked her shoulder, looking at the ceiling. "A dream."

"A nightmare?"

"No."

"Tell me."

"One of those recurring dreams. I dream I'm in Afghanistan, but I'm also in the Rockies—you know how dreams are. Wherever it is, it's so beautiful. I'm arguing with Garth. He orders me to get up. I believe I'm dead."

"Oh! Scary."

"No. That's the thing. It isn't. It's good. Really good."

A deep shiver trickled cold down her spine. "Good that you're dead?"

"Yeah."

She comforted herself with the reassuring solid warmth of his arm, the curved corrugation of his ribs, the firmness of his stomach moving under her hand with his breath. "I'm listening," she prompted.

"The thing is, even though it's mixed up, the dream feels real—hyperreal. Then stuff happens. The dream gets all confused." JJ had a feeling "stuff" was things he chose to leave out of the telling. "Then I hear someone say, 'Tell the lieutenant we've found him.'" Under her hand, his belly contracted in a soundless laugh. "It's so shocking, it wakes me up. Wide awake."

"And that's all?"

"Yep."

"What do you think it means?"

"I don't try to figure out what dreams mean anymore. On the morning that this happened," he touched his cheek, "I dreamed about my mom. It was one of those dreams where you dream you wake up, you know? I dreamed I could hear her sobbing, so I looked for her, and when I found her, she was crying because I was dead. I knew the dream meant I was going to die that day."

Again an icy trickle shivered along her spine. No so much because he was again talking about death as because of the matter-of-fact way he spoke.

He wasn't like most people who stop to notice death only when it happens to someone they knew. He was a man who lived with death. His acceptance of his mortality wasn't the passive, grudging acquiescence of most people. The life of a SEAL could get him killed. Without fanfare, without chest beating, he was ready to *give up* his life to do what he did.

In a flash of intuition, she saw that his relationship to death had been the source of that incandescent merriness she had first known in him. Being willing to die, he was also willing to live. The outlook had given him the willingness to ignore all boundaries, and to treat her with tenderness and respect while he did so.

JJ grinned inwardly. Respect was a funny word to use for some of what he did, and yet it was accurate. He had taken advantage of the moment, never of her. More than his overflowing animal vitality, more than his astounding masculine beauty, it had been his attraction.

The truth was, she hadn't asked him to marry her because his reappearance had been convenient—although, God knows, it had been. Seeing him again had shocked her into awareness that she could not live the way she had been going. No, the truth was she had been already close to being a facsimile of herself. She had buried the knowledge of what it felt like to be alive, called it something else for a year, but when she met him again, it had refused to stay buried.

Sometime in the last year, he had lost that merriness.

Oblivious to her wandering thoughts, he had continued down the path of his story. "I knew my mother was crying because I was going to die. Not a doubt in my mind."

"Well, you came close," JJ objected. "I'm sure she *would* have cried. In fact, I'll bet she did cry when she found out you were wounded."

"Yeah, she did. But I didn't die, and she did."

While they talked, the shadows of the room thinned in the barely perceptible lightening of the world that was first dawn. "JJ?"

"Hmm?"

"Tell me again about when we met—the first time."

It was eerily close to what she had just been thinking about moments ago. "What do you want to know?"

"Did we talk?"

"No. Not much."

"I'm really sorry I don't remember it. The thing is, I do remember, but it's like a slide projection. I know what it's a picture of, and yet I can't get it to come into focus. Of all the results of being blown thirty feet, that is the one I hate the most. That and the dream about a girl I probably shouldn't tell you about."

"What girl?"

"I dream I'm looking for a girl, but I can't see her face. I'm frustrated because I don't know her name."

"Have you had this dream only since you were injured?"

He thought for a minute. "No," he said in a tone of discovery, "I had it before—I'm almost sure."

He didn't remember her. She needed to remember that. She knew now he understood how temporary life and everything in it was. Which meant his feelings for her, such as they were, were genuine, but they were temporary. He wanted to go back to his life.

Her feelings for him, she finally realized, were permanent. She would have to go back to her life eventually. In the meantime, she was going to use one piece of what she had learned this morning. She would live to the fullest today.

Chapter 41

On Wednesday, JJ left Caruthers at noon to go home to the Topsail cottage.

Lauren had finally called, full of apologies for having missed JJ's message. She readily agreed JJ could have a dog in the cottage, so JJ stopped by her grandfather's house to pick up Brinkley.

With her awareness that life was fleeting, and that no matter how hard she tried it could not be held onto, she kissed her grandfather good-bye. She still didn't like his methods he had used to make her see that Caruthers wasn't the whole of existence, but she couldn't argue with the results, temporary though she knew they were.

He kissed her in return. He said something he'd never said before. "Your grandmother would have been so proud of you. I'm so proud of you."

Once at the cottage, David walked Brinkley prior to settling him down, while JJ enjoyed the warmth of the sunny deck. The calendar had turned. People were beginning to say, "Christmas is just around the corner," but the deck of the cottage, facing south, captured all the heat of the sun. JJ slipped off her sweater.

She turned to smile when she heard David come through the sliders.

"Is Brinkley okay? You don't think walking him on the beach hurt him?"

"He's fine. I've given him his morphine, but I'm

spacing doses further apart. I think in a couple of days, he'll be able to do without it."

In a couple of days, David would be gone. Her mind jumped to the future. But she would not be sad about what hadn't happened yet. She was absorbing a different message from the one she had learned at her parents' death. Everything could change in an instant. She had learned to be afraid of the future and to hold on with both hands to the most permanent thing she could find.

It was still true that everything could be lost in an instant. But that particular truth could also set one free.

She held out her arm, inviting him to come and stand beside her at the deck rail.

He carried her purple pashmina shawl, which he draped over her shoulders.

"I'm not sure I need this," she told him, touched at his care. "It's amazing how much the sun heats this deck even on the coldest days. I'll bet it's seventy degrees."

"You might need it." He stood behind her and pulled her back into contact with his front. "Are you warm enough?"

"Um-hmm."

He pulled her blouse from the waistband of her skirt. He ran his hands under her shirt and holding her against him, cupped her breasts.

"I want you," he said in that voice she had no defense against. "Here. Now."

"David, we can't. It's broad daylight."

"How far away is the pier?"

"It's almost exactly a mile."

"Do you see anyone on the beach between here and there?"

"No. But—"

He turned her in the other direction. "How about that pier?"

"More like three miles, I think."

"And...?"

Despite her rising excitement, she tried to force some steel into her voice, "I don't see anyone in that direction either. But that doesn't mean—" Her protest lacked a certain amount of conviction. He had only to touch her, sometimes not even that, for her body to begin to ready itself for him.

"Cottages on both sides are empty. We can't get much more alone than we are right this minute." He loosened a couple of buttons of her blouse. She understood the purpose of the shawl. It preserved her modesty and covered the action of his hands.

"What if we never get this opportunity again?" He whispered against her neck. "You're getting wet, right now, aren't you? Just thinking about it."

She was. Her heart was pounding. She pressed her bottom into closer contact with him. Against her buttocks, she could feel his hardness through her skirt, through his jeans, calling for entry.

"Brace your hands on the rail," he urged. "That's right. Lean over. Move your feet apart."

Unhurriedly, as if the action were accidental, unconsidered, he drew up the back of her skirt. An errant breeze evading the barricade of the house cooled the backs of her thighs. She understood the purpose of the shawl now. If anyone were looking up from the beach—which she was glad there wasn't because there was still time to refuse, and she didn't want to—all they would see would be the wide shawl draped from her shoulders to the deck.

—៳៳—

He worked the silk of her panties over her high, round butt. They drifted down her legs to make a puddle of red lace around her ankles and the yellow stilettos she wore. She'd worn these shoes the day she had announced she wanted to marry him. He did appreciate this woman's sense of style. "Step out of them."

When she had, he gently folded up the back of the skirt to make the fine wool frame the treasure he sought. "Widen your stance a little more, Jane."

"You can see…"

"Seeing is part of it. You know that. Do you want me to tell you how pretty this is? Blushing for me? Glistening because you're turned on."

He ran his hands under her blouse. Unhooked her bra. She grabbed for her front with one hand. "No, keep both your hands on the rail." He leaned over her. He pushed the cups up, freed her breasts to drop their full weight into his hands. Plucked the nipples into hard peaks and then rolled them between thumb and forefinger. "Wouldn't you like to feel me in you while I do this?" He smiled at the inarticulate gasping reply. "I can't hear you. What did you say?"

"I said yes."

."Good."

He gingerly lowered the zipper of jeans that by now were far too tight. He had trained himself to put on protection one-handed. He was never more glad. It allowed him to keep one hand playing over her. The sight of his own hand touching her swollen folds, the slick dew covering his fingers, was almost enough to make him come.

David was a man who loved sex. If he numbered his fantasies, this would make the all-time top ten. Again that crazy déjà vu feeling, like an earthquake deep in the bedrock of his being shaking him awake. The feelings seemed to get more far-fetched and yet more real all the time. Impossible though it was, he knew the fantasy hadn't been about some nameless, faceless woman. It was JJ in the sun, and he had fantasized the right to have her in the daylight and open air.

Carefully he spread her with one hand and positioned himself with the other. He grasped her hips to stabilize her. Slowly, relishing every centimeter as her tight, hot velvet took him, he made fantasy real.

———

JJ dropped her head, her neck no longer able to support its weight. Her whole awareness was on the place where they were joined: the sense of fullness, of heat, of pressure. She knew what she was: a woman completely yielded to a man's possession. Out of control.

She not only let it happen, she gloried in it, and if she was honest, gloried in the edginess of being in the sun and open air, the risk of being seen. Caught.

Caught in what? Letting her husband make love to her? Daring, yes. Illicit, no, enjoying sanctioned sex.

Each thrust moved through her whole body.

"You're coming, Jane." Sometime in the last week, Jane had become his very private sex word, a name he only used when they made love.

God, she *was*. The walls of her passage squeezed

with every withdrawing stroke. The crests of water made of light rose higher. She waited for the wave to break, to crash over her head, and still it rose higher. The waiting was unbearable, the intensity unbearable, the knowledge that when it came it would take everything in its path, unbearable.

"That's so good," he praised.

"Harder," she said, determined to claim the blessing she had been given.

He covered her, his hands on her breasts as promised. His breath was a harsh rasp in her ear. She was encompassed, inundated, the tsunami finally meeting its promise of destroying everything. It took her, and she gave herself to the taking.

Her legs threatened to buckle. He was heavy. Still he took. Still she took. Of this moment she took all there was. His fingers dug into her hips. He plunged wildly. Into the sunlight he hurled a triumphant shout.

—*w*—

Hardly more able to stand than she, he circled her waist as her trembling legs gave way. She gulped great shuddering breaths. She was so limp he feared this time he had gone too far. But he knew his Jane. Was attuned to her, body and spirit, as he had been to no one before. He pushed her skirt down. He prayed a wordless prayer. And then his legs refused to hold them anymore. He heard the sound he had been waiting for. Her laughter.

He lowered them to the deck, and there they sat with their backs to the railing, legs splayed out in front of them, howling with laughter.

The sun slid further down the afternoon. The ocean

whispered of eternity. A line of pelicans glided overhead riding the thermals created by the cottage roofs. They honked their rusty-hinge honks, unfazed by the doings of humans.

Brinkley woke and wandered to the sliders to look for them, puzzled that they were out and he was in.

"Admit it," JJ demanded. "Doesn't he look more intelligent now that his name is Brinkley?

———∿∿∿———

On Thursday, she had a meeting with the man from the bank that handled their floor plan. When she was done, she told her manager she would be gone for the rest of the day. She and David walked Brinkley. They ate scallops. During the afternoon, the sky and ocean turned dark, gunmetal gray. Rain turned the boards of the deck dark.

As day turned to night, there was less and less to say, because there was more and more that couldn't be said. They made slow, careful love and fell asleep early wrapped in each other's arms.

———∿∿∿———

On Friday, it was still raining when they got up. They ate the pancakes David fixed. They sat at the counter in the kitchen.

JJ cut her pancakes into smaller and smaller bites. It didn't help. They still felt like they lodged against the tight place in her throat with every attempt to swallow.

"When is Brinkley supposed to get his stitches out?" David asked.

"Tuesday."

"Tuesday?"

"That's what the vet said."

David looked confused, then whatever question he had, he let go. "Will you be able to manage him by yourself? Maybe you'd better call Ham."

"I won't be keeping him. The rescue organization called. The woman who's been out of town will be back Sunday. She'll pick him up sometime Monday."

"You're going to let him go? Grady gave him to you."

"I trust them. They have a no-kill policy. They'll find him a good home."

"He has a good home. With you."

"No." She couldn't explain why she couldn't hang on to Brinkley. Couldn't make him into the sea anchor of her life to keep her from drifting. She was moving under her own power now.

She cut a piece of pancake into a smaller bit. "You have your last post-surgery appointment today?"

"Yes."

"Do you want me to go with you?"

"Why would I?"

His eyes, especially the left, had that tight look it got when he was in pain. She had learned not to mention it, as she had learned not to notice his occasional lapses. "I just don't think you should go alone. What if it's bad news?"

"I'll deal."

That closed that subject.

He petted Brinkley and told him to be a good boy. Short, prickly hair was beginning to come in around the dog's sutures. David ran gentle fingers along it.

"This has been good," David told her as she walked

him down the cottage steps to his car. "I have a lot
to thank you for. Knowing you've got my back with
Riley—it means as soon as I'm operational, I can get
my life back."

Stay, her heart said.

He didn't want her to say he wasn't ready to return to
duty, and she didn't have the right. He had lived up to
his part of their bargain and more. Caruthers was safe,
and, because of him, she no longer needed to cling to it.
She had found a freedom to move on—with Caruthers,
and past it. Now she had to set him free to live the life he
wanted. To regain the life he felt he'd lost. She wasn't
part of that.

She kissed him carefully. The wrong touch could
be agonizing when whatever was causing his pain
started up.

He kissed her in return, already seeing a world she
could only dimly imagine.

Stay, her heart said. *Let me protect you and keep
you safe*.

He climbed in his car and drove away.

Chapter 42

CMDR. KOEHLER TURNED DAVID'S HEAD FROM ONE SIDE to the other. He had him smile, frown, make chewing motions, purse his lips.

"Pretty good," he pronounced. "Looks like you have full use of the masseter—that's the muscle that flexes when you clinch your teeth—but you're a corpsman—you know that. Purse your lips again. Still not perfectly symmetrical, but it looks like you compensate well enough to keep your spit in. And it may continue to improve.

"Cosmetically, the result is good." He consulted the chart. "The other reason we revisioned was we thought a portion of the trigeminal nerve might have been entrapped by scar tissue and be causing the neuralgia you've been experiencing." He pressed all along the trigeminal nerve pathway. "How's the pain now?"

"Better. None at all the last week. Steadily diminishing before that."

Koehler leaned against a cabinet. His dark, intelligent eyes narrowed. "Would you tell me?"

"Would I tell you what, sir?"

"Would you admit if the pain weren't improved? I know how you SEALs are. You deny pain anytime you think it will keep you from operating."

There wasn't much David could say to that. It was the truth. To become a SEAL, a man had to be willing to push past pain, past exhaustion, past being cold to the bone. He had to want to be a SEAL *more*.

"So what do you really think?" Koehler asked. "Do you think you're ready to operate?"

David thought he'd been a little too positive earlier, so he tried for judicious now. "I've kept up my weight training, but it'll take a while to build up stamina. Otherwise, I'm good."

"How about the mild TBI? Your records say the symptoms resolved by eight weeks post-injury, but blast TBI symptoms can have delayed onset."

"Want me to recite the months of the year backwards?" David grinned, naming a common TBI screening task.

Koehler folded his lips in a grimace. He shook his head. "My gut tells me you're not fit for duty." He studied David's chart again. "No pain at all for the last week, you say? A week isn't very long. If you are getting better I don't want you to do anything that could set you back. Okay, I can put you on LIMDU—"

Broken legs, arms, ribs, wounds put SEALs on limited duty all the time. Other SEALs understood how much the man wanted to operate and would help as much as they could.

But if he accepted limited duty, he had to accept that he couldn't operate in his present condition.

"Tell you what. Instead of LIMDU, just note you want to see me again in a few weeks. With two back-to-back deployments, I've got leave saved up. How about I take that? I'll use it to get back in training. When you see me next, I'll be a hundred percent."

Koehler paused in the notes he was making. "What are you covering up?"

"Not a thing." David added his best gleam-in-the-eye smile. "I'm a newly married man. Spending time with my new wife will be all the therapy I need."

Chapter 43

JJ WAS LATER THAN SHE SHOULD BE WHEN SHE FINALLY got to Caruthers. After David left, she had sat on the sofa in the great room, strangely unable to move, not thinking of anything, watching the ragged gray clouds move over the gunmetal gray ocean. Without the sun coming in the sliders, she grew cold, and still she didn't move until Brinkley got up and nudged her hand, whining.

At Caruthers, cars ranged row on row through the lot, reflecting gray light from a dull gray sky, and not a customer was in sight. Rainy days were not good for the car business.

"You brought the pooch," Kelly called from her position at the concierge desk.

"I couldn't stand the thought of leaving him by himself all day. Ham will be by to pick him up in a little while. Send him up to my office, will you?"

"Sure."

"Kelly, I noticed Red's car isn't here. Have you heard from him?"

"Uh, no."

The short answer wasn't like the normally chatty Kelly.

"Isn't he on today's rotation?"

"I don't know."

Another short answer. JJ became aware that throughout the showroom, people had paused in their work.

"Is there anything I need to know about?" Although her assistant Katherine was tireless and efficient, Kelly often had a better reading on what was happening over all.

"I just had two phone calls in a row, that's all. They wanted to know what would happen to their warranty if Caruthers was sold."

A warning chill ran down JJ's spine. "What on earth made them ask that?"

"There's a rumor going around. A couple of people have told me they've heard it and asked me if it was true."

If they only knew what she'd gone through to keep the dealership secure. "You told them not to worry, didn't you? Caruthers isn't being sold."

Kelly's eyes didn't quite meet JJ's. "I wasn't sure."

Her own people were doubtful about Caruthers' stability? "Well, it isn't. And you can tell anyone else who asks you heard it straight from me."

JJ didn't need to be a mind reader to guess the meaning of the compliant smile that passed across Kelly's face. She didn't believe her boss. She was thinking, if the rumor was true, but the sale not ready to be announced yet, that's exactly what JJ *would* say.

JJ wasn't used to having her word doubted by her people. It hurt, but not as much as it would have a couple of weeks ago. Caruthers wasn't her whole life anymore.

The rumor needed to be scotched. The trouble was, she didn't see how. She'd just seen how little effect denial had—even on a person like Kelly who had reason to trust her. But if there was one thing she didn't want, it was the appearance of not being willing to talk about it.

"Katherine," JJ said as soon as she arrived at her assistant's desk. "Would you call all the department heads and ask them to meet with me in, say, a half-hour? And also, would you check the sales rotation and see where Red is supposed to be?"

"Red?" Ham appeared in the office doorway. "I can tell you where he is now. He's over at Dunning Ford. Saw that BMW of his turning in there as I was going by."

There were a dozen reasons Red might have gone to Dunning. One was that he was looking for another job. JJ made a mental note to have a chat with him soon.

She passed Brinkley's leash to Ham. "I appreciate you taking him for the day. Are you sure you don't mind?"

Typical of Ham, he didn't answer any question he wasn't interested in. Instead he asked, "Did your man get off okay?"

"Early this morning. He had a long drive."

In a most untypical gesture, Ham laid a leathery hand on JJ's shoulder. "Are you brokenhearted?"

Tears sprang to her eyes, surprising her. *Yes*. Embarrassed, she pushed them away with the flat of her fingers before they could fall. "No, of course not. I will miss him though."

Ham nodded. "Well." He flicked Brinkley's leash. "Come on, dawg."

JJ checked her phone messages to see if David had called. He hadn't.

———

Though she wasn't sure how much she was believed, the meeting with her managers relieved some of the strange, tense atmosphere around the dealership and halted the wary sideways looks. At least the future of Caruthers wasn't something that had to be whispered and speculated about. They knew they could come to her directly with questions and concerns.

The meeting also pinpointed the source of the story at least within Caruthers: Red, although they seemed to think he had gotten it from somewhere else.

She checked her messages again after the meeting. No calls from David, but one from one of the most social of Wilmington's social butterflies, Taylor Vaughan. JJ returned it while she walked back to her office.

"I was wondering when we were going to get to meet that new husband of yours," Taylor said as soon as they had gone through the ritual greeting phrases. It wasn't the first inquiry of its kind. The holiday season was gearing up. Invitations to parties arrived daily— all including a handwritten note to be sure to bring her new husband. Naturally people were curious, but JJ expected the curiosity to die down once the word got out that he was in the Navy and wouldn't often be available for socializing.

"His leave was up," JJ told Taylor. "He returned to his base in Virginia this morning."

"Will he be home for Christmas?"

JJ found herself departing from her prepared answer. "If he can," she hedged, knowing she was expressing more hope than likelihood. "You know how it is with the military."

"So you don't know when he'll be back? No one seems to have seen him. Are you sure he's real?" Taylor laughed gaily.

His face was suddenly there in her mind's eye. JJ chuckled. "Trust me. I have all the proof I need. He is very, very real."

After wringing from JJ a promise to bring him to her Christmas party if he was in town, Taylor hung up.

Kelly had clearly been eavesdropping from her counter in the center of the showroom, so JJ grinned at her as she closed the phone. "Can you believe that? She just asked me if I was sure David was real."

"When people ask me that, I tell them I've seen him with my own eyes."

"People have been asking if he's real?"

Kelly shrugged. "You know how people are. You did marry him out of the blue. They've got to talk about something."

—◊—

Ham returned Brinkley at six. JJ kept the dog with her, where he was happy to lie under her desk while she worked on the books. December's early dark caused the lights across the fourteen-acre lot to come on. David didn't call.

"Brinkley," she said at last, rewrapping a half-eaten deli sandwich and stuffing it back in its white bag, "putting off going home isn't going to work, is it? No matter how late we stay here, he still won't be back when we get there."

Brinkley gave her a very patient look and yawned.

"Yes, you're right," she told him. "I know how I get attached. I should have known this would happen. I could call him." In fact she had punched in the numbers several times but stopped before hitting *send*.

She wanted to hear his voice and to know if he was all right. She wanted to tell him about her day. He would listen and then make some insightful remark or find the humor in a situation that had gotten steadily less funny as the day went on. If nothing else, he would tell her she couldn't do any more tonight.

She wanted to feel his warm, strong body and see his laughing brown eyes. She wanted him. When had she wanted something that wasn't directly tied to Caruthers? "The only thing is, he never once indicated to me that he wanted me in his life. Wanted me, yes. Wanted me to be part of his life, no."

Brinkley got to his feet a little stiffly. The problem was beyond the scope of dog duties. Feeling the need to do something, he laid his big, square head on JJ's thigh.

JJ gently pulled the amber velvety ears. "He's lived up to his part of the bargain. I promised him he would be free to go back to his life without needing to be concerned about me."

JJ swiveled her chair to gaze through the window overlooking the back of the Caruthers lot. Everything was shiny from the rain: the cars row on row, the asphalt. All she had ever wanted was Caruthers, and now it was all she had.

Back at the cottage, JJ moved Brinkley's bed into her bedroom. She opened the drapes after she had the lights turned out. The rain seemed to have tapered off to a light mist. She lay on her side looking out the sliders, trying not to notice that the other side of the bed was empty.

At last, knowing she was setting a terrible precedent, she patted the mattress. "Come here, Brinkley."

Chapter 44

IT HELPED TO HAVE A SENIOR CHIEF LOOKING AFTER YOU. True to his word, on Monday, Lon had David's leave approved, everything signed and ready to go. David would have liked to throw everything in the car and get out of Virginia Beach fast.

Instead, he methodically thought through what he would need.

He couldn't overcome years of packing in order and with care. He was a SEAL. Forgetting equipment was not tolerated. Mishandling equipment was not tolerated. And at the end of ops, packing gear that needed to be cleaned wasn't tolerated. Sometimes he thought half a SEAL's life was about packing.

He didn't have a lot of clothes except for jeans and work shirts, which simplified some of his choices. He packed his one old dress shirt and the two new ones he had bought for the wedding. JJ and her grandfather required a certain amount of dressing up. His one old blazer that was starting to look old. Dress shoes.

His hand hesitated over running shoes. He hadn't run since his last surgery. Before his doubts could take hold, he snatched up the shoes. He *would* be able to run. The pain was going to get better. He just needed time. He had the leave. He had time.

He gazed around his apartment, momentarily confused, having lost track of where he was. He calmed and centered himself as he had been taught. Emotions wouldn't help. Sticking with his training. Doing things in the right order. That's the way you managed moments when the shit hit the fan. Besides, stress made his difficulty focusing worse.

He carefully put the fear back behind its compartment door. What he had to do, what he was *going* to do, was get back in training.

He packed his wet suit. The proximity of the Gulf Stream kept the ocean off Topsail far warmer than Virginia Beach. And he needed his surfboard. His small set of weights, he left. He would join a gym.

Laptop, iPod. Time to stop being lazy about emails. He needed the practice typing. And reading. He could download remedial math and spelling. The big thing was to learn to catch mistakes. He didn't focus on what would happen if he didn't succeed.

He finished loading the car and realized he didn't know if he'd forgotten anything or not.

He should have made a checklist.

He'd never needed one before for this kind of packing.

His eyes got hot, but he fought the tears back. Nor did he give in to the urge to break something. He didn't allow the too-familiar protest that this was *not* his life. He wanted *his* life back. He wasn't going to whine about the hand he had been dealt. Instead, he was going to do something about it.

He centered himself. All right, he needed a checklist now. From now on, he would make one.

His BlackBerry! He'd forgotten it.

He took the stairs up to his apartment two at a time.

His new BlackBerry lay on the dresser. It had a couple

of dozen new apps he needed to learn to use. And wasn't that a kick in the teeth? He was of the generation born as the Internet was. He had never had to *learn* to use an electronic piece of equipment before.

He pocketed the BlackBerry. He glanced around to make sure nothing else had been overlooked. He opened a drawer at random and saw the shoe box. He had already given JJ the only valuable thing in it. Still, taking it might be a good idea. He tucked it under his arm.

He took U.S. 17 south. I-95 would be faster, but so what. There was no need to rush anywhere. Nowhere he had to be for twenty-nine days.

He'd always been content to live in the present, never having been able to see far into the future. If he couldn't be a SEAL, he had no future at all.

For much of its length, U.S. 17 was a two-lane blacktop. It strung together tiny coastal plain towns, skirted flat open fields where behemoth cotton-pickers toiled, and tunneled for miles through pine forests. Long bridges crossed one wide black-water river after another. He had driven through North Carolina numerous times. After graduating B/UDS, SEAL basic training, his combat medic training had taken place at the Joint Special Operations Medical Training Center at Fort Bragg. SEALs sometimes had training exercises with Marine Spec Ops at Camp LeJeune.

But he'd never before driven through North Carolina thinking he might be going home.

He told himself he should call JJ from the time U.S. 17 passed near Elizabeth City. He didn't know what to say. He didn't know how glad JJ would be to see him. It would be too easy for her to tell him "No" on the phone. It would be harder to turn him away face to face.

One mile added invisibly to the next. He was at Jacksonville, North Carolina, watching signs for Camp LeJeune, when he decided showing up at the Topsail cottage wouldn't be his best strategy.

The critical period would be the time between when she saw he had turned up after she thought she was rid of him, and when he brought it to her attention that she was happy to see him. She'd have a hard time giving him the boot in front of other people. He drove past the Route 210 turnoff that would have taken him to the island and continued on to Wilmington.

"JJ," Kelly said, calling from the concierge desk. "There's a man here asking to see you."

JJ stood and straightened the neckline of her white eyelet blouse. She debated only a second before she took the suit jacket from its hanger. The suit was a fine merino wool in deep purple—her power color. She'd put it on for her appointment at the bank this morning. She had needed all the power she could get.

She'd called the bank Friday, hoping to assure them of the rumor's falsity before they heard the rumor elsewhere. Floor-plan lenders took seriously having their borrowers be entirely above board. With the whole industry in a credit crunch, if a firm lost their lender, they weren't likely to find another one.

Unfortunately, the chilly tone of this morning's meeting made it clear that while she got points by asking for the meeting, she hadn't acted quickly enough. The rumors had already reached the bank. They had talked about reassessing the degree of risk. They could, if they assigned her to a higher risk category, raise her interest, or they could reduce her line of credit. Either would be a serious setback to the gains Caruthers had made. Either one could effectively put Caruthers out of business.

She could only assert that the rumors were not true and that she planned to operate Caruthers for many years.

Even after the bank meeting, she had been called to the front desk four times to reassure customers.

"You stay here and be good," she told Brinkley as she shut her office door. It was almost five. The coordinator from the rescue organization would be by to pick up Brinkley soon. She was going to miss him, but she couldn't ask him to stay alone all the hours she was gone or continue bringing him to work with her.

She was halfway down the stairs when she recognized the set of broad shoulders of the man leaning over the concierge desk. Hot bright joy expanded to the point of pain in her chest. "David?"

The last piece she needed fell into place. She loved him.

He turned at the sound of his name. For one half-second, naked supplication shone from his eyes. And then his teeth flashed white. When she was on the second step to the bottom, he lifted her in his hard, strong arms and swung her around.

She buried her nose between his neck and shirt collar, inhaling deeply of his comforting scent. Everything was okay now, not because she was some child who believed a place or another person would fix her world and keep it safe. Everything was okay now just because it was.

"Love bears all things, hopes all things, believes all things, endures all things." Words she had learned as a child, heard read at dozens of weddings, blossomed with meaning.

The piece that was missing from her life was her heart, and she had found it when she had irrevocably given it away.

Needing affirmation of his physical presence, she found his lips with hungry joy.

A long, loud wolf-whistle brought JJ back to awareness that she was standing in the middle of the Caruthers showroom floor.

David released her, a tender light in his eyes.

"I was a little scared you wouldn't be glad to see me. I guess I shouldn't have worried, huh?"

Chapter 45

"HEY, BRINK." JUMPING UP WASN'T YET IN BRINKLEY'S repertoire, David saw, but he bounced on his front legs and wagged his whole hind end when David followed JJ into her office.

"Now that we've got some privacy, let's see if we can get this right." He crushed JJ to him, relishing the way she fit in his arms and her spicy scent, the scent that was hers alone.

JJ found herself bent over the desk, her skirt being pushed up. "Whoa, we can't do that here."

"You never let me have any fun. That's a perfectly good desk. There's no reason that we can't put it to use."

"I'm expecting Luann from the rescue group to come for Brinkley any minute."

"Let's foster him. At least until he's prettier looking. Once his hair has grown over the scar, he'll be a lot more adoptable."

They hadn't been together fifteen minutes, and already he was remaking her plans and turning her world topsy-turvy. "You want him, don't you?"

"It's been a long time since there was any way I could have a dog. Don't you?" He saw her weakening. "Call Luann. Tell her you've changed your mind."

JJ turned around to retrieve her phone from her desk. While she looked for Luann's number, David pulled her back to his front. In a tour de force of dexterity, he had her jacket and blouse unbuttoned before she hit *Send*.

She batted his hands out of the way. "Not now."

His hands came right back from a different direction. "Why? Luann's not a problem anymore."

"Because—" JJ had to break off when Luann answered.

While JJ tried to talk sensibly, he insinuated one long-fingered hand into the cup of her bra. Cupping her breast, he kissed the side of her neck.

"Everything okay now?" David asked when she hung up.

"Luann was almost pathetically grateful," she told David, turning so she could put her arms around him. "Apparently she's been bending over backwards to find a foster home for Brinkley." JJ hid her face in his neck. "Do I walk over people?"

David rocked her in his arms. "You don't walk over me." He paused. "Might be fun to try sometime."

She began to re-button her blouse. "Since you've dealt with Luann, we need to go. Granddaddy is expecting us—me. Mary Cole Sessoms—you remember her from our wedding—is already there. We're having a war council. I'll explain on the way."

~~~

"I've found out the source of the gossip," Mary Cole announced when they were all seated in the cushy leather sofas of the family room, Lucas with his scotch, Mary Cole and JJ having red wine, and David his preferred soft drink.

"Who?"

"Blount Satterfield. First let me tell you what he's been saying. According to Blount, foreign interests want to buy Caruthers but aren't willing to work with an unmarried woman. The deal was threatening to go sour. That's when Lucas approached Blount and offered him one hundred thousand dollars to marry you. You two had been dating, and Lucas thought money would make you more attractive."

Hands shaking with anger, JJ carefully set her wine on the coffee table before she spilled it. "And what does Blount say happened next?"

"He says no amount of money could make you more attractive. He refused and broke things off. A couple of weeks later, suddenly you're married very privately to someone no one had heard of. Someone only a few people in town have even seen. It's obvious you or Lucas beat the bushes until you found someone who— for enough money—would accept a paper marriage and fade back into the woodwork once the deed was done."

It was a tissue of lies and half-truths—all of them impossible to deny.

It was her word against his, and she could offer not one shred of proof that he was lying. In fact, it was one of those stories that the more she denied it, the more questions she would raise in people's minds.

David put his hand on JJ's knee and squeezed gently. "Is Blount The Idiot?—the one who was careless enough to leave you by yourself?"

Lucas and Mary Cole exchanged glances. Obviously, there was more to this story than they had heard.

"That doesn't prove he's an idiot. *You* went off and left me alone."

David picked up her left hand and displayed it for all to see. "Not until I had a ring on your finger."

JJ snatched her hand back. "I can*not* believe you said that. Neanderthal."

This time David and Lucas traded looks. Very masculine looks.

"Do you honestly believe I'm property that you can stick a *Taken* sign on?" JJ demanded.

David captured her hand again. This time he brought her fingers to his mouth and kissed the knuckles. "I believe you wouldn't have accepted the ring if you didn't intend to live up to all it means." His beautiful, clear brown eyes were sincere. At the same time, they assessed her reaction to see if she was going to let him skate.

One corner of JJ's mouth twitched. "Good save."

He turned her hand over and kissed the palm. "I thought so."

"Well. All right!" Clearly delighted and a little bit wide-eyed at David's loverly gesture, Mary Cole slapped the padded leather arms of her chair. "Let's get back to the subject, shall we?"

"Right. What are we—what am I going to do? There's *just enough* truth in what Blount is saying. If I attempt to refute it, I'll only make the story juicier. The bank is holding off now, but they're nervous. It won't take much for them to pull our financing."

"Wait." David held up his hand. "Which part of the story is true?"

"I did promise him one hundred thousand dollars," Lucas admitted, "once he and JJ were married."

"And you did threaten to sell Caruthers if I didn't marry," JJ added.

"That's what I thought. You know, Lucas," David spoke in a quiet uninflected tone, "somebody ought to ream you a new one."

"I know. This whole mess is my fault."

That was so true everyone took a sip of their drink and avoided one another's eyes. A profound quiet settled over the room.

"Since we're dividing up the blame for this mess, I contributed too." JJ broke the silence. "Blount doesn't have anything to gain by spreading this tale. This is spite, pure and simple. I should have handled breaking up with him more considerately. I've been warned I walk over people. I'm trying to do better, but this lapse has come back to bite me."

"Don't be too down on yourself. And don't take too much credit either. Blount's not the kind of man it's safe to turn your back on." Mary Cole raised her eyes heavenward. "Blount Satterfield, Lucas? What were you thinking?"

"I admit Blount was a mistake. But I never expected JJ to pick him. He was there to offer her a range of choices."

JJ blew out a breath. "Regardless of who's to blame, we have the same problem. I can't see what to do about it."

Mary Cole set down her wine glass. "There's only one thing you can do. The part of Blount's story that makes the whole seem plausible is the 'invisible husband.' Make him visible, and the story collapses." Mary Cole tilted her head, a strategic light in her intelligent blue eyes. "Until tonight, I couldn't see how to accomplish that." She grinned at David. "How long is your leave?"

"As of tomorrow, twenty-eight days."

"That means you have to go back, when?"

JJ saw David hesitate. "January third." She filled in. "Isn't that what you told me?"

"And you didn't know he was coming home?" Mary Cole asked JJ.

"The docs thought I needed more time to heal," David fielded the question for JJ, "before I went back to full duty. Rather than hang around doing scut work, I decided to hang around my beautiful wife. A no-brainer, right?"

Mary Cole shook her head in wonder. "My pastor preached on Biblical miracles a few Sundays ago. He said miracles are natural events that happen at exactly the right moment. If this isn't a perfect example, I don't know what would be. You're home over the Christmas holidays. There will be parties all over town for you to be seen at."

Chapter 46

"MARY COLE, ARE YOU SUGGESTING THAT I SHOULD drag David around with me? He shouldn't have to satisfy a bunch of gossips. If you're right, wouldn't it be enough to have a party here, maybe a couple of dinners?"

"JJ, I don't think you realize how far this thing has gone—"

"Excuse me, Mary Cole," David broke in. "JJ, can I speak to you in the other room?"

———

When David had pulled her into a powder room off the wide entryway, JJ held up a restraining hand. "Stop. I'm not going to ask you to socialize night after night with people you don't know and have no interest in knowing."

David stifled ire and made his voice flat and even. "Correct me if I'm wrong. This whole thing rests on the question of whether you really have a husband or not. As it happens, you do. You're the one who doesn't seem convinced. Maybe if you start believing, it will be easier to convince others."

"It's just that this isn't any part of what you signed on for. And you don't know what you're letting yourself in for. Parties, dinners, events every night—sometimes two or three."

Did he know what he was getting into? If he had the gist of what had been said in the family room, Mary

Cole was suggesting his worst nightmare: hours and hours of unaccustomed, noisy surroundings in which he had to *stay focused on* what strangers were saying. And if he blundered because he wasn't keeping up, he would be a discredit to JJ.

He did okay one on one. As long as he knew the people and had background knowledge of the subject under discussion, he could handle a group. The person he could remember being had liked parties, enjoyed chatting with strangers—but he couldn't let his mind go there.

"Let me worry about jumping into Wilmington's social whirl. I already told you, this marriage will be as real as I can make it. A husband stands up for his wife. If you need me, then I want to be there."

She laid her palm on his chest—right over his heart. "Do you mean that?"

"I did then and I do now."

"Then, thank you."

"All right." He reached for the door. "Let's tell Mary Cole her work is done, and go home."

"Wait. I don't want to look a gift horse in the mouth, so to speak, but how did you happen to show up now?"

David had carefully prepared his story so that it would come out easily and seem reasonable. He didn't know what else to add. "I had leave coming. Is it so hard to believe I would choose to spend it with you?"

"Well, no—but it wasn't your plan when you left here."

"After I saw the doc, it made sense to me."

JJ's eyes narrowed. "So he didn't think you were ready to go back on duty either?"

"He was just being cautious." Before she could question him further, he drew her closer. He lifted her hair from her shoulder and nuzzled the scented skin of her neck. He had already learned her neck was her most vulnerable spot. Not necessarily what turned her on the most, but the place that got underneath her guard.

He couldn't believe he'd gotten lucky enough to choose to kiss her there the night they met on the beach — it was just as if he'd known what he was doing.

He kissed the place just behind her earlobe. She softened against him, and he cupped her breast. "We have twenty-eight days together. What do you say we make the most of it?"

Chapter 47

THE NEXT MORNING, JJ FOUND DAVID ON THE DECK. The sun, risen just above the horizon, trimmed purple clouds in vermillion and laid streaks of beaten gold on a flat, calm, peach-tinted ocean.

Her bare toes curled away from the cold, damp boards of the deck. She hugged her robe tighter. "Chilly out here." She took in the amount of skin exposed by David's khaki shorts, T-shirt, and running shoes. "Aren't you cold?"

"I'm already warmed up."

She yawned. "What are you doing?"

"Stretching."

"I can see that. Why?"

"Time for me to stop being lazy. Got to get back into running if I'm going to be fit for duty once my leave is up."

"Okay." Something about his casual tone belatedly registered. "You mean you haven't been running until now?"

"The doc didn't want me to until my face was healed enough."

Thinking perhaps one cold foot would be better than two, JJ rested one bare foot on top of the other. "Well then, are you okay to now?"

David looked up from his stretching and laughed suddenly. Tenderly. "You look like a little girl." He tilted her chin and dropped a gentle kiss on her lips. "Go inside now. Before your feet are frostbitten. I'll be back in a half-hour or so."

———

Dressed for work in a black skirt, black-and-white blouse, and red leather blazer, JJ looked up from filling her car coffee cup to see David, a towel around his middle, emerge from the guest bathroom.

Drops of water glistened on the backs of his shoulders. "Hey," she said.

He jerked. "Oh. Hey." He turned toward the guest bedroom where he had insisted on putting his things.

JJ followed him. He sat on the bed, staring at nothing, a pair of socks forgotten in his hands. He didn't look in the mood for a chat, but he had insisted they act married. That meant they had to make plans together. "Today is Tuesday. Brinkley is supposed to go to the vet to get his stitches out. How do you want to handle that?"

He finally looked up, his eyes lightless. "Handle what?"

"His stitches. Do you want me to come back for him, or do you want to bring him to me, and I'll take him to the vet, or what?"

"No need to pay for an office visit. I can remove them."

"Okay. Good. Today is also my ballroom lesson. Would you like to meet me there?"

The dark, distant look slowly left his eyes. "Sure you trust me after last time?"

JJ chuckled. "We won't go back to Lucas's house, that's for sure. I had to call an electrician to fix the sconce." Feeling a little more sure of her ground, JJ asked, "Are you okay? You seem a little…"

"Sure. I'm fine."

"Was the run okay?"

He shrugged. "Harder than I want to admit it was. You don't do it every day, you pay."

"Will you feel up to dancing?"

"I'm fine." He gave her a lazy up-and-down perusal. "Would you like a demonstration of just how fine I am?"

―――※※※―――

A couple of days later, JJ smiled at the man behind her in the bathroom mirror. Marriage was something she could get used to. He liked watching her put on makeup, he said. She understood. She liked watching him shave.

"Did I tell you I talked to Elle today?" she asked. It was nice to talk with a woman who knew him and could tell her stories about David as a boy. Was she acting like a woman in love or what?

She hadn't shared with Elle the vague disquiet she had felt the night before when she found a sheet of yellow notebook paper covered with numbers: 2x3, 2x4, 2x5… all the way through 9x2. He had written the multiplication tables. She considered mentioning it now but discarded the notion. She had already seen that if she asked anything about what he was doing or why, all she got were short answers. She was enjoying this intimate moment. Why spoil it?

"She and Harris doing okay?" David asked her.

JJ stroked on eyeliner. "They're fine. We talked about Christmas. I want Riley to come here."

"Here? To this house? That will never work. Riley hates sand. Even with shoes on, he can't stand the way it feels to walk on it. If it gets in his shoes, he freaks."

JJ did the other eye. "That's what Elle told me. I'll just have to find a solution."

"Nah. He'll be fine at their apartment in Charlottesville over the holidays. Whose party are we off to tonight?"

"Taylor Vaughan. She runs gossip central. After tonight, everyone will know you're here and you're real."

—◆◆◆—

The next evening, she decided to leave work a little early. When she arrived at the cottage, David was on the sofa, his laptop open. He blanked the screen before she could see what he was working on. It wasn't the first time. Not that she wanted to know any SEAL secrets, but his caution seemed extreme. JJ tried not to let his shutting her out hurt, but it did.

He set the laptop aside and rose smiling. No matter how secretive he was, it was impossible to believe a man who smiled like that wasn't glad to see her. She was making too much of it.

"Hey. You're home early." He circled her in his arms. She lifted her face for his kiss.

He studied her face. "What's the matter?"

"I finally had to fire Red today. It was hard."

"When you lose a man, no matter why, you always wonder what else you should have done. But you did the right thing. You've got a right to expect simple loyalty."

"I do. And I appreciate your showing me that."

"But you still feel bad."

"Yeah."

"Come in the bedroom. Let me make you feel better."

Chapter 48

THE SMOKY, VINEGARY AROMA COMING FROM THE TAKE-out bag of barbecue JJ had picked up on the way home was making her mouth water and her stomach growl. JJ shifted the barbecue to her other hand while she felt for her cottage key. She really should have a motion-sensor light installed for moments like this. By five-thirty these December evenings, full dark had arrived.

Finally she found the key and inserted it into the lock. For once, they didn't have anywhere they had to be. A whole evening alone. With her husband. The thought was almost as yummy as the barbeque.

Warm air and silence greeted her once she had the door open. The only light in the great room came from the hood over the cooktop. Making as little sound as possible—though she wasn't sure why—JJ put her bags and purse on the kitchen counter. She switched on a couple of lamps in the great room.

The door to the master bedroom was open. A quick glance told her David wasn't in there. Still not sure why she was being so quiet, JJ went down the hall.

David and Brinkley were stretched out on the bed in the guest room. This wasn't the first time she had found David doing what he called "napping," but this time she was sure he wasn't asleep. He was lying in exactly the too-still way Brinkley had when he had been in severe pain.

Brinkley raised his head when he saw her. He lifted his nose, caught a whiff of the barbeque, and jumped off the bed.

David opened his eyes. "Oh, hey. I must have nodded off.

JJ sat in the place Brinkley had vacated. "Are you sick?" She reached for his forehead.

He jerked his head away. "No, I'm fine. Fell asleep, that's all." He sat up.

"You ran today, didn't you? Don't give me that innocent look. You've got a headache again. You're always worse when you run. Maybe you're trying to do too much too soon."

David patted her hip with the back of his hand. When she moved out of his way, he stood, his back to her. "Running doesn't cause the headaches. I get them even if I don't run."

"Running makes them worse. You are not okay. You shouldn't be running."

"You don't understand. I have to be able to run 1.5 miles in seven minutes."

"But surely they don't expect a man who has just come back from sick leave to be able to do that? Surely they have trainers, or whatever you call them, who will help."

He ignored that as he did most of her suggestions. "I'm going to get better. The docs have told me I've just got to give it time. That's all." He walked out of the bedroom.

JJ followed him into the great room, aware she was arguing with someone who had turned his back on her. She ought to shut up, but she couldn't stand to see him putting himself through this day after day.

"You're not improving, from what I can tell. I'm not real impressed with Navy doctors right this minute—if this is the best they can do for you. Let me make an appointment with a doctor in town. If we don't like their answers, we'll go somewhere else. We'll find out who Bronwyn says is the best and go there."

"It won't matter what doctor I go to. They will say the same thing."

"And what will that be?"

David hesitated. Suddenly all the clues, the bits and pieces JJ couldn't quite make sense of, came together.

"You didn't *tell* the doctor the symptoms you were having, did you?"

"We discussed it, sure."

JJ had learned to recognize the answer that sounded like information but wasn't. "Did you tell him at all?" Her eyes narrowed. "*You didn't*. You lied. You told him you were fine."

"I am."

She disregarded that. "And he didn't believe you, did he? You didn't fool him." She was on a roll now. His face was stony, giving nothing away, but she didn't need him to admit it. She knew she was right. "You knew you couldn't even do limited duty—not if it meant you had to run. You wouldn't have taken personal leave otherwise. You'd just had thirty days. You wouldn't have returned to North Carolina."

JJ sank down on the sofa before her legs gave way. More to herself than him, she murmured, "I saw what I wanted to see. I believed you were so besotted that you chose to be with me." She had thought he chose to use his leave because he wanted the time, as she did, to grow closer, to establish a real foundation for a real marriage.

The irony that she was upset that she had gotten the marriage she bargained for, and no longer wanted, wasn't lost on her, but it did nothing for the squeezing pain that threatened to cut off her air. Not only was she second choice, he didn't want to share the most fundamental things about himself, the things that mattered most.

He had hurt her. She wasn't crying, but JJ didn't cry much. The main way he could tell was the bleak look in her eyes, the fragile way she had lowered herself to the sofa. He hadn't meant to. He would cut off his arm before hurting her. "Come on, JJ. You're bound to know by now I want to be with you."

"Oh, I don't doubt that you enjoy being around me, and you love the sex. I know you believe in fidelity, so if you were going to be on leave, of course you came here. I just thought, I hoped, when you came back, it meant there was something more."

More? It had been more in every way. Both easier and harder than he had had any idea. Easier because just being in the same room with her was satisfying and the sex was off the charts. In bed they had a flawless communication like he'd never before experienced.

But it was harder, too. He could *feel* her frustration when he couldn't tell her what was going on with him, couldn't explain why her suggestions wouldn't work. He hated what he was doing to her.

Now that she knew he might not ever be a SEAL again, he wondered how long it would be before she thought he was too much trouble—especially with all her other responsibilities. If she knew the full extent of his problems, she might even want to send him to a hospital for trauma cases. Some place that would straighten him out or at least take the burden of his care away.

He would take himself away before that happened. He'd go away now, but she needed a "visible" husband, and right now it was the one thing he could do for her. Every time he made love to her, he tried to show her how he felt.

"JJ—"

She waved him away. "Don't worry. You haven't done anything wrong. It was my mistake. I'll get over it. I think I'll change clothes."

In the bedroom, she pulled on loose jeans and an old sweatshirt. Back in the living room, she went to the box where they stored walking shoes so that they didn't track so much sand into the house.

David watched her impassively, his fists on his hips. "What are you doing?"

"I think I'll go for a walk."

"Alone?"

"Alone."

"It's dark. It's too dangerous."

"I'll take Brinkley."

"I know he would try, but he's not a trained guard dog." David pulled his much larger shoes from the box. "Okay, I'll go with you."

JJ swallowed a lump in her throat, trying to be as

low-key as he was. "I'd rather you didn't. I really need to be alone."

"No problem. I'll walk protection detail. I'll be behind you. If you want me to, I'll make sure you don't see me. You won't know I'm there."

"You would walk behind so I could be alone and be protected at the same time?"

He gave her a patient look and went back to tying his shoes.

"But we just argued. Or at least, I did. Aren't you pissed? Happy to have me out of your sight for a few minutes?"

"It doesn't matter how I feel."

The statement hung in the air. He had just stated a profound truth about himself. It wasn't that he didn't feel, didn't want to feel, or was afraid to feel. It was that, as far as he was concerned, his feelings were beside the point.

The clear brown depths of his eyes lit with the dry, understated humor she had come to love. It was so much a part of who he was. "I've protected people I like a whole lot less than you."

No matter how hurt she was that he wouldn't share what he was going through, JJ couldn't deliberately hold him at a distance. She chuckled. "I do need a walk. Why don't you come with me?"

The ocean was calm. Small, wide-spaced breakers made leisurely trips to deposit their cream on the shore. The tide was going out. They walked on the wet sand just beyond the pale glow of scallops of foam left by departing waves.

They walked the beach silently. JJ was still dealing with the newly revealed facts of her marriage.

After she thought about it for a while, she realized

no adjustment was necessary. She felt the same way she had felt for a long time. It distressed her that he closed off part of himself from her, but she didn't have less than she'd had before she married him. She had more. In every way. Which reminded her that she needed to talk to him about his brothers and sister—hers too, now.

"Lucas stopped by Caruthers today." He had taken to doing that again. Dropping in for just a minute. The staff enjoyed his visits. He was careful not to stay too long or get in the way. "I think I've got the Riley problem solved. Lucas wants to invite your brothers and sister to stay at his house over Christmas."

"You don't have to do this, you know. I'll pick up Riley and take him to Charlottesville."

David's objection was immediate and no surprise. However, JJ was ready for him.

"Sorry, no deal. You made me Riley's guardian."

"If anything happens to me."

"Well, as far as I'm concerned, it has."

"You think I'm incapacitated, don't you?"

"I think you're making poor decisions. There *are* other doctors. Other places you can go. But I'm not going to go around again with you. In the last couple of weeks, I've gotten much better at telling when someone is willing to listen. It won't matter what I say… you're not listening to me. Riley and Elle and Harris are coming here for Christmas. Deal with it."

"Does Lucas know what he's letting himself in for? Riley has a longer vacation than the twins do."

"He likes Riley. They get along. When he's had all he can stand of Riley going on and on about one of his enthusiasms, he just nods off. And Lucas has wanted a bigger family for years. I think he's delighted to have some honorary grandchildren."

"How do you fecl about it?" That was another thing. He might disregard his feelings, but David had no difficulty understanding her feelings or listening to them. In fact, he understood her remarkably well.

"I think it will work. Esperanza will love having guests to do for. We can go over there for dinner, and they can come here. You can take them around while I'm at work."

They talked over plans. After a while, David said. "It's going to be hard for them. Their first Christmas without their mother."

JJ didn't point out that it was his first Christmas without his mother, too. He'd have some reason that that was beside the point.

Chapter 49

JJ SURVEYED THE ENTRYWAY AT LUCAS'S HOUSE, TRYING to decide what to do about Christmas decorations. She had done nothing last year until she'd felt so guilty she'd called a florist and had them deliver a door wreath and decorated tree for Esperanza to put wherever she wanted to.

Her grandmother had always transformed the house into a Christmas extravaganza, an exuberant over-abundance of arrangements of holly, ivy, nandina, and magnolia in every room, boxwood garlands up the balustrade, spruce wreaths on every outside door, red velvet bows on *everything*, including the grandfather clock JJ was looking at right now. The plethora of red and green was so unlike her grandmother's usual understated elegance that the house had felt as if some excess of emotion within her grandmother had finally exploded.

After listening to her grandfather's story at breakfast the other morning, JJ thought maybe something *had*, and, instead of being so restrained, her grandmother would have been better off to find a balance between self-control and self-expression all year long.

JJ was finally learning that lesson herself.

Ham materialized beside her. He followed the direction of her gaze. "Me and Miz Beth, we always strung garlands up the stairs."

"I know. Unfortunately, what goes up must come down. It will make a lot of extra work for you and Esperanza."

"How 'bout I make some of those greenery arrangements? I know how. Miz Beth and me, we'd work on 'em together."

In the past, JJ would have told Ham not to bother; she'd order something from the florist. Now she said, "If you feel like it, that would be lovely."

"How many?"

"You know which vases she used. Make as many arrangements as you like."

The jerky little nod of his head was Ham's only sign of assent, but that was Ham. Ham didn't waste words. He also didn't walk away, so she knew he had another talking point on his agenda.

"Your man. He's got shell shock, don't he?"

"Shell shock?"

"That's what they used to call it. Guy had been in battle, shells exploding all around him. Sometimes there wouldn't be a mark on him. Afterwards he was a little strange—sometimes a lot strange. He couldn't sleep. Stared at nothing. Shook.

"In Vietnam, they told us won't no such thing as shell shock. It was 'combat fatigue.' 'Course, soldiers kept getting it, so then, they called it Post-Traumatic Stress Disorder.

"Guy feels out of it. Disconnected. He don't know who he *is*, but he's not himself. Can't focus. Can't make plans. Doesn't always remember what he did yesterday. Family can't put their finger on it, but they know he don't behave like he used to. Don't live up to his responsibilities. His wife leaves him. His folks, they try, but they don't know what to do. After a while, he figures they're better off without him. He's a grown man—they're not supposed to be looking after him. He doesn't make sense to anyone, least of all to himself."

"Ham, you're talking about yourself, aren't you? Do you think traumatic brain injury is why you drank?"

"I reckon why a man's a drunk don't make no never mind."

JJ saw that he wasn't going to answer. She didn't want to make him uncomfortable by probing further. Still, his nonanswer was an answer of sorts. His reaction to being asked to discuss his own experience and draw inferences from it was similar to David's. The fear that David didn't want her to know about his problems lessened.

"Watch out for your man, JJ," Ham told her. "He don't know how to ask for what he needs."

Chapter 50

"I AM BOUND AND DETERMINED I'M GOING TO FIND somewhere that can help David. I've read brochures on the Internet until I'm cross-eyed," JJ complained to Bronwyn. She was unloading on Bronwyn, and she knew it.

David stonewalled her every effort. She was in the dark trying to understand what he needed. But after Ham's revelations, she understood David was not deliberately being obstructive. "I see lots of therapies, but nothing that fits him. What's going on with him is so subtle, yet so pervasive. But the programs I can find are designed for someone much worse than he is."

"That's true."

"Being competent is so much a part of him. If they ask him questions about his self-help skills, they're just going to make him mad. One woman just wouldn't listen. She asked, 'Can he dress himself?' I told her he could put on his wetsuit by himself, surf for six hours, and remove it by himself."

She huffed in frustration. "Do you know what her next question was? 'How about preparing simple meals for himself?'" JJ laughed ironically. "I know they have their list they have to go through. It's just so frustrating trying to ask for what he needs, when I don't know exactly what that is, myself.

"And you know the other thing? I've finally realized the 'therapy' they are talking about is to teach him skills and strategies for coping with the brain damage. I'm not faulting that, but I finally understood nothing they do will actually heal the damage. It's like the difference between a broken leg and an amputated one. With both, you might need crutches, but if the leg was broken, it will heal. You will have two working legs again. Oh, Bronwyn. I understand why he wants to deny that the TBI is a problem. I want to deny it, too."

JJ swiped at tears she had sworn she wasn't going to shed. "You know what he told me? He dreamed he died in Afghanistan, and it felt wonderful. He was happy. I'm not sure he's happy he lived. And now I read about the high incidence of suicide in those returning from Iraq and Afghanistan."

"Are you worried about suicide?"

"I don't know. A little. He won't tell me how he feels, but I'm afraid if he becomes hopeless…"

"Okay, I've been doing some research, too," Bronwyn told her. "I've found what might be good news. Brain damage is not as inevitably permanent as was once thought. Some researchers feel that some of the injury associated with blasts is caused by damage to the nerve synapses in the brain, and they can regrow. Something that I think worth looking into is hyperbaric oxygen therapy."

"Hyperbaric—is that like the pressure chamber they use for divers who have the bends?"

"That's right. Also for diabetic wounds, gangrene. Helping broken bones to heal. Crush injuries. There are reports that hyperbaric oxygen therapy helps TBI. It's considered off-label, meaning it's not an FDA-approved use of HBOT—that's the abbreviation for hyperbaric oxygen therapy—but the Air Force has a grant to research HBOT's effectiveness with brain injury. I don't know when they are supposed to release their findings. No reputable medical person is going to tell you it will work, but there is reason to think it might—and no reason to think it will make him worse."

"Where do I take him?" Not that getting him to agree would be easy. He stonewalled her every suggestion.

"I found an HBOT center in California run by former SEALs."

"SEALs?" The upsurge of hope made JJ dizzy. "I think he would listen to SEALs!"

"Why don't you give them a call?"

JJ pushed the off button on her phone. She stared out the window a long time, thinking about all she had learned about HBOT, its role in treating TBI, and treatment protocols.

Raul Chavez, former SEAL and former hospital corpsman, had spent most of an hour listening to her and talking about hyperbaric oxygen therapy and how it worked.

Hyperbaric therapy forced more oxygen into tissues. It wouldn't restore lost brain cells—he was careful to make that clear. However, it could speed healing. A possibility with mild TBI was that many cells were still alive but not functioning because they were starved for oxygen or had lost connections to other cells. If they could get oxygen, the cells could, in effect, turn on again. They could regrow the tiny connections to other cells and the capillaries that supplied blood.

Raul wasn't surprised by some of David's attitudes. JJ was comforted to have someone who understood both the problem and what it meant to be a SEAL.

"He's in horrible pain sometimes," she told Raul, "and I've begun to think he's in *some* pain all of the time. Why won't he tell the doctors? There are medications that could be tried, but he refuses to consider them."

"Oh, I can answer that."

"Then please do."

"The docs have most likely suggested anti-seizure drugs or serotonin re-uptake inhibitors—antidepressants. If he takes either one, there goes his security clearance. Without security clearance, he can't operate."

"So, even if the drugs work, they will prevent him from operating."

"If they offer the drugs and he refuses them, he is seen as noncompliant. Which would be another reason for medical discharge."

"He really is between a rock and a hard place. I see now why he would rather try to live with the pain and hope it will go away.

"He either can't or won't tell me what it's like on the inside to have TBI. A Vietnam vet I know told me he has shell shock. He said it's the same thing as combat fatigue and PTSD."

"He might be right. Kevlar helmets make injuries survivable that wouldn't have been in previous wars, and since IEDs are the weapon of choice in Iraq and Afghanistan, there is even more possibility of the blast type of brain injury. Some of the symptoms of PTSD are indistinguishable from blast TBI."

"He keeps saying, 'I just want my life back.' At first

I thought he was saying he wanted to operate again, but now I think he means something more."

"Did you know him before his injury."

"Briefly. Not well."

"Is he the same man?"

"No."

"That's his problem."

When she finished the call, JJ understood what was driving some of the behavior that had seemed so unreasonable. She knew why David resisted consulting specialists. He wanted to leave no record of being treated for TBI.

Therefore, the best news of all was that it was possible to buy HBOT chambers for use in the home.

———

JJ thanked the technicians who had driven overnight to deliver and set up the hyperbaric oxygen therapy chamber in one of the upstairs bedrooms in her grandfather's house—the best location, she and Lucas had agreed. "Shoot, if it's here, I might try it myself," he'd said. "Maybe it will make my brain work better, too."

JJ had ordered a top-of-the-line, single-person chamber, made of a shiny white fabric that stretched over a metal form. The technicians demonstrated the set-up procedure and let her climb in to try it. It was roomy enough for two people to sit in, or for even a large adult to lie down.

Feeling the most hopeful and celebratory she'd felt in a while, JJ peeled the paper off the sticky-tab of a huge, red velvet bow. She placed it on the HBOT at a jaunty angle.

Chapter 51

"I HAVE SOMETHING TO SHOW YOU." DAVID ALLOWED JJ TO take his arm and lead him toward the stairs in her grandfather's house. Her cheeks were pink, she was smiling, and there was a light in her eyes he hadn't seen in a while. He knew she was fretting over him. He hated it. She'd married a SEAL because she wanted someone who would stay away. Nothing seemed to convince her he didn't want or need her to take care of him. She'd finally stopped with her suggestions of topflight neurologists and therapy centers a few days ago.

He'd already made up his mind that if the docs wouldn't return him to duty, he'd take the medical discharge and get out of her life.

The pain wasn't bad this afternoon. It was easy to go along with her lightened mood. Too frequently, he hadn't been able to. Getting back into shape was harder than he had thought. Running with a headache wasn't pleasant, but he'd done it before. He had thought if he stayed with it, he would eventually be able to run even when running brought on attacks of nerve pain.

He grinned. "Baby Jane, I think I've seen it before, but I'm perfectly willing to look at it again."

JJ poked him in the chest. "Not that. This is special."

"That's pretty special, too."

"Stop with the double entendre. I'm serious."

"Okay," he clicked his fingers for Brinkley to

stop snuffling around the hall and follow them up the curving stairs.

At the top of the steps, JJ led him to one of the guest rooms. She threw open the door with a big smile. "I imagine you know what this is."

"It's a hyperbaric chamber. What's it for?"

"It's for you, silly."

"Why?"

"I told you about it. That HBOT is useful in treating TBI."

"Oh yeah. The place the SEALs are running out in California." He'd made a note to work out how to use his Navy connections to try it.

He'd been a little chagrined that JJ had discovered this use for HBOT, but not because he was a SEAL and should have known. He was a combat medic. When SEALs needed hyperbaric treatment, the Navy had specially trained technicians. The real reason he didn't know was that his reading was still too slow and he lost his place too easily to use the Internet effectively.

JJ lovingly patted the cloth cylinder that looked like a cross between a backpacking tent and a space capsule. "You refused to go there, so I figured it would just have to come to you."

"You bought it?"

"Yes. I could have rented, but renting was so expensive—"

"You *bought* it?"

"Yes."

"A thirty-thousand-dollar piece of equipment?"

"Twenty-nine. But with delivery and insurance, yes, a little over thirty thousand."

"David needs an HBOT, so I'll just pick up the phone and order one?"

"What's wrong with that?"

"Any problem you see, you solve it by throwing money at it. Do you think you can make me better by throwing money at this problem, too?"

"Throw money at it! Where did you get the idea I do that?"

"You do it all the time." He mimed a phone to his ear. "'Would you send over an HBOT, please? I'd like it delivered in an hour.' You want an example? We can start with the fact that you wanted to pay me to marry you and then get out of your life."

"Don't go all holy and self-righteous on me! You married me to get the money for your brothers and sister."

"Haven't you figured it out yet? I married you because I friggin' wanted you. I don't want your money. I don't want your stuff. I don't want friggin' thirty-thousand-dollar Christmas presents. I want you, dammit. I love you."

"I know."

"You do?"

"Yes, and I love you, too," she snapped, obviously unimpressed by his declaration. "I'm not trying to buy love from you or prove my love or anything else. Your problem with this is your issue. Not mine."

"Issue? What do you mean?" Anyway, when had it become about him?

JJ crossed her arms under her breasts and tapped her toe. "When you were a kid, *you* decided that everybody was supposed to be part of the family but you. Everybody was supposed to get your mother's love and attention *but you*. They were younger, more fragile, and needed support more than you did. You came to that conclusion when you recognized that she was overwhelmed because *you* are strong and generous and willing to sacrifice *yourself* to look after people."

"Wait a minute. You've been talking to Elle. This is her theory."

"I happen to think she's right, but I had already concluded it on my own. If we're going to make a family, at some point you have to decide the family's resources are for you, too." She poked him in the chest with a sharp fingernail.

David backed away, but she came after him. "When are *you* going to figure it out?" She poked him again. "The money comes with me. Are we married or not? I thought we were. I thought that meant I was supposed to do things for you occasionally. You've given me so much the last few weeks. Out of your vitality, you've given me life. Not money, but a kind of abundance I didn't know existed." Her eyes shot out icy green sparks. "But you're saying it's only supposed to flow one way—from you to me.

"I guess it comes down to this. You married me, but are you going to let me marry you?" She threw up her hands. "What the hell. You don't want to let me share in your life. Fine. Use the HBOT. If it works, you can *have your life back*. That's what you always say you want. You got along without me before. We don't have to wait a year. I'll set you free to go have *your* life. We can be divorced by the end of January."

"You can't do that. What about your grandfather?"

"What about him?"

"He'll say you reneged. He'll carry out his threat to sell Caruthers."

"Let him. I can live without it."

"You can?"

"My umpty-great-grandfather built that business. I can build another one—or find something I like better. I can take the people who want to come with me and help the others to find something else."

"But you love it."

"I thought I loved the business because it gave me security and felt like a family. I found out it's the other way around. It gave me security and felt like a family because I loved it. Caruthers was a place that made my world safe and orderly when I was a child. But I'm not a child anymore. I have security inside myself. In my heart. In the love I feel for you, for all of you. I can lose the business... I can even lose you, but I can't lose love I give."

He went for the part of that he understood. "You love me?"

"Yes. I don't want to be married to you so I can save a business or save other people. Not anymore. I want to be married to you, just because I do. But no more deals. No more contracts. No more quid pro quo. Just love."

She peeled the giant red bow off the fabric cylinder and stuck it on the center of her chest, over her heart. "Take it or leave it."

Chapter 52

HERE SHE STOOD IN THE MIDDLE OF THE SPARE BEDROOM, bed and other furnishings shoved against the wall to make room for a contraption that pressurized air for the purpose of squeezing oxygen into people's bodies, with a red velvet bow blooming on her chest.

She had no idea what time it was or what she was scheduled to do next. This was life in all its confusing, chaotic, engrossing, heart-wrenching glory. And she was in the thick of it.

Before her stood the man who was her heart's desire. And in the confusing, messy way of love, all she wanted was to give him his heart's desire. She had begun only knowing that if the HBOT helped him, and he *got his life back*, he might decide he didn't want her at all.

And the next thing she knew, she had a bow on her chest and was offering, not her help, but herself.

The thing was, whatever was going to happen, however this was going to turn out, was in the future, and life wasn't lived in the future. Life was now.

Irrelevantly, she noticed that having shoved the furniture all around but having left the paintings hanging as they were, the paintings now looked unbalanced and haphazard. She thought that was a metaphor of some kind, demonstrating that life is all about relationships, and when one thing shifted, everything else did, too, whether it *moved* or not.

After what might have been forever or might have been no time at all, David's clear brown eyes lit. The corners of his mouth lifted. With one beautifully modeled arm, he reached out and plucked the bow from her chest.

"I'll take it. I'll take you and whatever comes with you."

"For better or for worse, for richer or for poorer, whether it makes *you* richer or poorer?"

"Yes."

"Together in sickness and in health, meaning *your sickness* and *your health*, as well as mine?"

"You drive a hard bargain, lady." He kissed her solemnly. "I do."

Chapter 53

Raul, the SEAL, had recommended sessions of one hour twice a day for at least forty sessions. Every brain and every brain injury was different. There was no telling what improvement there would be—or when they would see it—or even if there would be any improvement at all.

The experience of being in the HBOT wasn't unpleasant. There was a sense of pressure in the ears, much like diving, and in fact, the slang for HBOT sessions was *dive*.

David almost postponed the first dive because the nerve pain in his face was worse that morning. He wanted to give the process a fair chance.

In fact, the dive didn't make it worse. The pain was considerably better afterwards and didn't return for several hours. After the second dive, the pain was gone for longer. After the third, he ran. The pain returned but was much less severe and didn't last for hours as it had before.

He didn't get too excited. Though this wasn't typical trigeminal neuralgia, nerve pain of its type could go into remission for unknown reasons and return for equally obscure ones. He'd had a couple of days without pain before. And days when there were only a couple of very short episodes.

Like a lot of SEALs, he was obsessive about keeping statistics on his performance. At the end of a week, he checked his notes. There had been no pain at all for forty-eight hours. By the end of the second week, the nerve pain had not appeared for nine days. It never returned.

"Who knows?" was Raul's diagnosis. "Maybe there was inflammation or swelling. The hyperbaric oxygen does help reduce both. Maybe something needed to heal, and the dive speeded the process."

The dull, always present ache around his eye was less dramatic but steady in its improvement.

On Saturday, JJ came home to the cottage with presents for his brothers and Elle that she wanted to show him. After a few minutes she said, "You act like you're really enjoying hearing about this."

"I am," he said, and meant it. Thinking back, he could recall several conversations lately he had found enjoyable and entertaining. He had always been gregarious, extraverted. He had no idea how much of the pleasure of hanging out and talking he had lost until it was restored. Talking with JJ was the best. Sometimes they talked late into the night. He couldn't put his finger on why it was better. It was simply more interesting.

Numbers started to make *sense* again. They were just *there*, no fumbling around, the way they were supposed to be.

He and JJ drove to Riley's school to bring him home for vacation. On the way home, Riley announced he had decided to become a neurologist and talked non-stop for an hour about brain chemistry, brain structure, and nanotechnology, which he informed them was the future of neurology. Trying to focus for so long would have made David frantic even a couple of weeks ago. Instead, he enjoyed his younger brother's chatter and drew him out further with questions.

"Is everyone in your family medically oriented?" JJ laughed when there was a lull in their talk. "Did you ever want to go to medical school?"

"I had four semesters of premed," David admitted. "Then I wanted action. Excitement."

"Would you like to finish med school when you get out of the Navy?"

"I think I'd like to work with kids," he told her. "I love kids." He read the surprise on her face. "What? I never told you that?"

"David," Riley, who had been silent for a while, interrupted, "do you think I could try a dive? I have read about it on the Internet. Some people say it helps autistic kids. I read about one kid it made less sensitive to noise. Do you think I would be scared?"

"I'll do it with you. We'll play cards."

Later that evening, after seeing Riley settled in with Lucas, David and JJ returned to the cottage.

"What are you thinking about?" JJ asked David when she found him sitting in the darkened living room, looking out the sliders at the night beach, Brinkley at his feet. It was a question she wouldn't have asked him a couple a weeks before. He would have said, "Nothing," or in some way let her know he didn't want to go into it.

"I remembered something today when we were with Riley. I remembered waking up in the hospital, and Mom was there. I remember being real confused but not wanting to let her know."

Seeing he was disposed to talk, she sank down beside him on the sofa. "Why not?"

"I think it was what you said. I thought I had failed her in some way. I wasn't supposed to worry her."

"You were trying to protect her from knowing you were hurt?"

"I think so. Anyway, I didn't want to tell her I didn't know where I was—because that might worry her—so I asked her if she knew where *she* was."

He let his head loll on the thick back cushion of the sofa, his teeth showing white, laughing at the memory. Then he sobered. "I wanted to ask her about Riley and Harris and Elle, but I couldn't say their names. It wasn't that I didn't remember. I couldn't bring their names from the storage place. Does that make sense?"

"Yes, I think so."

"I asked her where were her babies. And she said," his voice thickened, "'you're my baby.'"

JJ took his hand. His hard, masculine, long-fingered hand. "You were her first baby."

"I kept trying to tell her about the dream I had in Afghanistan."

"The one in which you dreamed you died?"

"Yeah. I could tell I wasn't making any sense. What I wanted her to tell me was if that really happened, but all I could say was 'I dreamed I was dead and then I was awake.'"

"Do you think maybe you did die, or had one of those near-death experiences?"

"I think I came real close. Maybe I did and came back. Who knows?"

"I'm glad you came back." She lifted the hand she held to her lips. It was the kind of affectionate gesture he would have avoided a couple of weeks ago. Now he smiled.

"Me, too." He returned to his story. "I wasn't making much sense, and she kept saying 'It's okay, you're awake now,' and I was babbling on about dying and her being there, crying, and trying explain that she didn't have to cry because it was okay. If I died, it was okay… and she started sobbing."

"Then, you mean? In the hospital?"

"Right. I asked her why she was crying. She said because she was so happy I was alive."

"Was that the last time you saw her?"

"What happened when is still kind of confused, but I don't think so. I think she was there a couple more times."

"Why do you think you remembered this now?"

"I'm remembering a lot of things now. No, it's not so much that I remember. It's more like I can put things together now. I thought for a long time the wrong one of us died."

"You don't think that now?"

"No. She was glad I was alive. That's what I needed to remember."

"I'm glad you told me that. I like knowing more about your family."

"Yep." He stood and picked up Brinkley's leash. "Come on, Brink. Let's go out and water some bushes so we can go to bed."

Chapter 54

FOR HIS LAST TRIP OUTSIDE BEFORE BED, DAVID USUALLY took Brinkley to the street-facing side of the cottage, so they could walk along the traffic-less blacktop. The dog couldn't get the hang of wiping sand from between his toes. Walking on the blacktop instead of the beach saved the need to rinse him before he could come back inside.

Fog had rolled in. It blew in wispy chunks between nearby street lamps and turned the ones that receded into the distance into little more than glowing reminders of civilization's presence.

On the ocean side of the cottage, the sea kept up its ever-present murmurs. On the street side, every jingle of the dog's tags fell into emptiness of noise so profound that silence itself was an entity. It was so quiet David could hear himself think.

JJ had said she liked hearing about his mother. She might want to see the picture of his father, Carl. Carl had given David's mother the diamond JJ now wore. The shoe box of odds and ends was still in the trunk of his car where he had tossed it when he left his apartment in Virginia Beach.

While Brinkley sniffed bushes to make sure no other dogs had been marking his territory, and if they had, making sure they understood whose turf this was, David opened the trunk and retrieved the memories of love his mother had stored for him.

He heard JJ running water in the bathroom when he shut the redwood door on the damp, dark, deserted street. The cottage was warm. He inhaled deeply of the fragrance of contentment and JJ.

With Brinkley settled in his bed for the night, lamps in the living room turned out, and the lock on the sliders checked, he carried the box into the bedroom and laid it on the beach color-splashed bedspread.

In the closet, dropping his discarded jeans into the hamper, he suddenly wondered what had become of the jeweler's box the ring had been in. He'd like to keep it with the mementoes, since his mother had saved it all those years.

The last he remembered, he had put it in a pants pocket. He began going through his dress slacks. He didn't find the box, but in one pair of slacks he found a silk pouch with "It's all about the ride" embroidered on it.

He chuckled at the memory of purloining it from JJ's bedroom at Lucas's house. He probably ought to sneak it back where he'd found it and never admit to anything. He tugged at the tiny snap closure. Yep, that's what he ought to do—not that there was a chance in hell he would—not until he'd discovered what it contained first.

He studied the colorful scraps of lace and elastic thongs that fell into his palm, aware of that déjà vu tickle of memory, except, he realized, this wasn't déjà vu.

He had seen a thong like these, and recently.

JJ found him sitting on the foot of the bed, a Nike shoe box open beside him, when she padded barefoot from the bathroom. He was naked. JJ thought she was comfortable nude, but she'd never seen anyone who got naked as readily or as unself-consciously as he did. The lamplight gilded his powerful shoulders, noticeably browner these days since he often ran shirtless.

JJ unzipped her skirt and stepped out of it. "What do you have there?"

"It was you." His eyes were dark and full of pain when he raised them. "Why, JJ? Why didn't you tell me?"

"What was me?" She had never seen him like this. Never heard him sound like this.

He opened his fist. A little silken pouch slid from his fingers to the peachy-gray carpet.

She dropped the skirt on a chair and knelt to pick up what he had dropped. "This was a gag gift from Bronwyn. Where did you find it?" She laid her hand on his dark, hair-roughened thigh. "David? Tell me what's wrong."

Slowly he reached into the shoe box at his side. "Remember this?" He held out another thong, ecru. He stretched it between two fingers so she could see the Mustang logo.

For a minute, she didn't make the connection. Then she did.

She sat back on her heels. "You found that? And you've kept it? All this time?"

"Why did you lie? Why did you tell me we 'met'? Like it was no more significant than a handshake."

She rubbed her forehead. "If you will recall, you strolled up to me and said, 'Do I know you from somewhere?'" She rose to her feet. Trying to master her anger, she stalked to the closet and jerked out a skirt hanger. She rounded on him. "Give me a break, David!

What did you expect me to say? 'Yes, I know you, but only in the Biblical sense.'"

She inserted the skirt waistband into the hanger clips with short, jerky movements. "The question was something less than flattering, you know."

"I'm still waiting to hear why."

She hung the skirt in the closet and returned. "'Why?' Do you really think I should have greeted you with open arms?"

"That's not the question. The question is, why didn't you tell me the truth?"

"All right. You want to know? For one solid year I had felt disgusted with myself every time I remembered that night. I had sex with a total stranger. I didn't even know his last name." She turned her eyes heavenward. "Talk about wasting my upset on nothing. A turning point in my life—my absolute all-time low—was a non-event to you. You didn't even remember it happened! Do you really believe I had any reason to want to reminisce?"

He squeezed the thong in his fist, then opened his fingers and watched the flesh-colored elastic rebound.

"Your absolute all-time low was an evening with me."

"I didn't mean it like that."

"I didn't know your name. That was my all-time low."

"What? How?"

"In hindsight, I could see that something had been bothering you. I didn't know what was wrong, but I had only made it worse. But had I paid attention? No, I ignored it because I wanted you. And if I wanted a girl—hey, what other consideration was there?"

"Well, you offered to beat somebody up for me. That's got to count for something."

He smiled at her attempt to lighten the moment but shook his head. "Nah. I was careless. I was living way too fast. I thought getting to know someone just slowed me. And why should I have to ? I was so wonderful that girls were honored to spend an evening with me. God, I was an arrogant bastard. It was pathetically easy for me to believe you had been overcome by my charms." He snorted with disgust. "You set me straight. You defended yourself with a shoe. You said, 'Don't make me regret sex with you more than I already do.'"

"That really bothered you."

"Yeah. I dreamed about you. Dreamed I was looking for you everywhere. And when I was awake, I did look for you. I'd see a woman with hair the brown of yours." He lifted a lock of her hair. "For a minute, I'd think it was you—even when I was in—" He laughed apologetically. "Well, a really unlikely place for you to be." He stoked her cheek. "Didn't you have any idea how glad I was to see you? Or how crazy it felt?"

"I thought… I don't know… maybe you had so many notches on your belt, you'd lost count. At first I didn't know whether to be insulted or relieved, but once I thought about it, I was mostly relieved. I thought you could and would take any relationship we had lightly."

"You thought I was that shallow. I was. The only time I wasn't was when I was operating."

"No, David. I look back on it now, and I think I was the shallow one. I was the one who expected nothing real or meaningful from a relationship. I thought someone who cared about me would just be a burden. You kept saying there was more and expecting more of me. I haven't been deliberately withholding the truth about that night. When

I got to know you, the *truth* is, I kind of forgot, myself. Whatever had happened didn't matter anymore. You were a different person by then, and so was I."

"I never forgot you, even though my brains were scrambled. Every time I touched you, I'd have this crazy feeling like *I know her*. You want to know what else? The thong? I'd come across it and think, *I ought to get rid of that*. I'm not one to keep souvenirs. But I couldn't make myself do it."

"And it came together for you tonight?"

"Yep. My brain is clearer and making more connections all the time."

"I'm sorry I let you believe nothing happened that night. I didn't intend to confuse you. But I'm glad you remember it all now. Consciously. You see, I've worried, if you got better, if you got your life back, you would one day go off and forget me again."

"Never. I knew, even then, what a terrible mistake I had made. I knew I had been given the pearl of great price and dropped it. Now I know you, body, mind, and soul." He lifted her hand and kissed the finger on which she wore his ring.

The ring represented the full circle. The love which has no end. The love of the father he never knew, the mother's love he had reclaimed this night, the life that may have ended in Afghanistan but had begun again with this woman.

He lifted her hand so he could look into the green fire of her eyes. "I am joined with you, and you are joined with me, body, mind, and soul." He kissed the ring. "And we are SEALed with a ring."

Epilogue

"THIS IS THE LAST PARTY, I PROMISE." JJ HUGGED DAVID'S arm as they went up the sidewalk toward Senator Calhoun's mansion in the historic district of Wilmington. As directed, they had parked in the Baptist church parking lot a couple of blocks away. They had elected to walk instead of waiting for one of the courtesy vans that was ferrying guests to the door.

"I'm sort of looking forward to this one," David admitted. "Do you think The Idiot will be here?"

JJ didn't have to ask who The Idiot was. It's what David always called Blount. "That's what Mary Cole says. Why do you ask? You're not planning to do anything SEAL-ish are you?"

"I understand Mary Cole's battle plan perfectly. We're supposed to meet and greet him amicably in impeccable company."

JJ thought he looked a little too sincere, but she let it drop. She returned to the previous subject. "If you never want to go to another one, you don't have to."

"I haven't minded. I'm the envy of every man everywhere we go. Does great things for my ego, knowing I'm with the most beautiful woman there."

"I'll bet all the attention from the women doesn't hurt, either. The scar has healed amazingly."

"One of the effects of HBOT."

"It's almost invisible. It really does look like character

lines now. And I don't think either one of us knew how much swelling there was around your eye until it went away. I'm going to have to start carrying a baseball bat to beat the women off you."

He stopped her. "No, you won't. Not now. Not ever. You are the only woman I want. I already have the best one. The only one I want to go home with. The only one I want to wake up beside."

"Good—oh, look!" JJ pointed to a couple already at the top of the mansion steps. "Is that Jax and Pickett going in?"

On the inside, they surrendered their coats to a young woman and quickly found Jax and Pickett. Pickett's pregnancy was now clearly visible and displayed attractively in a peach dress with a vaguely Grecian drape.

The men shook hands and clasped shoulders. Pickett squeezed JJ's hands. "If you need anything, you call me. We SEAL wives try to stick together. The guys"—she waggled a hand at David and Jax—"wherever they are, they have each other. Are you going to move to Virginia Beach?"

"I'm going to go up on weekends, as much as I can."

"Are you okay with him returning to operating?"

"I understand he needs to do it. He's physically and mentally healed, but he won't really feel like he's recovered all of himself until he's tested himself. His hitch is up in a year, and we've talked about what he wants to do then."

"There's a saying. Officers get out when they want more. Enlisted, when they've had enough. Speaking of which, here come Emmie and Do-Lord. Do-Lord is doing some kind of research now."

Pickett and Emmie were best friends, so they had to hug and catch up.

JJ was momentarily left with no one to talk to. She couldn't help herself. She scanned the reception room for Blount. Mary Cole had assured her he would be there. "Turn down an invitation to an A-list party when he's never done better than B-list before? I don't think so."

Mary Cole's cynicism was merited. JJ had always seen that her A-list status was a huge plus to Blount. She didn't see him now though.

"Will you look who's coming! Lon!" David hailed the senior chief. "Did Mary Cole get you here, too?"

The older man shook hands all around. "Mary Cole? Pickett's mom? No. I came with Lauren. Her late husband was a big supporter of the senator's. She needs to start getting out again, but she didn't want to come alone."

"If I can have everyone's attention." Senator Calhoun's trained orator's voice carried easily throughout the room. He was obviously wearing a wireless mic and speakers were hidden. The effect was impressive.

"We are all honored to have with us tonight a number of our nation's heroes. My friend the Secretary of the Navy has told me that yesterday he signed the recommendation for one of them to receive the Navy Cross, our nation's second highest honor. I don't believe the date of the award ceremony has been set, but I assure you, Charlotte and I will be there. In the meantime, I wish to make him known to you so that you may thank him for his service to our country. Ladies and gentlemen, Petty Officer First Class David Graziano and his lovely wife, JJ, whom many of you know as the former JJ Caruthers. Thank you, JJ, for making this fine young man a North Carolinian."

An hour or so later, JJ finally caught sight of Blount. In fact, he was hard to miss. He was standing completely by himself, while other guests walked past him without seeing him. Mary Cole's strategy had succeeded past even her dreams. The very people who'd been entertained by Blount a month ago didn't want to be seen talking to him—not when one of the most powerful senators in Washington had made it clear that JJ and David had his patronage.

Mary Cole had told JJ she would know the right moment to speak to Blount. This was it. She crossed the room to where he stood near one of the tall Palladian windows.

She held out her hands to him. "Blount!" she said in a clear voice. "I'm so happy to see you!"

He had the bleak, fixed stare of a man who has watched his future go up in flames.

JJ laid her cheek against his. With her mouth close to his ear, she whispered, "Take my hands, kiss my cheek, and smile, you idiot."

When, like a sleepwalker he had done as directed, she pulled back. A quick glance around showed she had the attention of those closest. "Are you ever going to forgive me? Please say you will!"

"For what?"

"For what." Playing to her audience, she shook her head in wonder at his forbearance. "That is just like you. For treating you so badly, of course. I wouldn't say I *dumped* you, but I could have let you down a little easier. It was just… the man I'd loved for a year had miraculously reappeared in my life."

JJ heard her own words and knew she was speaking the absolute truth. "From the moment I first saw him, something changed for me, and nobody else would have done. But if I hurt you, I am most sincerely sorry."

Rise to the occasion, Blount, just this once. I've handed you your line. I've done everything I can to get us both out of this. She felt someone at her back and knew without turning it was David. She turned up the wattage on her smile as she said through her teeth, "Say you forgive me."

Blount finally demonstrated that his political ambitions were backed by a modicum of talent. "There really is nothing to forgive," he told her with a slightly chagrined smile. "My mother used to say that love will triumph over all. It's obvious that's what happened here." He stuck out his hand to David. "Clearly, the best man won."

—∿∿—

The four SEALs and their significant others found seats in a cove under the stairs. They had been polite guests long enough. They could be forgiven for being a little clannish for a few minutes.

David and JJ would be leaving soon. As was his habit, he checked everyone, needing to make sure they were okay.

Jax was with Pickett. One child was at home, and one on the way. Do-Lord was with Emmie, and they were perfect for each other. David didn't know how it had happened, but Emmie had found an elusive, fairylike prettiness. Not his cup of tea, but he could see the attraction. Amazingly, even Lon was once again with Lauren.

"Do you realize that this is the first time we've all been together in one place in over a year without somebody getting married?"

"There's no one left to get married, except Lon," Do-Lord pointed out.

"How 'bout it, buddy?"

"I've asked her." Lon smiled into Lauren's eyes, while she blushed like a woman half her age. "She says AA recommends no decisions of that sort until there's been one full year of sobriety."

"When will that be?"

The burly senior chief crossed his arms over his chest, a very strategic smile on his face. "Tomorrow."

That did it then. Everyone was squared away.

And he, David, had the best one of all.

David was alive. More alive than he had ever been before.

Life was good.

Acknowledgments

A book becomes real—moves from being scenes and characters rumbling around my brain to being an actual object that can be held in the hands—only with the help of a lot of people.

Readers are always interested in my research. I don't begin to have the military knowledge I would need to create my SEAL characters and their actions. Capt. Larry Bailey, USN Ret., former SEAL, helped me plot the Afghanistan chapter, explained motivations, and took me through the action step by step. Medical Capt. Hiram Patterson, Medical Service Corp, USNR, generously took his time to help me with specifics about Davy's injures—how they would happen and how they would be treated.

Sally A. Bulla, CDR, NC, USN-Ret., assured me a SEAL would lie through his teeth to cover up injuries. "For the most part, they can hide things pretty well—imagine lying to a doctor or nurse! Happens all the time with these guys. It's only when they know they are a danger to their comrades that they will tell someone that there's a problem. They always hope it's going to go away or get manageable so they can hide it." She also helped me with a time line for leaves.

When I encounter general military questions, an answer is always a *Send* away at RTMS, a Yahoo! group of writers of military romance. What would I do without you guys?

All credit for military accuracy goes to the above. Any mistakes are mine.

I don't know whether it's a commentary on me or our society, but in plotting, I always encounter a legal question. Angie Narron is my go-to lawyer, always ready with an answer.

Elizabeth Vaughan, MD, of Vaughan Integrative Medicine, suggested hyperbaric oxygen therapy as a possible treatment option. Gail Durgin, PhD, a neurofeedback therapist gave me insight into how it feels to have mild traumatic brain injury. It was she who told me, "Patients always say, 'I just want my life back!'"

JJ wouldn't exist without Elva Pugh. She's this larger-than-life beauty with black hair and green eyes, recognizable to everyone in her hometown, on equal terms with judges, mayors, and Walmart greeters, *and* she owns a car dealership. With her in my corner, I had the factual basis to create a fictional heroine who owns a car dealership, plus the idea for the sunglasses. You should see me wearing the ones she gave me. I am hot.

Affectionate gratitude goes to Alyosha Anatoliy of Fred Astaire of North Greensboro—"The Happiest, Friendliest Spot in Town"—for some of the most enjoyable hours of my life, unending encouragement of my writing, and the background needed to create the dance scenes.

I am unfailingly touched by the generosity of perfect strangers who take their time to answer questions online. With the help of April, of http://www.vintagevixen.com, I found the 1967 wedding dress JJ borrows. And guess what? It was a Priscilla of Boston, originally sold in Goldsboro, NC. (I love it when that kind of synchronicity happens!)

In addition, I must thank my tireless critique partners, Jennifer Lohman and Yvonne Harris. Talk about unsung heroes. They read my manuscripts almost as many times as I do.

Eternal gratitude to my agent, Stephany Evans. Without her repeated acts of faith, her persistence and encouragement, you wouldn't be holding this book in your hands. Although I'm sure there were times she wanted to snatch me bald, the fact that she didn't is proof that she is as kind and forgiving as she is indefatigable.

Speaking of snatching me bald, my editor, Deb Werksman, also exhibited massive self-restraint and, as always, could put her finger on exactly what revisions were needed.

Finally, about hyperbaric oxygen therapy, or HBOT. The treatment is real. And yes, though the one JJ contacts is fictional, a hyperbaric treatment center operated by former SEALs exists. Although there are individual case studies of people with TBI and stroke who have improved with HBOT, they cannot be considered clinical proof. Clinical trials of HBOT and TBI are being conducted, but as of this writing, neither effectiveness nor ineffectiveness has been proved. Health insurance is unlikely to pay for HBOT, and the Department of Defense's position is that it is ethical to withhold HBOT—meaning at present, it is not offered to veterans as a treatment option.

About the Author

Mary Margret Daughtridge, a Southerner born and bred, has been a grade school teacher, speech therapist, family educator, biofeedback therapist, and Transpersonal Hypnotherapist.

Since 2002, she has been a member of Heart of Carolina Romance Writers, Romance Writers of America, and Romancing the Military Soul, an online writing group. She is a sought-after judge for writing contests. *SEALed With a Ring* is the third in her series of SEALed romances.

She loves hearing from readers and can be found at marymargretdaughtridge.com.

SEALed
with a Kiss

BY MARY MARGRET DAUGHTRIDGE

THERE'S ONLY ONE THING HE CAN'T HANDLE, AND ONE WOMAN WHO CAN HELP HIM...

Jax Graham is a rough, tough Navy SEAL, but when it comes to taking care of his four-year-old son after his ex-wife dies, he's completely clueless. Family therapist Pickett Sessoms can help, but only if he'll let her.

When Jax and his little boy get trapped by a hurricane, Picket takes them in against her better judgment. When the situation turns deadly, Pickett discovers what it means to be a SEAL, and Jax discovers that even a hero needs help sometimes.

"A heart-touching story that will keep you smiling and cheering for the characters clear through to the happy ending." —Romantic Times

"A well-written romance... simultaneously tender and sensuous." —Booklist

978-1-4022-1118-8 • $6.99 U.S. / $8.99 CAN

SEALed
with a
Promise

BY MARY MARGRET DAUGHTRIDGE

NAVY SEAL CALEB DELAUDE IS AS DEADLY AS HE IS CHARMING.

Professor Emmie Caddington's quiet intelligence and quirky personality intrigue him. When he discovers that her personal connections can get him close to the man he's vowed to kill, will their budding relationship be nothing more than a means to revenge…or is she the key to his salvation?

Praise for *SEALed with a Kiss*:

"This story delivers in a huge way." —Romantic Times

"A wonderful story that will have readers experiencing a whirlwind of emotions and culminating with an awesome scene that will have your pulse pounding." —Romance Junkies

"What an incredibly powerful book! I laughed and sniffled, was turned on and turned inside out." —Queue My Review

978-1-4022-1763-0 • $6.99 U.S. / $7.99 CAN